HONEY FROM THE LION

ALSO BY JACKIE NORTH

The Love Across Time Series

Heroes for Ghosts

Honey From the Lion

Wild as the West Texas Wind

Ride the Whirlwind

Hemingway's Notebook

For the Love of a Ghost

Love Across Time Sequels

Heroes Across Time - Sequel to Heroes for Ghosts

The Farthingdale Ranch Series

The Foreman and the Drifter

The Blacksmith and the Ex-Con

The Ranch Hand and the Single Dad

The Wrangler and the Orphan

The Cook and the Gangster

The Trail Boss and the Brat

The Farthingdale Valley Series

The Cowboy and the Rascal

The Cowboy and the Hoodlum

The Cowboy and the Outcast

The Cowboy and the Dealer (Preorder)

The Cowboy and the Hacker (Preorder)

The Cowboy and the Wheelman (Preorder)

The Oliver & Jack Series

Fagin's Boy

At Lodgings in Lyme

In Axminster Workhouse

Out in the World

On the Isle of Dogs

In London Towne

Holiday Standalones

The Christmas Knife

Hot Chocolate Kisses

The Little Matchboy

Standalone

The Duke of Hand to Heart

HONEY FROM THE LION

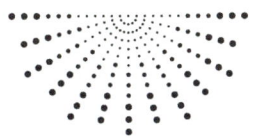

JACKIE NORTH

*All the best & happy reading.
Love, Jackie North xo*

Jackie North
MM Romance Author

Honey From the Lion
Copyright © 2018 Jackie North
Published September 21, 2018

All rights reserved. No part of this book may be reproduced, distributed, or transmitted in any form or by any means, electronic or mechanical, including photocopying, recording, or any information storage and retrieval system without the written permission of the author, except where permitted by law.

For permission requests, write to the author at jackie@jackienorth.com

This is a work of fiction. Names, characters, places, and incidents are a product of the author's imagination or are used fictitiously. Any resemblance to people, places, or things is completely coincidental.

Cover Design by Jay Aheer, Simply Defined Art

Honey From the Lion/Jackie North

ISBN Numbers:

Mobi - 978-1-94-280906-7
Print - 978-1-94-280908-1
Epub - 978-1-94-280907-4

Library of Congress Control Number: 2018956964

For all those who know that love is love...

And to Elin Gregory...
Who was the inspiration for Maddy

*Love knows not its own depth
until the hour of separation*

~~ Khalil Gibran

CONTENTS

Chapter 1	1
Chapter 2	9
Chapter 3	19
Chapter 4	27
Chapter 5	33
Chapter 6	45
Chapter 7	53
Chapter 8	61
Chapter 9	73
Chapter 10	83
Chapter 11	93
Chapter 12	101
Chapter 13	109
Chapter 14	119
Chapter 15	129
Chapter 16	139
Chapter 17	149
Chapter 18	157
Chapter 19	169
Chapter 20	181
Chapter 21	197
Chapter 22	209
Chapter 23	221
Chapter 24	245
Chapter 25	251
Chapter 26	261
Chapter 27	275
Jackie's Newsletter	281
Author's Notes About the Story	283
A Letter From Jackie	287
About the Author	289

CHAPTER ONE

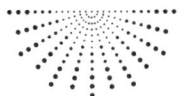

Feeling a little foolish in his brand new cowboy boots and hat, Laurie hefted his backpack, checked his pocket for his phone, and followed Maddy, who was the admin for the dude ranch, into the wood-lined office. She wore blue jeans and boots that looked authentic, and there was a smear of dust on her shoulder, as though she did manual labor on the dude ranch other than just in the office.

"You're a tad early, but that doesn't matter," said Maddy, laughing as she waved him to a seat. "Laurie, is it? I'll just check you in now, then you can go on over to the bunkhouse and have your pick of the lot."

"It's short for Lawrence," said Laurie for what seemed like the billionth time in his life.

The seat was made of leather and creaked when Laurie sat down in it. Well, groaned would be a better word. Also, it smelled old, of old animal, and was cracked in places, like it'd been left in the sun.

As Maddy rifled through the papers on her large wooden desk, Laurie gazed at the glass case that had a bunch of rusty, dusty junk in it, and at the sepia-toned photographs that hung in two rows on the wall above the case. The sunlight was pouring through the four-square windows with such fierce brightness he was unable to make out who was in the photos or what they were doing, even if he squinted.

He stopped squinting, sat up straight, and scuffed a line in the wooden floor with the toe of his boot. But gently so as not to mar it, as the wood, like the chair and everything else in the office, was old and well used. Which made Laurie think about the fact that the older something was, the longer it seemed to last. Anything new these days gave off the air of being about to break in short order. His phone for one, which was going on three years old.

If he didn't get it to a power source, it was going to go from fifty percent life to five percent inside of a heartbeat, and then he wouldn't be able to text his roommate Maxton that he'd arrived safely. Laurie could text him while he waited, but that would be rude, as the admin was looking at him and pushing over two sheets of paper and a pen.

"If you could fill those out and sign them for me, I'll file them," Maddy said. "You forgot when you made your final payment, and we need the info for insurance purposes."

The leather chair groaned as Laurie pushed off the wooden handles, and a puff of something dusty and ancient launched up at him. He took the pen and bent over the desk to sign the forms, which were the contact form, in case of emergency, and a release form, so pretty standard stuff. He filled in the info, putting his best friend Zach as his main contact, and Maxton, his roommate, as his second contact, just in case.

"Thank you muchly," Maddy said. She pulled the papers off the desk and put them into a folder, which she placed to the side. "Now would you like a quick tour? The other dudes will be here later, but—"

"I just need to plug in my phone," said Laurie. "And get my sunglasses out. The sun is really bright up here."

"Same sun as you'd find in Colorado," she said, her mouth puckering. "But up here there's not as much smog and such, so you'll be able to see the meteor shower pretty well after the chuck wagon dinner when they turn all the lights off."

He followed her out the door. He didn't know whether the chuck wagon dinner, a highly touted aspect of the dude ranch experience, was beginning to sound more hokey each time it was brought up, or less hokey. Regardless how it turned out, the idea of getting away from his software developer job at Duty View Software and going into the country where the skies were blue and there were no phones or computer screens had seemed especially good.

That he needed the break had become clear the morning after he'd come home from his friend Tyler's birthday party at the Dark Horse. He'd been exhausted just thinking about going to that party and left early, after only two margaritas and half a burger. He'd not even gotten wasted, but in the morning when he was standing in front of the door leading to the back step of his condo, coffee mug in hand, he realized that he'd left both of the locks on the back door unlocked.

For a long moment he stood there staring at it, the deadbolt and the lock on the knob both in the upright and unsecured position. His shoes were in their regular spot, and his keys were hanging from their usual hook, but the door was completely unlocked. The door could have been opened by anybody, *anybody*, in the night. It'd been a Saturday night too, when the partiers were out and cars zoomed up and down Main Street, revving their engines, trying to outdo each other with noise and celebration.

Even though nobody had broken in, that's when he knew he needed to take some time off and get away, not only from the never-ending software development cycle at his company, but also from everything and everyone. He needed to sleep, and he needed to be able to fall asleep, and to not feel the twist of work anxiety every minute of every day. The Farthingdale Dude ranch just outside of Farthing, Wyoming, had seemed just the thing.

He'd stumbled across the site for the dude ranch while searching online for something else. The website had promised blue skies, wide vista views, fresh air. It had also described demonstrations in riding and roping, a little bit of cowboy work, such as a mini cattle drive, and all the sundry tasks that went with it.

The most touted aspect of the dude ranch, besides the companionship of other dudes and dudettes, was the open-air eating, chuck wagon style. If the weather was bad while they were at the ranch, they could eat in the dining hall, but while on the cattle drive, and if it didn't snow, they would eat around a chuck wagon, and could even roast their own steaks over the open fire. It seemed like the civilized version of rough living, and he'd signed up as soon as he'd skimmed their gallery of photos.

He'd enjoyed buying the gear that came on the list the dude ranch had emailed him though, as he and Maddy stepped out of the office and went down the dusty wooden plank steps, he realized he might have gauged wrong. His boots were too new. Not only that, they were made for city streets, and the high gloss showed dust the second they hit the ground. His jeans were stiff and bright blue, and his coat, a nice Carhartt, was too fancy.

His cowboy hat, chosen after an agonizing search at the western apparel store at the south end of Harlin, was crisp and clean and stamped him as a greenhorn without him having to say a word. A cowboy they passed tipped his hat at them, and everything he wore was perfectly broken in and faded. Laurie felt like a cut-out doll in comparison.

"That's the main corral over there," said Maddy as she pointed. "And that's the secondary one, where we give riding lessons. This building is the main dining hall, that's the barn, and this is the bunkhouse."

"Where's the chuck wagon?" Laurie asked, scanning the circle of buildings that was to be his home, on and off, for the next week.

It was Sunday, and the bus would take them back in a week to the airport or bus station in Cheyenne, Wyoming. So, really, it was only seven days that he had to be there. Seven days to either unwind and relax, or suffer the consequences of a late night desperate search for someplace to go for vacation that wouldn't eat into his paid time off, cost too much, or force him to get on a plane.

"It's in the barn, for now," she said. "They needed to repair the canvas and also one of the axels had broken."

Laurie didn't say anything, but the fact that they were working on the chuck wagon was either a good sign or an indication that everything was run down and he'd made a terrible mistake. He took off his hat and noted that it already had a streak of dust on it, though he'd only put it on for the first time when he'd arrived at the dude ranch.

"That's some mighty auburn hair you have," said Maddy. "It goes well with your brown eyes."

"It's not—it's not auburn," said Laurie as politely as he could, though that kind of statement always irritated him. "It's brown, dark brown."

"Could have fooled me," she said. "Well, here's the bunkhouse. The door's not locked, none of the doors are locked except to the office." She shrugged as she opened the door, and it seemed to Laurie that she was pretending to be embarrassed, but was actually proud of that fact. Honest dudes and dudettes didn't tend to break into places and steal things. "This is the men's bunkhouse; the woman's is right next to it and is just the same."

She waved him into the bunkhouse. As Laurie stepped in, the wooden planks creaked beneath his feet and seemed covered with dust. When she flicked the switch on the wall, the light fixtures at either end of the bunkhouse, twisted curves of iron with a yellow shade on top that looked like thin cowhide bleached in the sun, flickered to life.

There were three rows of bunk beds, all made of wood, with one along each wall and one in the center of the room. From where he was, he could see there was a bathroom on each side, with a sink, toilet, and small shower with a plastic shower curtain. It was a far cry from his nice private bathroom back home, but he didn't say anything about that, as the point was to change things up, wasn't it? At least he had the chance to take the bunk bed furthest from the bathroom.

"I'll take the one in the corner," he said to Maddy. "Is there someplace I can plug in my phone?"

"There's only one plug and it's in this bathroom," she told him. "We discourage the use of mobile devices, anyway, as the point is to get away from technology, not to bring it with you." Watching her purse her lips gave Laurie a bit of a bad feeling that he was already on her shit list.

"I just need to let my roommate and my friend know I've arrived," he said. "Then I'll put it away."

"Well, okay," she said. "When you're finished, come to the steps in front of the dining hall, where the iron triangle is hanging," she said. "That's where everybody will be gathering around five o'clock."

When she went out, her steps echoed down the wooden stairs. She'd left the door open so the light came inside in bold, blue streaks. Overhead in the ceiling was a rather large skylight that let in even more light, which would, when the lights were off and it got dark, let in the ambient light of the stars and the meteor shower that was going on. That would be nice and might make the entire experience worthwhile, even if the chuck wagon turned out to be hokey and all the other dudes and dudettes turned out to be asshats.

In the meantime, he needed to pick out a bunk, text his roommate, and use the facilities. Then he planned to sit on the steps of the dining hall like he was one of the actual ranch hands and not a dude. He would look out over the dude ranch, gaze at the horizon, and squint at the bright blue sky from beneath his brand new and too-pale cowboy hat.

At least there wouldn't be phones ringing, at least there wouldn't be endless meetings, and there definitely wouldn't be any espresso. No, at a dude ranch, the coffee would be properly cooked in a metal percolating coffee pot, like he'd always seen in the movies. There would probably be raw sugar, and maybe even half-and-half, for the coffee, and baked beans to eat, and large, grilled steaks.

He patted his stomach, promising it something to eat soon and, going to the furthest bunk from the door, hefted his backpack onto it. Then he went into the bathroom, plugged in his phone, and laid it on the edge of the sink, where it teetered precariously.

The little white lightning bolt showed up right away, and the single bar turned into two bars. The phone would be up and running soon, but he didn't want to leave it, in case someone came in and chided him for having a phone, or perhaps knocked it into the sink.

He should put the phone on the toilet tank, and just trust that another human being would understand what he was doing with it.

Then he should go outside and sit in the sunshine and be part of the fun, like he'd planned to do.

Anybody who came up to a dude ranch in Wyoming in October probably needed to get away as much as he did and would likely not be an asshat. He'd be okay. He'd get some fresh air, do a little work, and fall asleep like a baby. It'd be okay. He was going to have a good time, yes, he was.

CHAPTER TWO

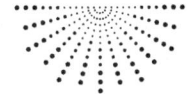

After Laurie kicked some hay bales, he walked around and found the newly repaired chuck wagon in the barn. It was a high-wheeled narrow wagon with new-looking beige canvas hung over the hoops. The sides of it were painted a gently faded green, and it looked as though it'd seen many miles on cattle drives and knew all about it. He talked to the real cowboys who were working on it and walked around some more, trying to imagine what it would be like to live like this all the time. He felt like he failed.

He went back to the bunkhouse and took a snooze in his bunk with the thin pillow propped against his backpack. By the time he woke up, his phone was fully charged so he quickly texted Zach to say he'd arrived safely.

Zach texted back using many laughing emojis, punctuated by some ever-funny poop emojis. He told Laurie to be careful where he was stepping, and then bet him twenty bucks that something would soon go haywire. *Get it, haywire?* Zach texted. All of which made Laurie laugh to himself, grinning as he found a gif of a laughing cowboy to send back.

Next, he texted Maxton, using fewer emojis, as Maxton wasn't a laughing kind of guy. But he was a good roommate, the best, so Laurie gave into temptation and sent the same laughing cowboy gif, and got a gif of a kid rolling his eyes in return. Awesome.

Once that was done, and feeling warmly connected to his friends, he put on his boots and hat and stomped out of the bunkhouse, across the dusty yard, and over to the dining hall. Overhead, the sun was still glaringly bright, and a brisk wind had picked up as it came out of the mountains to the west. Laurie practiced his best Clint Eastwood squint as a small bus, two taxis, and a minivan were pulling off, leaving behind a bunch of faux cowboys and a pile of too much luggage.

The dude cowboys milled around as though they didn't know what to do with themselves. With great interest, three were examining the iron triangle that served as a dinner bell. Several others were kicking the bales of hay that were attractively stacked near the stairs. The rest were sitting on the steps. One was going frantically through his overly stuffed suitcase. All wore too-new cowboy hats and boots, which made Laurie feel better about his own outfit. All were looking askance at each other.

Laurie had been in tour groups before, and sometimes it took a little while for the group to mesh. The dude ranch had the added aspect that all of them looked like they were dressed to go to a rodeo none of them was quite prepared for. Since Laurie had had some shuteye, as the local parlance might have it, he was ready to make a go of it and put everybody at their ease.

"Hi, I'm Laurie," said Laurie with a wave and a smile. "Did everybody else pay too much for their boots and not have time to break them in?"

The response was good; several men smiled, one or two snorted, and the rest waved back. As Laurie went over to the dinner triangle, he noted there were no dudettes. This was a shame, as the women he knew always had an interesting perspective on things, and could be a helpful buffer when he didn't want to flirt or hook up with other men. Though he could look, right? He could always look, and took the chance as he reached up to lift the rod and ting the triangle, just a little bit.

"That's not loud at all," said Laurie, conversationally. "How the heck is that supposed to call us to chow?"

"You really got to whack it," said one dude with a wry grin, as though he knew he was using an innuendo and was doing it on purpose.

As a reward, Laurie smiled at him, and got the typical reaction when he met someone who liked other guys like he did. Cowboy dude had that look of open-eyed surprise and delight as he cast his gaze over Laurie's features and then his whole body.

Laurie didn't go in for one-night hook ups and wasn't about to start now. There was no privacy in the bunkhouse for anything anyway, and Laurie also was not into sleeping bags and squished quarters. But window shopping, as he called it, could be fun, so he looked the other guy over in return, and they both smiled. Laurie had a feeling the other guy was just window shopping, too.

Presently, as all the dudes straggled in and out of the bunk house with their luggage, several real cowboys started rolling the chuck wagon from the barn. They dragged it over to the large fire pit that had been dug into the ground where it sloped away towards an open, wheat-colored field of grass.

Laurie felt a sting of disappointment that they'd not hitched up actual horses to pull the chuck wagon into place, but then supposed that since the fire pit was so close, it only made sense. But was the entire experience going to be half-assed like that? Had they all paid money for an experience that was a cutout of the real thing where only the hay bales were real?

Laurie shook himself mentally, and put a brave face on because yes, chuck wagons were pulled around by hand all the time, and cowboys, even dude cowboys, didn't cry foul each time things didn't go their way. But then Maddy came out with a sheaf of papers in her hands, and waved them all to come closer. Laurie felt another stab of disappointment. More paperwork. More real-world stuff to distract him from having a true western experience.

"Hi, everybody, I'm Maddy," said Maddy. She took the glasses that hung from a glittery cord around her neck, put them on, and began to review the top sheet of paper. Then she looked up at them and smiled.

"You've either emailed me or talked to me on the phone. I've got everybody's signature on the release and insurance forms, so we're all ready to go. Bill, our head cowboy, will come out in a minute and go over how to be safe around horses and cows, branding irons, swirling ropes, and the like. How to tell what time it is by the sun, and how not to get trapped in a ravine. How to properly wear your cowboy hat and, most importantly, how to break in your brand new boots."

This brought a low chuckle from the group of dude cowboys. In the meantime, Laurie could see that the real cowboys were carrying green Coleman coolers from the barn to the fire pit. They placed them beneath the chuck wagon, out of the sun.

The coolers probably had the steaks they were promised they could roast themselves over the open flames. Still, it put a damper on things that such modern elements were being brought, so soon, into the make-believe world of the western ranch and cowboys and horses and cows. But it would get better, right?

And quite soon it did, for out of the dining hall and down the wooden steps, breaking through the ranks of dudes who were all looking at Maddy, came the realest cowboy Laurie had ever seen. Literally.

He was shorter than Laurie was, barrel-chested, his snap-button and bright red cowboy shirt bulging at his belly. He walked with a half-hitch limp Laurie knew right away wasn't faked. His boots were worn, and one sole was just flapping at the boot tip. His jeans were thin, and his cowboy hat, by its sunburned brown color, had seen years of wear. Years of falling off bucking broncos. Years of being used to dust off the cowboy's jean's after he'd been thrown.

And his face. It was tan from the sun, deep wrinkles curving from his eyes and the side of his mouth. His eyes were bright blue and clear, and he smiled as he stopped in front of them. He waved Maddy off as though she were a mirage that was interrupting the wonderful story he was about to tell.

"You go on, now, Maddy," said Bill, the real cowboy. "I got this group, an' I'll take good care of them. Go on, now."

Maddy waved the papers at him and smiled, like this was a long-practiced and ritualistic handoff. Laurie barely noticed her trot up the wooden steps to the office as he turned every single bit of his attention on Bill.

"Hey, fellows," said Bill. "Don't think I have any ladies in the group, so I'll just say fellows and suchlike. I'm here to orient you to the ranch, to tell you how you're supposed to behave, and what to do if you get yourself into a spot of trouble, so listen up. Are you listening?"

The group of dudes all nodded in their cowboy hats, Laurie along with them, mesmerized.

"Did I hear you?" asked Bill. He cupped his hand to his ear and seemed to be waiting, as though listening for the long-distance howl of a coyote or a lost calf. "I don't believe I did, so here's what you need to know. When I tell you something or ask you something, you tell me Yes, Bill, or No, Bill, or whatever is appropriate. That way I know you heard me. And when I tell you to move, you say, Yes, Bill, and *move*, otherwise, you're liable to get your foot stomped on or your head kicked in. We'll be working with live animals, most of 'em with a mind of their own, and you always gotta be on alert, understood?"

"Yes, Bill," said every single dude cowboy, including Laurie. He felt better about everything already because Bill was a take-charge kind of guy and wasn't fooling around. This was more like it.

"Now, we're going to walk around the ranch, the main part of it, and I want you to pay attention to what I tell you. Where ropes are stored, how to close the barn door, how to climb over a wooden fence, and how to find the gate in a barbed wire fence so you don't rip your nuts off trying to climb over or through.

"Tomorrow, we'll introduce you to the cattle, but at the end of the tour today, right before we settle down to supper, we'll walk through the barn. Maddy has everybody's height and weight, and some info about you, so the stall with your name on it, next to the horse's name, is your horse. You'll start riding tomorrow, right around mid-morning, and we'll put you straight to work. Is everybody ready?"

Laurie was so ready, his smile felt like it took up his whole face. He felt the window-shopping cowboy dude looking at him, so he made a face to let him know that he could share in the smile, but it wasn't going any further than that. Laurie was here for himself, and he wanted to have a good time with no dating drama, nothing to distract him from the wide open spaces he'd signed up for.

"This way, boys," said Bill. He waved them to follow him, and as a group, they trudged up the slope of the hill to the corral just beyond the barn.

Dust kicked up from sixteen pairs of boots spun into the wind to be whipped away to the fire pit and beyond. The smell of horsehair and horse manure and leather oil and grassy hay swirled from the barn, while the odor of cow and muck and cow shit baked in the sun became stronger as they walked toward it. A small group of cows lollygagged in the corral, but Bill ignored them as he went up to the gate.

"Do you see this?" asked Bill.

"Yes, Bill," they all said.

"This here's a gate. You always go through the gate, if you can," he said. "Now I know in the movies, them dang fools are always climbing over the fence, but that wears down the fence, and it's got enough to go through surviving the cold of winter and the heat of summer. Use the thing as it's meant to be used and you won't go wrong. Use the gate, don't climb over. That is, unless you've got to get out or get trampled; every rule has an exception, you see. Your job is to know when to follow the rule and when to break it."

"Just like in life," said Laurie, loudly and with a grin.

The cowboy dudes were all silent, as though wondering whether it was okay to interrupt Bill like that. But as Bill smiled and nodded, they all laughed. The tone of the group settled into a feeling of camaraderie that might have taken a bit longer to achieve without Laurie's response and the laugh that followed it.

Laurie tipped his hat at Bill to let him know that Laurie had his back, but wouldn't be taking over the conversation. He should stop trying to lead the meeting, but it was a habit from work that was hard to kick. But he really should kick it, at least for the next seven days, and let somebody else take charge for once.

THE ORIENTATION HAD BEEN ENERGIZING, and the reason for the chuck wagon being dragged out by hand had been learned: the draft horses that usually pulled it were being shod in Chugwater, eighteen miles away. They'd be back in time to pull the chuck wagon for their cattle drive on Thursday and Friday. By that time, Laurie figured they'd all be settled into their routines, and at least mostly ready for the two-day stint on horseback with the charge of caring for and driving around 200 cattle.

They'd all gotten appropriately dusty during the orientation, which had included a serious talk about animal safety, and boot and hat care and maintenance. How to approach a horse. How to tell time by the sun. How to tell direction and pinpoint exactly where you were by Iron Mountain. That was the black and rust colored chunk of rock that rose out of the sandy bluffs and dusty, autumn-brown foothills to the west, and whose jagged top looked like it had been lopped off by a giant wielding a sharp axe.

There had even been a quick roping demonstration by one of Bill's cowboys, a wiry fellow who didn't talk but who could make the rope dance like it was alive, and who had been able to lasso anything Bill pointed him at. They'd been given a tour of all of the outbuildings, the tack barn, and the feed barn.

Finally, they went to the barn where animals were kept, and said hello to their horses. Laurie's horse was a lovely dun colored mare that went by the name of Gwen, and had sweet brown eyes and a silky black mane and tail. She'd whickered at Laurie when he'd cautiously petted her neck, and nuzzled his hand just as Bill came around with a pan of carrot chunks.

"You hold that in your hand, flat, and they'll eat it, gentle as anything. We don't have any biters here, so don't worry. Go on, try it."

"Yes, Bill," they all said.

Laurie, remembering that he'd always wanted a pony when he'd been younger, was thrilled when Gwen took the carrot from his flat hand. Her large horsey lips were soft as velvet and gentle, as though she knew he was a very inexperienced cowboy who didn't mean her any harm.

Afterward, they went to sit on the hay bales scattered around the fire pit. The bales were covered with brightly colored woolen blankets. Hay dust swirled up into Laurie's nostrils as the sun began to go down.

Three of Bill's cowboys were setting up the iron grills over the fire that was now banked coals. Later, Laurie'd been told, the fire would be built up, and Bill would tell ghost stories. That sounded kind of hokey, though fun, but for now the coals, blue and white and orange, looked perfect to roast steaks over.

They didn't actually get to hold the meat over the flames on a stick, as he'd imagined, but they were each given a fork and put in charge of making sure their own steak was done as they wanted it. This might have caused some crowding near the fire, and maybe somebody'd fall on the grill, but that never happened, as Bill was standing by, watching over them.

One of the cowboys stirred the baked beans, and another of them went to the chuck wagon and hauled out covered metal warming trays, one that held hunks of cornbread and another that was full of white rolls. A metal bowl of butter was propped on top of one of the hay bales, and one of coleslaw, along with eating utensils, and plastic glasses for water or tea.

This was all pretty standard stuff, in Laurie's experience, so he wasn't expecting that when he sat down with his medium rare steak, surrounded by a puddle of baked beans, and one each of buttered corn bread and white roll, that everything would taste delicious.

Maybe it was the fresh air, or maybe it was that he'd been away from a computer screen for two whole days. Maybe it was the cool breeze coming down as the skies overhead grew dark and the fact that one of Bill's cowboys actually began playing a harmonica to accompany them while they ate. This last was definitely hokey, but Laurie figured he was settling into the experience, and of *course* a cowboy would be playing the harmonica while they ate. That was as it should be, and the food was terrific.

CHAPTER THREE

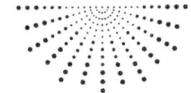

By the time Laurie finished his steak, and smiled a time or two at the window-shopping cowboy dude, he was full. And he was tired, though he didn't have much confidence he'd actually fall asleep when bedtime came. The stresses at work had been hammering on him for a while, and in spite of his best efforts, and how tired he was, he was always too edgy to unwind.

Maybe it would be a good idea to get together with window-shopping cowboy dude, just to blow off some of the tension in his body. But then he'd have to follow up when morning came, and it was just too much to think about. Besides, where would they go? The bunkhouse had no little side rooms, and all the other buildings were dark. The high prairie was pitch dark and cool, now that the sun had gone down. Probably it was full of snakes and bears or whatever, so it was off limits anyway.

While the cowboys cleared away the dishes and the grill, looking quite domestic in their long cotton aprons, Bill stepped up to the fire pit and built up the fire with thick logs. The flames curled up to the darkness. All the dude cowboys sat in a circle around the fire, either on the hay bales or propped up against one, as Laurie was, the cool dust making his butt feel cold.

Soon after Bill had sent the real cowboys away, all of the lights went off in every single building, even the one over the flat dirt parking lot. The night was so dark that Bill, standing beside the fire pit with the blue and yellow flames, actually glowed on one side.

"This is too high," said Bill. He leaned over and poked at the fire with a stick to settle it down, where, seeing it was Bill, it obediently collapsed into a low triangle of yellow and gold.

"That's better," said Bill. "Now, see how dark it is? Since you're one of the last groups of the season, we do this special just for you, make it all dark like this so you can experience it how the pioneers did. Later, out on the high prairie when we're on our cattle drive, it'll be even darker, but this is special."

Since this first night experience had been described in some detail on the website, it felt hokey again, and Laurie rolled his eyes, sure that nobody could see.

"Yes, it is special," said Bill, looking right at Laurie. "Because tonight I'm going to tell ghost stories, and while I'm telling 'em, look up from time to time at the meteor shower that's going on."

"The Orionids," said one of the dude cowboys, bravely interrupting.

Laurie wondered if the response had come from his window-shopping cowboy dude friend, because he liked smart guys, guys who knew things. Now was not the time to follow up on that, though, because with all of them seated, Bill looked tall in the darkness, the light from the fire blazing up and down one side of his body.

"That's right," said Bill. "Most of the cowboys back in the old west would not know that. But rather than be impressed with how smart you are, just look up at the dance of the heavens while I tell my ghost stories."

Laurie had the feeling if any more modern facts came in to break the mood and tone Bill was trying to set, that Bill would tell that dude cowboy right off and send him to the bunkhouse for punishment. Laurie also wanted to tell everybody that the meteor shower happened because of Halley's Comet, because he was geeky like that, but he didn't want to incur Bill's wrath.

More, he didn't want to ruin the mood for everybody else, or for himself. It was dark, the night was cool, it smelled like hay and horses, and it was the exact right setting for ghost stories. Laurie didn't believe in ghosts, of course, but it was fun to pretend he did and, besides, the atmosphere was perfect for it.

"This here's the story of Oooooold Joe," said Bill, drawing out the o's like the moan from a lost ghost. "Oooooold Joe," said Bill again, as if he himself liked the sound of it. He smiled and closed his eyes for a moment. When he opened them, they were brilliantly lit by the glow of the fire.

"Now, listen up," said Bill in a story telling voice. "The story of Old Joe is one I heard from my great-great-*great* Grandad Pete who ran the general store in the nearby town of Farthing in the late 1800's.

"He heard this story from a half-white, half Native American woman of the Arapahoe tribe. She made a living in his store crafting and selling Indian beaded work, like belts and moccasins. My grandad liked her. I even think he had a crush on her, but that wasn't done in those days, though they were good friends forever. She probably had an Arapahoe name that would have been given to her with great ceremony, but he just called her Adeline.

"Grandad Pete had met Old Joe a time or two, but Adeline knew him better and had learned his story, which I'm about to tell you. Old Joe had fought in the Indian Wars of the 1890's, after which he came away quite despondent over the senseless killings and the death of Native American men, women, and children. He had gotten a bullet in the leg from friendly fire and might have lost that leg but for the care of a local doctor. He carried that scar for the rest of his life, and had what we today would call PTSD, though they didn't know that then.

"All Old Joe knew was that he needed to be by himself so he could lick his wounds and recover from the horrible sights his eyes had beheld. He came out west, where he'd heard the air was clear and silent and a man could make his way on his own. He came by train and then by coach and then by foot and ended up in Farthing, Wyoming in the autumn of 1891. In his pocket he carried a letter of employment to take over the surveyors' cabin just outside of town.

"He was entrusted with making sure the blizzards of winter didn't destroy the cabin or the shed that contained the surveyors' equipment, scopes and rulers and lamps and the like. He was entrusted with keeping the land clear of mountain lions and wolves, and was asked to keep a journal about the weather and conditions, sort of an early meteorologist. He was gifted with supplies and a rifle, allowed to hunt antelope and snare rabbits, and he was paid twenty dollars a month.

"In short order, Old Joe had acquired a buffalo hide coat and wore the local version of the cowboy hat, which in those days might have been made out of leather or it might have been made out of felt. He moved into the surveyors' cabin that, until a little while ago, was right over there on that little hillock. We kept it for many years so folks could go in and look around and see how cozy it was, and what it might feel like to live there. But we tore it down because it's on government land and the government determined that it was too decrepit and therefore unsafe for human beings to enter."

"That's a damn shame," said one of the dude cowboys, and there were many cowboy hats, edged in yellow firelight, nodding in agreement.

"Time moves on, fellows," said Bill. "And that's a lesson of life you need to learn. But there are pictures of the cabin and of Old Joe in the admin office. Maybe before we get started in the morning, or if you get a chance before you leave, you can go and see Old Joe's likeness. Then you can admire some of what we collected from the removal of the cabin, trinkets and suchlike, that Old Joe used in his day-to-day life."

Bill stared in silence at the fire, then tipped his head back to look up at the night sky.

Laurie and all the other dude cowboys echoed him, their heads tipping back as they, too, looked at the blackness overhead dotted with starlight. It took a moment for Laurie to realize that there were streaks of silver zooming between the stars, glowing with a timid brightness for a second before shooting into brilliance and then dying away in a blue and gray line.

Over and over this happened until Laurie almost felt dizzy with it, his stomach a little queasy with the speed of the shooting stars, his heart swelling with the beautiful majesty of it. He lived in the town of Harlin, which was quite civilized, and worked in the city of Denver, which was almost too civilized. And while he wasn't a nature boy, there were some aspects of nature that man would never tame, and shooting stars were one of them.

"Now, pay attention," said Bill, drawing their eyes to him once more. "Oooooold Joe lived in that surveyors' cabin all on his own that winter. He came into town once or twice a week, and hardly ever spoke to anyone besides my Grandad Pete and Adeline. He would always stop to see her while she worked in the window of the general store my grandad owned, doing beautiful beadwork. It was museum quality and would be quite priceless today, though he was able to buy a piece or two from her to help her make her living.

"Early on that season a blizzard attacked the town, leaving everybody helpless and stranded for three days. Some were unprepared and perished, while others, adapted to life on the high prairie, knew what to expect and had stocked up. This wasn't the long winter of 1888, you understand, with blizzards every other day, as was described by Ms. Wilder in her children's books, no. This was the on-and-off winter of 1891-1892, where the snow and sleet and cold would come down off Iron Mountain without warning. Right quick, the town of Farthing began anticipating them. Nobody would leave their homes or businesses to go anywhere. Not that there was anywhere to go, you understand, but they grew cautious and anxious, and the rascal youth of the town would sometimes cause trouble just to blow off steam."

"Iron Mountain?" asked a voice. "Is it really made of iron?"

"Is this a classroom, Sunny Jim?" asked Bill in a haughty voice that made some of the dude cowboys chuckle, and surely made the offending questioner squirm on his blanket-covered bale of hay. "No, it is not. Quit ruining the mood. Let me finish my story, and I'll take questions afterwards, you hear?"

"Yes, Bill," came a single solitary voice from the edge of the hay bales. It was definitely not Laurie's cowboy dude window-shopping friend and, indeed, sounded like the guy who'd been anxiously going through his suitcase earlier.

"Old Joe," said Bill, continuing as though no interruption had happened. "Old Joe, in the midst of this first freak blizzard, heard a scratching at his door. He went to answer it, assuming it was someone who had lost their way. Instead he found a little red fox with its tail coated with snow, its ears drawn back in misery.

"Without a word, Old Joe scooped up the fox and used his fingers to remove the snow from its fur, which turned out to be a glossy deep red. This wasn't one of those wheat colored foxes, no, it was like a fox from the ancient stories, with an auburn pelt and dark brown eyes, and a little dark mask over its nose. Old Joe wrapped that little red fox in a woolen blanket and carried it to the fire and fed it warm water and a little broth and took care of it. And in return, that little red fox became his closest companion.

"Old Joe even brought the fox to town to show to Adeline how beautiful it was, and how smart. Adeline always told my Grandad Pete that the fox was tame, in a way, but was always getting into mischief, like foxes do, and Old Joe had to keep a close eye on it.

"You can imagine what a picture they made together, in town or in the surveyors' cabin, with Old Joe, the wounded man who swore he wanted to be alone, doting on this little slip of an animal who sometimes didn't know right from wrong, but who always turned to Old Joe whenever he wanted anything, that fox's smile on its dark face. The little red fox saved Old Joe, in a way, from being alone, and Old Joe and the little red fox were happy together.

"One day," said Bill, his voice lowering in a way that made a chill creep over Laurie's skin. "One day, the little red fox went missing, and though Old Joe hunted and searched all over, he could not find him. He looked everywhere, even when it snowed and sleeted, trudging into the night with a lantern, calling and calling for his fox friend.

"It wasn't until early spring when he gave up, though nobody in town, not even Adeline, knew this at the time. He pulled his cowhide-covered chair to face the door, wrapped himself in an old quilt, hitched his rifle over his arm, and waited. He waited forever without moving while the snows howled and the storms blew so hard they blew the windows in. But Old Joe didn't move, for he died, sitting there, waiting for his little red fox to come home. They found his body in the spring, starved and frozen to death."

Bill waited a long moment for the horror of that to sink in, and then used his stick to poke up the fire so that it jumped in long gold ribbons into the darkness.

"They say that if the stars are streaking overhead and the sleet and wind are coming off of Iron Mountain, you can see Old Joe walking across the snowdrifts of the high prairies around Farthing. He's wearing his buffalo hide coat and brown felt hat.

"Sometimes he carries a lantern lifted high so he can search for his fox friend, which is a portent of evil things to come. Most times, though, people say they see him carrying a little red fox cradled safely in his arms. Old Joe died alone, and though he thought he wanted to live alone, he found a friend and is searching for him still. Most times he finds him and sometimes he doesn't. And that's the story of Old Joe."

Laurie's throat felt thick. He could barely swallow, affected by the story to such a point where he felt it deep inside, though he couldn't reason why. It was just a story, after all, and probably not even true. Oh, sure, there'd been some guy named Joe, most likely, and he and the fox, or some animal, had crossed paths, but it hadn't been like Bill was describing, there was no way. Foxes were wild, and time had a way of shifting the truth of a story until it fit the situation that the storyteller wanted to tell.

But it definitely wasn't hokey the way Bill told it because Laurie was so moved he didn't know what to say, not even to step into his team leader role, like everybody at work always expected him to do. It was nice just to be able to sit there and let it sink in and feel the moment, just like it was.

Nobody moved or said anything; the silence settled over them, and they could hear the wind blowing, though it blew so gently it barely rubbed the dry grasses together.

"Did you like that story?" Bill asked. When all the dude cowboys nodded silently, Bill waved at the fire. "Good. And remember, if you see Old Joe carrying his little fox friend, and you walk straight toward Iron Mountain during a meteor shower and make a wish, it will come true."

Bill took his stick and poked at the fire, sending satisfactorily blue and gold and orange and yellow flames leaping up to light his face.

"Now, as a special treat, and in case it snows and we have to make other arrangements, it's a good night for sleeping out in the open. We'll set up blankets and pillows and little pads to keep you off the ground, though cowboys would have just had their own hats as pillows and one woolen blanket. You're all greenhorns and we don't want you to suffer, so visit the bunkhouse to use the facilities, and when you come back out, it'll all be ready for you. You'll settle in and look up at the stars, and I'll tell you more ghost stories, the way the cowboys used to sing the cattle to sleep, back in the old west."

CHAPTER FOUR

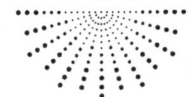

Bill let them get anything they felt they might need from the bunkhouse while his ever-efficient cowboys set up the dude cowboys' bedrolls for the night. Laurie wondered what it might be like to actually sleep on the ground with nothing between him and the dirt but a thin woolen blanket, though he was glad he would not have to find this out. The pads beneath the sturdy sleeping bags looked like a comfortable arrangement, and he had his fingers crossed that after all of his activity the past two days he'd sleep like a baby.

When he came back from the bunkhouse, he went over to Bill, who was standing beside the chuck wagon talking to one of his cowboys. It was interesting to approach them, with the low gleam of the fire shining on one side of their faces while the other side was in darkness, because maybe this was what it might have looked like, back in the old days.

Both Bill and the cowboy stopped talking as Laurie walked up. He assumed they were discussing business they didn't want him to know about, for confidentiality reasons, or because it might ruin the mood that Bill had set. With a tip of his hat, the cowboy walked off toward the barn. That left Laurie alone with Bill, which was nice. Bill was the kind of man who knew things, which Laurie always admired.

"Howdy, Laurie," said Bill in a cheerful way. "You ready for more ghost stories?"

"Howdy, Bill," said Laurie in a likewise manner, feeling the smile on his face on account of it was such a hokey way to greet someone. "I sure am. Is that story true?"

"You callin' me a liar?" asked Bill, but there was a twinkle in his eyes as he said it. This was probably part of Bill's persona, the rough, experienced cowboy, though Laurie had a strong feeling it was really how Bill was, with a veneer of dude-ranch-hokey laid over the top. "That story is as true as it was when my great-grandad handed it down to my grandad and he handed it down to my Dad, who handed it down to me. It's as true as it ever was."

Which meant, if Laurie cared to dig beneath the surface meaning, that it wasn't true at all, for if it wasn't true in the beginning, it was just a story now. Still, it had been a good story.

"Can you really make a wish on Iron Mountain?" asked Laurie, not because he really wanted to know, but because he wanted to hear Bill tell him about it.

"Well, no, you can't," said Bill with an open-mouthed but silent laugh, leaving Laurie unsure whether Bill was laughing at him or laughing because wishes were just foolish make-believe. "But Adeline always told my great-grandad that if you walked toward Iron Mountain under a meteor shower like this one we're having right now, it would show you your heart's desire. Do you understand the difference, son?"

"Yes," said Laurie, though he didn't think there was much difference, as a wish was the same as a desire, right?

"When you get more miles on your boots, you'll understand the difference," said Bill. His gaze on Laurie was so steady that Laurie had a feeling that Bill would one day be proven right, and Laurie *would* know the difference.

"Is the mountain really made of iron?" asked Laurie. He probably should leave Bill alone so Bill could get back to the responsibility of looking after sixteen guys from the city who wanted to experience the open west, only without snakes, cholera, dysentery, or doing without a proper bathroom and hot and cold running water.

"It's made of iron ore," said Bill. "That, and other good metals, but mostly iron. Just like a meteorite is. I always figure that when meteors fall around these parts, they are trying to get home to Iron Mountain, but that's just foolishness. Now, you gonna get into your sleeping bag with the rest of the fellows so I can finish up with my stories?"

"Yes, Bill," said Laurie, smiling and, with a wave, dismissed himself from Bill's presence and went over to the sleeping bag where his cowboy hat had been placed on top of a thin pillow.

The bedding had been nicely set up, though Laurie, rather than taking off his boots and climbing into it, settled fully clothed on top of it. He took his too-new cowboy hat and, with his head resting on the pillow that no real cowboy would have had on a cattle drive, settled it over his eyes in anticipation of more ghost stories from Bill.

While he waited, his eyes shaded by darkness, he could hear everything, as though the arrangement of the hat amplified it. The sound of cowboy boots walking across dry grass. The rustle of a sleeping bag as one of the cowboy dudes crawled into it. The low, saw-like sound of a zipper being pulled. Voices from the bunkhouse. The wind rattling the canvas flaps of the chuck wagon. And, way off, so faintly that he thought he might be imagining it, the high-pitched chorus of coyote howls.

Perfect, perfect, perfect. He was going to listen to Bill tell more stories, and fall asleep like a baby. In the morning, the sun would be shining, they'd do some cowboy chores, and then go for a ride on their horses across the dusty high plains. Just like in the olden days. With each moment, he felt more confident this vacation was going to be just what he needed.

LAURIE FELT the cold on his cheek, and a sting, as if the wind had been whipping around him for quite some time. He must have fallen asleep on top of his sleeping bag. He needed to wake up enough to pull off his boots and crawl inside, which he had to do quietly so he didn't wake up all the other dude cowboys. Except when he opened his eyes and lifted his head, his cowboy hat, now frosted with ice, jumped off his head and he had to grab it before it blew away.

Laurie sat up. All around him was an expanse of white snow coming down sideways from an equally white sky. It was freezing cold, and his butt was starting to go numb. The sleeping bag was gone, the fire pit was gone, and there was no sign of the bunkhouse or the barns, or the corrals, or anything. There was no circle of cowboys nestled in their sleeping bags. There was just the snow and the bone-deep cold and Laurie was all alone.

The brightness of the air seemed to suggest that it was morning, but if he'd slept the night through, why didn't someone wake him up for coffee and some breakfast grub from the chuck wagon? The chuck wagon was also gone, and there was no sign of anyone or anything. Nothing moved except the sleeting snow that came down and sifted through every place it could, into the neck of his Carhartt jacket, into his boots, up his sleeves, freezing him every place it touched.

The wind howled, always coming at him sideways as he staggered to his feet and used both his hands to keep his cowboy hat on his head. He squinted into the wind, his lashes clumped with snow, the warmth of his skin melting it and sending tears of icy cold water down his cheeks and his neck. He couldn't feel his face, and his lips were numb. All around him was nothing but a whirl of ice, snow, and bitter sleet. And cold, he was so cold and he knew he needed to get out of the weather before he froze to death.

But where was he to go? There was nothing, no buildings, no people, nothing.

He walked a few feet, then realized he didn't know how he was oriented. If he was facing the main part of the dude ranch and started walking, he'd be fine. But if he was facing away and started walking, he'd be walking for miles and miles, out onto the open high prairie where there were no houses or even roads, just acres of open grassland.

He'd probably freeze to death if he started out aimlessly, so he needed to think. Except thinking would cost him precious seconds he might need later. On the other hand, he'd stay warmer if he kept moving, so he picked a direction that felt like it was the direction of the office and the bunkhouse. He turned up the collar of his Carhartt jacket and, with one hand on that, keeping it closed, the other hand on his cowboy hat, he tucked his chin down and began to walk.

Except it was more like stumbling as the fierce wind pushed at him from his right side and threw him off balance with every other step. The snow was deep, besides, and crusted on the top so his boots sank as he walked. That meant he had to lift his legs high, up to the height of his knee, to get his boots out of the self-created holes. Snow went into his boots, and packed around his ankles, and melted only enough to make his socks wet and his calves feel like they were slowly freezing.

He knew about hypothermia. Anybody with an internet connection could find out all about it. Since Laurie was that type of guy, when insomnia hit him he'd spend the hours drifting through the internet looking up anything to distract him from the fact that he wasn't sound asleep. He was definitely awake now, though he couldn't feel his fingers where they gripped the brim of his hat.

Once in a while, a spike of snow flew up his sleeve, soaking his shirt cuff, making him want to complain bitterly that he was cold, only there wasn't anybody to complain to. Laurie was alone in this, and if he didn't find shelter soon, he was very likely going to die. An unfair fate for a guy who only wanted a break from his high tech job and endless meetings, who only longed for a bit of fresh air and interesting company. If he died, he'd never get to ride Gwen, his soft-nosed cowpony.

Hypothermia must have set in, for he imagined that he saw her ahead of him, her dun colored hide edged with white snow. There she stood, her head turned toward him as though she were indicating that yes, here was where they should stop to rest and warm up. *Here, Laurie, here.*

Laurie shook his head, for he knew that it was just the wind that was making him think he heard her voice because horses didn't talk, and certainly Bill wouldn't have been as cruel as to let Gwen out of her stable when the weather was this bad.

Laurie would have a bone to pick with Bill when he got back for not knowing that it was going to snow like this. It was probably a blizzard. He was going to die in a damn blizzard, which would be his own fault for thinking that an outdoor vacation in October in Wyoming was a good idea.

Walking toward Gwen, for there was nothing else he could see to aim for, Laurie squinted as the snow banged against his face. He could feel the weight of it in his hair and on his shoulder, the one that he kept pointed into the wind so he could make a straight line for Gwen across the growing drifts. Except as he got closer, he realized that he wasn't seeing Gwen, but instead something solid and brown, dense against the white.

Squinting and blinking, Laurie did his best to make out what it was. It was a cabin of some sort, made out of logs, though he didn't remember any building like it when Bill had taken them on a tour of the dude ranch. But the closer Laurie got to it, the sturdier the cabin became. Step by step he went, his knees sinking in deeper and deeper until he was right up against it. The snow pushed him hard against the wood, the drift of snow rising up to his chest just where the logs, overlapping each other, made a corner.

If he could get around the corner, he wouldn't be much more out of the wind, but there'd be a door. It'd probably be old and rotted, but at least he could yank it open and crawl inside to shelter. If he could outlast the storm, he could make his way back to the dude ranch and ask Bill for his money back because this was the worst vacation ever.

CHAPTER FIVE

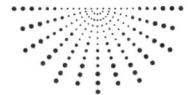

Laurie slid around the corner of the cabin, holding tightly to his hat. Feeling the way with his numb hand, he traced the length of the snow-coated log at shoulder height. Bill might applaud Laurie for his sense, even if he kept his eyes squinted against the icy wind that whirled around the corner logs. He didn't quite recognize the door when he saw it, for it was tall and broad and had no trim, save for the wooden handle that looked quite new and felt smooth beneath his hand.

Laurie gripped the handle and tugged. It didn't budge. Then he pushed. Then he tugged again. The door creaked, but it didn't move and it didn't open. Was it locked? What idiot locked a door to a cabin in the middle of nowhere? It was probably an empty cabin with nothing of value to steal; only an asshat would do something like prevent Laurie from getting inside so he wouldn't freeze to death.

In frustration, he banged on the door, barely feeling the slap of his hand against the wood. Then he kicked it, barely feeling the pressure of the kick on his boot. Only one toe, the middle one, had any feeling at all, and it was stinging, so he knew he'd kicked the door pretty hard.

He kicked the door again for good measure, and slammed on it with the heel of his palm, wincing as his skin began to sting and his wrists hurt. After another, single pound, he let his fist stay on the door, and stood there, unable to think it through further than that.

He had nowhere else to go, nowhere he could make it to fast enough to curl up into a ball and weather the storm. He might make a cave out of the snow, but that would be cold, so cold, and he did not have enough body warmth to keep him alive like that, not for very long, anyway. He was going to die, and they'd find his body when the snow was cleared away. He'd end up a story in somebody's news stream: *Lead Software Developer Found Frozen to Death, Was on Vacation Anyway*.

The wood beneath his hand creaked. For a second, he imagined he'd actually managed to open the door, but to his amazement, he heard metal clinking on the other side. Then he heard something that sounded like a latch, or maybe it was a bolt. Slowly, so slowly he thought he was imagining it, the door began to open.

It slid back, widening. A man stood at the door, holding it open, seemingly on the verge of slamming it shut. Behind him, Laurie could see the view of the interior of the cabin, and his gaze focused on the cozy orange and gold fire that burned in a stone fireplace.

"What in tarnation?" asked the man. "What are you doing wandering around in a storm like this? You another one of them fool city slickers thinking he can make it here when he couldn't make it back home?"

Laurie opened his mouth to explain how he'd gotten lost somehow from the dude ranch and that he was freezing to death and could he please come in. But no words came out and his whole body shuddered as a gust of wind bunched behind him. It slammed him in the back and pushed him over the threshold of the cabin, along with a huge drift of snow that in the warmth of the cabin began to melt into silver puddles.

"Damn it," said the man. He grabbed Laurie by the shirt collar, yanked him all the way in, and slammed the door behind him. He pulled the bolt closed, cutting off the wind and cold, and let Laurie go.

Laurie stumbled, his hands clenched together to try and warm them. Snow dripped from his too-new cowboy hat, and also into his boots, where he could feel it soaking his socks. He couldn't stop trembling and his lips were numb. The middle of his body, all up and down, was vacant and empty, filled with ice, and he knew he could never get warm unless he could get to the fireplace and hunker down in front of it.

"Damn it," said the man again. "All right, take off them clothes, and I'll get you a blanket. But don't go too near that fire too fast, you hear? You'll singe yourself trying to climb on top of them logs."

The man stepped away, giving Laurie a better view of the cabin, which was one large room with a fireplace on the far wall with a curtained window on one side. There was a long wooden counter against the wall, next to which was a farm sink.

On the other side of that was a little iron cookstove, with a table and two chairs in the corner. In the middle of the room was a leather chair, the kind that Laurie had seen in some of the more western-style hotels he'd stayed at a time or two, with a heavy, thick back, and a deep cushion that was more comfortable than it looked. Beside it was a small side table with a book, and a writing tablet with a thick pencil with no eraser.

Thinking he'd ended up in a portion of the dude ranch experience, which he might have to pay extra for later, Laurie started toward the fire. He was focused on that and nothing else, when the man yanked him back by the collar.

"What did I tell you?" asked the man. "Take off them damn clothes so you'll warm up all the sooner, and so you don't track snow on the rug. You hear me? Take them off."

Still shaking, Laurie looked at the man and scraped the melting snow from his eyebrows.

The man was wearing boots, canvas trousers with a thick brown belt around the waist, and leather suspenders over his blue chambray shirt. Beneath the open collar was another layer that looked like a union suit, the kind grandfathers liked to wear, with a tuft of dark chest hair peeking out. His face was sunburned beneath his dark, messy hair. He had a square jaw and looked tough, though there were small smile lines on the outer corners of his eyes, which were deep blue and cold as they stared at Laurie.

"You do as you're told, you hear?" asked the man. "I don't have time for this as it is, so take off them clothes and don't make me tell you again."

"You want me naked?" asked Laurie, not quite understanding, his mind still spinning at his brush with death and this sudden strange rescue. Then he did what he always did, which was to make a joke of the whole thing. "What, so you can have your wicked way with me? Aren't you at least going to buy me dinner first?"

Instead of making his audience laugh, as he usually did with a sassy comment like that, it had the opposite effect. With his mouth a firm scowl, the man yanked at Laurie's coat collar to get him to start taking it off. Which meant that he was quite close as a hard, red blush curled along his jaw and around his ears.

"I'm not that kind of man, d' you hear?" said the man, his words sharp as he pulled off Laurie's Carhartt jacket. "I'm *not* that kind of man."

The man took Laurie's cowboy hat from his head and shook it free of snow, then laid it on the kitchen table, and once he had Laurie's jacket off, he hung it on the back of one of the wooden chairs. For a moment they looked at each other and, startled, Laurie realized he'd overstepped a boundary.

The man might have leanings, but nobody liked being outed when they weren't ready. It wasn't just the worst manners, it was cruel, and Laurie was most definitely not a cruel person. Nor was he into trying to coax somebody to admit they were gay before they were ready. Or maybe the man wasn't gay and had just been embarrassed at Laurie's implication earlier that he was.

"I'm sorry," he said. "I'm really sorry, sometimes I go off at the mouth, but I didn't mean you any harm. But I'm really cold right now, so can I get in front of that fire?"

Laurie pointed at the fireplace that had been drawing him to it ever since the man opened the door. The river-rounded rocks that made up the fireplace front looked rosy in the firelight, and he found he was shuddering, wanting to go to it, but feeling unable to without his host's permission.

"Do as you're told and take off the rest of them clothes," said the man.

He sighed as he walked across the room and drew back the curtain to the left of the fireplace. This revealed a little bedroom where an iron bedstead filled the narrow space. From the bed, he grabbed a red woolen blanket and brought it over to Laurie.

"You'll warm up faster if you don't have to dry your clothes from the warmth of your skin," he explained. "Do you see? Now get undressed and I'll rub you down with this."

Laurie could see the sense in it, once it was explained to him.

"Okay, okay," he said as he began unbuttoning his shirt and slipping it off. "I remember now how it goes; you can freeze to death if you stay in wet clothes in the snow."

His mouth jerked as he spoke. Now that he was warming up, electric shocks ran through him, making all of his movements clumsy and undignified. He bent to slide off his cowboy boots, the leather shiny as the snow melted off them, and pulled off his wet socks which slapped against the wooden floorboards.

Lastly, his hands so numb he could barely manage, he took off his blue jeans and boxer briefs and gladly wrapped himself in the red woolen blanket that the man handed him.

"What are these?" asked the man as he held Laurie's limp, wet underwear in his hand. "Lady's pantalets?" The man shook his head as he quickly laid all the clothes over the other wooden chair at the table. "Never mind," he said. "Now, come here."

Laurie took a step closer, and then another one, and the man made him take the last step by clutching the fold of blanket that Laurie held close to his chest with both hands and pulling. Then he yanked the blanket back and, as briskly as any professional, buffed Laurie's skin with it. He started with Laurie's hair, then his shoulders, all the way down his ribs and around his hips.

When he knelt at Laurie's feet, he didn't even pause, but buffed and dried and warmed up Laurie's skin to the point where he felt glowingly warm all over. Even the insides of him, which had begun to feel like a deep freeze, began to thaw.

"There," said the man as he stood up and wrapped the blanket around Laurie once more. "You'll live," he said, the expression in his voice indicating that he wasn't sure whether or not that was a good thing. "Go and sit on the edge of the rug, and I'll bring you something warm to drink."

Laurie did exactly as he was told, now that following orders allowed him nearer the fire. He padded over to it, barefooted. His feet tingled on the wooden floorboards and then were warmed by the scratchy feel of the braided rug that was woven of many colors and looked like it had been made by hand. When he settled onto it, wrapping the blanket around him, he found that it was soft to sit on, and just the right thickness for him to cross his legs in front of him, the wooden floor cool beneath his calves.

The warmth of the fire licked at him, and he opened the blanket a bit to let that warmth soak into him. Everywhere the snow had melted, and where the man had buffed him dry, felt warm. Beneath his armpits even, and between his legs, where his balls nestled beneath his cock, which lay comfortably. Though normally he wasn't terribly shy about being naked when the occasion called for it, he felt rather wild and daring to be like this, naked and wrapped in a red wool blanket in front of a fire while a blizzard raged outside.

He heard the man clinking things at the stove and smelled warm coffee brewing and perked up. When the man hunkered at his side with a thick china mug full of the hot brew, Laurie took it, nodding his thanks.

"You have saved my life," said Laurie. "Which I very much appreciate because I don't think I could have found the bunk house or one of the barns even if my life counted on it, which it did. I'm Laurie, by the way. Pleased to meet you."

With one hand clutched around the coffee, Laurie held out his other hand so they could shake hands as gentlemen cowboys did.

"The *what* house?" asked the man, not taking Laurie's hand. His mouth scowled, and his dark brows drew together.

"The bunk house," said Laurie. "You know. The place where all the dude cowboys sleep when the weather is bad. There's one for the dudettes, too, which I'm told is pretty much the same, though I'm certain the bathrooms are nicer, which always happens. I couldn't find it, or the barn, or the corral when I woke up this morning. Everything was a whiteout, and your cabin was the only structure for miles."

"Well, this cabin *is* the only structure for miles," said the man. He stood up, pressing his hands on his thighs, and winced, like one of them hurt him. "Otherwise, I don't have any real notion what you just said. Except for your name. Laurie, was it?"

"Yes, Laurie. Laurie Quinn," said Laurie. "Say, do you have a phone I could use so I can call Bill at the dude ranch and tell him where I am?"

He held out his hand even further, though this time it was for the man's cell phone. The man drew his head back on his shoulders, which didn't surprise Laurie too much, as some people simply didn't like lending anyone their phone, no matter what the reason.

"I can't tell anybody where you are until the snow stops," said the man, as though Laurie were the worst of fools. "Drink the coffee, Laurie, but drink it slowly. Let it warm you up from the inside."

Laurie pulled his hand back and, holding the coffee mug with both hands, did as he was told. The man's reaction was puzzling, and he talked much slower than Laurie or anybody that Laurie was used to.

Also, why was he wearing grandfather clothes like an old-time cowboy? The cabin held only the bare necessities, so maybe the man was one of those minimalist types, determined to live in a one-room cabin like his ancestors did, as though to prove the point that modern civilization was the devil and only he knew the right way to live.

"My name is Laurie," repeated Laurie. He took a sip of the coffee, which was perfectly hot and just a bit bitter, the way good coffee should be. "And your name?"

The man stepped to the fire and took up an iron poker to move the logs. The fire burst into a bright flame that lit the room and cast long gold-edged shadows across the floor.

"My name's John," he said. "John Henton."

With his head down to study what he was doing, John poked at the fire and pulled a log from a wooden box to lie across the top. With the poker, he pushed that log so it was across the other ones, and the fire obediently began to burn with steady warmth. Laurie, sitting on the rug on the floor wrapped in only a red woolen blanket, had a good long moment to look at him.

John was tall, taller than Laurie, and seemed older than Laurie's twenty-four years, maybe being around thirty. He had broad shoulders and muscles beneath his blue shirt and suspenders. Everything about him was dense and strong, including his wrists as he held the heavy iron poker. His thighs were sturdy, though he cocked his hip and seemed to favor one leg over the other.

His boots were made for giants, which raised Laurie's eyebrows, as they weren't cowboy boots, no. They were working boots that had flaps to pull them on with, the kind you got from a western wear store, but with blunt toes and thick soles. The man, John, was dressed for work, but it wasn't for something as straightforward as riding horses or driving cattle across the high plains. No, it felt more complex than that.

When John looked down at Laurie sitting on the floor, Laurie looked up at him. His eyebrows rose and he felt a little expectant because if this was the extra portion of the dude ranch experience, then that meant that John worked for Bill. Since Bill liked to lead the way, probably John did too.

"I'll lend you my extra clothes, though they'll likely be too big," said John. "And you'll have to stay here till the snow stops." John shook his head as though deeply displeased by this notion.

"It's a blizzard," said Laurie, smiling.

He expected John to join in with him with a little sarcasm about the life or death threat of such weather. Instead, John shook his head and walked over to the table, pulling the plain, thick curtain back to reveal a wall of falling snow outside the window.

"That's not a blizzard, by any means," said John. "Just an early snowstorm, though a pretty heavy one at that."

"Not a blizzard?" asked Laurie. He took a gulp of his coffee and thought earnestly about this.

"I'll tell you when it's a blizzard," said John. "Though even a fool from back east, like yourself, ought to know better than to traipse about when the clouds gather over Iron Mountain."

"Yes, John," said Laurie, thinking to respond to John the way Bill liked his dude cowboys to answer him.

"In the morning, I'll take you into town." John gave the fire another hard poke. Then he put the iron poker back on the hook, where it swung back and forth once or twice, leaving another half circle of soot on the pale wall behind it. "We'll see if anybody there has lost a boy, though you're hardly a stripling, either."

With his mouth curling in displeasure, John went over to the tall wooden chest of drawers that was by the opening to the small room where the bed was. He slid open one of the drawers and pulled out clothes, presumably for Laurie to wear.

Next to the chest of drawers, Laurie noticed that there was a little wooden bookshelf that looked handmade, on top of which was a pen of sorts, and a brown journal. On the two shelves beneath were books. This arrangement gave the room a homey, welcoming air.

Laurie thought he would get dressed, and then he would look more closely at the titles. He'd borrow something to read to occupy his time until the snow stopped, then he could go home. He stood up, finished the last of his coffee, and, leaving the mug on the floor, went over to the bookshelf.

There was a row of calendars tacked to the wall above the shelf by long nails. The calendars were colorful, and probably had been hung to brighten the room. One was of playing cards, fanned out. Another showed a pair of women dressed in old-fashioned clothes, and the third one showed a boy in a sailor outfit riding a sturdy sled in the snow.

All of them displayed the month of October, and all of them indicated that the year was 1891. This was probably meant to give the idea that it actually *was* 1891, or thereabouts, when the old west was still the old west to give the dude ranch experience a sense of veritas.

"Why didn't you make it 1888 or something like that?" asked Laurie. "You know, because all those eights, eight-eight-eight, lined up together would look all old-fashioned and everything."

"Excuse me?" asked John, though as he came over to Laurie with the clothes, his eyes, with their flat expression, indicated that he wasn't much interested in Laurie's out loud conversation with himself.

"1888," said Laurie again. "Cowboys were at their height, and Buffalo Bill was doing his Wild West show, right?"

"You mean that fool Bill Cody?" asked John. He looked like he wanted to spit on the floor and cross himself. "That fellow don't know the first thing about being out west."

"I'd say he did," said Laurie. "He had that old west show and lots of people loved it. It was a big hit for years."

"*Lots* of people," said John, saying it in a way that mocked the way Laurie had just said it. "Lots of people are fools. Now get dressed. I need the table to finish up my work and then I need to get supper on."

"Supper?" asked Laurie. "Isn't it morning?"

"No, it's late afternoon, not whatever time you want it to be but the time that it is," said John, stern. "And the calendar says 1891 because it *is* 1891. Now get dressed before you catch your death of cold, and I have to explain myself to the sheriff in Farthing, which I would rather not do, thank you very much."

Laurie moved back to the fire and dropped the blanket to the wooden floor, his forehead wrinkling. He must have misunderstood what John had just said. It definitely wasn't 1891, in spite of the old-fashioned surroundings, where everything was sturdy and looked like it had been made by hand.

Why this isolated cottage and its occupant on a deserted corner of the dude ranch hadn't been described in the online brochure was beyond him. There must be more than one person who would have enjoyed the one-on-one experience with a real live old-fashioned man who worked and lived and breathed the era. He was handsome to boot, though a less stern expression on his face might make it easier to talk to him.

For now, Laurie would get dressed and eat supper, which was probably going to be more beans and steak. Then he'd read a book by the firelight, which sounded rather cozy. He'd probably have to sleep wrapped in a blanket on the rug, though that would be about as comfortable as he'd been the night before, maybe even more-so, when he'd fallen asleep on top of his sleeping bag.

When the snow let up, he'd get John to take him back to the dude ranch, where hopefully Bill wouldn't be pissed that Laurie had wandered off. Then he'd decide whether to continue with his vacation at the dude ranch or whether he'd be better off going home to sleep in his own bed.

CHAPTER SIX

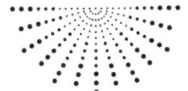

The clothes John handed to Laurie to change into were worn but sturdy. The woolen underwear was like John's except it was a yellowed-white and seemed thinner than what John was wearing. On top of being too big, it was also a bit tricky to get into because where was he supposed to put his dick so it wouldn't get chafed or pop out? Everything else he was given to wear, thank goodness, made sense, the long woolen socks, the belt, the flannel shirt, everything.

As he pulled up the thin leather suspenders, he realized John was watching, had been watching, the entire time. Laurie tugged on the waist of the dun-colored canvas trousers and smiled at him.

"I like the way these fit," said Laurie, trying to be nice, even though the underwear was too big on him. He was also careful not to point out that John's attention was bordering on stepping over that invisible line Laurie had drawn for himself. "Thank you, I'm a lot warmer now."

"You should be," said John. "That's what they gave me when I left the army. They are for summer, but they'll be warm enough for now. It's good to see them not go to waste."

"Oh," said Laurie. He wasn't sure what to say to that. Either John had really been in the army and they'd stiffed him because this wasn't the sort of goodbye package the U.S Army normally gave their soldiers. Or, more likely, John was playing the role assigned to him by Bill, and it was 1891, and yes, back in the day when you left after years of service, you got a stack of clothes that were completely unfashionable and, moreover, were for summer when it was almost winter.

"I'm going to get supper on," said John. "You want more coffee?"

"No, thank you," said Laurie. "But is there a bathroom I could use?" He jerked his thumb toward the middle of the room. He could not figure out where the bathroom would be, though possibly it might be hidden behind a curtain, the way the bedroom was.

"Outside and to the right," said John. He didn't take his attention away from what he was doing at the stove, where he was lifting round circles with a nickel-trimmed handle and shoving in thin strips of wood.

"Outside?" asked Laurie, trying not to let his voice rise in astonishment. Even the dude ranch had real bathrooms, so this whole old-fashioned thing was taking it a bit too far. Plus, it was still snowing. The thought of going out into what John had determined was a snowstorm, but what Laurie was sure was a blizzard, made his whole body clench up.

"Yes, outside," said John. He turned to look at Laurie, his brow furrowed. "Where else do you put an outhouse?"

"Holy Jesus," said Laurie under his breath.

"Wrap up, Laurie," said John, who either had not heard Laurie or was pretending he hadn't. "It's cold out there."

Laurie pulled on his too-new cowboy boots, the leather of which was squelchy and damp, and shook out his Carhartt jacket before putting it on. When he put on his cowboy hat, which was wet through, he shivered. The moment he stepped out the door, all that dampness would freeze, making him even colder.

It might almost be better to piss in a jar, though weren't there supposedly chamber pots or something back in 1891? Maybe, maybe, but Laurie didn't want to bother John, who turned back to his cooking with an expression that told Laurie he'd bothered him enough already. Which was strange because if the dude ranch wanted their customers to have a *good* experience visiting with this old-fashioned guy, then he'd have better manners.

"I'm going to go now," said Laurie.

John didn't say anything, still busy with the door on the cast iron stove, and Laurie thought he'd not heard. But then John turned around and went over to the chest of drawers where he pulled out a dark gray woolen scarf. Maybe it was another gift from the U.S. Army, but when he handed the scarf to Laurie, it was warm and soft.

"Wear that instead of your hat," said John. "Nothing will make you feel the cold worse than a wet head."

"Thank you," said Laurie.

He took off his cowboy hat and felt instantly better, especially when he wrapped the scarf around his head and clutched it beneath his chin like an old-fashioned grandmother would. He wobbled his head and curved his mouth in a little frown, as if he *was* a grandmother, displeased with what she saw before her.

"Now, you get supper on, young man," said Laurie in his best, creaky grandmother voice. He even shook his finger at John, wanting him to join in the fun. "It had better be ready by the time I get back."

John did not laugh, though he looked confused rather than disapproving, his dark brows drawn low, his mouth pursed.

Laurie laughed at himself and pulled the scarf back from his face, though he kept it clenched beneath his chin.

"If I don't come back," said Laurie with mock seriousness. "It means the wolves have eaten me."

"There are no wolves," said John as he came to the door and undid the bolt, making Laurie wonder if he was always going to be so staid and practical. "Maybe a pair of buffalo wolves who don't know any better than to leave an area that's going to be built up." With the door open, the snow swirling right outside, John stood there, and it seemed he was thinking of something to say about this. "You're too small a mouthful for them anyhow."

With a low, barked laugh, Laurie wanted to put his hand up so he and John could share a high-five. But because while John obviously had a sense of humor, a dry one at that, if he was going to maintain his role, then the palm-to-palm hand smack would be out of the question. Instead Laurie clutched the scarf as tightly as he could and stepped out into the swirling snow.

It was getting darker, which meant that, somehow, it was late afternoon, as John had said. Which Laurie didn't quite understand because he'd woken up in daylight after falling asleep, so it *should* be morning. But that was the lesser question. The more important issue was how he was going to catch his breath with the wind howling snow at him. The second he turned to the right and stepped out of the lee the cabin created and into the wind, he was pushed backwards and all the air from his lungs was sucked from him.

"Holy shit!" said Laurie, as loud as he wanted with nobody to hear. It didn't matter anyway because the words were snatched by the wind and whipped away to Kansas. Or, since he was in Wyoming, the wind whipped everything to South Dakota and then some.

Laurie squinted into the snow. The outhouse was on the top of a slope, about forty, maybe fifty feet away from the cabin and a little higher than where he was now. When the wind paused, and the snow swirled straight up around him, Laurie dashed for it, huffing to keep breathing, his mouth full of snow, his boots slipping with every step.

When he reached the outhouse, the wooden structure provided a small space of calm, but also slightly reeked. He didn't want to go in, but his bladder was bursting. His only other option was to pee in a snow bank, during which time he might very possibly freeze his dick off.

Holding his breath, Laurie yanked open the wooden door, which even had a crescent moon carved out of the planks, and stepped inside. He'd seen pictures of outhouses, but had never been in one, so the hole carved in the wooden seat was distressingly primitive, as were the sheets of paper from an old catalog hung on a nail. Well, he'd be going back to the dude ranch in the morning, so he could man up and pee into a dark seemingly bottomless hole for now, couldn't he?

Shivering, he unbuttoned his canvas trousers, fumbled through the buttons on the woolen underwear, and peed, breathing a sigh of relief. When he was done, he was shivering all over and could barely do himself up again. This was a mighty rough way to live, and while it might be fun for a day, or even seven days, it was nothing he would choose for himself for longer than that.

Laurie clutched the scarf to his ears, opened the door to the outhouse, and stepped out into the crisp swirling air of the snowstorm. He breathed in the fresh air deeply, which made his lungs hurt, it was just that cold. He hustled down the hill, kicking up snow as he went, keeping his eyes on where he was going. It wouldn't do to get lost, which would be easy to do, as he couldn't tell where the air ended and the ground began, especially now that it was getting dark.

The only solid thing was the brown logs of the cabin, and he headed for that. When he went around the corner, the wind seemed to have died but the snow was coming down like someone up above was shoveling out buckets of it.

The door opened, and John stood silhouetted in the firelight, beckoning Laurie inside.

With a grateful jerk of his chin, and shivering from head to toe, Laurie stepped over the threshold. He was startled when John grabbed the scarf from him without asking. But when John shook it outside before closing the door, Laurie understood. There was only so much snow that John wanted brought into the cabin, which seemed much warmer and far more cozy than it had before Laurie'd gone to the outhouse.

"Supper's ready. Wash your hands," said John. He pointed to where a blue and white china basin sat on the wooden counter.

Peeling off his Carhartt jacket and pausing a moment to tug off his damp boots, Laurie made his way over to the basin, from which steam rose. Next to it was a small wooden box that held what looked like soap, as he could see finger marks in it. When he used the soap, it felt greasy, and didn't lather very well.

Laurie was struck with the differences between John's make-believe world and his own, where every convenience was available at any moment, and soap bubbled up right away instead of never. With a shrug, Laurie dried his hands on the towel that looked like it had been made out of a flour sack and hung it back on the nail that had been pounded into the counter.

When he went to join John at the table, John had just placed the last of the food down, and was bending to light a kerosene lamp, which cast bright silver circles on the wood.

John sat down with his back to the fire, so Laurie took the other seat with his back nearest the door. He could feel a cold draft coming from somewhere, but was distracted by the meal John had prepared. There was a plate of fried bacon slices, a bowl of cornbread bricks, and a bowl of what looked like fried potatoes and onions. None of it resembled Laurie's idea of what supper was. Still, he didn't want to be rude.

"What's in the jar?" asked Laurie, pointing.

"Tomato preserves," said John with a bit of a grunt, as if Laurie should already have known that. "There's butter, if you want it."

Laurie looked where John was pointing, which was at a wooden bowl with several pale lumps in it. It might be butter, but it actually looked like old white frosting scraped from a can.

"That's not very yellow," said Laurie, reaching for it. "Butter is yellow," he told John, nodding his head to emphasize this.

"Maybe back east, where you come from," said John. "Out here, butter is the color that it is when it's churned."

Laurie gave John a mock salute and points off for being so gloomy and serious. And just as he reached for the plate of bacon, John lifted it and scraped off half onto Laurie's plate. He did the same thing with the hunks of cornbread and fried potatoes and onions, each dish divided neatly and fairly into two portions.

"Help yourself to the butter and tomatoes," said John. With his fork gripped in his fist, he began to shovel in the food, slowly and methodically, as though it gave him no pleasure at all and was merely sustenance. Which, as Laurie considered it, in 1891 was how it probably had been.

Laurie sprinkled the salt, which came in a little tin, on pretty much everything. He used the dull knife to spread butter on top of the cornbread which though hard, was steaming hot, and began to eat. Everything was a little on the plain side, though it tasted pretty good. When John used his spoon to spread tomato preserves on half of his buttered cornbread, Laurie did the same, and the sweetness of the tomatoes made the meal taste just a little bit better.

Eating with John became its own pleasure, as John, seated at his own table and not striding around taking care of an unwanted guest, was a little more calm. His expression while he ate was a little softer beneath the dark edges of his five o'clock shadow.

Once or twice he looked directly at Laurie, his eyes sharp and blue, but mostly he stared at the table, as if into a middle distance of other thoughts that would take him far away from where he was. The light from the lamp trailed gold ribbons across his face, bringing up shadows and secrets, making Laurie want to stare. Which he resisted as best he could as John, playing Mr. 1891, would not appreciate it.

When they finished the meal, John stood up, scraping the legs of his chair across the floorboards, plate in hand.

"Bring the rest of that over and I'll do the supper dishes," said John.

Laurie stood up, too, his mouth open. He was just on the verge of making a joke about where the dessert was and, if it was hidden, was John going to get up in the middle of the night and eat it by himself? But Laurie had a feeling that had there been dessert, John would have divided it exactly in two, as he'd done with the rest of the food. Besides, Laurie was full, and he was warm, and in the morning he would go home so he could get himself something sweet later.

He picked up his empty plate, which was made of china and did not match any of the other dishes or bowls on the table. One by one he gathered the rest of the dishes and placed them on the counter.

"What should I do now?" asked Laurie. He did not mention the most obvious fact that there wasn't a computer anywhere to be seen, so definitely there would be no Netflix, which would have been a very welcome distraction on any night in the middle of nowhere, especially on a snowy one like this one.

"Help yourself to the books," said John. His back was to Laurie as he worked at the stove, pouring hot water from what looked almost exactly like the large coffee pot Laurie'd seen on the chuck wagon.

"But don't touch the ledgers or the journal, as those are the property of the railroad."

"Okay," said Laurie, trying not to let himself feel put off by John's gruff manner, as it was probably all a part of the extra portion of the dude ranch experience.

Going over to the bookshelf, which was against the wall beneath a curtained window, Laurie hunkered down in front of it. As he expected, he recognized none of the books, for they were all old and looked like nothing he'd ever seen in a book store or in a library.

There were titles like *Millbank*, and *The History of the French Revolution* by Thomas Carlyle, and other books of that nature, all thick and studious looking, and certainly not very interesting. One bright green spine stood out, though, and when Laurie pulled it out to look at it, he saw that it was called *The Polar and Tropical Worlds* by Dr. G. Hartwig. Laurie wanted to groan and complain, for was there nothing fun to read?

He opened up the book anyway, as it was the only means of entertainment. The frontispiece showed a group of huskies pulling a sled, and the description indicated that there were over two hundred illustrations, as if this amazing fact was bound to make the book a best seller.

The words within the book were printed so small that Laurie almost had to squint to read, but he stood up with the book in his hand anyway. He went over to the edge of the braided rug and sat cross-legged in the firelight and browsed through the book, flipping the pages till he saw something interesting, and began to read.

CHAPTER SEVEN

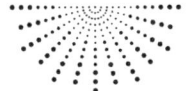

The book, as old and dreary as it was, drew Laurie in and absorbed him. He only looked up from the pages when John hunkered in front of the fire, inches away from Laurie, and began tucking the ashes together with a small dented iron shovel. Almost imperceptibly, the room became a little colder.

"What are you doing?" asked Laurie.

"Banking the fire so we can go to bed," said John. "Then I'll bank the stove."

"Is it that late?" asked Laurie. It certainly didn't feel like it.

John, still hunkered in front of the fire, turned his upper body, and reached down to a small pocket just at the waist of his canvas trousers and pulled out a pocket watch. It wasn't attached by a chain, as Laurie would have thought, just tucked away, ready to be used, close at hand. Rubbing his thumb across the latch, John popped it open, and the brass lid gleamed in the firelight.

"Nine o'clock," said John. He closed the watch, stood up and, pausing to wind the pocket watch, he placed it on the chest of drawers. "That's bedtime in these parts."

Laurie's eyebrows rose in his forehead. He thought about stating quite clearly that he wasn't tired. Not to mention, he'd just reached a very exciting chapter on polar ice caps in the book he was reading and couldn't he stay up another hour or two so he could get through it?

He was about to ask this and make a little joke of it, except John stood up. Stretching his elbows back, his blue shirt pulled across his chest. Then with a low chuff of his breath, he ran his hands through his hair, making it stand up.

Laurie tilted his head back and realized he was staring, his mouth open. In spite of this, John began unbuttoning his shirt, and pulling off his thin leather suspenders as he walked over to the counter next to the stove.

As though unaware that Laurie was watching him or, if he knew, he was disregarding it, John not only pulled off the shirt and laid it on the back of one of the chairs, he unbuttoned the top buttons of his red union suit and dragged it down until he was stripped to the waist. Then he pulled off his boots and stockings, and stood there, barefooted, his broad back naked in the firelight.

John tossed the dishwater from earlier into a metal bucket, and poured more water from the large coffee pot into the china basin. Laurie could hardly stand to look away, even when he realized what John was doing. Surely this moment of washing for bed was a private one, and not meant to be shared with anyone who was not also doing the same.

Oblivious to his audience of one, John took a small, rough cloth and a dollop of soft soap from the wooden box, and began to wash. He washed his face, and scrubbed it with the cloth. Then he splashed to rinse his face. With his chin dripping, he washed beneath his arms and across the back of his neck, always with long, calm movements, as if this was what he did every night and could have done it in his sleep.

Bending over the basin, he splashed with water those parts of him he'd just washed and then, bending down, he wiped the bottoms of his feet with the wash rag. Lastly, as Laurie watched with wide eyes, John unbuttoned his trousers and his red woolen union suit and applied the washcloth to his crotch. Rinsing the washcloth, he did this again with intimate, quick gestures.

Laurie was so mesmerized that he was unprepared for the moment when, after hanging the washcloth on a nail next to the drying towel, John turned to face him, buttoning up his union suit but leaving the trousers hanging open.

"You can wash now," said John.

Without waiting for Laurie's reply, John strode to the chest of drawers, moving across the braided rug behind Laurie's back, which sent Laurie's whole spine rippling with reaction. Obviously, it was expected that he do what John just did, though Laurie preferred to wash in private with the benefit of a hot stream of water steaming up the place.

Telling John that no, he wouldn't worry about it now as the shower at the dude ranch would be fine once he got back, didn't seem to be an option. Especially not when John came over to the stove to bank it for the night, as well. He'd slipped a nightshirt on over his union suit when Laurie wasn't looking, and now looked rather sweet in the collarless striped garment, which reached to his calves.

"I don't have a nightshirt for you," said John. "I only have the one, but let me know if you get cold, and I'll let you have it."

Laurie was quite able to imagine what it might be like to watch John pulling off the nightshirt, arms crossed as he pulled. And how Laurie would be left there, staring at John's chest, molded close by the thin wool of the red union suit, its jaunty metal buttons closing up the front and the little flap in the back.

No, he most definitely could not deal with that particular sight, so with a gulp, Laurie nodded. "I'm sure I'll be fine, but thank you," he said.

When he went over to the basin and touched the water, it wasn't very warm. Laurie knew it wasn't going to be very pleasant, but if he hurried, he'd get it over with fast.

While John puttered around, checking the bolt on the door, rechecking the fire and stove, Laurie peeled back his shirt and union suit. Using a clean cloth, he scrubbed his face and neck, doing it like John had done. He even washed his feet and his crotch, pretending he'd gone camping with one of his more outdoorsy friends and he was cleaning himself in the woods after a long hard day of hiking.

When he was finished, he dumped the water in the metal bucket as John had done, and hung the used washcloth over the one John had used. Wiping his hands on his union suit, thinking too late about drying them on the towel on the nail, Laurie turned to face the center of the cabin.

"Do we really have to go to bed now?" asked Laurie.

In another, different situation he would have made a comment that would have come out as a suggestion that they do something else, something more intimate to occupy the hours of the evening. But in this time and place the innuendo would be lost on John, who was pulling back the curtain all the way to reveal the bed fully. He took the two plump little pillows and placed one on each side of the bed.

"Why don't I sleep on the floor and leave the bed to you?" asked Laurie.

"Only animals sleep on the floor," said John as he tugged the bedclothes back. "Besides, morning comes early, so stop your chatter and get in the bed."

"Forceful," said Laurie under his breath.

Except John heard him and, with brows lowered, he shook his head.

"Back east you might have electricity and can do as you please till all hours. Here we don't, so we need to work when it's daylight and sleep when it's dark. Now take off your clothes and get into bed."

Laurie was half inclined to call the whole thing off and tell John that he really didn't want to participate in the extra dude ranch experience anymore. Except that wouldn't change anything, as it was still cold as hell out and snowing. Besides, he really didn't want to sleep on the floor, which was fine to sit on for a while, but would be too hard to sleep on.

Grateful for the golden light of the single kerosene lamp, Laurie took off everything except his union suit and, with nowhere else to put his clothes, went to drape them on the chair. While he was crossing the room, John snuffed the lamp on the table, leaving the room in total darkness. It was like being in a mine, and the only reason Laurie made it to the bed without tripping was because he had already touched the thin iron bedstead.

As he listened to the sounds of John crawling into bed, Laurie climbed in on the right side, unsure whether the double bed could really hold two men. The metal bedstead creaked. The bedclothes felt heavy, and he imagined that there were layers and layers of woolen blankets, or at least he hoped so or they'd freeze to death. When he lay back, his shoulder brushed John's, and his eyes were wide open in the dark.

"Sometimes," said Laurie, softly, wanting to be kind and warn John. "Sometimes I have a hard time falling asleep and toss and turn a little."

"You'd fall asleep a damn sight faster if you stopped talking," said John, not even whispering in the dark.

The sound of John's voice sent a little shiver up the back of Laurie's neck. He wondered whether it would be appropriate to respond to the guy Bill had hired to give Laurie a bit of extra in the visiting-the-old-west experience. And then whether Zach would have considered himself lucky to be in Laurie's shoes, as Zach liked dark and handsome. He probably would have said that Laurie should roll a little closer and see what happened.

Maxton, on the other hand, would probably advise Laurie in no uncertain terms to get out of the bed and sleep on the rug, as John wasn't somebody Laurie knew and trusted. Maxton, as well, preferred blondes, at least as far as Laurie knew because Maxton played his love life close and quiet.

Laurie was not up to either moving close or abandoning the bed. Besides, his union suit bunched around his middle, so he had to tug on it as he turned on his side to face the wall. The little bedroom was built in an alcove that jutted out past the fireplace. He imagined that it must have been added as an afterthought and built somewhat hastily because he could hear the wind howling quite clearly. In fact, as he faced the wall, even with the sheets and blankets pulled all the way up to his chin, he could feel a thin waft of very cold air.

When he rolled over the other way, he came face to face with John's back, his nose buried in a fold of John's nightshirt. But he was distracted from this by the fact that the thin waft of air was now dancing around his neck. This meant he definitely was not going to be able to fall asleep, not with the combination of the cold air, the strange bed, and the person he did not know in the bed with him only inches away. He whimpered as he burrowed down, and prepared himself for a long, uncomfortable, and wakeful night.

"What's the matter with you now?" asked John with a grunt.

It was so dark Laurie couldn't truly see, but it seemed John had pitched back in the bed, as though turning his head to listen. This also brought him closer to Laurie, all warm and solid in the dark.

"I don't want to complain," said Laurie. "But I have to because there's cold air coming from somewhere and it's right on my neck."

He felt bad because almost instantly John launched from the bed, leaving a blank space with the bedclothes pulled back that filled with cold, moving air. Laurie shivered as John walked around the bed, with no idea, no idea at all, what John was doing. He listened as John's bare feet moved across the wooden floor, and then he almost came out of his skin when John's body brushed his side of the bed.

"What are you doing?" asked Laurie, hoping his voice didn't sound as nervous as he felt. What if John was a murderer and was going to kill him in the night and hide his body in the snow?

"Feeling for drafts," said John. "Seems like a chunk of mud fell, creating a chink in the daub."

"A *what* in the *what*?" asked Laurie. He rolled over on his back and sat up, staring as hard as he could into the darkness. Now that his eyes had gotten a little more used to the dark, he could almost, it seemed, see John's outline, which was quite close, since the bedroom was so small. John loomed there, a vital, warm form that made Laurie catch his breath.

"There's mud between the logs, mud and grass," said John. "Some of it must have fallen out, so now there's a breeze coming in. Scoot over."

"What?" asked Laurie, his voice rising high in his confusion.

"I said scoot over," said John. "You're such a tenderfoot. I'll take this side, and in the morning, I'll fix it."

"In a blizzard?" asked Laurie, unable to imagine how John could fix something like that with the snow coming down and everything frozen."

"It'll stop by then," said John. "Now scoot over so I can get some sleep."

Laurie did as he was told, moving into the place where John had so recently been, the sheets still warm, the pillow smelling a bit like John. Laurie turned on his side once more so he could keep his eye on what John was doing.

John crawled in the bed, graceful in the dark, and when his head was on the pillow he pulled the bedclothes up. The bed heaved and shifted, and finally, when everything was still, Laurie realized their faces were only inches away in the dark. But where normally he might make a crack about it and get John to laugh, he only blinked a few times because already he was a good deal warmer with no icy breeze coming down his neck.

"Thank you," Laurie said. "I'm warmer already."

"You've got the manners of a lady," said John, unexpectedly.

Laurie snorted, thinking it ironic that John had gotten him to laugh, rather than the other way around. At least he was warmer. But more, he felt like burrowing close so that John's body completely cut out all the night-ness and the darkness and the coldness, and the whole stress of ending up here, in a cabin in the middle of nowhere. He would tuck his arms close to his body, and snuggle his head beneath John's chin, and keep his eyes closed till he fell asleep.

But that would startle John and cause him to curse, and Laurie didn't want that because as he yawned, he realized he was feeling sleepy. Which of course anybody would in the dark, like it was, with the wind howling outside like wild wolves trying to get inside the cabin. But the wind couldn't get in, so Laurie could go to sleep, and as he did, he thought that it was nice having someone like John to look out for him.

CHAPTER EIGHT

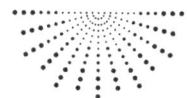

In the morning, Laurie awoke to find himself, yes, indeed, burrowed into the small of John's back, and though his whole body wasn't molded to John's, it was a pretty close thing. But the second he realized it, John surged in the bed, pushed the bedclothes away, and got up.

When he pulled back the curtain, the whole cabin was suffused in light. The sun was shining, the light bouncing off the snow which, as John had predicted, had stopped falling in the night.

Without a word and still in his nightshirt and union suit, John began walking around the cabin, easing the hitch in his step. Laurie could only see the door of the cabin from where he was, but by the sounds of it, dull clanks of iron, the hiss of a match, John was lighting the stove. Laurie could smell the woodsmoke almost immediately, and soon after heard the crackle of flames, and the creak of the pump.

Was he supposed to get up and help? Or stay in bed and out of the way? Well, it didn't matter, because by lunchtime he'd be back at the dude ranch where both light and warmth could be had by the flick of a switch. John must be pretty dedicated to the whole reenactment thing to not have at least one or two modern conveniences to offset the amount of time it took to do everything else.

"Better get up so we can eat and head into town before it starts snowing again," said John.

He came to the open doorway of the bedroom and began to raise his nightshirt over his head, just in the way Laurie had imagined it the night before, with the motions pulling the wool of the union suit close over John's chest. Laurie tried not to stare but it was hard.

Then John got dressed in the clothes he'd worn the day before, using brisk, practical movements. When he yawned as he ran his hands through his dark, witchweed hair, Laurie made himself look away.

There wasn't any use panting and pining; soon he'd be long gone from here, and John didn't need someone like Laurie wanting him when he didn't want, or couldn't want, Laurie back. Laurie had learned that at the beginning of his college days, a lesson hard learned and never forgotten.

"Get up," said John, turning to the bed as he buttoned his trouser buttons, fastened his thick belt, and pulled up his suspenders. He put his brass pocket watch in the little pocket of his trousers. "I'm not bringing you breakfast in bed, that's for certain."

His sharp blue eyes looked directly at Laurie as he said this, and for a split second, Laurie could imagine how it might be to have John bringing him breakfast on a tray, maybe with a little rose in a slender glass vase, the way it always was in the movies. But that would mean John would have to have a tray and a vase *and* the rose, not to mention the time it would take to wait on Laurie hand and foot. Which would probably only make him more grumpy than he already was.

Laurie sighed to show how put upon he was, and crawled out of the bed, now cold since John wasn't also in it.

While breakfast sizzled and popped on the stove, Laurie got dressed. Since his own clothes were dry, Laurie got into them, though the blue jeans were stiff and the shirt crackled when he put it on. Everything felt thin, right down to his boxer shorts and socks, and much less sturdy or able to keep out the weather than the clothes John had loaned him the day before.

"Come to the table and eat up," said John. "Daylight's burning."

Indeed, daylight was burning, right into the three windows cut into the walls of the cabin. Since the cabin faced east, the light was bright and intense, so Laurie reached up and pulled the curtain that was nearest him closed.

"Don't like the light?" asked John as he brought breakfast to the table.

"It's early," said Laurie. He was about to go into his don't-wake-me-till-I've-had-coffee shtick, which usually made everybody laugh, when John preempted him by pouring coffee directly from the coffee pot into a thick, sturdy china mug. There didn't seem to be cream or sugar, so Laurie drank it slowly, drank it black, and smiled at the bitter warmth of it.

"Thank you," said Laurie. "I'm not quite human till I've had coffee."

"You look pretty human to me," said John. He poured his own coffee, then put the coffee pot back on the stove. The drips down the metal side hissed when they touched the hot iron of the stove, filling the air with a faint scent of burnt coffee. "Now eat."

Eating meant working his way through the pile of food that John deemed breakfast, which was strips of something yellow and fried, along with bacon and more fried potatoes and onions. John was pouring what looked like real maple syrup over pretty much everything on his plate, but since Laurie wasn't sure, he pointed.

"What's this?" he asked.

"Fried cornmeal mush, what do you think it is?" asked John with his typical grunt. Then, his hand fisted around his fork, he began to eat in that same methodical style he'd used the night before, without any pleasure in the meal, as though it was something he had to do rather than something he enjoyed.

"I don't know," said Laurie, doing his best to keep the conversation pleasant, though that was proving to be hard to do with John. "I've never seen fried cornmeal mush before."

John gave a dubious snort and continued eating, so Laurie, being brave, took the syrup and drizzled it on the fried cornmeal mush and the bacon. Then he put a little salt on his fried potatoes and onions, took up his fork, and began to eat.

As with the night before, the food was simple and hot and filling, and so while the sun blazed through the windows, and the stove filled the air with smoky warmth, Laurie ate everything on his plate.

When they were finished, John took the dishes and cutlery to the counter, looked at the stove, and shook his head.

"I'll do those when I get back," he said, almost to himself.

Which made Laurie think John talked to himself more often than not and also that he intended their trip into town would be successful. Laurie would find his way back to the dude ranch, by sled if necessary, and John would come back to the cabin to continue his life alone.

When Laurie had put on his Carhartt jacket, also stiff, his thin, warped cowboy boots, and his cowboy hat, which had dried badly into a misshapen circle, John shook his head.

"Forget the hat," said John, handing Laurie the gray scarf. "Wrap that around your head. It's only a mile or so into town, but there's no point in you being cold. We should make it there before it snows again."

Laurie, unable to imagine more snow on the way, watched while he tried not to watch John pull on his boots, using their leather flaps, a grunt deep in his chest as he stomped on the heel to settle them. Then he pulled on a coat that looked like it was made of some kind of fluffy fur, the inside of which was lined with flannel.

"What kind of coat is that?" asked Laurie, wondering if it was warmer than his Carhartt, which it probably was.

"Buffalo hide," said John. "This kind has the hair left long, which makes it warmer." As he dipped his chin to focus on fastening the coat, he stroked the fur and added, "At least I think so."

This statement, soft-spoken, at least for John, did tender things to Laurie's heart for reasons that he couldn't really explain to himself. But there wasn't time to mull over it, as John quickly banked the stove, grabbed what looked like a burlap sack, which turned out to be a kind of rucksack, from a peg beside the door, and opened the bolt. Sun and wind swirled in the cabin as John stepped outside, Laurie close on his heels, into the bright sunshine.

Morning had brought wind, and already great swaths of brown grass were showing beneath the drifts of snow, as flecks of icy snow whipped across the surface. John motioned with his hand as he slung the sack on his back, and with John leading the way, they headed across the prairie toward the brown smudge of buildings in the near distance.

THE WIND BLEW from the west, howling over the drifts of snow and churning it up in the air so that while the snow wasn't deep to walk in, they were constantly surrounded by clouds of it. Laurie had to hold his hand cupped around his eyes to be able to see, though as he didn't have any gloves he often had to switch hands. Constantly leaning into the wind to keep it from blowing him over also gave Laurie a crick in his neck.

He kept his eyes on John's broad shoulders the entire way, walking one step behind, wondering why anyone would pay good money for an experience like this. Maybe there were guys who liked roughing it and testing themselves against the elements. His best friend Zach might have enjoyed the challenge, at least for a little while. Laurie was not one of those guys; he should have listened to his roommate Maxton and never signed up for a dude ranch in the first place.

He felt almost frozen by the time they reached the edge of town. As they walked along the buildings on the wooden sidewalk, his brain started whirling with confusion. The town they entered had the same layout that Farthing had when he'd come through on the ride share from the airport in Cheyenne. Not only was the layout the same, the width of the streets was the same, and the buildings were the same. The difference was that everything was new, as if it had been built quite recently.

Laurie pulled his scarf away from his nose and mouth, which made the slight layer of frozen mist from his breath crackle.

"Where are we?" asked Laurie as he tugged on the sleeve of John's buffalo hide coat.

"Farthing," said John, though he barely turned his head to speak.

That was impossible. Farthing was an old town where everything was worn by time. The stop signs were faded by the sun, the blacktopped streets had crumbling edges, and half the buildings held businesses that had closed. One of the few businesses still running had been the old-time general store, a sturdy brick building that had been full of tourist stuff like you found everywhere. Except John was leading them to that very building, and it was new, with two brick stories, and shiny clean windows.

In one of the windows was a Native American woman. She was sitting at a small table as though on display, and it looked like she was sewing beadwork. When John and Laurie tromped into the store, she nodded at them and smiled.

The owner of the store, as was obvious by his glossy mustache and his confident stride, came across the wooden floorboards to greet them.

"John," said the man. "I see you weathered the storm fairly well. Welcome."

"Pete," said John, in his typical gruff way as he shook the man's hand, though it seemed to Laurie that John was more pleased than he let on.

"What brings you to town?" asked Pete. He took a moment to straighten his white apron, which was tied around his belly with a black string.

"A few things, maybe," said John. He unbuttoned his buffalo hide coat, as though in echo to Pete's straightening his apron. "Mostly, I've come to see if anybody's lost a boy." John jerked his thumb to point at Laurie, and when he did this, more than one guy in the store turned to look at him, including Pete.

"Where did you find him?" asked Pete. "And where did he come from? It's too late in the season for railroad workers."

"I don't know, that's why I'm asking," said John. "He's some tenderfoot from back east, I reckon, as he came scratching at my door yesterday in the midst of the storm. As he was hardly dressed for the weather, I had to let him in."

"I'm standing right here," said Laurie, not bothering to hide his irritation.

He stepped forward, unwrapping his scarf and unbuttoning his jacket. The stares were getting to him, as was the store, which was filled with the kind of sensible things John had in the cabin, and nothing like the touristy things he was used to seeing. As well, other than the Native American woman sitting in the window, there were no women in sight, no music playing from the speakers, no signs to the restrooms.

A calendar hung over the open door to a little office, and it was one of the same ones that John had, the one with the two old-fashioned women. Like the calendars in the cabin, this one indicated it was October, 1891. The sight of this made Laurie shiver all over, as though he were out in the storm once more, though he didn't know why.

"So I see," said Pete, with his hands on his hips and a smile that seemed to say he was humoring Laurie like he was a youngster. "Where did you come from, young man?"

"From the Farthingdale Dude Ranch," said Laurie. He waved his hand to indicate that much should be obvious to everyone. "The one that organized this whole shindig where everybody makes like it's the olden days for the tourist trade. Like it's 1891."

"That's because it *is* 1891," said Pete, and though he didn't roll his eyes, from the tone in his voice he might as well have.

John made a little chuffing sound beneath his breath and took off his hat to run his hand through his dark hair.

"He's been talking this kind of nonsense since he showed up," said John. "Now listen, Pete, do you know anybody who'd claim him? Has the sheriff been by from Chugwater about him?"

"No and no, I'm sorry to say, John," said Pete. He gestured over John's shoulder. "Adeline, put that down and come on out of there."

The woman stepped down from her table in the window. She was not quite as tall as Laurie and was wearing a leather dress with fringe along the sleeve. Her black hair, streaked with gray, was done in two simple braids that hung forward over her shoulders. In her hands she carried some of her beadwork, clutched at her side.

"John," she said, tipping her head in greeting, her voice softly accented in a way that Laurie couldn't define. "How is the leg, I hope it fares well."

"Adeline," said John, with a small smile that told Laurie he was glad to see her. Maybe he was sweet on her, too. "The leg is good, thanks to your salve."

"You got lucky coming out of them damn Indian wars with nothing more than a bullet wound," said Pete.

"*Dude*," said Laurie, more irritated now than when they'd first come in the store. "Native American, please. She's standing *right* here."

"I see the little red fox you found in the snow has sharp teeth," said Adeline, and though her smile at Laurie seemed genuine, he couldn't understand why she wasn't insulted by what Pete had called her.

"Do you mean me?" asked Laurie, astonished as he pointed to himself.

"On account of your hair," she said and nodded, her dark eyes bright. "It's quite red."

"It's not *that* red, lady," said Laurie, hurt that after he defended her she'd insult him. "It's deep auburn."

"Just like a little red fox," said Adeline, completely nonplussed by his anger. "You're going to have your hands full with this one, John."

"I'm trying to get somebody to take him," said John. "And Laurie, there's no call to be talking to Adeline like that. I don't care if you don't think much of Indians, you don't speak to her that way, you hear?"

"For *fuck's* sake," said Laurie. "You guys can *stop* now. I guess back in 1891 everybody said insulting and derogatory things any time they wanted to, but you're taking it too far. She's a Native American. I mean, if she wanted to call herself an Indian, that'd be one thing—"

John grabbed Laurie's arm, and clutched it tight enough for the words to die in Laurie's throat. He gave Laurie a hard shake, and his grip hurt.

"Look around you and shut your mouth for once," said John, his voice low and hard. "Get it through your head what year it is. It's 1891. If you can't do that, and you can't stop pestering everybody about how they talk, then I will teach you how, you understand?"

Everybody in the store was silent, even the fellow at the cash register, with his sleeves puffed at his shoulders on account of he'd pushed his wrists back with little paper cuffs. And the man fishing in a barrel with a large pickle halfway to his mouth, and the guy at the counter looking at a half-unrolled bolt of dun-colored cloth. All of them stared at Laurie.

Laurie blinked, his mouth open, though no words came out.

It could not be true, of course, as time travel was impossible. It must be that John and everybody had been paid a great deal to stick to their roles, to stay submerged inside their personas.

It might be that Pete was really an accountant from New York who had a thing about the old west, and it might be that Adeline was really a high powered lawyer from San Diego who wanted a chance to see what it had been like for her people before the west had been taken over and civilized.

And John. John could have been a linebacker for a major league football team who wanted to see if he could winter it alone. Everybody in the store, all of them, could have back stories of homes in the suburbs, and mortgages, and every single one of them was probably a lawn-raking, card-carrying adult following their collective dreams of living in the old west.

Or.

Or, it could be that Bill had been right, and that Iron Mountain granted wishes. Only Laurie hadn't known his wish was to come back to 1891 to experience hardship, deprivation, outhouses, and not enough sugar in his coffee. Except that's *exactly* what he'd come to Wyoming for, and exactly why he'd paid for a true old west experience at the Farthingdale Dude Ranch.

Had his wish come true? For real?

"Let me go," said Laurie. He shook John's hand from his arm. He was sweating everywhere even though he felt cold again, as cold as though he'd just come through a storm.

"Looks like you're going to have to keep him, especially since you're the one who found him," said Pete. "Besides, nobody else is going to want a firecracker like that, I'd say."

"I reckon you're right," said John, though he was obviously far from pleased. "Damn it all anyhow."

"You can tame a little red fox easily, John," said Adeline. "If you're gentle with him."

"I'm not a—*fuck* it." Laurie snapped his mouth shut and rubbed his arm and, unable to figure out what to do with himself, glared at John.

John, in his John-like way, ignored Laurie as he admired the beadwork Adeline was showing to him, a long belt with an intricate and colorful pattern.

The work had been done by hand as Adeline sat in the store window like some kind of live display, a demeaning caricature of an animal in a cage. Though, if it was really 1891, such treatment was probably common. That didn't make it right, but it was, in a way, proof Laurie was back in the past. Which was impossible, simply impossible.

Laurie opened his mouth, but he knew if he brought up any protests about their treatment of Adeline or the way they talked about her, John would probably make him wait outside in the wind and cold. So Laurie glared some more, which John was completely unaffected by, and tried to focus on the beadwork, which showed Adeline's skill and experience.

"That's going to bring a pretty penny, Adeline," said John as he traced a finger along the edge of the belt. "Enough to take you through to spring, easy."

"This and the purse, I think," said Adeline. "Right, Pete?"

"That's true enough," said Pete. "Probably right until summer."

"I should return to my work so I can finish these," said Adeline. "And John, take good care of your little red fox, yes?"

John sighed as they watched the woman go back to her table in the window. There, she arranged her leather skirts and bent once more over her work.

"So," said Pete, echoing John's sigh. "Are you going to keep him?"

"Looks like I'm going to have to until, if ever, somebody comes looking for him," said John.

Laurie, who had never before felt more like an unwanted parcel, tried to keep his mouth shut, though in his rage and confusion he bared his teeth and snarled, which brought John's attention back to him.

"Kit him up," said John. His blue eyes looked Laurie up and down, as though measuring him. "Make sure he's warm. Get him something to replace those thin, east coast clothes he's got on. Thick socks, a warm hat, union suit, and so on. And boots, too, if you have any. And a buffalo hide coat, both like mine." John lifted his booted foot and tapped it, and patted the flap along the edge.

"Shall I put it on the railroad's tab?" asked Pete.

"No," said John. "I'll pay for the boy's gear. But if you got any tar paper for the cabin, the railroad can pay for that. For now, I'll take the boy outside before he tears anybody's head off."

"I'm not a boy," said Laurie through gritted teeth.

"Then quit acting like one," said John in reply as he started walking out of the store. With a gesture, he directed Laurie to follow him.

CHAPTER NINE

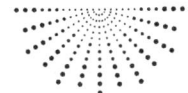

Laurie followed John out of the store. He didn't want to do as he was told, though as they stepped outside onto the boardwalk and into the cold, windy sunshine, he realized he didn't have anywhere else to go. Especially if it really was 1891.

At that point in history, as he vaguely recalled from history class, Wyoming was one big wide-open space. Farthing was miles from anywhere anyway, but in 1891 there wouldn't be any gas stations along the way or passing cars being driven by someone kind who would give Laurie a lift to Cheyenne so he could get home to Harlin.

There were no cell phones or cell towers, no convenience stores, no cash machines where Laurie could enter his PIN and get out a wad of cash to pay for a bus ticket home. Nothing that he knew or was familiar with, no culture that he knew how to navigate the way he normally would.

He couldn't call Zach up and ask him for advice—and it hit him that he might never see Zach again, with his fair hair curling over his forehead, his blue eyes full of affection for Laurie.

He'd never again stumble into the kitchen of the apartment he shared with Maxton. Maxton was always up early, making the best coffee anybody had ever tasted, a cup held out in silent greeting, waiting for Laurie to speak first, so as not to break the peace of the morning.

Laurie had nothing and no one, only John, who was now looking at him as though Laurie was the worst of inconveniences.

"Come on," said John, seemingly ignoring Laurie's state of shock. "While I'm in town I might as well tend to my errands. For one, I need to go to the apothecary to pick up some things. If you're good and mind your manners while we're in there, I'll take you over to the hotel for a piece of pie and a cup of coffee not made by me."

The last of that statement, which sounded more like an order, might have been meant to be funny, a light addition to make Laurie smile. But Laurie was numb all over, and didn't smile as he followed John along the wooden sidewalk.

The wood, still nearly frozen from the storm, creaked and popped beneath their feet dangerously, as if the sidewalk were about to collapse beneath them. But it didn't, and soon John stopped in front of a store that had a sign in the window that said: *Apothecary and Simples; Teeth Pulling*.

The smell of the shop was spicy and fragrant, and the shop had the same wooden floors as Pete's store did. There was only one other person in the store, a man in an apron much like Pete's, behind the counter.

Laurie didn't know what to do with himself while John went about his business. He waited by the door, almost hiding, and watched as the clerk wrapped several piles of what looked like brown dust in brown paper packets. John paid for the articles with silver coins from a leather wallet and put the packets in the pocket of his buffalo hide coat.

When he turned to look at Laurie, his expression, while not exactly one of dismay, was not happy. John had been saddled with him, but out of a personal sense of obligation, it seemed, would keep him. As Laurie had nowhere else to go, he needed to go along to get along until he could figure things out.

He followed John around the small town, which had more stores than Laurie could remember from before. John went into each and every one of the stores, filling his rucksack with supplies, and all the while, Laurie's mind churned, over and over, on the same useless facts.

It was 1891, at least that's what John said and the calendars all said, and here Laurie was, even though there was no proof that time travel existed. He had no idea how he'd arrived in this time, and no idea how to get back home. But time travel wasn't real. His brain kept trying to think it all through, and all the while he felt numb from the neck down, barely feeling the ruts in the street as he stumbled over them.

The wind was blowing, bringing clouds that packed overhead in anxious white knots, and which began drifting down a bit of sleet that would soon turn into real snow. Seeming to ignore this, John led them both back up the street.

At one point, he went diagonally across the whole street to the other side. Back in Laurie's time, this would have meant they might get run over by a car, but now only meant they had to dodge piles of horse manure and the occasional buckboard wagon.

They went into a two-story brick hotel on the corner opposite the general store. The sign over the door read *Farthing Hotel*. As John opened the door and they stepped in, Laurie was surprised to realize he was in what would be, one day, the gift shop and drug store he'd stopped at to get some aspirin on his way to the dude ranch. Only now the building was a hotel, with a small lobby with dull painted walls, and a board along the wall with ten nails pounded in, upon which hung room keys.

A sweet little girl in a blue dress and apron, her hair brushed severely back into a braid, surely too young to be working, led them to a table. She took their coats and John's rucksack, and hung them on hooks, though she placed the rucksack on the floor.

A woman came out, her hair scraped back into a bun, wearing a gray dress that went to the floor. Her likeness to the young girl was so close that Laurie presumed she was the girl's mother, and indeed, the woman clasped the girl's shoulder gently as she smiled at John.

"We've got chicken pot pie, Mr. Henton," said the woman.

"Surely it's too early for lunch," said John. He smiled at her in a gentle way he'd never used with Laurie. "We've just come in for pie and coffee, if it's available."

"You should eat first," said the woman. "I'll bring you the pot pie."

The woman and the young girl left. Laurie didn't want to draw attention to himself, but as he sat in the wooden chair and slumped, the chair shifted with a loud noise. John, who was unfolding a cloth napkin in his lap, scowled at him.

"None of your foolish talk in here, understand?" said John. "These are good people."

"I'm good people," said Laurie in retort. "I know how to mind my manners, so don't treat me like a kid."

Before John could answer this, the woman came back carrying two china plates with the pot pies. She also brought a bowl of mashed potatoes, and cornbread.

Normally, Laurie wouldn't have been impressed, but if it was 1891 —if it was *truly* 1891, then the amount of work it would have taken to prepare the meal was a lot. The woman had probably killed and gutted the chicken herself, dug the potatoes and mashed them by hand and on it went. Though Laurie nodded his thanks, when the pot pie was placed in front of him, his stomach was so upset he couldn't eat.

John started right in, holding his fork in his fist, his lips slick from the grease as he chewed. Laurie did his best not to stare.

"Are you not eating?" asked John as he licked his lips. "I don't know what you did back home, but out here we don't waste food."

"I'm not that hungry," said Laurie. "Besides, we can get a doggy bag."

"A *what* bag?" asked John, his eyebrows going up. Laurie imagined that John's mind was quite confused with the idea of wasting such good food on a dog.

"Never mind," said Laurie.

He did his best to eat, though mostly he just picked at the meal, as he hadn't the stomach for it. He managed half a bite of the pot pie, some of the potatoes, and gave up. When the woman brought out slices of strawberry-rhubarb pie, Laurie didn't even try, although he almost managed to enjoy watching John enjoy his pie and coffee.

When they finished, the remainder of Laurie's meal, including his uneaten slice of pie, was wrapped up to be taken to somebody who lived in town who'd broken his leg and couldn't get up to fend for himself, though Laurie didn't catch the name. Then they put on their coats and went back to the general store to pick up Laurie's new clothes.

Laurie quickly put on the buffalo hide coat, a smaller version of John's, and gratefully put on the pair of knitted mittens and the new hat. Then, loaded down like two packhorses, they headed back to the cabin.

By the time they'd hiked through the sleet-pocked drifts to the cabin, Laurie was shaking with cold, in spite of the coat. His stomach churned with his distress at arriving at the cabin with no real idea how to leave it.

Had this been when it was supposed to be, Laurie could have gotten a ride back to the dude ranch. Only now, the full-on realization that that wasn't going to happen hit him hard and he was freaking out. Was he going to be stuck in the year 1891 to live out his life with not only no modern conveniences, but also nobody that he knew?

He was all alone except for one grumpy, grizzled buffalo hide coat-wearing linebacker. Who was now scowling at him, yet again, as Laurie stood inside the door dripping snow on the floor.

"Take off your coat, and next time knock the snow and mud off your boots before you come inside, you hear?" John slung off the rucksack and put it on the table. "I've got to go walk traps, so put these supplies away. Then, after, you can either hang up or wear your new clothes. If you get cold, there's more wood in the shed, but be careful, the railroad's surveying equipment is out there, too."

With that, John took down the rifle from the pegs over the door. He cracked it open to check the bullets, and refastened his buffalo hide coat in a swirl of fur. He went out into the snow, closing the door solidly behind him, leaving Laurie alone for the first time in two days. He sighed deep into his lungs and, going to the table, sat down and buried his face in his arms.

The cabin smelled like cold, boiled potatoes and onions fried in rancid bacon grease. There was the smell of dust, too, and slightly warm ash. Outside, the wind was growing, keening around the edges of the cabin like a lost thing wanting to get in.

He wanted to call Zach on his cell and complain about the smell and the sound, and how the cabin seemed empty without John in it. How scared he was, how worried. How he feared he would never be able to figure out how to get home and would be stuck here forever.

He wanted to bump his shoulder in silent solidarity with Maxton, who would look at him in that steady way of his, holding back his words, but standing nearby, because that was who he was.

But neither of them was there, and Laurie was alone. He didn't know what to do or how he was going to survive. And he hadn't the energy to figure it out.

THE CABIN HAD GROWN cold as Laurie sat there with no fire in the fireplace, the coals in the stove gray and soft. Laurie made himself go out into the windy day to get more wood for the fire. When he came out of the shed, his arms full of wood, the wind came and yanked the shed door open with a loud crack.

With pieces of wood flying from his arms, Laurie managed to shove at the door to get it to close. Then, back inside the cabin, he crammed a lot of wood in the stove, hoping to get warmer more quickly. Except, instead of the fire behaving as it did when John was around, flames leaped up dangerously from beneath the stove lids. The stove began to smoke, large black clouds of it rising to the beamed ceiling.

Frantically, he propped the door to the cabin open with a chunk of wood. Then he went back to the stove and tried poking at it with the fireplace poker, but the wood he'd shoved in there was stuck fast and burning merrily away. Black clouds roiled to lace the windows and churn in a swirl into the open air through the doorway, and soot started to layer on the table and the floor.

If he burned down the cabin before John got back, John was going to be pissed and would toss him out into the snow, and what would happen to Laurie then? He wouldn't last a minute on his own in 1891.

Sparks rose to the ceiling of the cabin and fell to the floor, leaving little black spots. Laurie stamped them out, only he couldn't be sure they *were* out. But he couldn't get the red pump next to the metal sink to work so he tossed the remains of the coffee on the sparks. Which made the cabin smell like burnt coffee, ash, and Laurie's own sweat of desperation.

He stood with his hands on his hips and stared at the mess. Maybe if he got a bucket of snow and tossed it on the coals, then they would go out, and the stove would stop smoking. And maybe he could clean everything up before John got back. But John had already been gone hours, it seemed, and was probably due any moment, so Laurie had only minutes, if not seconds, to get the stove unjammed so it would stop smoking.

Except he'd not even that, for John strode through the open front door with his rifle over his arm, a large dead jackrabbit in his hand. Snow swirled around him, head to foot, as though he'd brought the weather indoors with him. One side of his face became damp as the snow began to melt and his eyes were filled with fury.

"What the *hell*, Laurie?" John laid the jackrabbit on the snow. Storming in, he quickly placed the rifle in its hooks over the door, shedding his buffalo skin coat, which sent specks of dampness onto the floorboards as he went. "What did you do to the stove, and why is the shed door open?"

Laurie stood back as John went to the stove. In under a minute, John wriggled the stuck wood free, and closed the door on the now-obedient fire. Smoke began to dissipate, though it was leaving a gray layer of soot and ash over everything. Soon the air would be clear, but the cabin was now cold and smoky, and John was glaring at Laurie so hard that he took a step back.

"Come with me," said John.

When Laurie didn't instantly do as he was told, John grabbed him by the back of the neck and took him outside and into the shed. The door to the shed hung open, and now snow had swirled in, covering the floor and the woodpile. The haystack-insulated boxes of railroad surveying equipment were splatted with snow, and though Laurie thought they would be okay, John obviously did not.

"That equipment's sturdy, but if it needlessly gets broken, it's worth a hundred dollars to the railroad company, which will come out of my pay come spring, do you understand?"

"Who *cares*." Laurie glared at John, shaken by the near-disaster, and the hopeless sinking feeling that overtook him as the smoke died down. "I certainly don't care because this is all probably a dumb dream in my head. Or maybe I'm stuck here in this *shitty* cabin and I'm never getting back home."

"You need a lesson in manners, that's easy to see," said John. His voice was level, but his face was tight.

Before Laurie could say anything else, John took off his belt, bent Laurie over one of the hay bales, and whipped him with the belt. Shocked beyond words, Laurie gripped the hay with his fists, wincing as the belt struck him, as it curled around his hips and bit into his skin. When John stepped back with a grunt, and Laurie heard him putting his belt back on, he stood up, his ass on fire, his hands clenched into fists.

"What the *hell* was that for?" shouted Laurie. "I'm not a kid, you can't do that to me!"

"If you're going to behave like a ten year old," said John, his blue eyes narrowing, "then I'm going to treat you like one."

"Fuck you," said Laurie, teeth bared. "It's not my fault the wood got jammed in the stove! At least I didn't let the cabin burn down."

"You don't have any call to talk to me like that," said John. Though his voice was low, he became dangerous, someone with no heart who would, at last, throw Laurie out into the snow and shut the door so he couldn't come back in. "You might be from back east, but I won't stand for language such as you'd hear from a street rat."

Laurie took a breath. "Fuck you," he said. "Fuck you and fuck this stupid cabin and fuck 1891! It's a fucking asshat of a year and you people live like animals!"

In a heartbeat, John was next to him, gripping Laurie's arm in a hard fist. Laurie raised his chin and stuck it out, but fear rippled through him that John was going to take his belt off again and give Laurie another whipping.

Laurie was so scared and so anxious—what if he never got home to his own time? What if he never saw his friends Zach and Maxton again? What if he was stuck here with a furious old-time linebacker who liked to order people about and enforce it with his might?

Laurie had gotten beaten up a time or two, both for being gay, and once or twice just because someone found him obnoxious enough to punch. But he couldn't put up with abuse. He'd grab his coat and leave and track back to Farthing to find someone to take him in till he could figure out how to go home. Determined, Laurie jutted his chin out. And then it trembled.

It might have been a small movement, but John's eyes caught it. He turned his head slightly away, as though trying to examine Laurie out of the corner of his eyes to understand what he'd not understood before.

"You don't quite know what to do with yourself, do you," said John, almost conversationally, though his voice was steel hard. "Well, you need to learn how, and you need to stop complaining about what year it is, because it *is* 1891 and that's all there is to it."

Laurie thought John might give him another hard shake just to prove his point. If that happened, Laurie felt like he'd snap and take off running back to town or just out across the high, white-swirling prairie until he collapsed and was covered with snow.

If this was all a dream, then maybe he'd wake up and it'd be morning around the campfire, with Bill's cowboys making them breakfast on the chuck wagon stove. Or maybe it wasn't a dream, and he was stuck here, stuck living this hard, horrible life, one miserable day after another until he died.

Except John didn't shake him. Instead, John sighed, his mouth tight. In that moment of stillness, Laurie could see that John was tired, just like Laurie was tired, for there were traces of exhaustion around his eyes. Laurie was obviously a trial to John, who was doing his best to deal with someone who must seem to him to be a crazy person.

John must have realized how close they were, and that Laurie was looking right at him because John looked away, let Laurie go, and stepped back.

"Go into the cabin and clean up," said John, the expression on his face saying that this was just another order, like all the others. "I'll get the snow out of the shed, fix the door, and skin this rabbit. Then I'll make supper."

Laurie could refuse. Part of him wanted to, just to make a point that you didn't leave someone alone who didn't know how to work a cast iron stove or follow instructions to build up the fire if he didn't want to freeze to death.

In John's mind, however, someone Laurie's age *would* know how, so there shouldn't have been any problem. But if Laurie started explaining this, then he'd yet again have to bring up the fact that he didn't belong in the year 1891, which might set John off. He'd said several times that he didn't want Laurie talking about it anymore, like it was bad manners Laurie had that John was trying to break him of.

So he had to do as he was told.

"Fine," Laurie said.

He moved past John out of the shed and went into the cabin and stood at the door, shocked at the sight. John's once-tidy cabin was now a mess of ash and soot, with snow sprayed across the floorboards and mud tracked in from both their boots. There were even streaks of gray on the curtains that would now need washing.

It was so many things all at once that Laurie stood there for a moment with his eyes closed, half hoping that when he opened them, the cabin would turn out to be one of the self-cleaning types, and the problem would be solved. But, alas, no. When Laurie opened his eyes, the cabin was still dirty, so he went to the little pantry off the long wooden counter to find a broom and some old rags to clean with, and got to work.

CHAPTER TEN

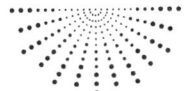

Laurie slumped in his chair at the table, though he tried not to. John, silently and efficiently, had helped him finish cleaning the cabin, using vinegar and water on the windows and flat surfaces, and applying the broom to the walls and floors. Together they unpacked the rucksack and put away supplies. Laurie's new clothes were left on the bed for him to wear or put in the chest of drawers, and his new boots stood by the door to try on later.

The cabin currently smelled only faintly of smoke, and John said they'd take the curtains and cleaning cloths to the laundress in town, and to never mind that now. He lit the kerosene lamp and served up jackrabbit stew in two equal portions in the mismatched china bowls, along with a plate with four biscuits on it, and the wooden bowl of white, lumpy butter.

The stew had a layer of oil on the top and looked like it had been made with cut carrots and onions. Laurie supposed it smelled good and would taste good, but he didn't have the stomach for it. He didn't want to eat anything, he was just that tired.

His heart hurt with the idea of never going home again. With never again being able to grouse with Maxton about the coffee shop downtown that didn't know how to do a proper pour-over. Or to joke with Zach about the local diner that kept sending them coupons for blue plate specials, but which always were expired by the time they arrived in the mail. All of the life he knew was gone and now he was faced with the prospect of this, a rough existence on the frontier, and screwing it up every other minute.

"You need to eat your supper," said John. He held his spoon in his fist and started scooping the stew into his mouth, getting a little grease on his chin, which made Laurie notice that there was beard-growth along his jaw, and how the hell did people shave in 1891?

"I'm not hungry," said Laurie. "Thanks anyway."

"You need to eat," said John, a little more forcefully. "You didn't eat hardly anything in town and have not eaten since breakfast."

"And I just told you I'm not hungry," said Laurie, and then he regretted saying it the way he had because what if John took it in his mind that Laurie needed another whipping? He was still aching from the first one. Overwhelmed, he pushed back his bowl of rabbit stew and buried his face in his arms on the table.

"I just want a salad," he mumbled from the cave of his arms, where the smell of the vinegar they'd used to clean the table was strong. "With tofu and ginger dressing."

"I don't have any notion what tofu is," said John, his voice coming through the dark. "And I don't have any fresh greens, so—"

"I just want to go home," said Laurie. "Do you understand that, wanting to go home?"

"I understand it right enough," said John. "But I don't have any cash to send you till spring, do you see? So eat your supper."

Laurie sat up with his hands in his lap, hopelessness swamping over him.

But then, as John looked at him, sitting there with his spoon gripped in his fist, it occurred to Laurie what John had just said. As he thought Laurie came from somewhere back east, he was, it seemed, offering to send Laurie back there, only he couldn't right now because he couldn't afford it. Which was kind of nice, considering that Laurie had been nothing but trouble since the moment he'd arrived, been rude to John's friends in town, and had almost burned the cabin down.

"Eat your supper," said John. He pointed at Laurie's plate with his spoon.

"I honestly can't," said Laurie with a shake of his head. "I'm just too upset to eat."

John suddenly got up from the table, scraping his chair across the wooden floor, startling Laurie into sitting up straight. But then John went past him and over to the pantry, and Laurie let out a slow breath.

John went down into the little root cellar, and when he came back up he had two canning jars in his hands, which he placed on the table with a clunk. He sat down and took one of the biscuits, sliced it, and slathered it with the white butter. Then he took a spoonful of something that looked like red vomit from one canning jar and drizzled what looked like honey from the other. He handed the whole mess to Laurie on a small blue and white china plate.

"You can't go to sleep on an empty belly," said John. "So at least eat that."

Laurie scrubbed at his chin, not knowing what to say to this sudden display of care. What if John was like one of those guys who beat their partners and then apologized with roses, only to have the whole cycle start again the next day? He couldn't deal with that, couldn't put up with that. But he was too exhausted to leave for Farthing, and besides it was dark out.

"What's the red stuff?" Laurie asked.

"Rhubarb compote," said John. "A woman in town makes it, along with the tomato preserves and suchlike that I have in the cellar. Try it, it's sweet, for she makes it with sugar."

"Sweet?" asked Laurie. "And is that honey?"

"I save it for special occasions," said John, and it seemed to Laurie he was somewhat defensive about this, as though a burly, strong man shouldn't have any weaknesses, or a soft spot for honey.

"Don't save it for special," said Laurie, in an almost scolding way. "Now is special."

He meant to say it in a way to explain to John how he felt about always putting off the nice things, like the people who bought super expensive towels only guests could use, which was ridiculous. Possibly John had been planning to save that honey to celebrate with when he got his pay in spring. Except now he'd opened it for Laurie, so now it was Laurie's duty as a guest to eat it.

He picked up the laden biscuit and bit into it. The inside of his whole mouth turned into a mix of flavors he'd not been expecting, the tart with the sweet, and the fat of the butter. He found he'd eaten the entire thing with a few swallows.

"Good, eh?" asked John, and he might have been smiling, only Laurie couldn't be sure. "Do you want the other one like that?"

"Yes, please," said Laurie, nodding.

"Fine," said John. He sat back a little in his chair. "You can have it, but eat some rabbit stew first."

Laurie, of course, could have made himself another biscuit layered with butter and honey and rhubarb compote, and eaten it before John stopped him. Well, almost. But not only would it have been rude to do that to his host, Laurie realized he was now a little bit hungry. He picked up his spoon and started eating his stew. Meanwhile, John prepared another biscuit and pushed the plate near Laurie.

Together they ate, a pleasant silence building between them. John finished his stew before Laurie did, after which he made himself two biscuits with butter and rhubarb compote and honey and, not saving them for later, ate them both, one after the other.

When Laurie's china bowl was empty, he enjoyed his final biscuit, eating it slowly and with more care, licking the traces of the rhubarb and butter and honey from his lips.

When supper was done, John got up and began heating water on the stove, shaving slivers from a yellow and white brick of soap into the basin. It occurred to Laurie, perhaps not for the first time, that everything John did took five times longer than it did back in Laurie's own time, back in the future. This realization made Laurie feel quite lazy to be sitting there while John worked, as the day had been as long ˙ⁿ as it had for Laurie.

help you with the dishes?" asked Laurie, though he wasn't

really sure how he could be of any help, since there were so few dishes, and only so much space at the sink.

"No," said John, with his back to Laurie. "You're so ham fisted you'll break them."

"No, I wouldn't," said Laurie, though he knew it was probably true. As tired as he was, and as unsure as he was how everything worked, he'd be more likely to dash a plate to the floor than anything else. "Why don't you use tin dishes?" asked Laurie as he watched John working away. "Then it wouldn't matter."

For a moment, John was silent, and when he turned his head to reply, he paused.

"I prefer the china," said John. "I don't like the sound of metal on metal."

With some astonishment, Laurie realized there was a red blush curling around the length of John's jaw and up behind his ear, disappearing beneath the thick, dark hair.

This stopped Laurie from his own darker thoughts about being stuck in 1891, and made him focus on John. The metal on metal sound could simply mean it was something that John disliked, though Laurie had an inkling that the aversion might have come from the wars Pete had talked about. Being in a war, *any* war, could make someone come away from it wanting to escape from the harsh sounds, and as Laurie looked around the cabin, it suddenly came more clear to him.

In the cabin there was very little metal that could scrape against other metal. Sure, the knobs had metal in them, and the bolt on the front door was entirely made of iron. There was a metal bucket near the counter, and that was it.

Then there was the set of mismatched china plates, some with a rose pattern, some with blue and white, as though John collected them along the way as he journeyed from the war to here. Unable to afford an entire set all at once, he'd picked those that had struck his fancy, but only those made of china rather than tin so he wouldn't have to hear the sounds of a fork being scraped across metal.

He'd brought the dishes to this cabin in the middle of nowhere, along with the plain curtains which, as Laurie looked at them now, were made of warm wool on the outside and soft flannel on the inside. The thick braided rug on the floor was very soft, as he could attest, and the leather chair in the middle of it looked comfortable. The cabin was a place for John to escape to, and the only hard things in the cabin were the floor, the table, and John himself.

When John was finished with the dishes, he set them on a towel on the wooden counter to dry. He motioned that Laurie should get up so he could sweep around the table, and generally settled the cabin to rights for the evening. Then he pulled his pocket watch from the little pocket in his trousers and opened it, then shut it with a snap before placing it on top of the chest of drawers.

"It's not quite bedtime," said John. "I'm going to oil my boots. You should oil yours so they keep out the snow better."

"You want me to do more work?" asked Laurie, in a way that was meant to be a joke, to get people laughing, as he usually did. Only he said it before he realized that John would likely take it that Laurie was complaining. John might determine to do something about that, which would require going out into the shed and for John to take off his belt again.

"Would you rather we sit here and twiddle our thumbs while the fire dies down?" asked John, either ignoring the attempt at a joke, or not having understood it. He went to the cupboard and took out a glass bottle of oil and two worn cloths, and sat at the table in his stocking feet, his boots arranged on the table in front of him. "You should oil yours and then try them on."

Unsure what else to do, Laurie got his boots from beside the door, and sat at the table with John. Taking one of the cloths, Laurie tipped the bottle of oil onto the cloth. The oil smelled a bit like a stable, or a place that had saddles, like the tack room at the dude ranch. But before he let this sweep him into despair, he began to spread the oil, a little bit at a time, over his boots.

new leather softened and darkened as he oiled it, and made supple beneath his hands. He felt somewhat better now that his hands were busy and his brain was occupied, even though the task was very simple.

John's boots were much larger than Laurie's and clunked when John turned them to oil the other side.

"Don't get any on the table if you can help it," said John.

"I won't," said Laurie, though he already had left little black dots of oil that would mar the table forever.

John put his boots by the door, and gestured that Laurie should try his on. Which Laurie did, pulling the leather flaps and stomping his feet on the floor to settle his heels inside the boots. They were a little tight, but they felt solid and good when he stomped his feet.

He wondered whether Maxton would have nodded his approval, or whether Zach would have made a joke about joining the local motorcycle gang, now that he had the boots for it. But he couldn't let himself feel sad, otherwise he'd never make it through this. So he stomped his feet again to hear the thud and to stave off the queasy feelings and to remind himself where he was right now.

When he looked up, he saw John had been watching him the entire time. Laurie couldn't tell if he was smiling or not, though it seemed he might have been.

"Those'll keep your feet dry in all weather," said John. "Now, put them away as it's time to get ready for bed."

"You sure are bossy," said Laurie. He was so tired he was unable to keep his mouth shut as he did as John had asked and took his boots off to place them by the door next to John's boots.

"And you sure are mouthy," said John, with a scoff and a shake of his head. "It's dark out. It's time for bed."

John poured water from the large coffee pot that had been heating on the stove into the china basin. He went through his ritual of half undressing, peeling away his suspenders, his shirt, and his union suit to bend and wash his face and neck.

Laurie knew what was coming and could hardly look away, though it was the more polite thing to do. He needed to give John his privacy, especially when there was so little privacy to be had in the cabin. He did everything he could not to stare, but was barely able to jerk his head away when he saw John take the washcloth and open his trousers to wash himself between his legs.

With his jaw tight, Laurie stared at the braided rug on the floor, only turning his attention back to John when he heard the used water being tossed into the slop bucket.

"Your turn," said John as he dried his face on a thin towel. "I'm going to shave in the morning. You can too, if you'd like."

"Okay," said Laurie, not feeling very enthused at the idea, as he didn't know how to use an old-fashioned straight-edged razor as John probably owned.

"You can also take off those clothes from today and we'll use them as dust rags. Your new union suit and nightshirt are on the bed."

Laurie washed at the basin, going through the ritual, echoing John's movements. He came out of his exhausted daze to see John standing there with Laurie's new underwear and nightshirt in his hands.

"You look plumb ready to fall over," said John. "Come on, now, here you go."

Laurie peeled off his clothes, too tired to care that he was standing there naked in the cabin with John so near, and put on the new red underwear. It covered him from neck to ankle, and was soft even if it was wool. It even had the little butt flap in the back, and had never been worn by anybody but himself.

When he put on the nightshirt, a long garment made of thick flannel that reached his shins, he felt warm all over. He put on the woolen socks that John handed him, and knew that he'd not realized how cold he'd been for the last two days; a shiver engulfed him from head to toe as the warmth kicked in.

John checked the bolt on the front door, banked the fires, and blew out the kerosene lamp on the table. When he drew back the curtain to the bed, John went to the right side, and together they climbed into bed in the darkness, the metal frame creaking beneath them.

After a moment, Laurie adjusted his hands against his chest as he faced John in the bed.

"You're right," said John. "It is cold on this side. I'll chink that hole in the morning." Laurie heard him settling his head on the pillow. "We'll use the tar paper I bought today to make a seal over it so the wind can't blow it loose again."

"Okay," said Laurie.

He yawned hugely, almost cracking his jaw. He should fall asleep right away, because if he didn't, he'd be so exhausted in the morning he might say more things to John that he'd regret, and get John mad at him, and then John would throw him out in the snow and Laurie would freeze to death. He'd be dead in 1891, and nobody would ever know what had happened to him. And then he'd never get back to his apartment, or to anything from his old life.

In the darkness, he missed Zach and Maxton so much his throat grew thick. Though he knew he was swimming in self-pity and that he needed to get it together, a small sound escaped his throat. He realized he was crying, hot tears slipping down his face in the dark.

There was no way to hide this from John, who was only inches away. The lack of privacy for anything, even nighttime tears, was frustrating, almost infuriating, but there was nothing Laurie could do about it except attempt to quietly wipe his face with the back of his hand and hope John just ignored him.

To his astonishment, John reached out and cupped the back of Laurie's neck. He pulled him close till Laurie's forehead was resting on John's chest.

Laurie thought to jerk back, all the while thinking of the kind of creeper guys who would smack with one hand and reward with another. He didn't want any part of that kind of relationship, especially if he was stuck here in this cabin with John. But even as he struggled with the impulse, he realized John's hand was quite gentle, and that John was talking, low, in the darkness.

"It'll be all right, Laurie," said John. "You're just wore out from today. Tomorrow will look better, I promise."

John must also have been worn out from that day, too, having to put up with Laurie for that long, and the day before. As he really must have just wanted to live his peaceful, old-fashioned life, this was quite a sweet thing for him to say. So Laurie stayed where he was, soothed by John's easy, deep breaths, and the warmth that grew between their bodies. For the first time in days, Laurie felt perfectly safe.

CHAPTER ELEVEN

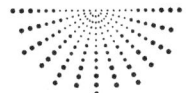

Morning came with a bang of light that found Laurie with his eyes wide open, the blankets pulled all the way up to his chin against the cold air. From beyond the partly drawn faded calico curtain he could hear John at the stove, clanging the iron lids, and smell the freshly brewed coffee. He was in John's cabin, and it was *still* 1891.

It would be time to get up, then, though Laurie barely remembered falling asleep. He remembered his tears, and John's hand at the back of his neck, and the comfort that had eased through him from that single touch. But now another day loomed, and Laurie knew he could either succumb to the morass of darkness that threatened to pull him down into it, or he could get up and face the cabin and the simple ruggedness of life in the year 1891. Face the day. Face John. Face everything.

He needed to survive, but more than that he needed to make life livable. Maybe he could find a way to make John laugh a little so John would like him, and life would be bearable until he found a way home. With this in mind, he got up, struggling out from beneath the warmth of the bedclothes.

He winced as he sat there for a minute, his ass sore from the whipping from the day before. At least he was warm and his feet were warm, and he had a feeling that maybe fried cornmeal mush might taste a little better today.

He got out of the bed and pushed the curtain all the way back. For a moment he stood there, rubbing the sleep from his eyes, attempting to figure out what John was doing at the counter, since he obviously wasn't cooking, as there were no sounds or smells from frying.

"What are you doing?" asked Laurie, his voice thick from sleep. He coughed, and John turned around. He was still in his nightshirt, a straight razor in his hand and a bit of soap on his face, his chin half shaved. "Oh."

"Leave your nightshirt on till you've shaved," said John. "In case you drip."

"I—" Laurie stopped at that, as he would have to admit to John there was one more thing Laurie didn't know how to do. Or maybe he should just pretend he did, and give it a try?

He went up to the counter and stood watching John shave with long, careful swipes of the razor, which glinted in a sharp, dangerous way beneath the soap that dripped from it into the basin.

John cast him a side-eyed look, quite serious, as he usually was. At the same time, as he looked into the small round mirror propped up on the counter, he was also making those faces that men made when they shaved. His eyebrows went high in his forehead as he drew his upper lip down, then he made a long mouth as he shaved the sides of his face, much like a small child who wishes to be amusing, making it impossible for Laurie not to smile at him. Which made him feel a little braver about just coming out with the truth.

"I don't know how to shave with that," he said. "Can you help me?"

If John was startled by the request or by the fact that Laurie had yet another lack of skills, he didn't show it, but only finished shaving and wiped his face with a clean cloth.

"Yes, I can do that," said John. He emptied the used water into the slop bucket and poured warm water into the basin. Then he took an old-fashioned shaving brush and swirled it around in a little ceramic jar that had a white lump at the bottom of it. "I only have a little bit of shaving soap left, as I forgot to get some when we were in town yesterday, but this should do. Come here."

Laurie stepped close, almost overwhelmed by the sight of John standing there with a razor and soaped-up shaving brush in his hand. The pale color of his nightshirt contrasted with his red union underwear, which was unbuttoned at the top and showed the warmth of bare skin around his neck.

Laurie looked up into John's blue eyes and for a moment his mouth fell open and he couldn't speak. He realized how awkward he was making this, as John had already given Laurie his opinion on the matter, that he wasn't that kind of man. After all John had done for him, it would be rude to press the issue, not to mention insensitive.

"Should I sit down to make it easier?" asked Laurie with a croak.

"Yes, that's a good idea," said John.

Laurie looked away as he sat in the chair at the table and tried to pretend, as John brought over the basin and the little mug of shaving soap, that he wasn't worked up. But then he saw that *John* was worked up, as evidenced by the deep red that curled along his jaw and beneath his ear.

John was as affected as Laurie was, it seemed, by their closeness, the intimacy of a quiet morning with both of them in their nightshirts. Though, given Laurie's mental promise to himself, there wasn't anything he could do about it.

With one finger beneath Laurie's chin, John tipped Laurie's head back and touched him lightly along his jaw, as though to tell him to keep his head right where it was. A pleasurable quiver raced through Laurie, though he tried to quell it because he didn't want John to know his stomach was tightening and his cock was twitching to life, as that would be awkward. He didn't want the razor to slip while on his face, either.

John took the soap-laden brush, which, as Laurie noted, had a little more suds on it than what John had put on his own face, and swathed Laurie's face with it. The soap was warm and a little bit itchy, and smelled, very faintly, of lemons.

John lifted the razor and nodded at Laurie, as if reminding him to keep quite still, placed his fingers on the side of Laurie's chin, and began to shave him.

"The important thing," said John, almost conversationally, though his voice had a tone of instruction in it. "You must always take the blade down across your face with the edge perpendicular, like this." John drew the blade across Laurie's face in a slow, steady motion. "Never go sideways, or you'll slice right through to the bone and leave yourself a nice scar."

"Oh," said Laurie, with a low grunt, trying not to move his mouth.

"And wipe the blade after each stroke to keep it clean."

Laurie made another sound of acknowledgement, because now John had pulled up Laurie's lower lip to get at his chin, then moved on to his upper lip, shaving with careful, deft motions. He finished shaving Laurie's face in this manner, always wiping the blade on a cloth after every draw of the blade.

He lifted Laurie's chin and carefully, with long strokes, shaved his neck. Laurie told himself he wasn't nervous but he couldn't help but swallow at one point, which drove the blade in with a sharp, sliver-edged nick.

"Never mind," said John. He wiped Laurie's face with a towel and pressed at the cut spot with the edge of it. "That can happen sometimes."

"That was my fault," said Laurie, looking up at John with wide eyes as John stood over him in his nightshirt, his dark hair wild from sleep, his blue eyes focused on what his hands were doing.

"How did you shave back east?" asked John. "Or I suppose you always went to a barber."

"Something like that," said Laurie, not sure how else to answer.

"That can get expensive," said John as he stepped back, tipping his head sideways to check his work.

"Yes," said Laurie faintly, a little chagrined that he had to keep lying to John. "It can."

John rinsed the brush in the basin, and then rinsed and wiped off the razor before putting it away in a slender leather case.

Again, Laurie found himself sitting down while John worked.

Feeling like he ought to be doing something to help, he got up and went over, enjoying the moment of standing at John's shoulder, focusing on what John's hands were doing, as the strong, sure movements were a tad mesmerizing.

"Can I help with anything?" asked Laurie.

"We'll eat first," said John. "Rinse your face to get the soap off, then get dressed, and I'll make breakfast."

Which was pretty much what Laurie expected him to say, except that around the corners of John's mouth, lush amidst his newly shaven face, was a small smile. That might be an indicator John was pleased to have been asked. In which case, Laurie might have found a way to make his existence a bit more pleasurable while he searched for a way home. He would always ask John if he could help, or get John to teach him how to do things. That way, if he ever had to leave, even if he never did make it home, he could survive on his own.

To stave off the dark cloud that bubbled up at the thought of being trapped in 1891, Laurie went over to the chest of drawers and pulled out his new clothes. He put them on, taking off the nightshirt and folding it up to put it away.

The canvas trousers felt snug over the union suit, and were high waisted in a way that made Laurie stand up straighter. The collarless flannel shirt, when tucked into the trousers, felt thick and sturdy, and the belt and suspenders made him feel as though he was ready for anything. Compared to being dressed in his old clothes, the cabin felt much warmer now, even in the cold of early morning. He couldn't resist pulling on his new boots, too, thudding his heels on the floor and stomping over to the breakfast table loudly for effect.

As he pulled out one of the chairs and sat down, he looked up at John, who was standing at the stove with his back to Laurie. Laurie was half tempted to get up and stomp around some more just to see if John was paying attention and if he found Laurie even the least little bit entertaining.

Except before he could do that, John brought over two mugs and poured them each some black coffee. He was shaking his head, and on his face was another kind of smile than what Laurie had seen before.

It was a little bit wry, as though John were trying not to show that yes, Laurie was amusing.

John served up breakfast that was the same simple meal it had been the day before, except now on the table was a little cut-glass bowl with a lid that had a wooden stick with a carved honeycomb at the end of it. The bowl held honey, and as the sun came through the windows, the honey shone gold through the glass.

It was pretty to look at, though Laurie wondered where the syrup had gone. He didn't ask because obviously John had taken some pains to pour honey from the canning jar and put it in the bowl. And while perhaps this was just for Laurie's benefit, maybe it was because it looked nice, too. Which was another break in John's armor; the man might live a rough life, but he had china plates and glass bowls, so there was a softness to him, somewhere inside.

Laurie ate his breakfast, and as he did, he considered what he'd decided before about asking more often if he could help. About asking John to teach him things. He took a swallow of coffee, wished heartily for half-and-half to put in it, and wiped his mouth with the back of his hand.

"John, I have a question," said Laurie.

John looked up from where he was scooping up a last bite of fried cornmeal mush with his spoon gripped in his fist.

"Yes?" asked John, displaying dimples that had not shown themselves before, but which did, now that he'd shaved. They were sweet, on each side of his mouth, and showed how firm and strong his jaw was, by contrast.

"Yes?" asked John again, and Laurie realized he'd been staring.

"I was thinking that if—" said Laurie. "If you're going to give me a place to stay till spring, then I should be a grateful guest and earn my keep. Except I don't know anything, so would you teach me what I'm supposed to do, teach me what *you* know?"

John looked down at his plate, as though the weight of what Laurie was asking was a grave and serious thing to which John needed to give every consideration. His dark brows furrowed together, and for a moment Laurie thought that he'd asked it wrong, or that he shouldn't have asked it at all. Except John lifted his head, and he was nodding, his mouth tightening, showing off his long dimples, as though he knew what Laurie had been staring at.

"I've been thinking, too," said John.

Laurie wanted to say *no shit, John*, but he kept his mouth shut. There was a time for sarcasm and this wasn't it, as his whole survival depended on John's answer.

"You're the worst tenderfoot I ever met, but you got this far, so that's something. And, moreover, this is what I think happened to you," said John, surprising Laurie with the focus on Laurie rather than what might or might not be learned. "Back east you must have done or seen something terrible, so terrible that you had to leave. Your mind was so scarred with it that you forgot it, and forgot a whole lot else along with it."

"What?" asked Laurie, for this was not the response he'd been expecting.

"When you see a man scalped so hard that his brains come off on the blade," said John, looking at Laurie in a steady way, his eyes blue in the morning sunlight. "Or you see a soldier bayonet a young Indian girl in the belly for no reason other than she was in his way, well, you want to forget you ever saw it. Parts of you come away as you leave the memories behind, and I think that's what happened to you. Something like that, anyhow. It's why you didn't know what fried cornmeal mush is and the real reason why you don't know how to use a straight razor or tend a fire. Something happened to you and parts of you came away as you left it behind."

John's response went way beyond anything Laurie had thought he'd say, and the only thing he could infer from the depth of the response was that John had been thinking about him. Maybe he'd not always seen Laurie in the best light, but he had been thinking about him, trying to figure Laurie out. And maybe he was doing that because he wanted to help.

"That's probably how it happened," said Laurie, lying again because the truth was so unbelievable, so out there, that he wouldn't be able to explain it to John. "So, will you teach me?"

"Yes," said John. "I will, and to keep it honest between us, I'll pay you five dollars a month and found."

"And found?" asked Laurie, moved by the offer and by John's desire to keep things honest.

"It means room and board," said John. "I'll pay you and teach you everything I know, but you have to promise me that when I tell you to do something you do it. Understand?"

"Can I ask questions if I *don't* understand?" asked Laurie. He wanted to make that clear, as he didn't want John to get pissed off at him because he'd messed it up because he'd gotten confused.

"Yes," said John. "Of course. That's how you learn."

Laurie smiled, pleased with John's answer. John smiled in return, showing his teeth but in a friendly way, as though he were pleased at the prospect of having such a student as Laurie, in spite of the fact that Laurie didn't know how to do anything, and could never keep his mouth shut.

In that moment of success, Laurie swallowed over the sadness that welled up inside of him, the sudden longing for home and everything familiar. He had made strides with John today, and was coming to grips with his situation. He needed to concentrate on where he was right now. He needed to survive.

CHAPTER TWELVE

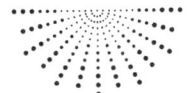

The lessons began directly after breakfast, but in an ordinary calm way, as though it was a perfectly natural thing for Laurie to need to know how to do things around the cabin. It was amazing that with as little as there was in the cabin, and how simple things seemed to be, how much there was to do, and how long it took to do them.

John showed Laurie how to prime the pump with a bit of melted snow to get it to work, and explained that the water came from an ancient well deep below the rocks, which was why it tasted so sweet. Then he showed him how to heat water and carve off flakes of soap, and how to wash an entire breakfast's worth of dishes in only a few inches of warm water.

How to clean a cast iron pan with no soap, and how to oil it up with a bit of bacon grease afterwards to keep it slick and ready to go. How to hang the pan on a sturdy nail in the wall to keep it free of dust. How to wipe the table and sweep the floor to keep winter mice from coming in the cabin. How to fill the kerosene lamp, and how to clean the chimney and trim the wick to keep it from smoking when it was lit.

John showed Laurie what was kept in the pantry, which was dishes and utensils and small bags of dried goods like beans, and rice, and flour. He showed him what was in the root cellar, a small dark space carved into the earth below the cabin that stored root vegetables like potatoes and onions and carrots, and canning jars of tomato preserves, rhubarb compote, and other delectable items that glistened in the light of the kerosene lamp that John carried.

John showed him how to clean the inside of the windows with vinegar and a cloth, how to take the used vinegar to clean the seat in the outhouse, and how pages from an old Sears catalog were hung on the nail to use as toilet paper. How to clear out ash from the stove and fireplace, and to take them to the ash barrel in the shed. What all the equipment in the shed was for, and why it was important to keep it stored safely until spring for when the railroad surveyors came out to measure the grade for the tracks across the high prairie.

Lastly, he showed Laurie how to chop wood for both the stove and the fireplace, as they took different sizes. How to properly close the shed door after he was done, and how to light a fire in the stove and bank it so that it would be ready to cook their lunch on when they were finished with their chores.

"Next we should chink that hole between the logs and then put up tar paper," said John as he closed the stove door. "Then, after lunch, when I walk my traps, you can cut more wood and get some practice with that axe."

"Okay, John," said Laurie. He was all warmed up and ready for anything. "What are we going to chink it with? The ground's half frozen."

John showed him how to gather the hard dirt in a bucket, and to stir it with a stick while adding water in the warmth of the cabin until it got soft. Then, both of them in their shirtsleeves, John took Laurie around to the back side of the cabin, which was sloped with snow. They had to break through the hard layers until they were close to the logs in the corner where the stone fireplace met the outside wall of the bedroom.

"Put the dirt in little by little," said John, using his bare hands to pack the mud in the small gap. "It's better if there's a little bit of grass or moss in there, but this will do for now. Go to the shed and get the tar paper and the hammer and nails while I finish this up."

Laurie slogged through uneven drifts of snow, pushing away sad thoughts as he focused on the now, and how pleasant it was working with John. He went to the shed and collected what John had asked for. He hung the hammer through his belt, stuffed a handful of nails in his pocket, and gathered an armful of tar paper.

Humming, he carefully shut the shed door, squinted into the cold, blue-streaked sunshine, and realized he was smiling. Yes, he was doing a lot of work, but John had been patient, and the way he taught things made them make sense to Laurie, so he was feeling good, like he could do this.

He could survive on his own if he had to, though he realized he would be better off staying with John. And it would be nice to stay with John and work together like this, though he would go home in a heartbeat if he found a way to.

When he got back to the far side of the cabin, John was eyeing the wall and measuring it with his hands.

"Good," said John, as he saw Laurie. "You kept those tar sheets flat. I should have told you that was the way to carry them, but you figured it out on your own. Now, hand me a nail and a sheet of tar paper."

With a quick, sure motion, John drew the hammer out from Laurie's belt, and Laurie had to clamp his mouth shut at the slithery sound the movement made, and how his skin seemed to shiver with it. Whether or not John was aware of this, Laurie didn't know, but he pulled out a nail from his pocket and handed it to John.

In the gap between their fingers, the nail slipped and dove into the snow. Laurie, after all he'd learned, even in just the past few days, realized that a store-bought item such as a nail would be expensive. He bent, shoved his hand in the snow, and found the nail. He brought it up in his fist and held it out to John.

"Caught it," said Laurie, pleased with himself.

"Be careful, Little Red," said John as he took the nail. "There could be cactus beneath the snow that you don't know about, and I don't want you to cut up your hand on it."

Laurie smiled, in spite of the fact that he usually didn't like being reminded how red his hair was, because John's whole face softened as he called Laurie by the nickname Adeline had given him. John seemed pleased with Laurie's eagerness and willingness to work, and maybe he was thinking they made a good team.

Together they worked at patching up the outside of the cabin with tar paper to keep out the wind and snow. First, they smoothed the layer of dirt daub that was already cold and stiff between the logs. Then, holding the tar paper over the mud, Laurie handed more nails to John.

John hammered in the nails with steady, strong strokes. Towards the end, John let Laurie take a try, and though Laurie had never been much of a handyman back home, he thought his nails had gone in pretty straight, and nodded his own self-approval as he handed the hammer back to John.

John smiled, showing his dimples as he shook his head, as though at Laurie's cocky attitude.

"We'll put these tools away, and go inside to warm up while I make some lunch," said John. "After, I need to go walk my traps and, while I'm gone, you could cut wood for the stove and fireplace. See if you can't clear out the ash and build a new fire in the stove so I can cook whatever I bring back for supper."

"Okay," said Laurie, though he was a little nervous at the thought of being left alone with the task of lighting a fire by himself. What if he burned the cabin down? But what he said was, "I can do that."

Lunch was a quick affair of leftover biscuits with butter and tomato preserves, washed down by mugs of cold water from the pump. John did the dishes, showing Laurie once more how it was done. Then he bundled up in his buffalo hide coat, looking even more burly with it on. He took down his rifle, checked the bullets, then put on his hat, and folded the gray scarf around his neck.

"I'll be back before sundown," said John. "If I'm lucky, the antelope herd will be passing through the valley. They usually do this time of year, so we should have fresh meat for supper."

John left, closing the cabin door behind him. Laurie saw him walk past the window, heading north. As the stillness settled over the cabin, he felt very much alone.

But John wouldn't have left him alone if he didn't trust him to do those tasks he'd set Laurie to do. It was as if he knew Laurie would do his very best, and that the chopping of wood and the tending to the fire in the stove would get done right. The only thing left for Laurie to do was to try.

He left his coat behind and went out to the shed in just his suspenders and shirtsleeves. He was glad for the purposeful activity to keep his darker thoughts at bay, to help him not think about how much he missed Zach and Maxton and his old life. He was also glad for the layers of clothing, as the wind brought brisk air along his neck.

Inside the shed, with the door propped open and, feeling very manly, Laurie put on the gloves that hung on the wall. He took up the small axe and began to split large logs into smaller ones, and to split those into even smaller slices of kindling that would be the right size to be used as fuel in the cast iron stove.

He split some more logs for good measure, in case they wanted a nice fire in the fireplace while they oiled their boots in the evening after supper. And he felt well pleased with himself as he wiped down the axe with a bit of oil and a cloth, put the gloves and the axe back in their proper places, and carefully shut the shed door as John had taught him.

Before he went back in the cabin, he stood at the threshold and dusted himself off, kicking the snow from his boots. As the sun began to slant low in the sky, the wind picked up and the chill deepened. John said he'd be home before the dark, so Laurie needed to get a move on. He realized he was pleasurably anticipating John's return and wondered if John would be eager to return to the cabin with Laurie waiting for him.

Taking care of the stove wasn't as hard as it might be, now that Laurie knew how. The ashes were still warm when he carried them out to the ash barrel in the shed, so he made sure to bury them in the center so they wouldn't char the barrel. Then he carried in an armful of kindling and a handful of wood chips to light the fire with, sweeping the snow back outside before shutting the door.

He was well pleased at his own success when he was able to do everything right, as the stove began to heat up and warm the cabin. Then he puttered about before taking the book about Antarctica from the shelf, and settled in the leather chair to read and wait for John.

It grew dark before Laurie realized it, too dark to read, so he got up from the chair and went to the table and lit the kerosene lamp. While he was standing there looking at the way the glow from the lamp spread itself across the floor of the cabin, he heard stamping feet and the creak of the shed door, and raced to the cabin door to fling it open.

In the cold air, thick with the smell of snow, he saw John stride into the shed. Laurie went across to the shed and peeked around the door. John was placing his rifle carefully against the wall and, at the same time, was attempting to lift an antelope from around his shoulders.

"Bring the lamp," said John. "But be careful with it."

Laurie hurried into the cabin and carried out the lit kerosene lamp in both hands. He placed the lamp on the dirt floor near the door, where hopefully it wouldn't get knocked over. The golden glow of the lamp lit up the interior of the shed like a secret cave, and Laurie felt pleased when John smiled his approval.

Laurie helped heft the antelope from John's shoulders. He'd never gone hunting before, and the feel of the still-warm dead animal beneath his hands made him want to drop it and back off. Except if he did that, then John would become unbalanced, and the antelope would fall into the dust, and this might ruin the meat.

Consequently, Laurie did his best to help John hang the animal upside-down on a hook, and didn't wince when John pulled a bucket beneath the animal's head and sliced its neck open. Ruby-dark blood trickled into the bucket, the smell of warm blood rising in the cold air, and Laurie had to swallow to keep from gagging.

"Sometimes you have to field dress an antelope," said John as he straightened up. "But it's easier to gut the animal in the shed because we put the little we don't want in the privy. That way, we're not going to attract wolves or mountain lions. Do you understand?"

"I've never butchered an animal before," said Laurie. He put the back of his hand to his mouth because while he didn't want to make John think he wasn't willing, he also didn't want to throw up in front of him.

"I'll teach you, so watch," said John.

It wasn't a very big antelope, so there wasn't much meat on it. John took his time and carefully demonstrated how to cut the skin away and slice the meat so it could be cooked right away or dried for later, whatever was needed.

The bucket of entrails was entirely too full and smelly when Laurie carried it to the outhouse to dump. It was quite dark as he wiped the bucket out with snow and tossed that in the privy, as well, before going back to the shed to help John finish up.

"We'll have steak today and tomorrow, as there's not enough meat for more meals than that," said John. "Which is good, in a way, as I don't have a way to smoke the meat, though I should have thought of that."

"Steak'll be good," said Laurie, his mouth watering as John salted the pieces of meat and wrapped them in waxed paper. "I wouldn't mind steak and eggs for breakfast."

"We only have a few eggs," said John. "We'll have to go to town in a day or so."

Together they cleaned up the shed and carted the wrapped meat into the cabin, where John took half of it down to the root cellar to keep cool for the morning. Then he came up from the cellar and drew and heated water, nodding his approval at how quickly the flames in the stove grew when he poked at the coals.

"Well done, Laurie," said John. "You're a quick learner, I'll say that for you."

"Thanks," said Laurie, smiling.

His face was warm as he ducked his head and tried not to show how pleased he was at the praise, but his whole body leaned into it. He felt a delightful tingle up his back at having done well in John's eyes.

Normally, Laurie's first goal with anyone he met was to get them to like him by making them laugh at his antics. And Laurie did want that with John, as there was way too little laughter in the cabin. However, earning John's trust and praise seemed its own reward, and was very satisfying, besides. He wanted more of that praise, more of that feeling of working with John, learning what John knew, and earning more of that trust that had been so hard won.

CHAPTER THIRTEEN

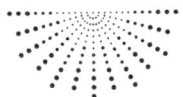

The antelope steak, which John carved thin and fried quickly in bacon grease, was delicious though a little bit tough. Laurie ate everything on his plate, including the requisite fried potatoes and onions. And realized he was happy sitting there across the table from John, eating in the light of the kerosene lamp with the oval-shaped shadows flickering across the table and wall.

"We'll get one or two more meals out of this meat, then we'll be eating store-bought meat from now on," said John as he used a bit of biscuit to soak up the last of the juices on his plate. "That herd of antelope is long gone."

"Did they go south for the winter or something?" asked Laurie.

"You mean like geese?" John asked in return. He tipped his head to one side and seemed to consider this. "It's somewhat like that. The herds are only about twenty head or so, so there's lots of places they can fit into."

"Oh, I see," said Laurie, though he was far less interested in information about a herd of antelope than he was in listening to John talk about something he knew.

There was something thoughtful about it, careful and sure, and John's face relaxed into such a handsome strength that Laurie was finding it extra hard not to stare. At the same time, it seemed that John, in the still, low dark of evening around the supper table, was trying not to stare in return. But company was company, so whether it was him specifically, or whether he could have been anyone, the fact was Laurie couldn't be sure whether or not John actually liked having him there.

"The other day in town," said Laurie in his best extra-casual way as he put his knife and fork on his plate and pushed it away. "Pete said something about the war. I'm just figuring out that you might have come out here to get away from all that, to be alone. And here I am, busting in on you, so I wanted to tell you how much I appreciate you letting me stay."

John drew his head back and looked at Laurie with narrowed eyes, as though discomfited by the fact Laurie had been paying enough attention to remember that part of the conversation. There was a flicker in his eyes that spoke of deep, dark memories. Then it vanished, as though John was well practiced hiding away his past. Or it might have been that there'd never been anybody to really listen to John talk about it. With Pete, the conversation must have been quite general, but Laurie wanted to know more.

"I don't know anything about those wars," said Laurie. His memory of any history class he'd ever taken had quickly disappeared beneath the layers of day-to-day responsibilities when he'd taken his first job after college. "Which ones were they?"

John's jaw moved as he looked down at his plate. Laurie expected his question would be rebuffed, that John would draw back, and Laurie would never be allowed to know. After all, who was he to John but some east coast tenderfoot who had barely any notion how to survive out west? He waited, thinking that if John didn't answer, he would offer to do the dishes while John oiled his boots and cleaned his rifle, and they would go on as they had been, just two guys sharing a bed as winter drew near.

John surprised him by looking directly at Laurie, his eyes so dark and blue in the gentle light of the kerosene lamp that Laurie had to catch his breath.

"I was in the cavalry," said John. "We rode up and down, from North Dakota to Kansas, patrolling the plains to protect settlers from Indian raids." John stopped and shook his head, his expression grave, a hard look in his eyes. "At first it seemed good, the right thing to do, protecting settlers, farmers, and suchlike. Only it turned into slaughter. No matter how I looked at it or tried to resolve it in my own mind, it was just killing people for no reason."

"Was that where you saw somebody get scalped so hard you saw his brains?" asked Laurie, unable to stop being totally pushy about it. He kicked himself as John scraped back his chair and shoved his plate away with a clatter.

"I'm sorry, I'm sorry," said Laurie. He got up as well, and wanted to do something with his hands, only he didn't know what. "I'm not just asking to ask, but if we're going to live together in this cabin all winter, maybe we should get to know each other a little bit. I really do want to know."

John didn't say anything, but began clearing the table in his usual way. He was focused on the task at hand, as though that would help him block out memories of the past, his eyes dark, his jaw hard set.

"Let me do that," said Laurie, both to give his hands something to do, and his brain something to focus on so that he could leave John alone for a minute.

He couldn't push, he couldn't insist, like he would do back home when he'd perform his antics and get people to open up to him that way. John wasn't like that. Either he'd talk or he wouldn't, and all Laurie could do was to be there when it happened.

While Laurie heated up the water and gathered the dishes and frying pan to wash, John moved away from the table, silence lingering in his wake. After he built a little fire in the stone fireplace, he went to the door, pulled down the rifle, and sat in the leather chair in the center of the braided rug to clean it.

As Laurie washed and dried the dishes, and oiled the frying pan, he could almost hear John thinking. He wiped the table and swept the floor as fast as he could, blew out the kerosene lamp to put the cabin in darkness, and went over to the leather chair.

John looked up at Laurie. In the golden glow of the fire, the wash of vulnerability that swept over his face made Laurie realize that he needed to be so, so careful with this gruff bear of a man who had probably seen more bad things than Laurie could even imagine. This was not a game Laurie could play and leave behind; this was real, and Laurie wanted more than games. He didn't care much for games, anyway.

"Take off your boots and give them to me," said Laurie as he stood there, quite close to the chair. "I'll oil them for you. I've learned how to oil mine, so I'm a real pro at it by this time." Laurie raised his eyebrows for emphasis, exuding his willingness with all of his might. "Let me help you. Please? After you got us fresh steak for supper, it's the least I can do."

This was one of John's weak spots, an offer to help, and Laurie knew it. He didn't want to exploit this as he might have done back home. He had no real idea what it would be like to trek through the snow to follow a herd of antelope and bring one down and then carry it back to the cabin, but it could not have been easy. Everything in John's life seemed to be hard, and Laurie really did want to help.

When John shrugged and placed the rifle to one side to pull off his boots, Laurie stifled his whoop of delight. Instead, he knelt at John's feet and began pulling John's boots off with his hands.

John seemed surprised but let Laurie do it, and by the time Laurie got back from the cupboard with the bottle of leather oil and a clean cloth, John had taken up his rifle again, and was tending to it in the firelight. The flickering flames glittered on the barrel of the rifle and warmed the edges of John's face and shoulders as he bent to his task.

Laurie sat cross-legged at John's feet, full on the rug, his face to the fire, his shoulder brushing John's knee. Pleased that John didn't move his knee away, Laurie made himself focus on putting oil on the cloth, stroking the leather of the boot with it as the scent of leather oil rose in the air, warming it.

Either John would start to feel comfortable with Laurie sitting so near and relax, or he wouldn't. In the meantime, the darkness of the cabin, lit only by the flames in the fireplace and the low coals of the cast iron stove, was cozy and quiet. This was probably how John liked it, as he made no comment that the kerosene lamp was not lit as it usually was when they tended to their evening chores.

When Laurie turned John's boot over to oil the other side, John shifted in his seat, and Laurie heard him place the rifle to one side, carefully leaning it against the leather chair. Then John began to talk, his voice low in the semi-darkness as he related the story of how he ended up in Farthing.

In the beginning, the raids on Native American encampments had seemed to have a true purpose. But the raids had quickly escalated into mass killings of women and children, after which his job with the cavalry became a wasteland of bodies needing to be disposed of.

John's growing horror at these atrocities rose in his voice, and Laurie felt the skin along the back of his neck start to crawl. He'd always known it had been bad, in the back of his mind, but now, knowing more of the truth of it, he knew John was right; the whole of it had been a slaughter.

"It was after the engagement at Wounded Knee that I knew I had to leave the cavalry," said John. His voice was so tight and unhappy that Laurie restrained himself from asking any more questions, especially when John was so upset. Even Laurie, with his spotty recollection of American history, had heard of the battle of Wounded Knee, and he was amazed that John had been there.

"I couldn't leave right then, or even the next day, when we were at the Drexel Mission," said John. "But I left as soon as I could, and came here."

"How did you end up in Farthing?" asked Laurie, thinking the question was pretty neutral, or at least he hoped it was.

"I was looking for a job," said John. "One where I didn't have to listen to the sounds of battle anymore. I found one here, where it is quiet."

"Except for me," said Laurie, smiling to himself as he laughed under his breath. "I've ruined all that for you, haven't I." He wanted to make sure that John didn't mind him being there, filling the cabin with unwanted chatter and the presence of another human being. "Have I?"

A long, low silence grew in the darkness while the firelight flickered on the walls and the floor, and a spark jumped from one log to the other. Then Laurie felt John's hand on his head. The weight of his touch was gentle, as John seemed to be reaching out, perhaps waiting for Laurie to reject the touch or accept it.

"I don't mind, Little Red," said John. "I've grown to like your company, actually."

Laurie tipped his head back to lean into John's hand, and rested his head on John's knee to encourage him. It had been lonely before because even if John was nearby, he'd been holding himself so distant. Which made every thought about home and his friends feel all the more painful.

He quite expected that John would pull away. But John surprised Laurie by curling his fingers in Laurie's hair, a sweet gesture that made Laurie feel a pang in his heart that a man such as John, so alone and wounded, trusted Laurie enough to do this. Maybe John would open up to Laurie, and they could go on together that way, and survive the winter together, and that would be enough for him.

Laurie pressed against John's knee again, and then looked up at John and gave him a smile to encourage him and let him know that Laurie was enjoying this, this small moment between them.

"Your hair is so red in the sunlight," said John, softly. "But now, in the firelight, I can see the gold in there. It's the color of a summer fox's coat, Little Red, it is."

"Guess that nickname's going to stick, isn't it," said Laurie, but he smiled up at John to let him know he didn't really mind. "My burden to bear," said Laurie in mock resignation.

He finished oiling John's boots, after which he got up to put them near the door, hung John's rifle above the door, and resumed his place at John's feet. Boldly, he wrapped one arm around John's calf, and felt John's whole body twitch.

Was it too much too soon? If John pulled away the least little bit, Laurie would let go and pretend it had never happened. Except that

John, instead, put his hand back on Laurie's head and gently combed his fingers through Laurie's hair. He did this over and over, till in the flicking gold of the firelight Laurie's eyes began to close and he thought he might fall asleep then and there.

A peaceful quiet filled the cabin, broken only by the crackling sounds of wood burning, and the howl of wind outside the curtained windows, announcing that a change in weather was on the way.

After a time, John slowly stood up, and tugged on Laurie's shirt to get him to stand up, too.

"Time to wash up for bed," said John. He drew out his brass pocket watch to check the time, then clicked it closed and looked at Laurie directly. A trace of trepidation glinted in his blue, half-lidded eyes, as if he wasn't sure he was doing the right thing letting Laurie get so close, or for the evening to get so intimate.

Somewhat breathless himself, Laurie decided to go on as he usually did, and yawned and petted John's arm, casually, the way he would do with Maxton.

"I *am* tired," said Laurie. "After all the hard work I did gutting that antelope today."

This made John laugh, which he did low in his throat as he put the pocket watch on the chest of drawers. Laurie smiled at the unexpected gift of the laugh and of John's bright smile, for all it was so quick.

"Let me heat water for the basin," said John. "Can you bank the fire while I tend to the stove?"

Laurie raced to do as he was asked, hurrying through the chore, feeling John's eyes watching him the whole while. Then, stumbling his way in the half-dark to collect their nightshirts, he brought them back to John, eager as a kid.

John had already peeled back his suspenders and undone his shirt, and stood there, chin tucked down while he unbuttoned his union suit and shrugged it off his shoulders. Laurie did the same, and together they washed in front of the stove as the last of the warmth oozed from the black iron.

Laurie still looked away to give John his privacy while he washed, but he didn't move away, not even when he washed himself at the same time as John. Being close to John felt good, and he liked it, liked the thought of them being in bed together. Focusing on that, on them keeping each other warm till morning, helped keep his loneliness at bay.

John slipped off his trousers, and Laurie did too, and then he put them on the chest of drawers. When he came back, John had dumped the used water in the slop bucket, and was tugging up his union suit, pulling on his nightshirt. John then helped Laurie on with his nightshirt. Laurie totally didn't need help, but he appreciated the gesture, especially when John gave the cloth on Laurie's shoulders a tug and then smoothed the cloth with his warm hands.

"I saw some buffalo wolf tracks today, and I need to follow them," said John. "I'll head out after lunch tomorrow. Do you want to go with me?"

"Yes," said Laurie without hesitation.

His mind filled up with images as to how it might go, him and John trekking through the snow, the two of them in the wilderness together. He imagined John pointing across to the mountains, telling Laurie something and teaching him what he knew. Then, after, they'd come back to the cabin and eat another quiet supper together, and spend time in front of the fire.

All of these ideas and images filled Laurie with a sense of desire so dizzying that he stumbled forward and almost fell into John's arms. Which made John draw back, though his hands went to Laurie's shoulders to steady him.

"Easy there, Little Red," said John in a way that let Laurie know he'd not messed everything up. "It's time for bed, now."

In the now completely dark cabin, Laurie followed John to the little bedroom. As John climbed into the cold side of the bed, Laurie knew that it probably wasn't so cold, now that they'd nailed the tar paper in place, but it was the gesture that mattered. John didn't want Laurie to be cold in the night and would take it upon himself to block the wind, and if that wasn't the best kind of kindness, Laurie didn't know what was.

As they settled in the bed, Laurie tugged up the bedclothes and, with his body facing John's, inched forward. And then inched forward some more, shivering as though he was much colder than he really was, because with the tar paper in place and John's body so near, he was really quite warm, warm enough to fall asleep just like this. Except he wanted more of what they'd shared in front of the fireplace, more of John, more of that.

John needed his rest, on account of he worked so hard all day, so instead of attempting to start a conversation, Laurie ducked his chin until his forehead was on John's chest. He sighed, long and low and deep, as though he'd finally arrived where he'd wanted to be all day.

Laurie didn't have to wait long for John's response. With an echoing sound that might have been a sigh, or a small murmur meant only for Laurie's ears, John shifted in the bed. As he settled, he drew Laurie into his arms and pulled him close. Their legs tangled together beneath the bedclothes, and Laurie slipped his arms around John's waist, which felt like solid muscle, and gave a small squeeze to let John know how content and happy he truly was.

John's warmth surrounded him, along with the smell of soap that John had used to wash with, and the lingering sweat of the day from his work. All of this Laurie was quickly coming to associate with a sense of peace and of safety, for if John was near, then everything would work out for the best.

Laurie knew he would fall asleep fast, being held like this.

He would just have to be polite enough to ignore the fact that John's hips jerked, as if he was holding himself back. He also needed to ignore the warmth of John's groin, and not act on his own growing-into-awareness cock. That would be the worst of bad manners, and nothing that John deserved. So Laurie pressed his cheek against John's chest, and sighed, and yawned, felt John's chest move with John's answering yawn, and let the darkness, peaceful and quiet, take him into sleep.

CHAPTER FOURTEEN

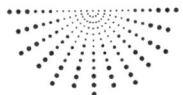

After lunch the next day, they bundled up for the weather in their hats and gray woolen scarves and buffalo hide coats. Though it wasn't snowing, the wind was blowing and it was cold as they left the cabin. They went up the slope past the outhouse and headed north along a flat, ice-clogged river that John said was Sand Creek.

Wading through the drifts of icy snow at its banks, they held their scarves to their mouths, heads tucked down as they walked against the wind, the air smelling like crisp snow. Laurie realized that while it was cold, he was warmer in his new sturdy trousers than he had been in his blue jeans, and understood a little better how the pioneers had made it through the rugged winters of long ago.

Their boots crunched in the snow. Sometimes Laurie slipped on hidden ice, but he did his best to keep up with John, whose broad back sometimes blocked the wind and sometimes aimed it right at Laurie. But John's long legs just kept going, the slight limp in his step easing as they went, so Laurie kept going too, until they paused by the bank of the river where the light glinted off crusts of ice thrusting into the crystal blue water.

"This is Horse Creek," said John, pointing across to where the river broke into two branches. He leaned close so Laurie could hear him, and Laurie leaned right back.

John pointed down at the sharp marks in the snow, which Laurie quickly realized were the paw prints of large, clawed animals that he would not want to meet without John and his rifle nearby.

"Though some of the tracks are blown away, this is the direction the buffalo wolves were headed," said John. "We'll come across them soon enough."

They walked for another two hours, forever it seemed, until John led them over a snowy rise. On the other side of the rise, the land dipped down into a flat, sheltered valley that was bounded on one side by the banks of Horse Creek, and on the other by tall, jagged hills.

"That's Iron Mountain over there," said John. He pointed at the sharp, snowy purple and blue-hued bluff that rose higher than the low hills around it.

The wind was starting to die down so he pulled down his scarf and wiped his mouth with the back of his glove as he settled his rifle over his arm. The wind swirled snow around his feet, then settled and blew, settled and blew.

"The tracks lead to that mound, which is their den, so we're going to wait it out and see what we can see."

"We're going to *wait*?" asked Laurie, unable to stop his dismay at the prospect. There was nothing for miles, it was cold, and the air was becoming sharp. "What are we going to do till they show up, and what will we do when they get here?"

"We're going to build a small snow fort over there to wait in," said John, pointing to the south-eastern side of the little valley. "And then when I see them, I'm going to shoot them."

"*What?*" asked Laurie. He realized he shouldn't be astonished that this was what John wanted to do, but he was. "Why the fuck would you do that? They never hurt you."

"I can't have them attacking and eating railroad workers in the spring, Laurie," said John, his eyes serious as he looked at him. "That's part of my job, to remove wild animals that pose a threat."

"Wolves don't eat people," said Laurie. "You've just been reading Little Red Riding Hood too many times."

"Actually, I've never read it," said John, scowling.

"Well, anyway, it's just a fairy tale," said Laurie, not letting himself be held back by John's disapproval. "Name me one time, just *one* time, you've ever heard of a wolf eating a person. Just one time. One." Laurie held up a gloved finger. "One. Go on, I bet you can't. Bet you."

"I don't gamble," said John in an almost dismissive way, though as he scanned the horizon where snow was drifting off the river's bank, he seemed to be considering what Laurie had said. "But I can't leave employees of the railroad, or the citizens in town, in danger."

With a scoffing sound, Laurie shook his head. He realized he'd have to leave it for now, and figure out a way to talk John out of what he felt to be a necessary killing, but which Laurie knew to be an unnecessary one. Besides, in Laurie's time, buffalo wolves were extinct, so why hasten the process?

They built a snow fort where John decided they would, and he propped his rifle carefully against a small, winter-bare tree. Together they formed the snow cave, digging into a low bank, piling snow on top and scooping out the center. Laurie quickly grew warm pawing in the snow with his mittened hands, flecks of ice speckling on his coat, melting on his face.

By the time they were done, the sky was rimmed with deflected sunlight that glinted on the opening to the small cave, which was just big enough for two men to either crouch inside or lie flat. The walls of the fort would keep out the wind, so although it was chilly, it would be bearable for a little while.

They crawled inside, lying on their bellies, propping their chins on their hands. While Laurie liked the stillness inside the cave, the feel of his shoulder brushing John's, and the sound of John breathing steadily, his hips got cold, and the front of his thighs soon felt frozen. The air grew still, damp with the smell of cold ice.

As they waited within the cave for the buffalo wolves to show up, there was nothing much to look at but the other side of the small valley. Laurie grew bored with just lying there, even with John so near, so he crawled out and set about building a little snowman.

He rolled miniature balls, one for each part of the snowman's body, and then dug around along the icy river for the right color of pebbles to be used as the snowman's features. He quickly got flecked with icy water. That wasn't too bad, but the snow balled up on his mittens so he had to take them off and hold his bare hands cupped in front of his mouth to blow on them.

All the while, John watched him, a smile twitching along his mouth, as though he felt he ought to disapprove of Laurie's antics but just couldn't bring himself to continue being grumpy just to stay grumpy. In the end, John crawled out, as well, and helped Laurie find enough little pebbles, brown and deep red, to make the snowman smile. He took off his gloves and placed the pebbles into place, one after another, carefully with his cold, bare fingers, and then grinned at Laurie, showing his teeth.

Which of course was exactly the moment that the buffalo wolves showed up. They appeared to be lumps, dark gray against the snow, and Laurie first thought they were old tree trunks with legs. But they were wild wolves coming down into the valley on silent paws, their ears pricked forward. As they came closer, Laurie opened his mouth, breathless, his heart racing, every nerve alive.

"Tarnation," muttered John.

He grabbed his rifle from where it had been carefully propped against the tree. With his legs braced in the snow, he lifted the rifle, set it against his shoulder and cocked his elbow, one finger on the trigger.

For a moment, all was still while Laurie squinted against the brightness of the snow. The two buffalo wolves, so gray and silver and white, like the day, barely stood out against the background, but he could see them moving around the opening of their den. They looked enormously tall, especially as they came closer. They didn't seem to be aggressive as they sniffed and trotted round and round, as though giving their place a good going over before entering, like humans did back home.

Everything came into focus, and one of the wolves nuzzled the other one. Their eyes glinted silver and bright, the gesture of affection wild and good all at the same time. When the other wolf ducked its head to return the touch, Laurie's heart was thick with the beauty of it. When Laurie heard John pull the trigger, at the last second, Laurie pushed the rifle up with his arm.

He jerked back as the rifle went off, the bullet shooting off into the sky. The wolves started, and stared in their direction before racing away, their gray tails flicking in the air. John cocked the long lever on the rifle and aimed at the retreating wolves and, again Laurie deflected the bullet's trajectory with his arm, sending it high into the sky as the sounds of the shot ricocheted off the hard edges of nearby Iron Mountain.

As the echoes of rifle shot died and the wolves disappeared from view, John whirled, the rifle clenched in his hand, teeth bared.

"*Damn it*, Laurie," said John with a snarl. "What the hell did you do that for?"

John advanced. Laurie backed up, tripped over the heels of his own boots, and fell back into the side of the snow fort. His landing crushed the wall, sending snow up into his face. Suddenly afraid of what he'd just done, and that he'd earned another whipping from John, Laurie, determined to show he *wasn't* afraid, jerked his chin up, and braced his arms behind him.

"You don't *need* to shoot them," said Laurie, half-shouting, his voice loud in the sharp, cold air. "Wolves don't eat people, don't you *get* it? Besides, they're going to be extinct in a couple of years anyway, so there's no point killing them now. They get pushed west and west and west and then they die out. Or are you killing them to gratify your own manly ego? Huh?"

"What on earth are you talking about, extinct?" asked John, dark brows drawn together, his puzzlement making him squint at Laurie. "There's plenty of wolves. And no, it's not gratifying my ego to kill them, it's my job. It's what I'm paid for."

They looked at each other in the still, blue air, Laurie open-mouthed and panting, a bit of fear rushing through him, John scowling, his head cocked as he looked at Laurie, as though attempting to figure Laurie out.

"They're gone anyway, John," said Laurie. "They're gone, so they won't hurt anybody in town. They won't hurt us."

"I wouldn't have *let* them hurt us," said John, and his face softened a fraction as he looked at Laurie and reached out his hand for Laurie to take. "I wouldn't have let them."

Laurie took John's hand and let himself be pulled to his feet. Adrenaline was still rushing through him, so he was quite close to John as he shuddered a breath, trying to calm himself down. John's eyebrows went up, and his eyes were blue and gentle.

"Were you afraid, Laurie?" asked John. "I would have shot them before they got too close—"

"No," said Laurie. He licked his lower lip. "I just really didn't want you to shoot them."

John let go of Laurie's hand and clasped his shoulder, almost petting it, and did not move away from Laurie being so close.

"What a soft heart you have," said John, though the way he said it felt like he didn't think this was a bad thing.

"You have one too," said Laurie, quite softly, his chin tipped down as he looked up at John through his lashes, smiling. "I think you let me deflect those bullets."

"I didn't," said John, though there was a blush curling along the length of his jaw.

"I think you did." Laurie smiled, calmer now that the danger had passed, and John didn't seem angry with him anymore.

John grunted and picked up Laurie's mittens, shook them off, and handed them to Laurie. Then he picked up his own gloves and put them back on.

As he settled his rifle on his arm, he went over to the snow fort and kicked it down. He went to the little snowman that Laurie had assembled and that John had helped him decorate, his foot poised to kick it down as well, as though no trace of them must be left behind.

Laurie held his breath. He debated protesting the destruction of the snowman, but John shook his head as he backed away. He looked at Laurie, his mouth firm, but his expression told Laurie he was uncertain why he was giving in to Laurie's unspoken request to leave the snowman intact. He might be unable to figure out why he was indulging Laurie so, but at the same time he seemed equally unable not to.

"We need to head back before it gets dark," said John. "We'll leave the snowman to guard the valley from any intruders."

Laurie laughed, open mouthed, and waggled his hands in victory, which earned him an answering smile from John, and a twinkle in those blue eyes. Settling his hat on his head, wrapping his scarf around his neck, Laurie pulled on his mittens and followed John out of the valley and along the path by the riverbank.

Their previous footsteps in the snow had been softened by the wind, but it was much easier to walk in them than to break the snow. They made their way slowly, and Laurie kept close behind John, glancing up every once in a while to trace the breadth of John's shoulders, snug beneath his buffalo hide coat. While the wind settled, the air around them became still and cold as the sun began to set over Iron Mountain and the scrabbly foothills around it.

They walked forever, it seemed, stomping eternally through the crunchy snow. When they got to the junction of Horse Creek and Sand Creek, the sun dipped entirely behind the mountains. Twilight grew dark, the clouds turning purple and dark blue, faintly orange at their edges where they stretched to the east. Without any light pollution, the colors were pure and clear.

When John stopped, Laurie stopped and looked where John was looking, at the ridge of hills and the bulwark of Iron Mountain growing dark in the lengthening shadows.

"Mountains make a good sunset," said John, as though to himself.

He looked at Laurie. Laurie, who'd grown worked up with worry at being out in the wilderness when it got dark and, at the same time, was moved by the wild beauty of the sky overhead, began to babble, unable to stop himself.

"It really is pretty, don't you think, John?" said Laurie. "Do you think we'll be able to make it home before midnight? Will we freeze? Will there be more wolves?"

John slid off a glove and, without a sound, placed his warm, bare hand over Laurie's mouth.

"Hush," said John. "Watch and listen."

Blinking, Laurie shut his mouth. John kept his hand in place for a good long minute, as though letting Laurie savor the feel of it, and note the calluses along the edge of John's palm. Feel the warmth of his skin.

Laurie kept silent and listened to the quiet of the darkening sky, the slight breeze on his cold cheek. Then John took his hand away, his rifle crooked in one elbow, his outline sturdy and capable, his strong face etched against the dark mountain.

And then Laurie heard it. A whir. A low, silky thrumming sound that grew louder as the sky filled with a cloud of geese coming in to land on the wide expanse of silvery, ice-edge water flowing slow and glassy where the two creeks joined. Wave after wave they came, thickening into the reality of it, the noise of the gray-dark wings of a thousand geese, tired after their airborne journey south, coming down out of the sky to settle on the water for the night.

Laurie stood there, completely silent. His mouth fell open as the roar of wings filled the air, loud as a jet engine, dying slowly away as the geese settled on the wide, flat river.

"That was unbelievable," said Laurie. "I've never seen anything like it."

"Happens all the time, when winter's near," said John, softly.

The expression in John's eyes seemed to invite Laurie to agree, and to draw him near. Laurie stepped closer, his shoulder brushing John's as they watched the last of the geese settle, folding their wings to their bodies as they drifted into stillness on the silvery water.

"We best head on home," said John. He hefted his rifle on his arm once more and nodded. "It's going to be past dark by the time we get there."

"Won't we get lost in the dark?" asked Laurie, unable to keep himself from expressing this very small worry of his.

"No," said John. "We follow the river back to the cabin, just the way we came. The ambient light will show us the way as our eyes get used to the fading light and, besides, we might catch the meteor shower on the way."

John led the way as the skies went from ruddy and rose-streaked to blotched and purple and finally to black. That blackness was lit by a million stars, the night sky a stark, black line against the snow, which seemed bright by comparison. Laurie kept close to John, walked in his footprints, and thought about reaching out to hang on to John's buffalo hide coat like a little kid, but didn't.

At one point, when it was completely dark and the cabin not yet in sight, John stopped them both. He brushed Laurie's chin with his gloved hand to get him to look up, and when Laurie did, he lost his breath all over again.

The dark velvet of the night sky was filled with stars. Between them zipped shooting stars, sharp, silver threads spinning into the void, fading as quickly as they'd come. One after the other in quick succession until the sky was nothing but silver threads.

"Happens around Iron Mountain, like this, I'm told," said John, his voice quiet. "They say the mountain is made of iron, and meteors are made of iron, so the shooting stars are trying to get back home."

"Like me," said Laurie, shivering, though whether it was with cold or the fear that he might not ever make it back to his own time, he wasn't sure.

"Come spring," said John. "Come spring, we'll get you home, but you can bide with me till then."

Laurie wanted to hug him for the offer of comfort, but only petted John's coat sleeve and nodded. Then John turned into the darkness, and began leading Laurie back to the cabin, to home.

CHAPTER FIFTEEN

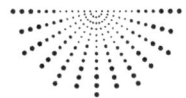

When the hard edges of the outline of the cabin loomed in the darkness before them, Laurie whooped. He kicked up snow as he sprinted past John so he could get there first and wrap his arms around the solid wooden logs that jutted out from the side.

"Oh, thank God," said Laurie, not even caring as the snow on the logs drifted along his neck. "Thank you, cabin, for showing up before I froze to death, thank you, thank you, *thank* you!"

"What're you going on about, Little Red?" asked John. He must think Laurie had gone crazy, though he laughed out loud, amused and probably too tired to stifle his reaction. "Come along inside, now. I'll build us a fire and make a quick supper. It's late."

It was late, and the cabin was dark as they went inside, though Laurie managed to take his boots and outdoor things off and put them away without too much stumbling. He was so grateful for the shelter from the ever-present wind, and the bit of warmth the cabin offered, even before John had lit a fire in the stove.

Laurie moved close to the table as John bent to light the kerosene lamp. When he did, their faces became bright in the dark. Laurie found it hard not to stare at John, lit with gold, his eyes dark blue beneath his almost-black hair. John was smiling, as though pleased at how their adventure across the snow had turned out. Neither of them mentioned the missed shots at the buffalo wolves.

"The last of the meat should still be good though there won't be much of it," said John. "I can whip us up some biscuits that we can have with butter and honey."

Whereas normally Laurie might consider this quite a heavy meal to have right before going to bed, his stomach, growling and ravenous, disagreed with him, so he nodded.

"What can I do to help?" he asked, fully happy to offer, and happy that John nodded, seemingly quite pleased with Laurie's question.

"Go fetch what we need from the cellar and the pantry," said John. "And set the table."

Laurie did as John asked, padding about in his stocking feet, sighing as he relaxed into the evening chores, gratefully inhaling the smell of steaks sizzling in the cast iron pan and the biscuits baking in the little oven in the cast iron stove.

He set the table with the mismatched china dishes and the flat cutlery and thick white mugs, which he filled with water at the pump. Sitting in his usual spot, he propped his head in his hands, and watched while John finished cooking. His movements were efficient, and he did not seem to mind that Laurie, his audience of one, was rapt in his attention.

Quite quickly, John brought the steaks and hot biscuits to the table, and while it was odd to eat steak with no steak sauce from the fridge, there was plenty of salt and pepper to make each bite delicious.

Laurie slathered the white, lumpy butter on his biscuits and drowned them in honey from the cut-glass bowl and ate them with huge bites. He chewed with his mouth open, wanting John to laugh at him and perhaps to join in with the show of bad manners. While that wasn't who John was, he was relaxed enough that he smiled, and there was a sound a little like a laugh as John wiped his mouth with the back of his hand as he ate the last of his steak.

"Will you wash the dishes while I bank the fire and go out and check the shed?" asked John. "There was quite a wind today and I want to make sure the door is secure."

They both got up from the table in tandem, and while John banked the fire, Laurie washed and dried the dishes. He also heated up extra water for them to wash with before going to bed. John wiped the table, and Laurie swept the floor, and then John went out in his shirt-sleeves to check the shed.

A gust of cold air swept into the cabin as he went out. Laurie hurried to give himself a wash, and made sure to leave enough water for John. Then he scrambled out of his clothes and slipped on his nightshirt, shivering the whole while.

When John was outside and not nearby in the cabin with Laurie, the cabin felt cold. Dark thoughts of missing home, of missing Zach and Maxton, began to crowd in on him, and he listened for John's step outside the door, anxious the whole while.

When the door opened, John kicked the snow off his boots on the threshold, and then came striding in, shutting and bolting the door behind him. His presence filled the room, making Laurie feel better, feel safer.

John was shivering as he took off his boots and left them by the front door. Rather than making some smart-ass comment about needing to have worn his coat, Laurie went up to him, dressed in his nightshirt and in his stocking feet, wrapped his arms around John's waist, and pressed his body to John's. John was cold from being out in the night, but Laurie had just been by the fire, so he knew his warmth would soon soak into John.

When John went quite still in Laurie's embrace, Laurie thought his action might have been too abrupt, their positions too intimate. But instead of pulling away, John wrapped his arms around Laurie in return, almost gingerly at first, but then his grip tightened as he hugged Laurie.

"You're quite toasty," said John, his voice a little high pitched, a little tight, as though he wasn't quite sure he should be saying what he was saying. "From being near the stove, I reckon."

"There's warm water for you to wash with," said Laurie. He tipped his head back to look up at John, smiling his pleasure, his whole body sighing with the contact of another human being. "I left it for you in the basin on the stove."

"You might crack the china, Little Red," said John, touching the pocket watch in his trouser pocket, though he didn't draw it out. Instead, he pulled out of Laurie's arms, though his hands trailed along Laurie's shoulders for a moment, a gentle, heavy weight, before he moved to the stove.

Laurie stood at the edge of the thick, braided rug, and watched John move the basin to the wooden counter. His movements were steady as he began his ritual of unbuttoning his shirt, slipping off his suspenders before peeling his garments back from his upper body. He bent over the basin, took up the soap, and washed himself.

This time Laurie didn't look away. Instead, he allowed his eyes to linger across John's shoulders, the dip of his spine above the roll of red woolen underwear, the twitch of his skin as water dripped from his hair. He was careful, though, to not let John see he was staring, as that might make John feel shy, and this Laurie most definitely did not want.

When John was nearly finished, he dried himself with the thin towel. When he hung it on the nail in the wooden counter, Laurie brought him his nightshirt. John put it on and took the clothes to the chest of drawers to put them away. Carefully, he placed the pocket watch on top of the chest of drawers, where it gleamed in the low light of the lamp. Then he came back to the table.

When he started to reach for the kerosene lamp to blow it out, he stopped, as though suddenly realizing Laurie was simply standing there, looking at him.

"What is it, Little Red?" asked John, his voice quite low. "What is it?"

Without a word, Laurie stepped quite close, close enough to see the round, dark pupils in John's blue eyes, to feel John's small breath, indrawn and quick. Laurie took both of John's hands and placed them on his face. John's fingers were tender on Laurie's ears, his palms warm and rough on Laurie's skin.

"We-we-we oughtn't to—" said John, and then he stopped, seemingly lost for words for the first time since Laurie had met him.

They might not continue as Laurie wanted them to. If John said no, then Laurie would stop, as that was the polite thing to do.

But John flicked his tongue along his teeth, leaving a tender spot of moisture on his lower lip. And he had *not* said no, so Laurie rose up on his toes, as though John was drawing Laurie close with his hands on Laurie's face. He kissed John on the mouth, gently, quietly. He drew away, blinking in the light of the kerosene lamp, his heart thumping hard, totally unsure what John's reaction would be.

John looked surprised, though the expression on his face spoke more of an unexpected pleasure, rather than something he'd dreaded the arrival of. His hands tightened on Laurie's face, though gently, and his eyes softened.

"You have such a sweet face," said John, almost whispering. "So bright, so bright in the darkness."

This might not be merely the darkness in the cabin at night, but the darkness in John's life, and Laurie felt his heart catch at the thought of it. Of having seen so much, been through so much destruction that the sight of Laurie, with his self-proclaimed goofy features, was enough to make a man like John melt to the point where he would admit it openly.

John kissed Laurie again, gently, with his plush mouth, the taste of him like salt and honey together, his warm breath stirring across Laurie's cheek. He took his hands from Laurie's face, and wrapped them around Laurie's waist, and for a moment held him close in rough, strong arms, kissing him the whole while.

Laurie felt his own hard erection beneath his nightshirt. Since they were standing so close, he knew that John was aroused, too. His heart sped up at the thought that they might soon be tumbling in the bed, pulling each other's nightshirts off, touching each other in the dark.

Instead of this happening, John took a deep breath. He drew back, though his hands stayed on Laurie's arms as he looked at Laurie, his eyes so blue, his hair wild about his forehead.

"We shouldn't do this," said John. He firmed his jaw, as though to emphasize he meant what he said. Except in his eyes was desire, and there was that dark red blush curling beneath his ears.

"I won't tell anybody," said Laurie. "It's no business of theirs anyway. It's nobody's business but ours."

Laurie's small spark of defiance made John smile, though there was a lingering wariness that drifted over that smile, as though he knew better than Laurie how it was everybody's business, and what could go wrong if folks found out.

"I won't tell," said Laurie again.

"I know," said John. "But we're both tired, and I need to sleep on the idea of it." He stopped and ducked his chin, his eyes a little wide. "If that would be—if I could—"

"Yes," said Laurie, quick to agree. If John needed to sleep on it, then it meant he was thinking about it. And that meant maybe, just maybe, they could be together that way, and Laurie wouldn't feel all alone anymore. And John wouldn't be all alone anymore, which was the more important thing.

"But—" John started and stopped, then swallowed hard. "Might I hold you while you fall asleep, Little Red?"

Laurie was riveted by John's bravery, and the flush on his cheeks, and by the determination in his eyes. And then he realized what John was asking him, and when he did, he flung himself at John and wrapped his arms tightly around John's neck.

"Yes, yes!" said Laurie, almost squealing in John's ear with joy, wriggling, his whole body flush against John's.

John's eyes were bright as he held Laurie close and bent to douse the kerosene lamp. He half carried Laurie through the dark cabin to the bed, whereupon he lifted the bedclothes and tucked Laurie beneath them with the strength of one arm. He climbed in quickly after to gather Laurie to him, with Laurie's head tucked against John's chest beneath his chin.

Laurie went still so he could hear John's heartbeat, fast and rapidly beating beneath his ribcage, his breaths a little sharp. Not from exertion, it seemed, but from nerves.

Laurie settled him as best he could, reaching up to pet John everywhere he could reach, his fingers soothing the bare skin along John's neck. He petted the flannel along John's arm, drawing his palm across John's chest, imagining he could see little sparks from static electricity.

Soon, as John settled and his breathing steadied, Laurie let himself relax as well, on his side pressed against John, his hand drifting to John's waist, where it lay comfortably. He thought he could fall asleep in seconds. He might have, except John shifted, bringing Laurie's whole body into alert. Where was his hand? Where did John want his hand to go? Anywhere? Or was he just getting comfortable on the lumpy mattress?

Unsure, Laurie waited. Then John shifted again, and Laurie's hand slipped lower to John's hip, and he was sure, quite sure, that John's arousal was the same as it had been when they'd been standing at the table. Only John couldn't ask for what he wanted, not in the year 1891, when it was illegal, so Laurie would ask for him.

"May I touch you?" Laurie asked, whispering. "May I?"

For an answer, John turned on his side away from Laurie, except he gripped Laurie's hand and pulled it down to his groin that, even beneath the layers of nightshirt and union suit, was hot and hard.

From John came a small sound, a cry, even, that rippled an echo up and down Laurie's spine. It might be shame John was expressing, or it might be fear. But even though Laurie was a little surprised at how quickly *maybe* turned into *now*, he was determined to take care of John in every way possible, to calm his fears, and soothe his need.

Laurie curled his hips forward to tuck his thighs behind John's thighs, and pressed his face close against John's back. He reached around, tugging up John's flannel nightshirt, fumbling and cursing inwardly as his fingers struggled with the metal buttons on John's woolen underwear. There were so many damn buttons, but finally he sighed as he undid a few of them and slipped his hand inside, his fingers tangling with John's pubic hair.

John's cock was warm in Laurie's palm, the pulse of John's heartbeat just beneath the thin skin. John was uncut, as only made sense considering what year it was, so Laurie stroked him gently, mentally cursing the restraint on his wrist by the space made by the few buttons he'd managed to get undone. But it was enough, both to slip his fingers up and down, and to feel John's cock harden.

He drew his hand out to lick his palm, then slipped back inside of John's garments, where the faint moisture made the movements of stroking John a little easier as Laurie's hand slipped up and down. With each push and pull, John's hips surged, pressing forward, pushing himself into Laurie's hand harder, as though wanting more.

Laurie wasn't sure if John had ever had sex with a man before, though his body seemed to know what it wanted, how to get more of what it wanted. As Laurie thought to go more gently, John clamped his hand on top of Laurie's hand, and Laurie knew that he wanted more, harder, *now*.

Laurie gave John what he wanted, clutching at John's nightshirt with one hand while he rode John's cock with his other hand, fingers tight, stroking him up and down until John's cock pulsed in Laurie's fist, hot semen spilling over his fingers. John grunted low in his throat, and then sighed as his whole body relaxed, head tipping back as he sank into Laurie's embrace.

Laurie released John's now-soft cock, gently. He did up the buttons as best he could, swiping his hand on the sheet. He kissed John's mouth in the darkness as John turned in his arms, and imagined he could see John's eyelashes around his wide-open eyes.

"Okay, John?" asked Laurie. He felt desperate to make sure he'd not marched over some invisible line John had drawn, on one side of which was *yes, please*, and on the other side of which was *no, thank you*. Laurie would stab himself in the heart if he'd wounded John in any way, and he needed to know. "Are you okay? Did I do okay?"

"Yes, Little Red," said John, sounding a little breathless. "Yes, yes."

Though it was John who might have needed comforting, he rolled toward Laurie and gathered him in a gentle embrace, as though Laurie was quite young and had awoken from a bad dream. He kissed the top of Laurie's head, and pressed his cheek there, locking in the kiss so it wouldn't get away.

Laurie sighed, and felt his neck relax, and snuggled close, as contented as he could ever remember being. His cock, which had been quite demanding of its own turn only moments before, began to soften, and Laurie found he didn't mind so very much because the anticipation was its own pleasure.

Until it was Laurie's turn, John would keep him safe in the dark, protective against all dangers as he had been in the low valley along Horse Creek, when he thought Laurie had been afraid of the buffalo wolves. With John near, Laurie never had to be afraid of anything again.

CHAPTER SIXTEEN

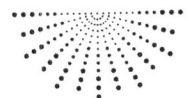

Laurie awoke the next morning, blinking at the light coming through the window. A swirl of icy wind outside indicated that the clear skies the night before had turned into a boiling snowstorm, which meant they might be stuck in the cabin all day. Which would not have been a bad thing, except Laurie wasn't quite sure what John's mood might be.

John was not the type to play games, though he was the type to stand for what he said he would. Which, in this case, was that he wasn't the type of man who went around kissing other men. Except he'd kissed Laurie quite thoroughly the night before, and had, in fact, drawn Laurie's hand to his very hard cock, and not stopped Laurie when Laurie had jerked him off.

John wouldn't have called it that, of course, he'd refer to it using some old-fashioned term that would be quite sweet and endearing when he said it, melting Laurie into a puddle on the cabin floor. So while the wind was most certainly blowing from the north and west outside, who knew from which direction it was blowing inside. There was only one way to find out, so Laurie crawled out of bed and stood at the open curtain, rubbing the sleep from his eyes, just as he had before, to see what was what.

John was sitting at the kitchen table fully dressed, a steel-nibbed pen in his hand and a bottle of ink at his elbow. His sleeves were rolled up, and his red woolen union suit pushed up on his forearms. He was writing in the brown, leather-covered journal, the pages spread flat, making cursive motions as he went, pausing from time to time to dip the pen in the ink, tapping it on the rim of the ink bottle before taking up his writing again.

"Can I make you some breakfast?" asked John. "There's coffee, if you want some."

John didn't look up from his work, but of course he knew exactly where Laurie was. His words had been said as if this were an ordinary morning, as though they'd not kissed and had sex the night before. Almost as mysterious was the fact that it was well beyond their usual time for breakfast, so it appeared John had let Laurie sleep in.

A little baffled, Laurie came close to the table in his nightshirt, and waited until John looked up at him. John's expression startled him. His blue eyes were filled with worry, as though he thought Laurie would scorn him, now that it was daylight. Or that he would head off to Farthing and tell everybody what happened.

"I'd like breakfast, please," said Laurie, offering his sweetest smile in an effort to reassure John while at the same time giving him something to do to distract him from his worries.

When he laid his hand on John's wrist, John suddenly scraped the chair back and stood up, as though he desperately wanted out of Laurie's reach. The table got bumped, and the ink splashed out of the well, and John placed the pen down with some firmness.

Had this been early days, when Laurie had been so newly arrived, he would have expected a firm scolding how to mind himself and not go barging about knocking into things. Except as John stood there, his breath came hard and there was a blush to his cheeks. Laurie knew right then and there that they were each besotted with the other, such a lovely old-fashioned term and entirely appropriate to their situation.

"You should get dressed, Little Red," said John with a gulp, his eyes on his journal and the newly formed splotch of ink on the table. "It isn't right to go around in your nightshirt all day. Besides, I don't want you to be cold when you go out this morning to chop more wood, as I'll want to keep a fire going in the fireplace, as well as the stove, while the storm lasts."

When he finally looked at Laurie, his half-lidded eyes were so blue, and while the whole of him was handsome and strong, there was an expression of wariness in those eyes. A hesitation that seemed to want consideration and reassurance, though John was definitely not the type of man to ask for something like that, so vulnerable, out loud. Laurie took John's hand and kissed it, and felt that he'd be willing to look after John all the days of his life in this regard.

"Yes, John," said Laurie.

He lifted on his toes and kissed John fondly on the cheek, and then went obediently to get dressed so he could have breakfast, and afterward chop wood, and after that? Well, they were going to be stuck in the cabin together while the storm lasted, and who knew how long that would be. Laurie hoped it would be a good long, long while.

After a quiet breakfast where neither of them spoke very much, and John kept casting glances at Laurie as though he'd grown two heads, they did chores. They split up the work, as usual, with Laurie doing the dishes and John sweeping the floor. Then after they made the bed together, Laurie bundled up to go chop wood for the fire.

When he stepped outside the cabin, the wind had died down and the sky was full of fat flakes that tumbled down in slow-motion in the cold, still air. Everything was white, and the snow was almost up to Laurie's knees as he plowed his way to the shed. It wasn't a very long way he had to plow, but what if it had been? How would he have managed on his own?

He was on the edge of panic when he sternly told himself he didn't have to manage on his own, as he and John would manage together. Then he had to tell himself it wasn't fickle of him to miss his friends one minute, worrying about being stuck in the past forever, and then, the very next minute, be glad to be living on the frontier with a man such as John.

When he was nearly finished chopping wood, John came out in his shirtsleeves to help Laurie carry in several armfuls, which they stacked near the fireplace. After which John swept out the wet snow before it had a chance to melt. Then there was lunch to get on, and eat, and clean up after, and again Laurie was amazed that while they lived simply, there was so much to do to occupy their time.

When the table was cleared, John got out his journal. He spread it out and sat down to write in it again with his pen and ink, going back to the task Laurie had obviously interrupted before his late breakfast.

"What are you writing in there?" asked Laurie. "You were already writing in it this morning, what is it?"

He sat down at the table and looked at John. He was flirting a little but not too much, yet in a way that would let John know it would be okay to flirt back. John, who had been acting fairly normal all morning, now seemed flustered, so Laurie focused his attention on the journal. He put his finger on it, and at John's nod, pulled it to him.

Laurie flipped to the front and saw that the first entry, for it was like a diary of sorts, was dated a month earlier, when John must have arrived at the cabin. Each day or so, John wrote down the weather, noted the temperature and wind direction, how hard it had rained or snowed, and anything he'd spent on the cabin's upkeep, or how much tar paper he'd used to winterize the shed. What he'd hunted or trapped. How many antelope had passed the cabin. How he'd tracked the buffalo wolves to their den.

"You've written a lot today," said Laurie. He flipped to the last pages where the fresh ink showed him that John had written a report describing every day since Laurie had shown up, There was nothing personal about the entries, no thoughts or observations, no meditative writing. Just facts about the day, and certainly nothing about Laurie.

"I was catching up," said John. "As it's been rather busy around here, since you arrived."

John smiled, as though pleased at this, showing his teeth and his adorable dimples, and Laurie smiled back. He let John have his journal, though he did play a game of tug-of-war, not quite letting John have it back right away, and when John tugged, his thumb left a smear of ink across the corner of the page.

"Sorry," said Laurie. He stood up, peeved with himself. He was always taking it too far like that, and what was meant to be a funny little joke turned into a ruined journal or whatever. "I'm sorry, I didn't mean to do that."

"It doesn't matter, Little Red," said John. "It's just the corner. It's just paper."

Feeling pleased, Laurie left John alone with his journal, grabbed the green-covered book about Antarctica and the tropics and settled in the big leather chair in the center of the room to read it. After a time, John came over and built up the fire in the fireplace, making it a nice warm, crackling one. For a long while, the room was peaceful, the smell of woodsmoke in the air. And with the snow falling slowly outside the window, it was quiet outside as well, with no wind for once.

There was that moment, however, when Laurie needed to visit the outhouse. He groused to John, bundled up, and trudged up the small hill to use it, and trudged back down again under the white fall of snow. Except when he got back to the cabin and shook out of his coat and stomped the snow off his boots, he found that John had taken his place in the big leather chair. He'd even picked up the book Laurie had been reading, holding it high in his strong fingers.

"Hey," said Laurie. This was more for the effect than to get John's attention, for John was already side-eyeing him. His mouth twitched as though he'd been enjoying the anticipation of this moment and had planned it the second Laurie had set foot out the door. "That is my seat, I'll have you know."

"You left it," said John, and he went back to his reading, as calm as anything.

Laurie took off his boots and stomped over to the stove in his stocking feet to get a cup of coffee from the new pot John had made, which he drank standing up, leaning against the counter. Then he went over and hunkered in front of the fire, and poked at the logs with the iron poker just to watch the flames spark and dance.

They could tiptoe around each other all day, or he could flirt just a little harder. He'd show John how it was done, being ever so careful to watch for any signals that it was too much for John, or too soon. Besides, it was no fun if he was all the way over *here*, when John was all the way over *there*.

Putting the poker back in its place, Laurie stood up and dusted off his hands. With as much stealth as he could manage, given the size of the cabin and the fact that John was sitting in the center of it, Laurie sidled up to the chair and waited. He flicked at the leather of the arm of the chair with his nails.

When John loosened his hand to turn the page, Laurie took the green book from him and sat on the round leather arm of the chair. And then slowly, ever so slowly, as though gravity alone was to blame for everything that was happening, he slid into John's lap. Gently, though, so his bony hips didn't poke John in any of the wrong places.

Smiling the whole while, looking right at John as he did it, he sputtered with laughter as John spread his arms wide, as though he was astonished at what Laurie was doing. The look on his face was perfection, too, with his mouth trying to screw itself into one of displeasure while his eyes danced happily.

Laurie knew then and there he'd gotten it right. John had been waiting for him to make the first move, and whether that was because John was just that shy or because he wanted to be sure of Laurie didn't matter because he'd gotten it *right*.

Laurie gave himself many gold stars as he handed the book back to John. He slid even further into John's lap, settling on one of John's thighs while tucking his stocking feet beneath the other one, his ankles between John's legs. Then, curling himself with his head on John's shoulder, he spread his hand on John's chest, and looked up through his eyelashes, smiling a little.

"There is only one chair, as you know, John," said Laurie, as solemnly as he could without bursting into outright laughter. "It's selfish of either of us to hog it, so why don't we share for a while?"

"That sounds fair," said John, his voice rising a little, as though he was asking a question.

"It is fair," said Laurie. "More than fair."

To prove his point of exactly how fair it was, he tilted his head to press a kiss on John's neck, and then on his chin, and then on his cheek. Gratitude and pleasure filled him when John turned his head to return the kiss, almost casually, though he was blushing hard when he did it. Satisfied, Laurie tucked his head beneath John's chin, settled himself more comfortably, laughing when John grunted, for Laurie was not as light as a child, by any means.

"Read," he commanded, placing his hand beneath the book in John's hand, lifting it. "Read to me."

"Yes, sir," said John, and began to read in a low voice from the somewhat dull but soothing *The Polar and Tropical Worlds*.

Facts filled Laurie's head, and his eyes closed, and he knew he was going to fall asleep, then and there, which wasn't quite the flirty plan he'd had in mind. But it seemed a good compromise, as John's voice grew steadier, and his body relaxed beneath Laurie's. He didn't even seem to mind when Laurie shifted to snug his arm behind John's back, and hugged him from the front, and patted his belly before settling down again.

Laurie began to doze off, coming a little to wakefulness when John leaned to put the book on the table beside the chair. Both of his arms, warm and strong, came around Laurie, and there was a whisper of a kiss that Laurie felt on his temple, and the gentle words from John that he heard in his ears. In time, John's words faded away and he fell asleep, snoring a little with his head tipped back on the big leather chair. Laurie soon followed him; all in all, a satisfactory afternoon.

When he awoke, it was with a start, as he realized John was stirring beneath him and that he'd drooled on John's blue shirt. One of John's suspenders was digging into his scalp, and his foot had fallen asleep. But it was all worth it to have John's arms tighten around him, and for John to bend close with a small smile on his face.

"Time for supper, Little Red," said John. "Do you want to help me make stew? We'll use the very last of the antelope, and I'll put in extra carrots that you like so much."

Laurie didn't particularly care for carrots and had eaten them because he was hungry. However, he was prepared, then and there, to declare them his very most favorite food just to see that smile again, and hear the sweet way John made the offer.

"Yes, thank you," said Laurie using his best manners. "Have I crushed you very badly?" he asked, sitting up in such a way as to dig his butt bones into John's leg.

"Ow!" said John, laughing as he scooped his hands beneath Laurie's bottom to protect himself. The expression on John's face quickly turned into something else as he realized what he was doing, and that he might be allowed to continue doing it. Laurie wiggled to emphasize that it was perfectly okay for John to touch him anywhere, and leaned forward to rest his forehead on John's forehead.

"You have my ass in your hands, you know," said Laurie, waggling his eyebrows suggestively.

"I do, don't I," said John. He stood up, looping his arms around Laurie's waist to bring Laurie with him. Then he slid Laurie to the floor so he could stand on his own feet, and stretched, blushing a little as Laurie watched him. "I've not had that good a nap in a long time," he said. "I hope we didn't nap so long we can't go to sleep when nighttime comes."

Laurie laughed and shook his head. John was all innocence and wide eyes, but he was just laying it out for Laurie to knock it out of the park.

"Well," said Laurie with mock seriousness. He fiddled with the buttons on John's shirt, and then stroked John's chest to smooth the cloth. "If that happens, I'm pretty sure we'll figure out something to do to occupy our time."

"I'm sure—" said John. He was doing his best to join in Laurie's play, but he blushed hard instead and ran his fingers through his hair, so Laurie stepped back to give him a little space.

He trailed happily after John as he went over to the stove and began feeding it with slender bits of kindling to urge the fire into life. He stuck close to John's side as John gathered the ingredients for the stew, carrots and onions and meat from the cellar, flour and salt and pepper from the pantry. At one point, Laurie was so close on John's heels in the pantry that when John turned around with the box of salt in his hand, Laurie was right there, and John almost fell over him.

"For Pete's sake, Little Red," said John, as though he were half exasperated and half pleased.

Laurie gave him a quick kiss to reward him, both for being patient with Laurie and for being so handsome as he made them supper. It wouldn't be a fancy meal, but sharing food with John at the small kitchen table was its own pleasure.

With his usual seriousness, John showed Laurie how to properly peel potatoes with a knife, and how to peel carrots as well and cut them into strips. How it was good to boil the potatoes for a short while first before putting them into the stew, and how cooking carrots long and slow in butter made them soft and sweet. By the time John got around to searing the meat in the cast iron pot, Laurie's mouth was already watering, and his stomach was growling.

John, who was not oblivious, took a moment to pat Laurie's stomach.

"I'll make dumplings," said John. He tilted his head back, as though with pride. "You've never had dumplings as good as I can make them."

"That I do not doubt," said Laurie loudly, winking for effect, and was pleased to see a bit of blush curling its way beneath John's ears. "Now, what else can I do to help get supper on?"

"Set the table," said John with an expression of fondness. "Then come be near me."

With great haste, Laurie set the table, being careful with John's mismatched china. After he was finished, he went to stand at John's side while John assembled the stew, showing Laurie how he used leftover coffee to darken it. Then he made flour dumplings, and when the stew was bubbling, he placed large spoonfuls, one by one, on the surface of the stew, then put a lid on the pot.

Everything smelled wonderful. It was cozy by the stove, and entirely pleasurable to press his shoulder against John's, to feel John press back, and to stand that way together, side by side to wait for their supper to finish cooking.

CHAPTER SEVENTEEN

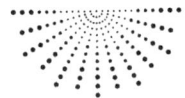

When the supper dishes were done, they shared the chores of wiping the table and sweeping the floor, and John went out to get more wood. When he brought in two armfuls at the same time, Laurie closed and bolted the door after him, mentally admiring John for being just that strong, and for the way the tendons in his forearms corded, his dense thighs spread to carry the weight without dropping it.

Laurie enjoyed the sight so much, he didn't even mind having to sweep the snow from the floor that had been left by John's boots for the nth time. But as they half stripped and washed for bed with water warmed on the stove, Laurie sensed John was getting nervous. As he checked his pocket watch and put it on top of the chest of drawers, he was not looking at Laurie, and though his motions were steady, he seemed uneasy.

"Hey John," said Laurie as he bent at the basin to rinse his face. "It's just me, you know. I'm not going to hurt you."

"I know," said John with unexpected honesty, rather than denying he knew what Laurie was talking about. He slipped on his nightshirt, and looked directly at Laurie finally, being brave, it seemed, which was his nature. "It's just that you've been looking at me all day and I don't know—that is, I'm not quite sure what is to happen next."

As this was the sweetest, most endearing thing Laurie had ever heard, he felt all soft inside. Wanting to make sure John was okay, he went up close and placed John's hands on his face, as he had before. He looked up at John.

"Nothing you don't want to happen," said Laurie. "Not ever, I would never, you see?"

To emphasize this, Laurie took his arms and hugged John around the waist, enjoying the strong feel of John's body, the warmth of him beneath the flannel nightshirt and red union suit.

He laid his cheek on John's chest and was gratified when John embraced him, for he was growing to adore John's hugs, those strong arms and the steady way John held him. There was nothing like it, not in the whole world, to compare with how safe he felt when he was in John's arms.

"Now," said Laurie, his voice muffled by the flannel of John's nightshirt. "Is it bed time or isn't it?"

"It is," said John, somewhat faintly. Then he coughed, and Laurie could feel him nodding. "It is," he said more firmly. "We've had a long day."

Laurie laughed under his breath as he let John go and looked up at him. John's eyes were shining, perhaps because he was nervous, but he also seemed happy because when he looked down at Laurie, he was smiling.

John bent to blow out the kerosene lamp, using one hand to cup the top of the chimney. As the light was doused, the image emblazoned in Laurie's brain was of John smiling, contented, his dark lashes long on his cheeks, and that made Laurie happier than he could have imagined.

He trailed John to the bed and clambered in on his side. As John tugged the bedclothes over them both, he propped himself up on his elbow. In the dark, he sensed John's rapt attention.

"Say, mister," said Laurie conversationally. "What's a handsome fellow like you doing in a place like this?"

John made a sound in his throat, and Laurie realized that being all funny and entertaining wasn't quite the way to treat John, not when he was so new to sex, not when he was being so brave as to allow Laurie this close to him.

"You're the handsomest fellow in the place," said Laurie, lowering his voice to a whisper as he scooted close and cupped John's face in his hand. "And the warmest," Laurie added, for John was as warm as the cast iron stove on a frosty day. "May I kiss you, kind sir?" he asked, for a little humor never went amiss, just not, in this case, the over-the-top kind.

"Yes," said John, so simply and quietly that Laurie's heart was moved almost to the point of pain. He couldn't imagine having gone as many years as John surely had, fighting his own nature, fighting the world. Well, now he was in Laurie's care. Laurie could treat him as he deserved, with gentleness, a little bit of fun, and a whole lot of love.

Laurie kissed John's chin, and heard John sigh, then scooted closer and kissed his warm, plush mouth in the darkness. He moved up and finally was almost on top of John, kissing and kissing him. John stopped him for a second, his warm hands on Laurie's hands. He might have been looking up at Laurie to make sure of him, but there was almost no light, so Laurie could not see his expression.

It might be nice to make love by the light of the kerosene lamp and without so many clothes on, but this was how they started. Laurie meant to go on and kiss John and pet him and make him feel good all over. So he kissed John, kissed him hard, and felt John respond and surge beneath him, his thighs strong. John's arms went around Laurie's waist to pull him close, to keep him close, though he was almost shaking, as though with desperation.

"John," said Laurie, his mouth moving against John's mouth. "Are you okay, is this okay?"

He felt John nod and then pause, his whole body going still. Just as Laurie was about to open his mouth to ask again, John surged and, grabbing Laurie, turned them so John was practically on top of Laurie.

His solid weight pressed on Laurie in the darkness, a delicious, almost dangerous power that stole Laurie's breath. John was hot all over, the scent of soap and sweat and woodsmoke surrounding Laurie as John kissed Laurie with powerful, deliberate kisses, mouth firm, tongue warm, his hands clasping Laurie's lower back. John was hard, all muscle, everywhere, and through the layers of their union suits and nightshirts, his cock pressed against Laurie's cock.

"Need to undo some buttons, John," said Laurie, muttering almost to himself as he groped down John's body to tug his nightshirt up. He didn't care about himself, or his own needs; he had to get to John, had to touch some skin, had to free John from the layers of his clothes.

John kept kissing Laurie, and petting him, and rose up to kiss the tender skin beneath Laurie's ear, which almost made him come in his union suit, then and there. But then he realized John was lifting up to help him, so he pulled off John's nightshirt and tossed it any old how, sighing when John settled back on top of him.

Now he could get at those damn buttons. He almost broke his wrist doing it, but finally the top half of John was free from his union suit. Though there really wasn't much ambient light, Laurie imagined he could see John above him, propped up on his elbow, half naked, neck exposed, sweat on his brow, his eyes gleaming with pleasure, his mouth moist and plush from all the kissing.

John deserved something for being so brave, deserved something so marvelous that it'd blow his socks off, something he'd remember forever. Laurie decided quickly and rose up to push John back on the bed. Then he straddled John, his thighs on each side of John's thighs, and scooted down John's body, double-checking that the buttons on John's union suit were undone as he went.

He couldn't quite bring himself to break the silence by explaining what he was about to do, so he went slowly enough so John could stop him if he wanted, or push him off if he didn't like it. Then, when he was on John's calves, Laurie swung off, bent down, his hands spreading John's union suit open. With his mouth, he traced the hair leading from John's belly button to his cock, swirled his tongue around the tip and paused, inhaling the close scent of John's body.

The garbled words from John's mouth were more than of surprise, they were of astonishment, followed by three quick indrawn breaths that contained a thin keening sound, as though John had been lost and now Laurie had found him. Found him and would keep him, keep him safe from the dark, from being alone in the cold of winter.

As such, having gotten permission to continue, Laurie reached into the opening in John's union suit where the buttons ended and wrapped his hand around the base of John's cock. He cupped John's hip in his hand to balance himself, and began to suckle John. He started softly at first, quietly. He shifted to get comfortable, to make sure he could do this nice and slow, to drag it on forever so John's first time would seem never-ending and sweet and eternal.

Laurie swirled his tongue around the foreskin of John's cock, tasting him, tasting the clean taste of him, like linen, and the bitter tang of pre-come that formed at the slit. He licked and stroked and petted, and all the while smiling inside at the sounds John made, the low moans, the quickened breaths.

John's thighs trembled beneath the union suit, and oh, how Laurie wished he could get John completely naked. Laurie soothed him with his hand, and stroked John up and down as he sucked, clutching at the base of his cock as he felt passion surge through John, collecting itself all on its own, as though nobody, not even John, could stop it.

John's hips jerked forward, much as they had their first night together, an almost involuntary movement, as though John couldn't help himself, crying out as though at his own weakness.

When he came, Laurie covered John's cock with his mouth and swallowed. It was always polite to swallow, especially if you cared about someone, if you loved them, and they tasted good, which Laurie did and which John did. As Laurie finished swallowing, he wiped his mouth with the back of his hand and thought about collapsing in a heap next to John and just pulling up the bedclothes to fall asleep.

Except that wouldn't be very gentlemanly of him. John needed tending to, he needed sweet whispers in his ear, and slow careful pets anywhere that Laurie could reach. More, Laurie wanted to be close to him as the shudders in John's body eased, and his breathing eased, and he became calm in the dark.

Laurie began to pet and to touch and to soothe, moving close into John's arms. When he was, at last, able to pull up the bedclothes, John held him quite tightly, almost too tightly, squeezing him hard before releasing him.

"What is it, John?" asked Laurie. He sensed John had something he wanted to say, as John seemed to be trying to catch his breath so he could talk. Laurie scooted up so that their mouths were almost touching, so that when John did speak, Laurie could hear him, with his body, with his whole heart.

"You—" began John, and then he stopped to swallow. "You put your *mouth* on me," said John. There was no denying the astonishment in his voice, though Laurie was very glad to realize there was no anger, no recrimination. Just a sense of wonder and, if Laurie would let himself admit it, a touch of awe.

"Yes, I did," said Laurie. He couldn't quite hide the smugness in his voice as he smiled and kissed John anywhere he could manage, three quick kisses.

"Where did you learn to do such a thing?" asked John, suddenly. Laurie could almost hear him thinking about how it might be possible for Laurie to be skilled at this, and who he might have been with to learn it. "Were you—did you—?"

John couldn't quite articulate what he wanted to ask, but Laurie had a good idea as to why. Back in 1891, being a prostitute was the one occupation where one might learn to give another person a blow job. Though, of course, John wouldn't refer to it that way. Oral sex was not a conversation for polite people, not in 1891, not even if they were two men in a winter-locked cabin in the middle of nowhere.

"I heard about it," said Laurie, as casually as he could manage, his heart pounding with fear that the whole evening might be ruined if he could not explain himself quickly enough. "You know, fellows at the, uh, barber and places like that. Or when you're standing in line to buy, um, coffee or whatever? You hear things, and I'm a good listener, you know, so I thought you'd like it if I tried what they were talking about." Laurie finished his hastily cobbled-together explanation with a whoosh of air, doing his best to imagine an old-fashioned street corner somewhere with guys in bowler hats standing around talking about blow jobs."

"You know, in the city," said Laurie, continuing on, because John hadn't said anything. It was looking like he didn't believe Laurie, either, and soon he would denounce him as a liar and all the good feelings between them would come to a halt. "You hear things in the city because there are so many people, and you get used to that, you forget you're not alone. People say things they don't realize other people can overhear. And you know how guys are, always talking about sex at the drop of a hat. So I listened."

Laurie waited, but didn't have long to worry, because John sighed, and tipped his head to rest it against Laurie's forehead.

"I reckon it is different back east," said John. "I'd not thought about it like that."

As he rolled into John's welcoming arms, Laurie tried to forget he'd just lied to John again. He didn't let himself think about what would happen if John found out the truth about where he came from. But he'd never find out, right? To find out, he'd have to discover that Laurie came from John's future, where blow jobs and similar activities were, at least in Laurie's world, what guys talked about.

Guys talked about sex all the time, as casually as they might make arrangements to go play computer games or when to see the next sci-fi movie that was coming out. In the future, sex was everywhere, at least it seemed to be in comparison to the past, the *now* where Laurie was living, where it was an intimate, private thing to be shared in a double bed barely big enough for the two men cuddling in it.

"Do you need anything?" asked Laurie. He was ignoring his own hard on, which would simmer down in time, if he let it. While usually reciprocity in the bedroom was in order, this was John's night, and Laurie wanted to take care of him and not have John worrying about taking care of Laurie. "Get you a glass of water or anything?"

"No," said John. He shook his head so gently it became a caress that turned into a kiss, John's mouth on Laurie's temple. "I feel as though I have lead weights attached to my eyes and they're sinking fast."

"That's how it should be," said Laurie with a pleased smile.

Of course, John couldn't see the smile. He must have felt it, though, for he reached up to cup Laurie's cheek in his warm palm, a gesture of love without words. Laurie leaned into the touch, sighing out loud.

He let his head fall into the curve of John's neck, and sighed again as John pulled up the bedclothes. John tucked the bedclothes close around the two of them, snuggled as they were, warm in the cold, dark night, together and not alone.

Sleep took Laurie. How easily it came with John to protect him against whatever nameless night fears and stresses that used to torment him into night upon night of insomnia back in his other life. It might be that the constant chores and occupations during the day contributed to the lack of insomnia, like a full day's worth of exercise at the gym might.

Or maybe it was just the fact that John was near. Yes, that seemed the better reason. Did Laurie even need a reason? Why was he overthinking it? He was happier than he ever had been, and staying with John felt more important than trying to get back home. Who needed to go back home? Not Laurie, that's for sure.

CHAPTER EIGHTEEN

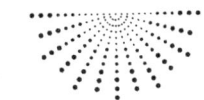

The storm lasted until mid-morning the next day. The wind stopped blowing, the skies suddenly cleared, and the sun shone, reflecting off the packed snow as though it were polished glass.

When Laurie opened the door to look out upon the day, he wished, quite hard, for sunglasses, even a pair of cheap ones. Then came thoughts of a string of items that would have proven quite useful back in 1891. Dental floss, for one, real dishwashing soap, for another. Sriracha sauce. Central heating and hot water. Toilet paper that wasn't made from pages of a Sears catalog. Maybe some lube.

Laurie smiled to himself as he swung on his coat, borrowed John's scarf, and trudged out to the shed for firewood. He gathered up as large an armful as he could. The pile of wood was so big he could barely see over it, and he staggered dramatically into the cabin, making high-pitched sounds of distress so that John would run to help him. Which John did.

"What are you doing, going out without buttoning up?" asked John, blustering and scolding as he took the wood from Laurie's arms and put it in the firebox. "You'll catch cold. Now take those off and come close to the stove."

Doing as he was told, Laurie hurried to hang up the coat and scarf, and went over to John. John was cooking them breakfast, his shirtsleeves rolled, his union suit sleeves pushed up to his elbows, handsome and sturdy in the warmth of the stove. He handed Laurie a mug of hot, black coffee and went back to his work.

The sun streamed through the windows. The whole place felt warm with the bright light, the cheery snap of wood burning, and the smell of coffee percolating. On impulse, Laurie wrapped his arm around John's waist and rested his head in the curve of John's shoulder. Which meant John had to put down the spatula where he was turning the cakes of fried cornmeal mush. When he did, he enveloped Laurie in that wonderful embrace, the smell of wool and soap and woodsmoke surrounding him.

John kissed the top of Laurie's head, and then pressed his cheek there for a second, as though to keep the kiss in place. Laurie sighed at the thought of locking in kisses like that, and kissed the closest place he could reach, which was John's warm, strong neck.

"I need to get breakfast done, Little Red," said John, though he didn't push Laurie away. "Or it'll burn and that'll be food wasted."

"Don't want to waste fried cornmeal mush," said Laurie, laughing as he eased himself out of John's arms.

He thought about omelets and whether they could be made in cast iron pans, though he didn't mention it. They probably could be made in a cast iron pan because people had been making them since forever. What if it turned out he'd been the one to invent the Denver omelet? His mouth began to water at the thought of fresh green peppers and tomatoes, all fried up with cheese and egg.

He dismissed this thought because it wasn't helpful, as there were no fresh vegetables to be found in 1891, at least not at this time of year. He distracted himself by setting the table, and went around to make sure all the curtains were wide open. Then he went to the front door again and opened it, just to look out. The cold air rushed inside the cabin, fresh and wild, and Laurie took a deep breath, and knew he was happy.

"What are you doing, Little Red?" asked John from the stove.

"You're letting all the cold air in, so close that door and come to breakfast."

"There's so much snow," said Laurie as he sat down and started eating the plateful of fried food John served him. "It's so white, just *white*."

John shook his head because, of course, to him, what other color would it be? In Laurie's world, snow was a variety of colors, depending on whether it was on a chemically salted road, or the humps and piles along the side, where it had been plowed. Or if it was in the city, it usually had that gray tinge to it. Which was exactly the opposite of what was just outside the door to the cabin, layer upon layer of white, pure white snow, the sun glinting off it making diamonds in the air.

"We'll see plenty of it tomorrow," said John as he took a sip of his coffee. "I need to go into town for more flour and butter and the like before the next storm hits. Perhaps we could pick up a few extras, if you'd like to come with me and help me tote everything home."

"That snow's up to our asses," said Laurie with a laugh. "We'd never make it," he added, being dramatic again, just for fun. "I'd get stuck!"

"The wind'll pick up and blow most of it away before we head out," said John. "Besides, I'd carry you."

John's expression was quite solemn because, as Laurie well knew, he never said anything he didn't mean. But there was also a look in his eyes, quite tender, that Laurie hoped wasn't entirely due to the sexy fun times they'd shared the night before. He wanted what was developing between them to be more than that.

He didn't think John would be overly comfortable with Laurie saying anything like that out loud, though, at least not yet. So, for the moment, Laurie admired his old-fashioned man with his shoulders the width of an axe handle, and his deliberate, careful motions as he ate his breakfast.

John had left the top buttons of his blue chambray shirt undone, as well as the buttons on his red union suit. With his neck exposed, and everything else covered up, that swath of skin became a draw to Laurie's eyes. As did John's strong jaw, shadowed with morning beardgrowth, and the delightful mess of his dark hair as it tumbled over his forehead.

As John felt Laurie staring, he lifted his head from his steady pursuit of his breakfast and returned Laurie's gaze. In those blue eyes was a deep and wonderful purity Laurie could not define in words, but that he felt, deep inside. There was nobody like John, nobody in all the world.

If Laurie had been brave enough, he would have told John he loved him, then and there. But it might not be the time, might not be the *right* time. John wasn't ready for that and maybe Laurie, stuck in a time not his own, wasn't ready either. If he said the words, then that meant he was ready to stick around, ready to stop hoping to go home. Which he didn't even know how to do, since he'd no idea how he'd ended up in 1891 at John's door in the first place.

Laurie swallowed, and did his best to focus on where he was, and not on the fact that he'd never see his friends again.

"What are you thinking about, Little Red?" asked John, his voice soft.

"You," said Laurie, not telling the entire truth, for it did no harm, no harm at all to flirt and show John how much he cared that way. "How it'd be if you carried me in the snow. You might drop me, you know."

"I'd never drop you," said John with all seriousness, though there was a twinkle of a laugh in his blue eyes. "Never."

"Such words, such words," said Laurie, shaking his head. He put the back of his hand to his forehead like a heroine in a play who was resisting the pursuits of the evil landowner. "I cannot, I mustn't!"

John laughed, ducking his head, a wonderful curl of a smile on his mouth as he looked at his plate and then at Laurie again.

"You sure do like to play up, don't you," said John, though this was with pleasure rather than with recrimination at Laurie's antics. "Never knew a fellow to have such rambunctiousness as you."

"Well, luckily, now you do," said Laurie, smiling, pleased at the result, which was getting to see John smile more with those lovely dimples of his and that light in his eyes, the one that told Laurie he was happy.

After breakfast, they cleaned up together, sharing the sweeping and the dish washing. This left Laurie feeling more domestic than he ever had in his life, though he had to quickly swallow a pang when he remembered there was no Zach, no Maxton, to share the joke with. They would have laughed; Zach would have elbowed him in the ribs, and Maxton's small smirk would have sent joy rushing through Laurie. But he couldn't think about that now, or he'd lose it.

Instead, he focused when John showed him how to clean the floor with vinegar and water and cloths. Together they both went on their hands and knees, sharing the task. After which, John showed Laurie how to wipe the chimney of the kerosene lamp. How to fill the reservoir with kerosene from the jug, how to put in a new cloth wick from a little tin box, and how to properly light it so that it didn't smoke.

Lunch was a simple affair of the rest of the antelope, fried in thin strips with flour gravy. It was the thickest mess, tasting mostly of salt and gamey meat, but Laurie ate his share, not only so he wouldn't insult John's cooking, but because he was hungry and that was all there was to eat.

In the afternoon, John cleaned his rifle, which he brought to the table, along with a tin of oil and a clean cloth. Laurie sat at the table to watch John work, so steadily and slow, as though he had all the time in the world, nothing to hurry, nothing to rush. Afterwards, Laurie cleared the ashes from the fireplace and the stove, then shrugged on his coat to go out into the sharp, cold air of the shed to cut wood, and time flew by.

When he was done with his chores, Laurie pulled out a book with a deep purple cover from John's bookshelf and sat on the braided rug at John's feet. The book was called *Millbank*, and though Laurie wanted to read it, it was so boring he was soon curled up on the rug, the opened book in his hand, watching the flames in the fireplace. He leaned against the arm of the leather chair, where John sat making notes in his journal with a lead pencil.

He'd never been so relaxed, so at ease without something specific to think about, without his mind having to buzz from one activity to the other, from his phone to his laptop to his email—with every minute filled with something. Here, time seemed to expand to fill the whole cabin with stillness, with the fire flickering steadily away, and John in the leather seat above him. He'd put the journal down and was now reading one of the books, turning the pages slowly, one by one, and Laurie's mind was still and peaceful.

When it got darker as the sun went down, twilight filled the windows where the curtains had been drawn back, great swaths of purple and blue with bands of bright pink streaking across. Laurie got up and, without thinking about it, went to the door and stood there with it open so he could watch the brilliant sunset as it faded to shades of gray and dark blue and blood red.

Back home, he seldom took the time to watch a sunset, as he was typically involved with rush hour traffic, trying to shake off the tensions of the day as he hurried home to heat up a frozen dinner. Sometimes, if his roommate Maxton had ordered a delivery pizza, they'd both eat that while watching something on Netflix and Laurie texted Zach and his other friends to blur out the day. And on it had gone while he'd skated across the surface of his own life.

Now it was different; every gesture, every act, seemed to take its own time. Laurie could find that stillness and let it sink into him. Plus, it was wonderful that when he got into bed, he fell asleep. Except for the fact John was letting him closer, and their actual falling asleep was delayed some, but even that was peaceful and left Laurie feeling more contented than he'd felt back home.

Behind him, John got up. Laurie felt some hesitation in John's movements, which he didn't like. This was John's cabin, John's world, and he should do whatever he liked, though it might be thoughtful if Laurie encouraged him.

"Come and see," said Laurie.

He turned and gestured that John should come closer. When John was behind him, Laurie reached back and took John's hand to pull around his waist. As John took a step, Laurie tugged until John's body was flush against his.

Laurie's front was cold from the darkening air outside the cabin, but his back was warm from John. He pulled both of John's arms around him, happy when John's arms tightened and he felt a small, warm kiss along the side of his neck.

"That's another beautiful sunset," said John, his breath ghosting warm across Laurie's skin. "I usually never stop to see them, not like this."

"Me either," said Laurie. "I was always too busy back home for sunsets."

"Not to mention all those buildings in the city getting in the way," said John. "I couldn't make it if I didn't have all this sky to look at."

"I can see why, it's so beautiful," said Laurie. "But maybe that's enough talking for now."

Laurie turned in John's arms so that John's embrace enfolded him, and he was face to face with John, toe to toe. He tilted his chin up so he could smile at John and John could smile back with his cute dimples showing. But even as Laurie realized he could feel John's erection through his sturdy trousers, John lowered his eyebrows and grew serious.

"We oughtn't to carry on so," said John, low, his eyes hooded.

"What, do you mean like moonstruck lovebirds?" asked Laurie with a grin, using the most old-fashioned words he could think of. "Two turtledoves, billing and cooing, or a suitor and his swain kissing and holding hands? Or do you mean something more daring, like this—"

Laurie stood on his tiptoes and circled his arms around John's strong neck, giving John plenty of opportunity to pull back or to stop Laurie in any way, but he didn't. As Laurie kissed John, John's embrace tightened, then, with a low sound, John dipped his head to kiss Laurie back.

For a long, sweet moment, they kissed in the open doorway with the sky darkening to black outside and the cabin growing more bright and warm, drawing them inside.

John pulled away, but gently with a last little touch of his lips to

Laurie's, his hands clasping Laurie's head, fingers trailing through Laurie's hair.

"We need to get supper on," said John, as always ever practical. "I have three eggs left, so we can make flapjacks and bacon."

"Flapjacks?" asked Laurie, though he quickly realized that John meant pancakes. "I love flapjacks."

Laurie hurried to set the table, and brought in more firewood to put it in the wood box by the stove, generally making himself useful while John was getting supper ready. Though, truth be told, he got in John's way to steal a kiss or two, and pretended more than once that there wasn't enough room to get by John and that he had to rub up against his front, or close behind him, with long pets to his belly and touches to his arm.

John, for his part, shook his head at Laurie's antics, and smiled indulgently, but he didn't move away, or push Laurie away. Instead, he moved into Laurie's touches, and stood firm and still when Laurie brushed against him, and held his arm in place when Laurie caressed him. Which meant, in the end, that the half a dozen flapjacks John managed to make from the few eggs they had were slightly crispy on one side, and a little underdone on the other.

As they sat down at the table, John divided the pancakes in half, exactly, and divvied the last of the bacon, so that it was fair. They ate mostly in silence, but it was a pleasant silence. Laurie felt his own smile was quite goofy, while John looked a tad bashful, like a schoolboy who is about to get his first kiss. This endeared him to Laurie all the more.

Could he have found such a man in his own time, he would have been over the moon. But all the guys he knew, guys in bars or at the gym, were all very sophisticated and acted half-bored with everything, pretentious in all of their reactions, as if they'd seen it all before and none of it mattered.

That was not how it was with John. Everything he did was deliberate and sure, as though his life depended on it, which it did. Who was now eating his half-burned meal with his full concentration on it, because in 1891 food was survival and John was not the type of man to ever forget that.

When they did the dishes and cleaned up together, John's full concentration was on what he was doing, what was in front of him. Which, as Laurie realized, watching him, was how he was with Laurie now—he was focused on Laurie.

This realization made Laurie's heart speed up as they washed at the basin and got ready for bed because, perhaps, it was his turn tonight. Having that concentration focused on him was almost too much to anticipate, as he could already imagine John's hands on him, John's closeness in the dark.

John did not make him wait for soon he checked his pocket watch and put it away, banked the fires, and blew out the lamp. Directly after they'd climbed into bed in the darkness, pulling the bedclothes close against the cold night, John turned to Laurie.

"Little Red," said John, his voice catching in his throat.

Laurie's insides felt soft and tender when John sounded like that. He knew it was hard for John, so he scooted forward till the warmth of their bodies joined in the dark, and their faces were so close he thought he could hear John lick his lips.

"Yes, John," said Laurie. He thought he might make a joke, leaving the moment open so that John would have to come to him. Then he realized how brave John was being already, and changed his mind. "Will you kiss me?" asked Laurie. "I'd like that, I'd like that very mu—"

In response, John took Laurie in a giant hug and held him close. They stayed like that for a long moment, as though John was absorbing Laurie into him while his soft breaths stirred Laurie's hair. Laurie stayed as still as he could with his hands on John's waist. John gathered him up and tucked Laurie beneath him, giving Laurie the feeling of being in a cave of safety and warmth, John's shoulders above him.

John dipped his head to kiss Laurie, firmly, as though he knew exactly what he was doing, had been doing it for years, even, and kissed him so hard it left Laurie breathless. John's hands were everywhere it seemed, until Laurie figured out John was trying to get through all the layers of Laurie's nightshirt and woolen underwear. Laurie arched his back to try to help, but then came the inevitable rip of flannel nightshirt. John froze, as though he'd been caught doing something wrong.

"Tsk tsk, John," said Laurie, but with affection mixed in with the teasing so John would know he wasn't serious. "That's going to take some stitches in the morning, but can you sew? I can't."

"I can sew a little," said John, whispering. "And I have thread in my kit in the cupboard."

"Until then," said Laurie, whispering back. "Let's get rid of this so it's not in the way."

It might be against some law Laurie was unaware of not to wear layers and layers of clothing to bed, but he wanted John's hands on him anywhere John wanted them to go. He pulled off his nightshirt and felt instantly cooler as he threw it on the floor.

"I'll put it away in the morning," said Laurie before John could say anything about it. "Now, what were you just doing? Let's go back to that, okay?"

"Okay," said John, saying the word the way Laurie said it, though he sounded a little breathless at the same time. "Okay."

John kissed him again, and with one hand began undoing the buttons on Laurie's woolen underwear. Laurie's eyebrows rose on his forehead, but though surprised at John's boldness, he didn't stop him. Instead he encouraged him with little sounds in his throat and a deep, heartfelt sigh when John got to the last button at his groin.

John's hand was warm as it wrapped around Laurie's hard and lonely cock. John's touches were a little gentle, but that was okay, John could be timid this first time out. At least, Laurie assumed it was John's first time doing this, though he wasn't about to grill him as to whether or not he'd ever done anything like this before. Besides, John moved close and half covered Laurie with his body, and the weight of him settled Laurie.

John's kisses were driving him half-crazy at the same time John's hand stroked him up and down, a little jerkily at first. As John grew more confident, the strokes got more firm. Laurie arched up from the bed, thrusting into John's hand, John's harsh breaths in his ear, his whole body gathering up, jerking forward as he came in John's hand.

Laurie heard John let out a shuddery breath, as though he'd climbed a mountain and could hardly believe he was there. Gently, Laurie clasped John's hand and wiped it along his woolen underwear, for hadn't John said something about taking clothes to someone in town who would launder them? Laurie shrugged off these practical thoughts and moved close, reaching beneath John's nightshirt one handed because he was already a pro at this.

"Now you," he said kissing John's neck and then his mouth. "Now you."

John made little sounds in his throat, and maybe he was a tad startled, but he mostly sounded eager. Laurie unbuttoned John's woolen underwear, just the three buttons where he needed them to be opened, making a little space for his hand so John wouldn't feel overly exposed. He put his hand in and took John's hard cock in his curved fingers and smiled as John gasped.

Pressing close, using the smallness of the opening as a kind of delightful torture, Laurie began to stroke John. He moved his hand gently up and down, making as though he felt timid about it, until John reached to open a few more buttons, which made Laurie smile.

He began to go harder, which was what John seemed to want and, as John clutched Laurie to him, Laurie stroked and pulled. He moved his hand in all sorts of lovely ways, drawing the kind of sounds from John that let Laurie know that this was good, very good, for John.

Their closeness grew in the dark as John came in Laurie's hand in hot, hard pulses as John's body tensed for a moment and then relaxed. His shudders shifted the bed a little, his breath warm in Laurie's ear as John held him close.

"Oh, Little Red," said John. "What you do to me, I hardly understand it, I hardly know—"

There was a time, back home, when Laurie would have filled the space of words that John left with something very funny and self-aggrandizing, or a joke at his own expense at how he left his bed partners witless. But with John, the impulse to do this was easily squashed, for John deserved better than jokes all the time. Besides, in those words, Laurie could hear John's heart was laid quite exposed, and John deserved only the sweetest response.

"I hardly know myself," said Laurie, echoing John's words. "But I know I feel good when I'm with you, less empty, less—"

"Empty?" asked John as though he had no idea what Laurie meant. "You feel empty?"

"Kind of," said Laurie. He scooted close and did up the buttons on John's underwear and settled his flannel nightshirt back into place. Laurie petted John in all the ways he wanted to pet him, reaching up to tug at his collar, to comb his fingers through John's messy hair.

"It's hard to explain, but when I'm with you, I don't feel like there are parts of me that are unnecessary. I don't feel rushed. I feel contented and happy when I'm with you. When we're like this, or doing chores together, or when we went looking for the buffalo wolves. It means something, my life means something when I'm with you."

"Little Red," said John, his voice thick with emotion, and though he might not have said in return how he felt about Laurie, his reaction was enough.

He pulled Laurie close in the darkness, and kissed his mouth, settled Laurie's head on his shoulders, and petted him over and over.

Laurie felt a kiss to the top of his head. His whole body sighed as though that was the kiss he'd been waiting for, followed by the press of John's cheek to the top of his head to seal it in. That was the kiss, the last one of the day before he fell asleep, delivered by John to protect him in the dark.

"I'll take care of you, Little Red," said John, soft and low. "Sleep now, sleep now, yes? Sleep now."

"Yes, John," said Laurie, yawning into John's nightshirt, and drifted into sleep with the smell of woodsmoke and the salt from John's skin, John's warmth all around him.

CHAPTER NINETEEN

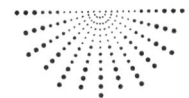

Getting breakfast ready and doing their morning chores afterwards was done with as much speed as could possibly be had. Laurie could not get over his own excitement at the anticipation of such a simple outing, going to town to get supplies with John.

John gave Laurie a rucksack to carry, shrugged on his own, then checked his pocket for his leather wallet of gold coins. They were bundled up, their scarves wrapped around their mouths, their hats firmly in place as they stepped out into the windy morning. Again, as before, John's limp became less pronounced while they walked, as if the walking was good for him.

As John predicted, the wind and the sun had erased a great deal of the snow from the storm. What was left was scalloped banks of snow spread out across the grass as though the plains were a palette and some invisible artist had come in the night to sculpt curving shapes out of the white.

The landscape was so bright, so still, that Laurie had to squint as they walked the mile or so into town, wishing again all the while for a pair of cheap sunglasses. Mostly he kept his head down and concentrated on stepping where John had stepped.

Every once in a while Laurie looked up at the breadth of John's shoulders beneath his buffalo hide coat, enjoying the exercise and being outside in the fresh air rather than in the cabin for a change.

Before long, they arrived at the edge of Farthing, which was brown and gray against the snow-streaked prairie, with wooden sidewalks in front of the buildings on Main Street, and piles of refuse in the alleys. Smoke rose from all of the buildings in thin wisps that were briskly swept away by the low ever-present breeze.

A buckboard pulled by two muscled horses went up the street while a man pushing a wheelbarrow walked briskly down it. Bits of activity pulsed all around, people in old-fashioned clothes on errands or standing beneath the awnings in front of one of the stores, some of them stopping to stare at John and Laurie as they came into town.

Laurie followed John, his eyes wide now that he understood that yes, it *was* 1891, and this was what a town looked like and smelled like back then. This was his life now, with John. Which made him want to stop and think whether he would stay if given the opportunity to go home. He didn't know, and besides, thoughts about his own life were constantly being swallowed up by this place, this time. Though perhaps that was for the best.

John, sensing Laurie wasn't following him so closely, paused on the wooden sidewalk and turned, waving Laurie to come close.

"Yes, John?" said Laurie, trotting to catch up, coming to a halt only when he was at John's side.

"We're going to order groceries and dry goods at the store," said John. "Then we need to send a telegram to the railroad folks. After that, we can have lunch at the hotel, then pick up our groceries and haul them home. How does that sound, good?"

Laurie liked the fact that John referred to them as *our* groceries, and that the cabin was *home*, and that John was checking in with him about the plan for the day.

"That sounds great," said Laurie. The idea of eating out had become such a novelty that he half forgot about everything else. "What are we going to have for lunch?"

"That depends on what the special for the day is," said John. "But we need to tend to the groceries first, so let's go."

Laurie snapped John a mental salute, as John sounded as formal as a military general. Being in town might have made John a little anxious, what with how intimate he and John had been at the cabin. But since the first store they went into was Pete's general store, this vanished as soon as Pete saw them and came over.

"Another snowstorm you've survived, I see," said Pete as they shook hands. "They've come so early this year."

"Indeed they have," said John by way of a greeting, nodding. "Little Red and I have come for supplies. Can you set us up with the usual? Then I have a few extras to add."

"Sure enough," said Pete. "Step over to the counter, and I'll help you out."

As John went over, Pete slipping on his spectacles as he took his place behind the counter, Laurie allowed himself the opportunity to stare.

The first time he'd been in the store he'd been so freaked out he'd barely noticed anything. Now he noticed the barrels lining the walls, with labels that said they held crackers or pickles, the wooden shelves containing boxes of salt and tins of peaches, jugs of kerosene. From the ceiling, hung on strings, was an arrangement of baskets and kettles and pots and frying pans.

The whole of the store bustled with items for sale that anyone living on their own without the benefit of electricity, microwaves, and hot and cold running water might need for survival. He'd not noticed all of this before, but then he'd been newly arrived and in a state of shock. Now that feeling seemed to have faded away for the most part, though staring at the items that were part of the current idea of civilized living made him think about it all over again. How had he arrived here? Was he ever going to find a way home?

He was distracted from these thoughts by watching John at the counter, his buffalo hide coat unbuttoned, his hat in his hand. Even with the tangle of his dark hair, he was the handsomest guy in the place, but then that was easy as Pete was no contest. John, dark haired and blue eyed, shone in comparison.

Two men came in with an empty burlap sack. They had the dry, dusty faces and clothes of men who had no access to water to wash with, nor would they have found it important. When they came up to the counter, they smelled so awful that Laurie made a face and tried to breathe through his mouth. He was about to turn to go outside when he spotted Adeline coming up from the back of the store.

She was dressed like a man from head to toe, the belt, the boots, the trousers, everything, and was carrying a full burlap sack over her shoulder. This she placed in front of the two men, dumping it on the wooden floor. In return, they gave her the empty sack they were carrying, and some money. Soon after, another man came in the store with an open basket full of lumps of clothes, which he handed over to Adeline.

The burlap sacks, as well as the basket, contained laundry in various stages. The realization surprised him, as he couldn't imagine Adeline, who could do such lovely beadwork, being forced to put her talented hands in hot water and soap to make a living. It just didn't seem right.

After she carried the basket to the back of the store, she quickly returned.

"They'll have it done by tomorrow," she told the man, who gave her some money and left.

When she noticed Laurie watching her, she came over with a smile, just as confident, even in men's clothes, as she'd been the first time he'd met her. Her dark hair was gathered in a single braid down her back, and she wore a little necklace of blue stone that was half hidden beneath the brown kerchief around her neck.

"Are you doing laundry now, Adeline?" asked Laurie before he could stop himself. "I would have thought—" He wanted to go on asking questions to find out more, but John came over and Laurie realized that it would be quite rude, so he finally shut his mouth.

"Hello, John," said Adeline.

"Hello, Adeline," said John. He had the same expression of fondness

Laurie had seen the last time they'd talked, which had given Laurie the idea that John was sweet on Adeline, but oh, how he knew better now. "How goes the laundry business?"

"It goes well," said Adeline. Then she gestured to Laurie. "This one's eyes nearly popped out of his head when he saw me with the basket. But what he doesn't know is that when the whores aren't working, they do laundry to make ends meet. Men don't want to associate with a whore in the light of day, so I am the go-between and make good money doing it."

She smiled at John as if he'd been the only one she was talking to, but she had a sideways glance for Laurie and a warm smile to welcome him into the conversation.

"How's the beadwork going?" John asked her. "I noticed you weren't working on it today."

"Some days I need to give my fingers and eyes a rest," she said. "But with the storm, I was able to finish a few pieces. Would you like to see them?"

"Yes, please," said John. His eyes lit up, showing his dimples to Adeline.

While Laurie wasn't the jealous type, he made a little face that he could have explained to nobody. But then, neither John nor Adeline noticed as Adeline hurried to her window seat and gestured that John and Laurie should follow her.

Gently, she brought down three pieces from the table. They were a small beaded pouch, a pin in the shape of a flower. Then, at the last, she showed them the beaded belt that had been only half finished the last time Laurie had seen, though now it was completely done.

The last time Laurie'd been in town, he'd thought her situation demeaning. Now he knew better, for she was in charge of her own life and had time to make beautiful things.

"Those are indeed beautiful," said John. He touched the beaded pouch with a gentle finger. "Your work is so delicate, I can't hardly see any stitching atall."

"They're for sale, of course," said Adeline with a wink at Laurie. "Should you have need of a gift to give."

John lifted his head, as though startled, and looked at Laurie.

Within his eyes shifted myriad expressions and thoughts that Laurie knew he would not have been able to understand when first he'd met John. But now he could, and he understood that the idea of a gift had not been planted there, but had previously existed and been stirred to life by her suggestion. John was seriously considering buying the belt for Laurie, only he didn't quite know how it would be accepted.

"These are all beautiful," said Laurie as he examined the pieces. He knew he meant what he'd just said, though before, in his old life, beadwork was the last thing he'd ever been interested in.

Very carefully, Laurie traced the edge of the belt, which had a brightly colored arrow and diamond pattern that looked a little bit like a snake's skin, or maybe it looked like lightning. In the midst of the dull brown store, with its homespun and simple articles for sale, the belt stood out, its delicate lines and bold swash of colors inviting ideas of adventure and movement.

He had a bad case of the *I wants* at that moment, but then figured the belt would be too expensive. John would quickly determine the cost outweighed the foolishness of buying something that could only be used for one thing, and that they'd leave the store to go on the rest of their errands without the belt. Besides, John had already given Laurie everything he ever thought he'd needed, and then some.

"I'll take it," said John, completely unexpectedly. "Little Red here's got such a slender waist that he's swamped by the belt I bought him last time we were in town. This one will fit him better, and be more pleasing to the eye."

Laurie's mouth fell open. As Adeline put the other two articles away while John dug out his money wallet, Laurie didn't know what to say. Adeline handed the belt to John, took his money, and put it in her pocket. Then John, the belt trailing over the edges of his broad palm, held it out to Laurie.

"Thank you, John," said Laurie as he took it. "Thank you, this is beautiful."

And indeed it was, silky and heavy in his hands, too, not incidental or lightweight or made cheaply in another country. This was the real deal with true craftsmanship.

Laurie fumbled to push his heavy coat back so he could slip the new belt on over the old one, which was indeed a little too big and sagged in the belt loops of his trousers.

John moved forward to help. It was quite the thing to stand there with John's hands around his waist, but hopefully nobody was looking. Quickly, John finished the task of sliding the belt through the belt loops and buckling it so they could both stop blushing.

When John stepped back, he was smiling and his eyes were bright.

"Do you like it, Little Red?" he asked.

"I'm the belle of the ball," said Laurie with his usual humor. When John looked a little confused, he amended what he'd just said. "And now I'm the best dressed fellow in the entire state of Wyoming."

John took a little step forward, though he stopped himself. A hard blush curled around his ear, and Laurie knew John had just stifled the impulse to kiss him, right there in the general store.

With a smile at John and a slap at his own waist, which was supposedly slender enough to warrant such a colorful decoration, Laurie wanted to strut around the store. But people were coming in, in particular two women wearing dark skirts and bonnets. They had serious expressions and went right up to the counter with their baskets, and Pete waited on them before some other men who were already in line.

Had Laurie been watching a western movie, he would have marked them as the schoolmarm character and her friend who was a seamstress. And suddenly it all felt a little surreal, and he wanted fresh air. Except he didn't want John to think he was running off, so he waited while he and Adeline finished chatting and then followed John out of the store.

They stopped at several stores along the main street, and Laurie was getting used to the low rhythm that sounded when he walked with his boots along the wooden sidewalk.

Storekeepers and clerks gave John respect whenever he entered. It might have been because he was so tall and somewhat imposing, or it might have been that his money, all in gold pieces, was very welcome. Regardless, Laurie was also welcomed, and together they purchased items to be tucked in their rucksacks, packing away carefully the wooden box of salt, the ball of hemp rope, the tin box of sulphur matches, everything they would need to survive the next blizzard.

Laurie waited to one side and watched while John chatted and exchanged pleasantries in each store, though only with the male storekeepers, it seemed. He never chatted with any of the lady storekeepers, even if there weren't very many of these, though he did tip his hat to every female he met.

"We'll stop at the telegraph office next," said John as they left the barber shop, where John had picked up a cake of shaving soap. It came packaged in a blue and white box that looked expensive. Laurie didn't say anything about it, and together they went into the telegraph office.

The small building was only big enough for two men to stand on one side of the counter, with the telegraph operator on the other. Behind the operator was a large box that had wires going up through the roof, and a shelf with a box of paper, and another shelf that held pencils. Below that was a table with what might be a Morse key, and another machine that had a ribbon of paper coming out of it.

The telegraph operator ignored them for two whole minutes as he busied himself with his writing while the brass arm clicked and jumped up and down, and a narrow ribbon of paper spun slowly from a shiny brass reel. Finally, he greeted John with a nod of his head and pushed a slip of paper at him, and a stub of a pencil.

"Fill it out, base rate is a dollar, with a penny a word over thirty words."

John, who had obviously heard this before, bent and quickly wrote his message. He paid the telegraph operator from his wallet, and hustled Laurie out of the store, their boots clomping loudly as they left.

"That fellow gives the hair on the back of my neck reason to rise," said John, low and only to Laurie once they were on the wooden sidewalk. "But he does his job all right, never a word wrong. We'll check back later for the response, so how about we eat some lunch now."

Laurie nodded and patted his belly, both to show that he was hungry and also to show off how nice his new belt looked.

"Yes, thank you," said Laurie to be polite. John's response was a smile, along with the accompanying dimples, both of which, this time, were meant only for Laurie.

They strode down the street and crossed it, dodging what there was of foot and wheeled traffic, and went to the hotel across from Pete's grocery store. Laurie remembered it from before, and smiled because this time maybe he could eat something.

John led Laurie through the front door, and they went into the small dining room that had square tables all in rows. There was the smell of cabbage frying, and Laurie's stomach gurgled in anticipation.

The two rough looking men who'd picked up their laundry from Adeline were already seated at one of the tables, and they had a friend with them. Laurie tried not to wrinkle his nose or to stare at the three men who looked like they spent half their lives rolling in the dirt, and the other half gearing up to eat without washing their hands. Laurie didn't want to say anything rude, so he just went where John directed them, to a small table near the window.

They took off their buffalo hide coats and hung them on brass hooks on the wall, and then hung their hats and scarves on top of the coats. All in all, it was nice to sit down out of the wind, someplace that was not the cabin, and where food would shortly be forthcoming. And to be with John, who looked at Laurie with some expectation, as if he'd just delivered to Laurie a bag of gold.

"Smell that?" asked John as he took the cloth napkin that had been folded on the table and laid it on his lap. "I do believe it's fried chicken day."

Laurie hid his groan; the last time he'd had fried chicken, it had been from a convenience store after a party with some friends. They'd been drunk and the convenience store had been the only place open. The fried chicken must have sat in the display case for days, and in retrospect had been greasy and disgusting, and ever since then, Laurie had lost his taste for it.

"It's good, I promise you that," said John. "What's the matter, don't you like fried chicken?"

"I do and I don't," said Laurie, though he knew that didn't make much sense. "Don't worry about it, I'm sure it's good."

The same waitress who had served them before came out, her hands on her hips and a smile on her face.

"Our special is fried chicken today," said the woman. "Would you gentlemen care for that, Mr. Henton? And how about a glass of milk and apple pie for desert? The cook baked the pies just this morning, and the milk is straight from the cow, fresh as a daisy."

"We'll take two of everything," said John. "But no milk for me. The boy will have milk."

As the waitress walked way, Laurie shook his head.

"The *boy*?" he asked, his voice rising. "Dude, I'm twenty-four."

"Should I have instead told her that my Little Red will have milk?" asked John with a broad smile. The delightful twinkles in his blue eyes told Laurie John was teasing him. *John* was teasing him in the middle of a restaurant with people around.

Laurie played it up by rolling his eyes and huffing in his best teenage manner, which made John laugh. Laurie settled back in his chair, well pleased with himself.

Soon the woman brought their lunch on a huge platter, which she set on the edge of the table, as if putting it on display for her customers. There was a large oval plate with fried chicken so crispy and brown and perfect that Laurie was hard pressed not to reach for a piece, his trials and tribulations with fried chicken vanishing in that instant. But there was also a plate of sliced pickles, one of coleslaw, a bowl of mashed potatoes, and a larger bowl with a ladle of brown gravy. And, of course, one tall glass of milk.

"Let me know if you need anything else, gentlemen," said the woman with a smile as she hurried away to serve her other customers.

"Eat up, Little Red," said John. "It's delicious, I promise you."

Laurie obeyed with some pleasure, picking up a drumstick to bite into it with a loud crunch. And discovered that this was, perhaps, the best fried chicken he'd ever had. It was so crispy on the outside and juicy within that he had to use his napkin every other bite just to keep from staining his trousers. The potatoes were fluffy and dotted with butter, and both he and John added enough gravy to make their plates swim with it.

Laurie couldn't eat fast enough, though when the apple pie came, and another glass of fresh milk along with it, he slowed down to savor every bite.

"Oh, John," said Laurie as he wiped his mouth one last time and folded his napkin to put it on the table. "*Oh*, John."

"Good, eh?" asked John. "I figured this might make a nice change from my plain cooking, which I learned how to do when I was in the cavalry."

"Your cooking is just fine, John," said Laurie, both to reassure John and to move the subject on from memories of the cavalry, which was making John's eyes a little sad around the corners. "But maybe we could buy some bread."

"Buy bread?" asked John. "But why? We can make biscuits ourselves."

"Maybe one of the ladies in town makes extra for sale, or maybe we could get the right kind of flour and make that instead of biscuits." Laurie had no earthly idea what kind of flour might be needed to make bread, though it only made sense that there would be a special kind that was used. "Either way, then we could have toast in the morning with our coffee. Toast and jam."

Laurie enjoyed watching the expression on John's face changing as he considered this new idea. He looked at Laurie as though Laurie had given him a present.

"That sounds like a fine idea," said John. "We can check with Pete as to who might be selling bread, and buy some jam from him."

"Okay," said Laurie. He could already picture in his mind the cozy mornings they would have, talking over cups of coffee next to the stove, licking crumbs from their fingers as the day warmed.

John paid for the lunch with a gold coin, collected the change, and gestured to Laurie that it was time to go. They bundled up in their buffalo hide coats, wrapped up in scarves and put on hats, gathered their rucksacks and strode out into the street to the telegraph office.

While Laurie waited in the bright sunshine, John went in to check on the response to his telegram, but shook his head as he came out.

"We'll go get the bread and jam, and by the time we're done, I'll have a response to the telegram I sent," said John.

They went back up the street to Pete's store. There, to Laurie's delight, they discovered that Pete had both bread *and* jam to sell. John bought two loaves and a jar of raspberry jam, and tucked the articles carefully in his rucksack. Then they headed over to the telegraph office.

"I'll wait out here," said Laurie, for the sun was warm and the buildings on Main Street blocked the wind. It would be nice to stand still and just look around him. "I'll watch your rucksack and mine, if you want to give it to me."

"Thank you," said John. "I won't be a moment, and then we can go home."

Home was where he and John could be alone and share quiet moments together. Home was where he could tease John into kissing him, and home was where he could fall asleep in John's arms when the day was done. Home was where he wanted to be. With John.

CHAPTER TWENTY

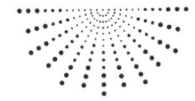

When John came out of the telegraph office, he was shaking his head and settling his hat on his brow.

"Did you get your telegram?" asked Laurie.

"Yes, but there's an issue I need to check at the bank about," said John. "It won't take me but a moment, so you might as well stay here with our things."

"Okay," said Laurie. "I'll be fine right here, so you go on. But you owe me a kiss when you get back."

In response to this, John took a quick look up and down the street, tipped his hat, and kissed Laurie hidden by the shadow of its brim.

"There's your kiss now," said John, blushing as though at his own boldness. "There'll be another one when I return."

John strode off, his strong legs taking him quickly up the street on his errand. Laurie, a tad breathless and smiling, was overcome with the pleasure of the quick kiss and the anticipation of more to come. He leaned against the outer wall of the brick telegraph building, his coat open and his thumbs hooked in his belt. He drew his fingers across the silky beadwork along his waist, and knew he'd never felt so good in his life, so well loved.

From around the corner of the building next to the telegraph office came three men who Laurie recognized as the three dusty customers at the hotel restaurant. They came over to Laurie as though they had been looking for him, or had been looking for trouble and found Laurie instead, he wasn't sure. They crowded up to him, and one of them gave Laurie a shove.

"What're you doing here, punk?" asked one of the men. He had a black tooth and Laurie tried hard not to stare or draw back at the man's bad breath.

"He's waiting for another kiss," said one of the other men.

"Yeah, waiting," said the third man as the first man gave Laurie another shove. "Waiting till he can bend over and take it up the ass like a good molly."

Laurie's whole body tightened up. The men must have seen John and Laurie in the hotel restaurant being all cozy together and giving each other sweet glances as they ate their lunch. Worse, they had seen John kissing Laurie, and now had come to make trouble. His head whirled as he tried to figure out what to do, and quickly, before everything escalated out of hand.

Had this been back home, Laurie would have walked away and caught the next cab he could, as there was never any sense getting into a fight when it could be avoided. Had he been cornered and there'd been no cab available, no ride, or no friend to come at a phone call's notice, then he would have walked right into it, fists ready for a fight.

What made this all worse was that this was 1891, and being gay was illegal. It was also three to one. Laurie didn't want John to come back to find Laurie getting mixed up with these guys. All in all, it was a bad situation that wanted defusing as soon as Laurie could manage it.

But before he could open his mouth to say anything, the three men dragged Laurie into the alley, knocking over one of the rucksacks, causing the loaf of waxed-paper wrapped bread to fall out. They cornered him against the wall.

The first man, the one with the black tooth, punched Laurie in the face, sending him reeling, holding his mouth. Then the man punched him again, clocking his jaw, sending his hat flying and sending a fist into Laurie's stomach. Laurie doubled over while one of the men grabbed his hair and yanked his head back.

"This will teach you, punk," said the man.

Laurie felt the slam of a fist in the middle of his face, leaving black stars dancing in front of his eyes and blood pouring from his nose. He struggled to stand up and to fight back, but it was three against one, and he was going to lose this battle. Where was the sheriff? Where was John?

"Better leave town, punk," said the first man.

Two of the men grabbed Laurie, one on each side, and just as the first man clenched his fist, John came around the corner, eyes blazing, buffalo hide coat flying. He grabbed the first man, punched him hard, and flung him to the ground. Then he ripped Laurie out of the men's grasp and shoved him out of the alley, returning to slam one man against the wall, and to punch the other one so hard that he staggered and half fell, blood oozing from broken flesh.

"Get lost," said John. "Get lost on your own before I make you. You hear? Now *go*."

The three men clutched at each other and scrambled off, the wind whipping their jackets as they went around the corner.

Once they were gone, John pulled Laurie to his feet and gently leaned him against the wall of the telegraph office. He steadied Laurie's shoulders with both hands and used his thumbs quite gently to wipe the blood from beneath Laurie's nose. Laurie blinked and tried to focus, unbelievably grateful that John had come, for he'd been losing that fight from the get-go.

"What was going on there, Little Red?" asked John. "Why did you get into a fight with them?"

"They got into a fight with *me*," said Laurie. He stopped and spat into the icy dust in the alleyway, his head pounding, his face half numb. "They called me a punk and told me to leave town, but jeez—"

He was about to make a joke about it, drawing on his vague

knowledge of western movies, when he realized John had gone pale white, and that he was clutching Laurie's arm quite firmly.

"What is it, John?"

"They called you a punk?" asked John, his voice harsh. "Did they see me kiss you?"

"Yes," said Laurie. "And yes, I guess they must have, but—who cares, right? They just called me a punk, it's no big deal. And then they called me a molly, whatever that is."

"They called you a punk *and* a molly?" asked John. "Damn it and tarnation."

John whipped off his hat and wiped his forehead with his fingers, and Laurie realized that John was sweating, that he was scared.

"Hey," said Laurie, wanting to soothe him. He knew John might be a little worried about someone finding out about them, but he'd never thought it would be this bad. "They're nobody. Who cares about them."

"They *know*," said John. "And they'll talk, and that's our reputation ruined." He gave Laurie a hard look and Laurie knew then and there how angry John was.

"Don't be mad," said Laurie. "I'm sorry I flirted with you and made you kiss me—"

"You didn't *make* me do anything," said John, and while his voice was low and perfectly level, there was a dark edge to it that shot anxiety into the middle of Laurie's belly. "But we're finished, do you hear? We're finished."

"What do you mean, we're finished?" asked Laurie, his eyes wide though he had a terrible feeling he knew exactly what John meant.

John paused as he put on his hat. He swallowed hard, set his jaw, and then completed the motion, all the while not looking at Laurie. When he did look at Laurie, his eyes were shuttered and his expression was closed off.

"You said that nobody would find out," said John. "Well, they've found out. Even if those three fellows aren't the biggest of gossips, it won't be long before the word gets around. If the railroad company finds out, it'll be my job. Then where am I supposed to go, Laurie, tell me that."

"I'd go with you wherever," said Laurie.

His heart sank. John had called him Laurie instead of Little Red, and was turning away and walking out of the alley. Laurie followed him and picked up his hat and then his rucksack from the steps of the telegraph office, roughly repacking the loaf of bread as John was picking up the other rucksack.

"I'd go with you, John," said Laurie, his voice full of hope as he hefted his rucksack over his shoulder.

"The only place we're going is to the cabin," said John. "Now."

Without another word, John hefted his rucksack onto his shoulders and began marching down the wooden sidewalk, looking neither left nor right. Men tipped their hats at him as he passed, but he ignored them, his face like stone, as though he was already prepared to be hated and ostracized.

Laurie saw Adeline waving at them through the window of Pete's store, but John ignored her as well. He walked with long strides till he reached the edge of town, and then stepped off the wooden sidewalk into the snowy grasses of the prairie and kept on walking.

It was all Laurie could do to keep up with him, his heart aching at the idea that John thought the situation was so bad. That John would be so scared he would push Laurie away. That everything they had built between them was now in pieces to be scattered by the high winds, to vanish in the grass and snow, never to be seen again.

THE MARCH BACK to the cabin was done in silence. John went so fast, and the wind was blowing so hard from the north that Laurie could barely breathe let alone try and talk sense to John. With his thumbs hooked in the straps of his rucksack, Laurie attempted to walk alongside of John, to talk to him that way, but the ground grew rough and he had to concentrate on walking. Worse, John's scowl was too dark, his mood too dour to break through. In the end, Laurie walked behind him, hustling the whole way.

By the time they got back to the cabin, snow had begun to fall, flopping to the ground in large messy flakes, coming down sideways on account of the wind. John unbolted the cabin door, and Laurie followed him in.

Together they put their rucksacks on the table and divested themselves of their buffalo hide coats and outerwear. Then, though silently, they unpacked the rucksacks and put away the jug of kerosene, the tin box of lamp wicks, the brick of butter wrapped in waxed paper, the eggs, the small canvas bag of flour, and the rest of it. The cabin was stocked with enough for ten more guests, should they show up in the snow.

John continued to be angry. His mouth was curved into a hard frown, his movements jerky and stiff as he reached up to the shelves or dug into his rucksack again. The whole while, he didn't say anything, which Laurie knew was the worst way to settle an argument. The loaves of bread and the preserve jar of jam were left to sit on the wooden counter, a forlorn reminder of what had been lost that day.

"C'mon, John," said Laurie in what he considered to be his best reasonable tone. "Those guys don't know what they saw and who's going to believe them anyway? People respect you in Farthing, I could tell, so you don't need to—"

But John just continued putting supplies away, almost as if Laurie wasn't there. This was frustrating all by itself, but what if Laurie wasn't there? What if this whole thing was a dream and now the part had come where Laurie would wake up to discover that it wasn't 1891 and John was long dead? Laurie felt cold all over with the horror of it, and in response he grabbed John's arm, tugging hard to get him to stop.

"John, listen to me," said Laurie, filled with desperation that rose and rose. It had nowhere to go because John clearly did not want to listen. "They don't know anything. They can think anything they want, but they don't know anything. Besides why do we care what they think anyway?"

Stepping away from the table, John whirled, pulling his elbow out of Laurie's grip with a snap. His fists were clenched and he looked ready to produce whatever violence was necessary to get Laurie to stop pestering him. His blue eyes were flat and expressionless, his dark hair spilling across his forehead.

"Now, *you* listen to *me* and listen good," said John in a low, hard voice. "They know. They *know* about us. Don't you know what a punk is? What a molly is? Punks are young men who have sex with older men, and a molly does it for money. This town barely tolerates what whores it does have, so what do you think the sheriff is going to do when he finds out you're here with me? And that we're doing what we've done?"

"He's not going to find out. And even if he does, he's not going to believe them," said Laurie, almost shouting. Then he realized what John had just said. "Besides I'm not a whore. I'm not having sex with you for money. And that's a *shitty* thing to say."

"Don't you use that type of language with me," said John, stabbing his finger in Laurie's face.

"Well, don't call me a whore, then," said Laurie. "And quit acting like an asshat."

Shaking, he was unable to believe that as close as they had grown, they'd quickly slid down the argument slope to the name calling stage. But there seemed no other alternative. John was too powerful a target for Laurie to wrestle to the couch and kiss into submission, and he didn't seem to want to consider anything remotely resembling reason.

"A what? *What* did you call me?" asked John, his eyes dangerously narrow.

"I called you an *asshat*," said Laurie, enunciating the word for emphasis and because it felt good to hiss in John's face. "Which is exactly what you're being, allowing some jerks you've never even met to call the shots on who you can be, and who you can care about, who you can love—"

Laurie stopped, closing his mouth so hard he almost bit his tongue.

John had never said anything about love and although Laurie had thought about it, they'd not yet exchanged those kind of sweet words or made promises, like lovers did.

They'd grown close, been intimate in bed, but they were only at the beginning stages of that slow, crazy-good tumble into a forever kind of relationship. Laurie didn't know what he would do if John insisted on them being apart.

He couldn't force John into a relationship; he couldn't make John love him. But how could he stay if there was no love and affection between them where once there had been? Except leaving was entirely out of the question, especially when he had no place else to go. John would never budge, and all of a sudden, the cabin seemed way too small.

Laurie grabbed what he thought was his coat, only it turned out to be John's. It was so huge that it hung to his calves as he walked out the door, slamming it behind him. The coat was still warm from John's body, and smelled like woodsmoke and warmth and John. Laurie pulled the furry lapels up to his chin with both hands and took a deep breath as he looked at the high prairie that stretched on for miles.

The wind was blowing fat, cold flakes of snow right against his face. The only shelter was, obviously, the shed, so he opened the shed door and went in. He carefully shut the door behind him because heaven forbid he disturb the railroad's precious instruments.

There in the dim stillness, he paced, kicking the straw on the ground and crunching on bits of kindling scraps. This made satisfactorily rude sounds, and gave Laurie something to concentrate on other than his heart. It was slowing down from its hard-beating state, though his mouth was still screwed tight, as though he was trying to convince himself he was too old to cry.

John was ridiculous. The whole thing was ridiculous. If they'd been found out, all they had to do was pull up stakes—wasn't that how they said it in all those western movies Laurie had only half paid attention to? Pull up stakes and head out and go somewhere where nobody knew them and make a new start. Except John seemed settled, and might not have enough money for such a drastic solution.

Besides, Laurie couldn't imagine anybody would care all that much. In reality, what with all those cowboys on all those long cattle drives, and all those ranchers with nobody to talk to but each other, surely some of them got up to hanky-panky. You just never heard about it. Even if word had gotten out about it, nobody would have cared, Laurie was sure of it.

But John was like a rock *and* a hard place. If he couldn't see sense now, how was Laurie supposed to convince him? John seemed the type of guy who when he made his mind up, made it up for good, and there might be nothing Laurie could do about it.

Defeated and cold, Laurie sat down on a bale of hay and pulled John's buffalo hide coat around him. It was warm and heavy, holding him in place in a gentle way. It smelled nice, of woodsmoke and leather oil, and the salt of John's sweat, a good combination that made Laurie close his eyes and take a deep breath. He'd figure out a way to convince John that it was okay. Then they could go on as they had been, like friends, like lovers, in the sweet little bubble of isolation in their cabin in the snow.

Laurie would go back into the cabin and he'd be polite and friendly, and he'd help John to see what was true and real. They cared about each other, and Laurie wanted to be with John, but only if John stopped being an asshat.

The door to the shed opened. John stepped into the doorway, filling it with his height and his shoulders, his messy hair almost brushing the top of the doorjamb. He looked calm and maybe a little sorry, like a little kid who had done something bad that was easily forgiven, but he wasn't sure if the time was right to ask yet.

"I'm just about to get supper on," said John in a soft, almost diffident voice. "Today in town I bought a little wooden box that has an oilcloth checkerboard, and checker pieces carved out of soapstone. I thought we could play after supper."

The idea that John had purchased something without Laurie knowing about it, with an eye to making the secret become a gift, touched Laurie, sending a balm to his heart. John cared about him to have done this so he could make it a surprise later. Which meant he cared, had never stopped caring.

In spite of the tender feelings the gift evoked, all at once a small fury rose in Laurie. He didn't think John would throw him out, but it was scary to think that John could be influenced by someone else's opinion like this, that he would stop what had been growing between them.

"That's priceless, John," said Laurie, his anger getting the better of him. "You let a couple of guys in town scare you? Those are guys who nobody will believe because guess what? They don't have photographs of the big event. And even if they did, who cares? Who cares?" He stood up, feeling mean. "I can't believe you'd let them tear us apart, and now you think you can replace what we had with a game of checkers?"

John looked like Laurie had slapped him, his eyes down-tilted at the corners. He opened his mouth as if to speak, but only sighed. He looked at Laurie, then looked away. Slowly, he backed out of the shed and closed the door behind him, leaving Laurie alone in the low gloom.

By the time it got near dark, Laurie was shivering with cold even while wearing John's coat because he'd been sitting still for so long. He knew he needed to go in because he had nowhere else to go and that was the problem. He was completely dependent upon John for everything, the clothes he wore, the food he ate, the place where he slept. Which now that they were arguing was probably going to be on the floor, in spite of the fact John had clearly indicated, right from the beginning, that only animals slept on the floor.

But he had to go in, so he did, crossing from the shed to the cabin. He kicked the snow from his boots before he stepped inside, which drew John's attention to him.

That certainly felt better than being ignored, so as he hung up John's coat, he coughed loudly. Then he went and made a great deal of noise snapping kindling and scrabbling for a match from the box on the mantelpiece. He hunkered in front of the fireplace, throwing chunks of wood about as he built a small fire.

"What're you doing that for?" asked John, scowling at Laurie. "It's already warm enough in here."

"I'm going to be bunking down in front of the fire for the night," Laurie said, scowling back, undeterred. "And I don't care what you think about it."

"It'd be too cold for that when the fire's banked," said John, though this was entirely without emotion and he did not bring up his prior point about who or what did or did not sleep on the floor. "Anyway, supper's ready."

Laurie's stomach was entirely too used to eating regular meals now, and it growled to let its wants be known. There was nothing for it but to wash his hands, go to the table, pull out a chair, and sit down.

Except the meal that had been laid out was not what Laurie was expecting, for John had gotten the hotel to wrap up an entire meal of fried chicken, mashed potatoes, pickles, and coleslaw. There was even a small wooden bowl of ground-cherry preserves that glistened with sugar. John had gotten fried chicken *to go*, and he'd done it for Laurie.

Laurie's throat closed up at the amount of effort John had gone to, doing it behind Laurie's back to keep it a secret, and all because he'd seen how much Laurie had enjoyed the meal at the hotel. Staying angry and suffering through another meal of fried cornmeal mush would have been preferable to experiencing what he was feeling, which was a tender softness at John's thoughtful gesture.

"Thank you, John," he said. "It's really nice of you to—"

"Just eat," said John and, in his dour, despondent way, he picked up his fork in his fist, eating methodically, chewing silently while staring at the middle of the table, as though the food gave him no pleasure whatsoever.

Laurie ate his supper silently, and while it was good, very good, it wasn't pleasant to sit there with John so silent, all his fears crowding in as to what would happen next. Now that he knew John better, he knew John wouldn't throw him out into the snowy night, but it was going to be mighty uncomfortable to live side-by-side like this if they weren't speaking, let alone kissing.

Maybe they could fix up the shed and Laurie could live out there till spring came? Or maybe he should man up and actually figure out how to get home to his own time. Except that would mean he'd have to leave John. He didn't think he could bear that, so he swallowed his thoughts and made himself eat the gift of a meal of fried chicken and fixings.

When supper was over, John continued in his silence as they cleared the table. Not leaving any room at the sink for Laurie, John washed the dishes by himself with the unspoken understanding, it seemed, that Laurie would wipe the table and sweep the floor. When they were finished with their chores, John banked the cookstove, and for a moment, with no other tasks to occupy them, they stood there, looking at each other.

"Should—" began John. He stopped and swallowed as though gathering his courage, which normally would have made Laurie feel like kissing him. Only now, this time, seeing John unsure filled Laurie's head with a cloud of anxiety and frustration he couldn't quite define.

"Should we play a game of checkers?" asked John.

"I suppose," said Laurie. There wasn't any point in saying what he felt because John wasn't going to budge.

John got the checkerboard off the shelf and laid it out on the table. The checkerboard was made of pale yellow oilcloth that had been painted with squares of red and black outlines to look like a real checkerboard. It had been made by hand, and someone had taken the time to decorate the edges with gold and red scrollwork, which made it look festive. The checkers themselves were hand carved out of dark gray or rusty beige soapstone, and felt dense and solid when Laurie picked one up.

"You can be red," said Laurie as he sat down.

"No, you—" began John, as though he'd been about to sally forth making a joke that since Laurie had the red hair, he should take the red checkers. But John snapped his mouth shut, and kept it shut as they set up the game, and the moment was lost.

They played checkers for a while. Although it should have been more comfortable, not to mention romantic, to play checkers in the light of the kerosene lamp with the golden flames leaping in the fireplace lined with river rock, Laurie could barely stay focused.

He was worried about John kicking him out, though he knew that wasn't likely. He was also growing a little more worried about what would happen if the guys in town *did* talk. Mostly, if he was honest with himself, he was worried about John.

John kept his head down the entire time they played, as though he was afraid Laurie was going to keep yelling at him. Though Laurie wanted to, John looked too vulnerable and it made Laurie's heart hurt too much to think about yelling when John was so upset, so he didn't say anything. John didn't say anything either, and so the entire evening was spent in silence.

John announced it was bedtime by losing the last game, standing up, and checking his pocket watch.

Laurie looked up at him.

"It's bedtime," said John.

"I'm going to sleep on the floor," said Laurie in reply.

"No, you're not," said John. "It isn't fitting, and it'll be too cold. And you need to wash your face again, for you've still got blood on your chin, and on your new belt. I should have said something before."

Laurie touched his nose, and felt a throb of pain. The low-level headache that he'd had since the fight in town spiked into life, and he winced.

"You heat the water while I get some snow for that," said John.

Although it felt a little too late to bother about it, Laurie heated the water and poured it in the basin on the wooden counter. John took a cloth and went outside and came back with a ball of snow wrapped in the cloth. He made Laurie stand there while he pressed the makeshift ice pack on Laurie's jaw and then on his cheek and on the bridge of his nose.

"I should have thought," said John. "I should have taken care of you sooner."

"Never mind," said Laurie. He took the ice pack from John. Their hands brushed as he did this, but only barely. It was too painful to think about what he was losing with John that the headache he'd had all evening didn't matter at all.

"At least give me the belt to wipe off," said John, reaching for it.

"I'll do it," said Laurie. He turned his body away like a three year old who didn't want to be touched, and was sadly rewarded by the unhappy look on John's face as he began his nightly ritual of washing for bed.

Laurie refused to let himself watch because what did he care? If he didn't watch, then he wouldn't be moved by the simple, intimate sight of John undoing the buttons on his shirt and union suit, and how vulnerable he looked with soap on his face.

As John rinsed himself, Laurie took off the Indian beaded belt and, with a corner of snow-soaked cloth, wiped off the blood. He dried the belt carefully, then he left it along the edge of the table to dry straight instead of curled, and took his turn at the basin. After which, he slipped on his nightshirt and scooted over to the bed.

And realized that the worst part of the day was not when the three men had beaten him up, no. The worst part was now as John banked the fires and blew out the kerosene lamp because now the two of them were standing on either side of the bed, continuing their argument in the dark.

"I can sleep on the floor; that way you won't have to be near me," said Laurie, regretting the harshness of the words as soon as he said them.

"It's not that, Laurie," said John, though the name sounded strange the way he said it, because that was not who Laurie was. He was John's Little Red, and he wanted to go on being that, only John wouldn't let him.

"I don't care," said Laurie.

With a hard, sharp sigh, he climbed into bed. He'd not really wanted to sleep on the floor anyway, with or without John's permission, because the bed was more comfortable. More comfortable, and warmer, and it had John in it.

As he pulled up the bedclothes, Laurie thought about just throwing himself in John's arms and making John touch him that way. Then he'd say a joke or two about long-lost lovers and where had John been all his life—but he stopped himself. John didn't deserve to be joked into changing his mind. John deserved better.

"I do care," said Laurie as he settled himself on the pillow facing John. "I care a lot."

He waited for John to reply that he also cared, or something like that, but John just took a deep breath and rolled away from Laurie to face the wall. Laurie moved into the pocket of warmth at John's back but was careful not to touch him and held himself very still until he fell asleep, which took a very long time.

CHAPTER TWENTY-ONE

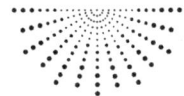

Laurie woke up with a stiff neck from holding himself still in bed so that he wouldn't roll into John's arms. He also had a headache, one that pounded right down the center of his face. He was pretty sure there wasn't any aspirin in 1891, so after he'd gotten dressed and was setting the table for breakfast, he didn't complain, and didn't say anything about it.

John must have known, as he always seemed to, what was up. He brought Laurie a thick china mug that didn't look like it had coffee in it, even though Laurie could smell coffee brewing on the stove.

"What's this?" asked Laurie, and though he'd not meant it to, his voice came out almost like a growl.

"It's willow bark tea," said John, kindly. "It's not sweet, but it will help your headache, so drink up."

John also went out in his shirtsleeves to gather another cloth bag of snow, which he handed to Laurie. Laurie sat down at the table, leaned on his elbow, and held the bag against his forehead while he sipped the bitter tea. Right away it seemed to draw the headache down to nothing, so he finished it off obediently.

John didn't ask Laurie to help with breakfast. He seemed to be giving him the time to recuperate and come to life, all without making too much of a fuss, which was thoughtful of John, but that was how John was. Which made Laurie's heart ache as he stared at John's broad back while he stood at the stove. Not only was Laurie going to be cut off from that, but John would continue his life alone, being gentle and sweet on the inside, only nobody knew that but Laurie.

John had been in battles where he'd had to shoot his rifle and kill people and live rough. But he'd created a life that had what he liked, his little cabin in the wilderness, where there was plenty of silence and stillness and nobody scraped their forks across metal plates. It almost made Laurie cry to think of it.

If only he'd not been so stupid as to flirt with John in town, then none of this would have happened. And if he'd not fallen in love with John, then his heart would not be breaking now.

John served up breakfast, which was hot cornmeal mush served in bowls, and the inevitable slices of bacon. There was white butter and golden honey to put on everything, along with the last of the sugared cherries in the wooden bowl.

Except there was more. John got up to toast slices of bread in the oven, carefully tending them, and carefully not looking at Laurie the whole while. He left the room only long enough to go to the pantry to bring out the preserve jar of red raspberry jam and place it on the table near Laurie's elbow. Then he brought over four pieces of brown toast, which he cut into slices. And then he placed half of the slices on the edge of Laurie's plate.

John was trying to make it up to Laurie in every way that he could, down to serving Laurie the special treat he'd asked for. When Laurie didn't move, John pushed the bowl of white butter toward him.

Laurie buttered his toast and spooned on the ruby red raspberry jam, but he could hardly make himself eat any of it. But that would be wasteful, and he didn't want John scowling at him so, putting the ice bag aside, he ate his breakfast. Then, he crunched his way through the now-cold toast with absolutely no joy at all.

It wasn't even any fun to lick his fingers after, though he did because that was part of the ritual. Back home, Zach would have thrown a napkin at him, insisting he remember his manners while

Maxton smirked and patted his mouth with his own napkin like an overly fussy lady. Laurie jerked his thoughts away from this image, jerked them hard, for they were of no use, and wiped his mouth with the back of his hand.

After breakfast, they cleaned up in complete silence, each moving around the other in almost robot-like ways, though of course nobody had any idea about robots in 1891. Then John settled at the table with his ink and pen and journal and began writing down his notes.

While Laurie already knew there would be no mention of him anywhere, the idea of it, of John ignoring him as though Laurie wasn't even there, made him sad and furious at the same time. He thought about going back out to the shed for some privacy, but there wasn't anything to do out there, and besides it was too cold.

Instead, he pulled a book from the bookshelf, settled in the leather chair, and read till lunch, doing his best to focus as the silence in the cabin grew. The distance between him and John seemed insurmountable, but forcing John to close that distance would never work. Not with someone like John, who was too stubborn and maybe too scared to change.

At lunchtime, they finished up the last of the fried chicken meal from the night before. John washed dishes and Laurie wiped them and put them away. Then, into the silence that had built up all morning, John coughed. Which drew Laurie's attention to him so sharply he almost hurt his neck turning to look.

"I need to go walk the traps this afternoon," said John. "Would you like to come with me?"

This wasn't the normal invitation that, along with the task of marching through the snow to hunt buffalo wolves or check the traps along the river, suggested there might be secret, cold-nosed kisses, no. It was a simple invitation to attend to an outdoor chore that provided them with fresh meat and nothing more.

"Okay," said Laurie. "Sure, I'll come with you."

"We might get some rabbits. If we do, I'll make rabbit stew," said John as he dried his hands with the towel. The sad expression in his eyes told Laurie that John hoped this would be enough because it was all John had to offer. All that he had.

Laurie's memory went to the last time they'd had rabbit stew. John had thought that Laurie liked carrots and so added extra for him. Laurie, who didn't consider carrots to be his favorite, had mentally promised himself he'd eat carrots all the day long if it would make John happy. Which was how love was, right? Or was it better to be honest?

"I actually don't like carrots that much," said Laurie. "I mean, I like them fine, but I like potatoes better, if that's okay by you."

"That's all right by me," said John. "We've got plenty of potatoes down in the cellar, but why didn't you say?"

"Because I was trying to—never mind," said Laurie.

As soon as he started to explain, he could see John already understood that sometimes you made sacrifices for people you cared about and sometimes you lied just to be nice. At least you lied about the little things, and never the big things. Because that's what love was.

"Are we going now?" asked Laurie, for it would be nice to be out of the cabin, which had become, overnight, quite small and cramped with no room for privacy, no space to be alone. Outside, they would be in the wild, fresh air, and would both be focused on the task at hand, and not forced to look at each other for hours on end. Why more people hadn't gone completely crazy back in the old west was beyond Laurie to comprehend.

"We might as well, in case another storm roars in come sundown," said John. "By the way the clouds are sitting over Iron Mountain, it looks like it will."

Laurie pulled on his boots, and then looked on the table for his beaded belt but couldn't find it.

John was busy at the chest of drawers while Laurie searched frantically. He looked under the edge of the table, beneath the chairs, everywhere. His heart sank and he didn't know what to do. Should he tell John, or just be nonchalant about the fact that he wasn't wearing it? Would John even notice?

John was waiting at the door, all bundled up in his buffalo hide coat and scarf and hat, with his rifle bent over his arm. Laurie's heart was beating hard, but he wasn't going to say anything about it and would look later. After all, how far could a simple belt go on its own in one night?

Buttoning his own coat and wrapping his scarf around his neck and face, Laurie jammed on his hat and hurried to follow John out into the cold, still air of afternoon. The sun was glowing through a haze of clouds and the snow crunched beneath their feet.

They headed south along Sand Creek, going slightly in the direction of town but keeping along the banks of the river. John was silent with his own thoughts. Laurie stayed silent as well, and stuck close, putting his boots in John's footprints, struggling to keep up with John's long-legged and steady pace.

He tried not to stare at the back of John's head. Tried not to pretend they were having a conversation where John pointed out landmarks, explained the sundogs that flanked the sun, or demonstrated how to find a rabbit trap that had been covered with snow. Instead John remained silent and led the way, stopping from time to time to kick at the snow, or to brush the snow away from the bent grasses with his gloved hand.

They headed west, where the river led into the ragged foothills and became deep in places, so deep the water ran cold and black beneath the icy sheets that covered it. It was even colder by the water because the rocks cast shadows over the snow.

Laurie shivered, tucking his chin low in the collar of his buffalo hide coat as he waited while John tugged on a trap to release a jackrabbit. The animal must have been caught hours ago because now it was frozen stiff.

"Here," said John, holding out the rabbit by its ears. "Carry this."

"Me?" asked Laurie with a squeak, but there was nothing else he could do but grip the rabbit's thick, furry ears in his mittened hand. "Ug."

"That's supper," said John. "Let's walk on a little while to see if the last trap has something."

With his rifle bent over his arm, John led the way. The path grew narrow and rutted with stones and the gnarled roots of several trees that had sprung up amidst the rocks. On one side was a low but steep hill, the other side led right into the river.

Laurie almost lost his balance a time or two, but managed each time to grab a ragged pine tree branch or the edge of a large boulder so that he didn't fall on top of John. Who, in his steady, methodical manner, kept walking, taking his time as he stepped over a tree branch buried in a mound of snow.

At one point, John turned to say something to Laurie, perhaps about the jackrabbit, or the fact that they might turn back soon. Laurie saw a flash of his blue eyes, and thought it was better than nothing. At least John was looking at him.

When John stepped forward, hope sprang in Laurie's heart just as the bank gave way beneath John. The nearest pine tree gave a mighty groan and the whole thing collapsed into the ravine in a tumble of ice and rocks and dirt.

John's rifle flew against the tree with a hard crack. Laurie flung the jackrabbit away as he tried to grab John's hand. But he missed, and John fell down and down and crashed through the ice into the cold, dark water.

"John!" cried Laurie, already halfway down the bank, grabbing on to any root he could find. Snow and ice and wet dirt spilled onto his boot tops, his heart pounding fiercely as the debris settled in an icy cloud around his shoulders.

At the bottom of the ravine, John was half in the water, one side of his body submerged beneath the cracked ice. Water rushed around him and seemed to want to tug him into the icy dark depths. But he was alive and moving, lifting his head to wipe the blood from his mouth and to grab his hat that was in danger of floating away. A large granite-gray boulder in the middle of the river was all that was keeping him from being dragged downstream.

"Stay where you are," said John with a croak, water dripping from his buffalo hide coat. "The whole bank could collapse and take you with it."

"Fuck the bank!" shouted Laurie. "I'm getting you out before you freeze to death."

"And I said stay where you are."

"Screw you, John," said Laurie. "I'm coming to get you."

The way was tricky as great sheets of dirt followed Laurie all the way down, threatening to engulf him and send him sprawling forward to hit his head on something hard and unyielding. Rocks and stones were everywhere, coming alive, spinning around his ankles as he went down to the river.

He'd created a mini landslide by the time he reached the river with a splash, his feet teetering on the unseen rocks beneath the muddy water along the ragged bank. When he took a step forward onto the ice, it cracked beneath him. He seemed to be on a kind of pebble-strewn shoal on this side of the river, though, and the water was shallow enough that he would be all right. So he kept going.

It was in the middle, just shy of where John was, that the bottom of the river plunged deeper, and the ice turned into dark, rushing water that could drag Laurie away with it. But it could drag John away if Laurie hesitated too long. John wasn't getting up and needed his help, so Laurie took a breath and leaped across the black water, scrabbling on the other side for purchase, almost on his hands and knees as he made his way to John.

"You're a damn fool," said John. His voice growled, but in his eyes, which were focused on Laurie, there was something else.

"Why can't you move?" asked Laurie as he scooted forward on the ice and rocks.

"My foot is caught in something," said John. "But you should just go back. I can make my way out."

"You haven't so far," said Laurie. "Here, I see it."

Beneath the water was a thick, forked branch that was caught in the ice at one end, and jammed beneath a large rock at the other. John's foot was pinned beneath the branch.

Laurie took off his mitten and reached down to shake the branch loose, and quickly got wet all the way up to his elbow. His head was pillowed against John's damp thighs as he jerked and tugged the branch loose, his heart beating against the cold all the while. If he was that cold, John was freezing, so it was important to get him out and back to the cabin as fast as possible.

"Can you move your foot?" asked Laurie. "Try to move it now."

John yanked his knee up and rolled across the ice toward the bank. The ice cracked and the dark water beneath threatened to take John with it, so Laurie grabbed John's hand and pulled with everything he had, until he was half on the far bank. His legs were still in the water, and he was coughing and shivering and soaked through.

"We need to get out of here," said John, his teeth chattering loud enough for Laurie to hear quite clearly and become even more alarmed. "The sun'll go down and the temperature will drop."

"No shit, John," said Laurie, muttering his frustration, his heart pounding, his mind racing with anxiety. What if he couldn't get John back to the cabin before hypothermia set in? "Here, roll toward me and I'll help you stand up. C'mon, try. Then we'll climb up the bank together."

With his hands under John's shoulders, Laurie urged John to pull his legs out of the water. He moved back, inch by inch, his knees digging into the icy pebbles, cold water going up his coat sleeves. John moved with him slowly until he was half across Laurie's lap, shivering with cold.

Together they helped each other stand up, teetering on the loose rocks as they made their way across the shallow, ice-flecked water, then leaped across the dark deep part of the river to the bank. John's teeth chattered as they started up the side of the ravine. While that was a good sign, if they didn't get out of their wet clothes soon, his body wasn't going to be able to warm itself up.

Laurie went first, and held out his arm for John to take so he could pull him up. John grabbed Laurie's forearm, clasping the whole of his elbow with his wet, gloved hand. Though the muddy bank was slippery and icy, they made it to the top, half collapsing in the knee-deep snow by the uprooted tree where frozen black earth was splatted against the white snow.

"We need to get back to the cabin," said John between shudders that shook his whole body. His face was white and there was blood on his cheek from where he'd scraped it on a rock.

"Okay, okay," said Laurie. "Let's go then, hustle, hustle."

He circled his arm around John's waist and kept him moving as fast as he could while John stumbled beside him, his arm around Laurie's shoulder for balance. John limped as he walked, holding hard to Laurie, and Laurie knew his leg had to be hurting.

Together they followed the path beside Sand Creek, though at one point the path narrowed and Laurie walked in front with John's hand on his shoulder so they didn't lose contact in the growing dark. Then, side by side, they hurried down a small dip and up the other side, going by the outhouse and then down the small slope to safety, the evening wind whistling at their backs the entire way.

By the time they got to the door of the cabin, Laurie was cold all the way through and could barely feel his own feet, and his hands not at all. But John, who'd gotten drenched, was now half frozen, and was shaking so hard he couldn't speak.

Laurie undid the bolt on the door and shoved them both inside. Before he did anything else, he bolted the door behind them, wanting to keep out the dark and the cold while he took care of John.

"Take off those clothes," said Laurie as he hurried to the stove to build up the fire and light the kerosene lamp. When John didn't answer, Laurie said, more forcefully, "Take off those clothes or I'll take them off for you."

He turned. John was standing at the edge of the rug as though frozen in place, his whole body shuddering. The golden fur of his coat was sopping wet and dripping on the wooden floor, and while John had slipped off his gloves and let them drop, his fingers were too stiff to manage as he tried to undo the buttons.

"Here," said Laurie. "I'll help you."

He was cold, too, but he was not wet through as John was, so Laurie quickly unbuttoned John's buffalo hide coat, pulled it off him, and flung it to the floor. He peeled his own coat off, and continued taking John's clothes off, first his shirt, then boots and wet stockings, and then finally his trousers, leaving John in his wet union suit.

"You need to take that off too, it's soaked all the way through," said Laurie. "I'll get your nightshirt—"

Laurie stopped. John was looking him with wide eyes, shaking his head. Laurie figured it wasn't that John was shy, but that he didn't want to stand there in the altogether, as it wasn't what a gentleman did. He was too much in shock to reason it out that this wasn't the time for niceties.

Laurie didn't have time to argue about it, so he was going to do what he had to do. He got John's nightshirt from the chest of drawers and the red blanket from the bed. Then, without saying anything, he stripped John to the skin and buffed him with the blanket, ignoring John's sounds of protest because he had to get John's circulation going and surely John knew that.

John's skin was almost white beneath Laurie's hands, a contrast to the dark hair on his chest and his legs and the thin line beneath his belly button. It almost broke Laurie's heart to see the bullet scar in John's right thigh, half an inch deep and almost a hand's length long, which might have been part of what John wanted to hide from him.

Laurie buffed the scar gently and dried John's feet, and went up and down his legs with the blanket, being businesslike about it at all times, for John's sake. Then he dried John's chest and back, and his hair, and slipped the nightshirt over his head and drew him to the stove as he pulled a chair up.

"Sit here, the fire is going strong now, and I'll heat up some coffee," said Laurie as he raced to get a dry blanket from the bed.

He wrapped the blanket around John, and got him dry stockings from the chest of drawers. Kneeling at John's feet, he rubbed his hands quickly over John's calves.

As John's hard shudders faded to faint shivers, Laurie looked up at John. He'd expected to see something fierce in John's eyes rather than the sad expression and the defeated slump to his shoulders as he pulled the gray wool blanket tightly around him.

"Are you going to make coffee?" asked John with a croak.

"Yes, of course," said Laurie.

He sprang to his feet and poked up the fire in the stove to get it really going. He made coffee in the large coffee pot, all the while hopping on one foot or the other as he peeled off his wet boots and stockings. He needed to change out of his clothes too, or he'd catch a cold because in 1891, even a mere cold could be a death sentence.

"You'll need to stuff our boots with cloth so they don't dry misshapen," said John.

"Yes, okay," said Laurie.

He hurried to do this, and then peeled off his wet clothes and slithered into his nightshirt. It was dry and soft, and although there wasn't the warm layer of woolen underwear beneath it, he thought he could manage now that they were both safe in the cabin.

CHAPTER TWENTY-TWO

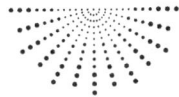

While the coffee heated, Laurie built a fire in the river rock-lined fireplace. Then he draped their wet clothes over every available surface and from every hook and nail. Soon the cabin was warm throughout, and a bit humid as well, reeking of wet wool and canvas. With the smell of fresh coffee going, Laurie sighed and allowed himself to relax. He poured coffee in the thick white mugs and handed one to John.

"Where's the rabbit?" asked John as he took the mug and sipped from it. "And where's the rifle?"

The rifle had been thrown in the snow and Laurie remembered it hitting the base of the tree with a snap. As to where the rabbit was, that was anybody's guess.

"I'm sorry," said Laurie. "I didn't think to grab them, and I think the rifle got broken."

"That's a brand new rifle," said John, his voice almost cracking. As he rubbed his forehead with the heel of his hand, a long silence fell.

They were without rabbit stew for supper, which was fine by Laurie. Rifles didn't matter, either, not when compared to someone's life, and John ought to know that. Laurie opened his mouth to begin explaining it to him, in no uncertain terms, when John shuddered a sigh and bent forward all the way to his knees, his shoulders slumped, dark hair spilled over his forehead.

"I really could use some whiskey right now," said John, as though to himself.

"So could I," said Laurie, joining in on what sounded like a small joke because he'd seen no sign of whiskey since his arrival.

"Well then, go and fetch it," said John.

"Where?" asked Laurie looking around the cabin.

"It's in the cellar behind the box of salt," said John. "I bought it for medicinal purposes."

"Well, I'd say this is one," said Laurie, with only a trace of sarcasm. While he wanted to make a joke about it, the fact that John felt it was time for medicinal whiskey meant that he'd been brought low, both by what happened in Farthing the day before, and almost freezing to death in an icy river because the path had collapsed beneath them.

Laurie trotted down to the root cellar and to the shelf that held the box of salt. Lo and behold, behind it was an amber colored bottle with an honest-to-God cork that was sealed with red wax. The bottle had raised letters that said *Kinsey*.

Laurie grabbed the bottle and headed back up to the kitchen where John was still sitting in front of the stove. He was curled forward with the blanket pulled hard around him, head bowed, looking at his stocking feet.

Quickly, Laurie broke the seal on the bottle, dumped out the coffee from the china mugs, and poured them each a finger of whiskey. He handed the mug back to John, and brushed John's shoulder with the back of his hand to get John to look at him.

"Here, John," said Laurie. "This'll warm you up." He made his voice light so John would know that he was okay, that both of them were okay, and that it didn't matter if they couldn't be together like Laurie wanted as long as they were safe and alive. But it was hard to put all of that into a wordless expression, and rather thoughtless of Laurie to expect John to unravel it all in his current state.

Laurie pulled the other chair close to the stove. When he sat down to huddle near the warmth, his knees almost bumped John's knees as he sipped his whiskey and thought about how to say it another way.

The whiskey was bitter, but it warmed his throat and his insides. Sighing, he watched the flames jump and dance in the stove where he'd left the door open. He noticed John had not yet drunk any of his whiskey, and reached over and lifted John's mug with his fingertips so that he would drink some and feel warm, too.

The second Laurie's fingers touched the mug, John lifted it and swallowed the contents all in one go. Then he barked a cough as the heat of the whiskey hit his throat.

"Do you want some more?" asked Laurie.

"Maybe mix it with some coffee," said John, his voice blurry with the whiskey.

"Sure, John," said Laurie.

He jumped up to pour coffee into John's mug, then added another slug of whiskey, and got the same for himself. He sat back down, scooting his chair a little closer to John's. Together they sipped the coffee and whiskey, and Laurie slowly began to feel warm all over and relaxed inside.

In the silence, the fire flickered golden and blue in the stove, and the snap and crackle of sparks jumping was the only sound to be heard. The room was warm and Laurie was starting to feel drowsy when he noticed John was looking at him. His eyes were sleepy and very blue, his dark hair slipping over his forehead in a tender way that pulled at Laurie's heart.

"What is it, John?" asked Laurie. "Should I make something for supper?"

"Perhaps in a while," said John. "After my stomach unclenches."

"Are you all right?" asked Laurie. Alarm bells began to ring in his head. "Did you—are you hurt inside from the fall?"

Laurie put his mug on the table and slipped to his knees in front of John, looking up into his face earnestly. If John was badly hurt with internal injuries, there was no hospital close enough that could save him, and no way to get there even if the right kind of help had been available.

Laurie's hands were on John's knees. He was probably too close for John's comfort and should move away to give John his space, but he needed to make sure first.

"Are you in pain?" asked Laurie with a shake in his voice. "What can I do to help?"

"You don't need to do anything," said John. His eyes were half-lidded as he looked down at Laurie. His fierce expression from earlier had changed into something quite soft, as though John was looking at something he held dear. But since the only thing John was looking at was Laurie, it was confusing.

"Then why is your stomach clenched?" asked Laurie. "Are you hungry, or—?"

"I'm hungry for you," said John, completely unexpectedly. As Laurie jerked back in surprise, John placed his hands on top of Laurie's hands to keep them where they were. "And I need to tell you something."

"Okay, John," said Laurie. He was uncertain because at the end of what John had to tell him, Laurie might be packing his bags and shuffling through the snow to Farthing to find a place to stay and work to do to earn his keep. "Okay."

"Yesterday," said John, petting Laurie's fingers with his own. "I was so in love with you I couldn't even see straight. Which was probably why I kissed you in town. My mind was so full with my love for you, I couldn't see the wrong of it."

"John," said Laurie, completely shocked at John's confession.

"When I caught those fellows beating you up, I already knew why they attacked you. It was because they *knew*. And when you confirmed it, well, I got scared."

"It's okay to be scared," said Laurie in a small voice. He kept his hands quite still on John's knees so that John would keep petting them. When John stopped, Laurie curled his fingers through John's so they were holding hands, as lovers did.

"I wanted to take off running, but there weren't no place to go except the cabin," said John, low. "With you close at my heels, there weren't no place to hide."

John swallowed hard and looked right at Laurie, which Laurie figured was the bravest thing John had ever done. He squeezed John's hands to comfort and encourage him. He wanted to fling himself into John's arms, but he needed to let John finish what he needed to say. Then he'd smother him with kisses and affection and all the love in the world.

"You were everywhere I went," said John. "Even though I didn't let myself touch you, I could still feel your skin against my skin. I could see the gold in your red hair, and the shine in your beautiful brown eyes. But all I could feel was the loss of you, for I had tossed you away with my own hands. And all because I was scared of three fellows I didn't know from Adam and what they might tell folks about what was between us."

Laurie's eyes were wide at this confession. A warmth suffused him, both that John trusted him to say all this, and that John described him as though he was beautiful, something lovely to be treasured.

"I would lie to keep you," said John. His eyes grew bright with tears that he blinked back, as though angry at himself for being so foolishly sentimental. "If they asked me, *do you love him*, I would lie and say no just so I could keep you."

Laurie surged forward into John's arms, sprawled across his lap, and felt John's arms come around him in response. John hugged him tight, and Laurie heard one hard sob from John's chest, and then John's lips were silky soft against his ear.

"I want to put my mouth on you," said John quite fiercely. "And draw you close and keep you near all the days of my life. Say you'll forgive my foolishness and stay with me. Say you'll be mine, Little Red."

"Yes, John," said Laurie, his voice as sure and steady as he could make it, given that he was shivering all over, his whole body reacting to John's confession and his proposal. "Forever and forever."

Casting aside the blanket, John stood up with Laurie in his arms, and carried Laurie to the bed and laid him on it. He tugged off Laurie's stockings and pulled the bedclothes back, though he seemed not to know what to do with them after that. As always, being intimate in John's world was a great deal more complicated than it was in Laurie's own time, what with all the folds of cloth and buttons and other fastenings.

"Will you be cold?" asked John.

"Not if you're near," said Laurie. He patted the lumpy mattress with a smile, savoring the sight of John in the firelight. "Come on in, the water's fine."

John's brow wrinkled in confusion, but he smiled and shook his head as he crawled into the bed next to Laurie and pulled up the sheet and blankets. Face to face in the bed with only their nightshirts on they were, in terms of 1891, nearly naked.

Laurie laughed a bit at being so excited at the thought of it, him and John nearly in the altogether, which was enough to make his cock hard and his mouth water and his breath go all jittery with anticipation.

John didn't make him wait. He encircled Laurie's waist with both of his strong hands, and tugged Laurie nightshirt up, pulling Laurie close to him.

Laurie's skin shivered with the feel of the flannel that John wore against his own bare skin, their hips brushing together with only flannel cloth to separate them. John was hard, too, Laurie could feel it, and he sighed with pleasure and kissed John's throat and his chin and everywhere he could manage.

Laurie reached up to clasp John's face in his palms, kissed him on the mouth. He kissed him again, loving the feel of John's plush lips, the scratch of the stubble of his beard, the warmth of his breath.

"You told me you loved me," said Laurie. "That was very brave. I want to be brave, too, and tell you that I love you and I will *always* be your Little Red."

John kissed him, hard, clasped Laurie's face in one of his hands, and made Laurie look at him. John's eyes were wide and dark and blue, and there was a question in them.

"Does it matter how I—" began John, then he stopped and started again. "I want to put my mouth on you, may I?"

"Yes means yes," said Laurie. "Do anything you want, John, anything at all."

With permission given and received, John tugged Laurie's nightshirt further up till it was bunched around his neck. He pulled the sheet up as well to keep Laurie warm, and sank down in the bed. His hands were on Laurie's hips and his silky hair brushed Laurie's belly and his cock, rough and warm.

Then with hardly any warning, John's mouth was on Laurie's cock, a deliciously warm pressure, and Laurie shuddered out a breath. John's mouth was gentle and sweet as he sucked and licked Laurie, his hands tender as they touched him and went between his legs to touch every part of him.

He was being careful, it seemed. Not because he was being timid, this his first time, but because he didn't want to hurt Laurie. Laurie sensed this with all of his being, and the sensation made him feel all soft inside, even while his cock grew hard beneath John's tongue as John suckled him and licked and kissed, and began stroking Laurie up and down, up and down.

This was the best, brightest love and it gave Laurie a fierce joy. He wanted to tell John everything he felt, but he could not find his own voice. So instead he carded his fingers through John's dark hair and tipped his head back and let the pleasure from John's mouth ripple through him.

When John cupped Laurie's bottom with both hands, his mouth drew Laurie's cock all the way in. The sudden warm circle of passion and heat made Laurie's body jerk all the way up his spine, and he came with hot, pulsing streams into John's throat. John swallowed then coughed and pulled off Laurie.

In the low light of the cabin, golden and warm, Laurie looked down at John, who was between Laurie's sprawled thighs, the back of his hand to his mouth.

"No time to warn you, I'm sorry," said Laurie, realizing that while John had probably pleasured himself a time or two, this was the first time he'd gone down on another man. "So you could draw off, you know."

"Tarnation," said John, smiling as he wiped his bottom lip with the heel of his hand. "You've a mighty spend there, Little Red."

"A mighty spend?" asked Laurie, his voice rising and his eyebrows going up. He knew right away what John meant, of course, but making a little joke out of it would give his heart time to slow down. He needed to be able to collect himself because he was on the verge of crying at the beauty of it, of John and him in bed together. "What am I, coins?"

John laughed out loud and climbed up Laurie's body to smother him with a broad, warm embrace, planting loud kisses to his forehead, and then to his mouth, where Laurie could taste himself on John's lips. In the low golden glow of the fire in the fireplace and the light from the lamp on the table, he could look at John to his heart's content, his entire soul soaking up John's nearness, the warmth of him, the steady bravery in those blue eyes.

With a tender hand, he pushed John's dark hair from his forehead and traced the curve of John's strong jaw with his fingers. A stillness came upon them both, and Laurie's breath slowed as he smiled, all the happiness in the world coursing through him.

"Your spend is mighty, too," said Laurie. "Which I already know." He waggled his eyebrows for emphasis to make it a little funny, as he could already see the lovely blush creeping along John's jaw. "So? Is it my turn? Yes, I believe it is."

John nodded, his eyes never leaving Laurie's. The connection between them was so strong, Laurie felt it hook into him to hold fast there forever. He kissed John on the mouth and scooted down in John's arms as he lifted up his nightshirt.

John wasn't wearing his union suit, so his skin was bare and warm beneath Laurie's hands. Though the skin on his face and arms and hands was brown from the sun, the curve of his torso was pale as marble, the dark curls around his groin dark in contrast.

All of him that normally hid beneath his clothes was soft on the surface with hard muscle beneath; his uncut cock stood up against his belly, dark and rosy red, and vulnerable beneath Laurie's touch. Laurie blew a breath along the length of John's cock and petted it, and clasped John's hip to steady him, for John had made a small, sharp sound when Laurie's fingers circled around his cock.

John shouldn't have to feel startled, so Laurie made sure to go a little slower, to be more careful, more gentle. He touched John's cock with his tongue, and then licked the length of it before circling his mouth over the top, lavishing it with the moisture in his mouth, tasting John, absorbing him.

Laurie stroked and suckled and kissed and petted, and drew John's cock even tighter in his mouth as he felt John's whole body stiffen. Then he eased his hand between John's legs, the hard corded muscle of John's thighs pressing on his wrist, and swirled his fingers across the little pucker of flesh between John's buttocks. John came in Laurie's mouth so hard he almost jerked back, but loosened his throat instead and swallowed.

John's legs trembled as Laurie took his mouth from John's now-soft cock. Then he eased John's nightshirt down across his thighs, and scrambled up and into John's arms, pulling the bedclothes up with him. Those arms circled around him and held him close.

As they breathed together, Laurie could feel John's heartbeat slowing down. He absorbed the sound of it, the steady rhythmic feel of it, his whole body humming with joy that John was alive and had not died in the ravine, and that the two of them were safe and warm and together.

"Little Red," said John with a sigh as he kissed Laurie's temple. "Oh, Little Red."

Laurie tilted his head back so he could look up at John. He knew he was smirking because he was so very pleased that John had changed his mind about them being together.

"Thank you for saying yes to us," said Laurie. "Thank you for changing your mind. I know it wasn't easy."

John looked a little chagrined and chewed his lower lip. As he glanced over at the kerosene lamp, his eyes were bright.

"I meant it when I said it," said John. "That we shouldn't be together."

"I know that," said Laurie. "I know you mean what you say, but what changed your mind? I know it wasn't me. I never bugged you about it. I was very good and patient, I'll have you know."

This came out a little more flip than he'd meant it to. He was about to explain himself further, that while he might like to know why John changed his mind, John didn't have to tell him. After all, John was entitled to his own private thoughts, just as Laurie was. At that point, he wondered whether he'd ever tell John the truth about where he'd come from.

"Before you came," said John. "I just wanted to be alone, and so I was. But I know now that if I'd fallen in that ravine and you'd not been close by, I would have stayed there, right where I was."

"You mean you wouldn't have—?" Laurie stopped, unable to even finish the question. Behind the answer was the threat of darker thoughts about how John would have let himself just stay in that icy water and freeze to death.

"I would have died," said John. "I would have died, and we would not have had this, so maybe it is better not to be alone."

"It is better," said Laurie, feeling fierce about it as he squeezed John's waist and pressed his cheek against John's chest. "It's always better, always."

"Easy now, Little Red," said John, the fondness in his voice sweeping over Laurie like a warm ribbon of love. "We're together, you and I, and I won't let any man take that away from us."

They lay in each other's arms in the golden light of the kerosene lamp and drowsed while the fire in the stove crackled and the flames in the fireplace glowed low.

"I need to bank the fires," said John, ever practical. "And douse the lamp, unless you are hungry for that supper we never had."

"I'm not hungry," said Laurie. "I will be in the morning, so be prepared to make me toast and jam, okay?"

"Yes, sir," said John, with a smile in his voice.

He got out of the bed and tucked the blankets around Laurie, shaking his finger at him to make sure he stayed where he was. John padded barefoot across the wooden floor, checking to see whether their clothes were drying properly, and that the door was bolted shut.

Then he banked the fires and doused the lamp and, in the darkness, came back to Laurie.

When he crawled beneath the bedclothes again, his skin was cold, so Laurie drew him close and warmed John's body with his own, curling around John like a vine on an oak tree. John's arms came around him and, in the darkness, they warmed each other up. Laurie fell asleep with a smile on his face.

CHAPTER TWENTY-THREE

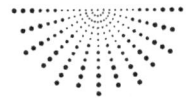

A s they were cleaning up the breakfast dishes, John stepped back from the basin, small white suds on his knuckles. He looked Laurie up and down as he swept the floor.

"Where's your new belt, Little Red?" asked John.

"I don't know," said Laurie, and he had to fight to keep from squirming like a second grader brought in front of the principal. The belt had been John's gift to him, and if John couldn't afford to send Laurie back east until spring, he certainly hadn't been able to easily afford the belt. "I took it off to wipe away the blood. Then I put it on the table to dry, but the next morning I couldn't find it. I'm sorry, John, I looked everywhere."

"We'll find it," said John. He nodded. "Don't worry about it, Little Red, it's just a belt."

It wasn't just a belt. Laurie shook his head and vowed that he'd tear the cabin apart if he had to to find it. He was not a careless person, and he didn't want John to think that the belt didn't mean anything, because it did. Money was hard to come by in John's world, and that was a fact. But he was distracted by the fact that John was getting dressed to go out, and was buttoning up his buffalo hide coat, which had dried a little stiff around the edges.

"Where're you going?" asked Laurie. "Wait, I'll get my coat and come, too."

"No, Little Red," said John. "Because you put my clothes closer to the fire, all of mine are dry, including my underwear. Your underwear didn't dry, so you need to stay indoors. I'm only going to fetch the rifle and the rabbit, anyway, so you should stay by the fire and keep warm till I get back."

"You'll be careful, right?" asked Laurie. He smiled at the thought of going commando in his trousers and that John *knew* he was going commando. That probably wasn't the word John would use for it, though, as he'd say Laurie was in a *state of nature* or *in the altogether* beneath his trousers. He'd rather go commando, though, than put on John's summer underwear, which were too thin and didn't fit him anyway.

He went up to John and encircled him in a hug, which was hard because the buffalo hide coat was so thick and the fur tickled his nose. John kissed Laurie on the forehead and pulled on his gloves, wrapping his face and neck with his gray scarf. Laurie handed him his hat, kissed him soundly, then held the door open for him.

As John walked past the shed and up the hill to get to the path that went along the river, he looked back, tapped his gloved hand against the brim of his hat, then turned and kept walking. The snow blew around his heels and the sun sparkled against the starry snow, making Laurie blink at the brightness of it.

Shutting the door, Laurie took care of the rest of the chores, wiping the table and sweeping the floor so that when John got back they could skin the rabbit and make stew. Breakfast had been delicious, especially with the toast and raspberry jam they shared, but that had been ages ago, it seemed, and soon he'd be starving.

Laurie fluffed the pillows and made the bed, and generally picked up, all the while keeping his eyes out for the beaded belt. As he got on his hands and knees to wipe the floorboards with a mixture of vinegar and water, he smiled at the thought of explaining this domesticity to Zach and Maxton. What would they say if they could see him now? Zach would laugh out loud, and Maxton might smile, though he'd probably not say what he was thinking. Both of them would wish him well in his new life.

These thoughts were quickly followed by the sudden desire to share John with his friends and anybody who would care that Laurie had found the love of his heart, a good man who only wanted to do the right thing and who cared about Laurie.

But did Zach and Maxton miss him? What did his work think about his lack of showing up day after day? Laurie had been so wrapped up in surviving and falling in love with John that he'd hardly thought about that aspect of it.

John's presence had been keeping those thoughts at bay. But now that he was gone from the cabin, Laurie began to wonder what everybody at the dude ranch made of him being missing. Had they called the police? Had they told his friends? Were Zach and Maxton worried?

With some trepidation coursing through him, Laurie got busy with his chores, and kept going at it until the only thing left was to dump the slop bucket and get more wood from the shed. So, bundling up in his now-stiff coat and mittens, Laurie wrapped his face in his scarf and stepped outside with the bucket in his hand.

Without the red woolen union suit beneath his clothes, the wind went right through his canvas trousers and bit at his skin, so he hustled up the slope to the outhouse. The slope seemed to go on and on, and something was snapping at his skin as though there was an electricity in the air. A hard wind came, dancing around his heels. It rose up, swirling the snow in front of his eyes, and he realized he was lost because he should have reached the outhouse by now.

But how could he get lost? The outhouse was only a little ways away from the cabin, and they were within eyeshot of each other. Even if it began to snow hard, which it was, he'd been headed straight for the outhouse. The ground beneath his feet leveled out, and for a moment he felt dizzy and reached into the snow for something to grab onto to steady himself.

Just as the wind blew snow into his eyes, he realized the slop bucket was gone. The wind went right through him and he should have been freezing, but he wasn't. In fact, as the whiteness dropped away, he was quite warm, almost too warm. The ground was brown and stretched out before him and there was not a speck of snow to be seen anywhere.

He stood on the top of a slope. A cool wind blew tags of cottonwood leaves around and, in front of him, neatly arranged beneath the crisp, blue sky, were the buildings of Farthingdale Dude Ranch. There was nobody around, so it seemed the place was deserted, but it looked exactly the same as he remembered it.

The large main lodge was right next to the little office, and on the far side of that was the bunkhouse and the corrals, where several brown horses were nibbling at tufts of grass and scraps of strewn hay. There was one car in the flat dirt parking lot, a blue Honda that he recognized from before.

"No," said Laurie, his voice half a whisper. "No, oh, no, no, *no*—"

With his arms wrapped around himself, he whirled, spitting up dust beneath his heels.

"John," said Laurie, then he cleared his throat and tried again. "*John.*"

He carved a line across the brown landscape with his eyes. The winter-dead grasses limped toward the west as the cool breeze whistled across them. But as hard as he looked, and as familiar as the line of the slope was, he could not find the cabin. Could not find the outhouse or the shed. Did not see John's tracks in the snow because there was no snow, not a speck of it. And worse, there was no John. Not anywhere.

There was the haze of smog along the cloud-gray horizon, and the smell of exhaust fumes, the low buzz of a light-winged aircraft flying overhead on its way to the nearest municipal airport. There were telephone poles and, toward the south, power lines supporting rows of steel wires.

But no cabin, no evidence of the life he'd lived there. No John.

"Laurie," came a shout from behind him. Laurie whirled around with a sharp indrawn breath, thinking that John, against all odds, had come into the future with him.

A woman was running toward him. Maddy. She was wearing blue jeans, like before, and her silvery hair hung in the same thick braid down the back of her neck.

"Oh, my God, Laurie," she said as she came closer. "Where the *hell* have you been?"

"I don't know," said Laurie, shaking, tears stinging his eyes. Where was John? Where was the cabin? Had it all been a dream? Was John lost to him forever? "What day is it?"

"It's Sunday. You disappeared a week ago," said Maddy. "The sheriff has had sniffer dogs looking everywhere for you, and they made us send everybody home. They thought you'd been murdered or abducted *and* murdered, and they didn't want anybody else to be at risk."

"Murdered?" asked Laurie. If that's what they thought happened to him, then everybody back home would be going out of their minds. He needed to take care of them. "If that's what everybody thinks—did you call my friends, my roommate?"

"Yes, of course. Hope it's okay, but we used the contacts on your phone," said Maddy. "Which is the first time I gave thanks for a cell phone. Your friends Zach and Maxton wanted to come up right away and help look for you, but the sheriff said they'd only be in the way. I'll call the sheriff now and tell him you showed up and then we'll have them reach out to your people in Harlin."

With one hand on Laurie's arm, as if she was afraid he'd run off, Maddy tapped her phone then held it to her ear and started talking.

Her voice was brisk as she explained the current situation, which gave Laurie a sense of what panic must have ensued when he'd gone missing. They'd been worried. Everyone he knew thought he was most likely dead, but he'd been alive the whole time. When he'd been with John, he'd felt more alive than he could ever remember being.

But what had happened to him? What had taken him back in time? And what had brought him home again? He had no idea. All he could remember was after Bill had told his ghost stories, he'd gone to sleep in front of the bonfire next to the chuck wagon.

It had been chilly, but the air had been still, the velvet night sky full of shooting stars. Then he'd woken up and walked through a snowstorm, thinking he'd lost his way and had wandered off from the dude ranch. Which was when he'd seen John's cabin in 1891 and knocked on the door. Except he was here, now, in the present.

Relief shook him that he'd be able to see Zach and Maxton and tell his funny jokes to make them laugh. And that he could take a hot shower any time he wanted to feel clean, or flick a switch to brighten an entire room. And use the internet to order pizza to be delivered right to his very door. He'd missed pizza and not even realized it.

But *John*. If Laurie was in his own time, then John was not ever going to be there, would never listen to Laurie or watch his antics with that solemn expression in his blue eyes, his mouth struggling not to smile.

Laurie's heart ached as though claws were ripping through it. John was going to come back from fetching the rifle and the jackrabbit, and Laurie would be gone. What would John do then? Would he search for Laurie? Or would he shrug in his practical way and go on as if Laurie had never been there? John's journals never even mentioned Laurie, so maybe while John had been Laurie's dream, Laurie had been John's and they'd never really ever met.

Numb and cold all over, Laurie felt as if he were standing in the middle of a blizzard. His breath whistled in his throat, and he could barely hear what Maddy was saying, though he could see that her mouth was moving as she talked. She tugged on his arm, and petted him, and he wanted her to reach through the numbness he felt and drag him out of it.

Very quickly, between blinks as though he'd lost track of time, the sheriff and his deputy arrived in an SUV with the county logo emblazoned on the side. An ambulance arrived, as well, and two paramedics got out.

The paramedics got first dibs. They dragged Laurie to the back of the ambulance, opened it up, and used their equipment to check him over.

One of the paramedics was asking Laurie questions about the bruises on his face and who had given them to him. The other paramedic kept trying to distract him with a conversation about his antique buffalo hide coat and brown felt cowboy hat.

His voice echoed in Laurie's ears as the first paramedic unbuttoned Laurie's shirt and checked his heart, listened to his lungs, used a flashlight on his eyes, and turned his wrists to check for needle marks. Nobody laughed when they found out he had no underwear on, though Laurie could hear them saying to Maddy that he ought to be admitted to the hospital for shock.

Laurie knew he had to speak up or they'd whisk him back to civilization before he could figure out what was going on.

"I'm—" he said. He stopped to swallow the fist in his throat. He pointed to his lip "I'm okay, I swear. This is from when I fell. I don't know where I was, but nobody hurt me. Nobody. And I don't want to go to the hospital. I don't need to go."

"What do you want to do, Laurie?" asked Maddy. "I won't let them do anything you don't want to do."

"Ma'am," said the sheriff. "Maddy, we need to question him, and it's best if we take him to Chugwater to do that."

"Not if Laurie doesn't want to go," said Maddy. Her voice was firm and clear in Laurie's ears and he looked at her. Her mouth was a straight line and her eyes glinted; for so sweet a lady, he was glad she was on his side. "He's not a criminal, is he? You're not charging him, are you? Then you can question him right here, in our dining hall. I'll make coffee."

The sheriff paused, looked at his deputy for a long moment, then back at Laurie. Finally, he nodded.

"Only because it's you, Maddy," said the sheriff.

As Maddy smiled, her chin lifted high in satisfaction, the sheriff said that the paramedics should release Laurie from their care. They reluctantly allowed him to button his shirt, shrug on his suspenders, and gave him back his hat, coat, and scarf. The sheriff then waved the paramedics off, and gestured to his deputy to lead the way to the dining hall.

All the while, something hummed in Laurie's brain, like a low and distant signal that he could not locate the source of. He shook his head to clear it, but it remained like a memory drifting away and then swooping closer as the wind took it.

They took Laurie into the dining hall, and Maddy stuck close to his side until they were all seated at one of the long dining tables. Then she went off to make coffee, leaving the door to the kitchen open so as to keep a sharp eye on Laurie, and he was glad for her presence nearby when the interrogation started.

Laurie answered the sheriff's questions as best he could. No, he didn't know where he'd been all week. No, he hadn't been kidnapped. No, nobody had hurt him. No. No. No.

He didn't tell them about John, or the cabin, or the iron bed, or the kerosene lamp, or the careful way John had held him. He feigned amnesia, which was the best thing he could figure out to do until he could straighten out the memories in his mind.

John had been real, the cabin had been real, and the kisses and love and affection that they had shared had been so real Laurie's heart was breaking at the thought of losing all of that. Worse, the thought of John being all alone made him want to cry. He didn't want to cry in front of the sheriff and his deputies, not because he would be embarrassed, but because there was no way to explain the why of it: John was lost to him forever.

AFTER A GOOD LONG WHILE, and way after Laurie's head began to ache and the questions they were asking began ringing in his ears, the sheriff and his deputy prepared to depart.

"Here's my card," said the sheriff, handing it to Laurie, whereupon Maddy snatched it up. "If you remember anything, give us a call, okay? We're going to follow up any leads we find, and might ask you to come up to Chugwater for that. Sound good?"

"Yes," said Laurie as clearly as he could, though he had no intention of giving them any information about what had happened to him. It was none of their business anyway.

Laurie also had the feeling that since the marks on him were minor and he had no real explanation for them, they were quite close to dismissing the entire event as a hoax or a grab for attention. Maddy just shook her head as they left, and guided Laurie into the office, sitting him down in the old leather chair. She gave him more coffee, and took his buffalo hide coat and hung it up on a brass hook on the wall.

"This coat is wet through. How did that happen? It looks like it's new but the style is so old. Wherever did you get it? And those pants—never mind, give me your hat and scarf and I'll hang those up to dry as well."

After she'd done this, she wrapped a warm red fleece blanket around him.

"You haven't stopped shivering," she said, and her eyes were kind as she tucked the fleece below his chin. "Now drink that coffee while I finish up this paperwork."

The sight of Maddy at her desk was as familiar as his own front door, or seeing Maxton slink through it at six in the morning when he'd been out all night. She shuffled some folders, and spread the sheets of paper to review, then wrote something quickly as scratching sounds filled the air.

"Now, I've talked to Bill," she said, glancing up at him. "He agrees we're going to give you a one hundred percent refund and ship you home in style. I've arranged for a plane to take you from Chugwater to the Boulder airport tomorrow, and a van will drive you straight to your door in Harlin."

"I'm not going to sue the dude ranch, Maddy, if that's what you're thinking." Laurie took a long sip of his coffee. It was served in a thick china mug that reminded him instantly of the ones John used, but the coffee tasted sweet instead of bitter and strong. "It's not your fault I went missing."

"I didn't really think that you would, Laurie," said Maddy, kindly. "But we've had so many calls—would you believe that our reservation rate has shot up fifty percent? People like the drama, so we're not hurting by any means. But Bill said I should take care of you so that's what I'm going to do. Give me a minute and I'll get the rest of these papers ready for you to sign."

"Can I use the phone to call—?"

"Yes, yes," said Maddy. She shoved the old-fashioned push button phone at him, smiling at his raised eyebrows. "I keep this one because sometimes we don't get a signal way out here. Just dial nine to get out."

Laurie called Maxton first, as Maxton was a night owl and had probably not yet gone to bed, while Zach usually slept in on his day off. The phone rang twice and then Maxton picked up.

"Yes."

"Maxton," said Laurie, suddenly breathless. "It's Laurie. I'm okay. I'm calling to say I'm okay."

"Laurie?" asked Maxton, his voice rising with rare emotion. "Seriously? Dude, where the fuck have you been?"

"I don't know," said Laurie. "I was gone and now I'm here. But I'm okay. I'm not hurt or anything."

"That sounds like—were you taking anything? Smoking bad dope, maybe?"

"No," said Laurie. He laughed a little under his breath, soothed by the sound of Maxton's voice sinking back into its usual low, careless tone.

Maxton liked to pretend to the world that he didn't give a rat's ass about anything, except he had a heart like melted butter. Laurie'd sworn to take that to the grave, which meant he had to pretend he'd not heard the care and concern in Maxton's questions.

"I've talked to the local law, and couldn't tell them anything," said Laurie, doing his very best to sound casual about it all. "They're probably convinced I'm trying to become internet famous or something."

"When're you coming home?" asked Maxton. He didn't care about social media or anything like that because he was too cool for school. And he didn't care about the local law either. But he cared about Laurie, this Laurie knew with certainty. Maxton wanted Laurie *home*.

"They're shipping me home tomorrow, right to my door," said Laurie, tears pricking his eyes. "Will you be there?"

"Yes," said Maxton. "I'll be here all day so I can take care of your sorry ass when you get here."

"What about your job?"

"Fuck the job," said Maxton. "I never liked it anyway."

"Maxton."

"Don't fucking care," said Maxton. "Now call Zach before that shithead gets wind that you called me first."

"I will," said Laurie, his jaw trembling as he held back the rush of affection he felt. "See you soon, my friend."

Without saying goodbye, Maxton hung up, which was how he was. If Maxton was acting like himself, that helped Laurie *feel* more like himself, more like he could now call Zach, his oldest friend.

He tapped in the number that Zach had had for years, and waited while the phone rang over and over. Zach never picked up before the fifth ring. Not because he was too busy but because the number on his phone would be one that he'd not recognize, and he'd have to decide whether or not the call went to voice mail.

Laurie primed himself to leave a message, hoping he could get through it before he started crying, when Zach answered the call.

"Zach speaking," said Zach. "Who is this? I don't recognize your number, so you sure as hell better not be a telemarketer, not this early on a Sunday."

Laurie opened his mouth, barely able to breathe.

"Fuck this shit," said Zach, muttering to himself, and Laurie knew he was about to hang up.

"Zach it's me," said Laurie, the words coming out all in a rush. "It's me, Laurie. I'm calling from the dude ranch. I'm okay. All right? I'm not dead. I'm okay."

"*Laurie?*" Zach's voice was a whisper. "Laurie, is that really you? You're really okay?"

"Yes, yes," said Laurie. "I'm sorry I made you worry."

"What the hell happened to you?" asked Zach, his voice rising the same way Maxton's had, though with Zach Laurie didn't have to pretend he didn't hear the love and affection. "Where'd you go? Where the *hell* did you go?"

"I don't know," said Laurie. "I went to sleep and when I woke up there was this blizzard and—and I was somewhere else for a while and now I'm here. In Wyoming."

"Somewhere else?" asked Zach, instantly focusing on the very point of Laurie's explanation that nobody, not even Zach, could understand, let alone believe.

"I don't know," said Laurie. His breath caught in his throat and he had to scrub at his eyes, turning his back so he didn't have to look at Maddy trying not to look at him while he cried in her office. "Look, I'm coming home tomorrow. Maxton plans to lose his job to be there when I get there, so if you guys could not fight until then, that'd be the best homecoming present ever."

"He's already lost that job, my dear," said Zach somewhat dryly. "I don't know how he does it—actually I do. He can't keep his mouth shut, and he can't keep his sticky fingers from the till. That's how."

"Zach—" said Laurie but it was a meek protest at best. While he'd been away, Zach and Maxton had kept in touch long enough for Zach to know Maxton's current employment status, which could only be called progress.

"He was doing something he shouldn't," said Zach, going merrily on as though he knew 100% what Laurie needed, and that was to hear the news from home in a chatty, casual way, as if everything were normal. Later, he and Zach would have a heart to heart, and maybe he'd tell Zach about the time travel thing, or maybe he wouldn't. He didn't think he could bear talking about John.

"There's this motorcycle gang, you know, the one that hangs out at that diner? Now, I don't know if he lost his job because he was hanging out with those guys, or he's hanging out with them because he lost his job. He won't tell me, and believe me I asked and asked because I knew you'd want me to."

"I did and I do," said Laurie. "Thank you for that."

"I tried," said Zach with a heavy sigh, as if all the world's burdens were encapsulated in the single solitary human being that was Maxton Barnett.

Laurie wiped the tears from his chin and tried to remember how to breathe without his chest shuddering.

"What time will you be home?" asked Zach, ever practical.

"I don't know," said Laurie. "Tomorrow, sometime in the afternoon probably. They're flying me into Boulder County Airport, so at least I won't have to come all the way from DIA."

"I'll pick you up," said Zach.

"No, better not," said Laurie. "I don't know what time I'll arrive, and I don't want you hanging out in a craptastic county airport. They don't even have internet at those places, I hear."

He waited for Zach to laugh at this very small joke, and when he heard it, he smiled and took a deep breath.

"It'll be good to have you home, my friend," said Zach. "I can't wait to see you. I'll be waiting at your apartment with Maxton, just for you."

"And pizza," said Laurie.

"And pizza, of course," said Zach, pretending to be shocked that Laurie would assume they would forget how much he loved pizza. "Canadian bacon and pineapple, right?"

"And sausage and onion for Maxton," said Laurie.

"And pepperoni and garlic for me," said Zach.

"No garlic," said Laurie. "We'll be up all night talking and I don't want to smell your smelly garlic farts."

"I'll aim them at Maxton, as usual," said Zach, laughter in his voice.

Laurie was about to reply with his usual comeback that Zach was an asshat, or something similar, when he stopped and swallowed.

"I missed you, Zach," he said. "Love you, buddy."

"Love you too," said Zach. "Now let's hang up before we both start crying, 'cause I can hear the tears in your voice just like a little girl."

"I'm hanging up now," said Laurie, smiling at the phone, blinking fast.

"Me too," said Zach. "See you tomorrow."

The phone went dead with a click. For a moment Laurie just sat there, then he replaced the phone in its cradle. Maddy was still busy with paperwork, or pretending to be busy, obviously giving Laurie a moment to collect himself, which he appreciated.

But within a minute, he was restless. He stood up with the coffee mug in his hand and the red blanket wrapped around his shoulders like a shawl. His mind looped around in crazy circles, going over the same thoughts again and again. His heart kept racing as it ached. Right smack dab in the middle of it all was John's face, and how he would worry about his Little Red and be hurt when Laurie never came home.

He looked around the office, desperate to distract his brain. The leather chair was still cracked, still gave off an old, dusty smell. The office had the same two rows of sepia toned photos along the wall above the glass display case. Laurie went over to it.

He found himself looking at the photo in the upper left of the arrangement. It was of a cabin made of wooden logs that had fallen into a tumble on one side where the roof had caved in. The next photo was older, and the cabin was more intact in that one.

Some of the photos showed black and white images of Iron Mountain. One or two had pictures of horses that were almost too small to make out. Most were of the cabin in various stages of disrepair.

"What's this cabin?" asked Laurie. He felt warm enough to lay the blanket on the back of the leather chair and put his mug on the corner of the desk. He went back to the photo, crossing his arms over his chest while he stared at it. "Where have I seen this before?"

"Oh, you haven't," said Maddy, not looking up from her paperwork. "That's Old Joe's cabin. You remember the story of Old Joe, right? That's his cabin. We left it up for a long time till it got too dilapidated. Our insurance wouldn't cover it if someone got hurt, so we tore it down. That's what it used to look like, though."

"Old Joe," said Laurie half to himself.

"The stuff in the case is what we found in the dirt beneath the cabin when we tore it down," said Maddy. "I love to collect old things. When Bill found that case in an antique shop, I knew exactly what should be displayed in it to give the people coming to the ranch a sense of the history of the place. It's mostly old junk, but there are nicer things, too."

Laurie appreciated the distraction. His heart wouldn't settle down, and his stomach ached. All he wanted to do was go home to John, but how? He didn't even know how he got back *here*, let alone how he'd gotten *there* in the first place.

He made himself look down at the case, focusing on the things inside it in a way he'd not done the first time he'd been in the office. The collection was mostly rusty, dusty, and old like Maddy said.

It was easy to imagine Maddy taking the time to create the display simply because she thought her customers would enjoy it. Each item had an index card in front of it with tidy printing that explained what it was. Everything was laid out with some reverence on a large sheet of faded green blotting paper.

There was a tin of matches, and a long rusty spoon. A pile of bent iron nails with square heads, like they used way back when. There was half of a blue and white china plate, and a small cut glass bowl that was mostly intact, except for a tiny chip along the rim.

The chip caught the light and drew Laurie's gaze to it, so delicate a thing to have lasted all these years almost intact. He was sure he'd seen the bowl before, but where? He tried looking at the other things in the case, like the half-opened brass pocket watch, but that also seemed familiar and didn't help distract him from the odd twist in his stomach.

Then Laurie's heart stopped, for there, laid in a flat line at the back of the display case was an Indian beaded belt.

No. It wasn't just any belt, it was *his* belt. It had been here in the glass case the entire time, from before his arrival at the dude ranch to this very moment.

Though the leather looked brittle and stiff, curled up at the edges, the colors of the beads were as bright and crisp as the day Adeline had finished the belt. The vivid pattern, meant to look like snakeskin or maybe like lightning, was exactly the same. It was *his* belt, he knew it, the one that he'd lost almost as soon as John had given it to him.

Which meant—the cabin in the photographs was *John's* cabin. The cabin they'd shared, where they'd been so intimate, had fought and ate and lived together. Everything was true. *All* of it.

Laurie looked at the pocket watch, turning his head to see the slender black hands stopped at nine o'clock. He could almost hear John saying, *It's late, it's time for bed, Little Red,* and he wanted to cry.

"Old Joe, you say?" asked Laurie, doing his best to keep the shake out of his voice as his fingers gripped the edge of the display case.

Maybe he'd dreamed the whole thing and had awoken into this nightmare. But while his brain told him one thing, his memories and his heart told him something else.

"Oh, that wasn't his real name," said Maddy, obviously having no idea the effect her response had on Laurie's state. "But Bill decided that Old Joe had a better ring to it, not to mention the fact that we'd be conjuring up John's ghost every time we told that story."

"His real name was John Henton," said Laurie, his stomach dipping hard enough to hurt.

"Yes, but how did you know that?" asked Maddy.

Laurie turned to look at her, and though she seemed a little surprised, she wasn't the least bit suspicious about how he knew.

"Oh, maybe Bill told me," said Laurie, his mouth trembling as he told the lie. *I would lie to keep you.*

"That's not like Bill to reveal something like that, but yes, that was his name," said Maddy. "He came out to work for the railroad, so that part is true. Most of the story is true, but some of it we changed to make a better story, and also, because some people have issues. You know."

"No, I don't know," said Laurie, for he had no idea what she was talking about.

"Here," said Maddy in a way that told Laurie she was completely oblivious to the state he was in as he shook with the effort of holding still. "I'll bring these to you."

She came over to him and spread the papers like a fan on top of the glass case.

"Sign here and here. Don't press too hard or you'll break the glass on the display case."

Laurie signed without looking, his heart beating wildly the entire time. He handed the sheaf of papers back to her, but paused before he let go of the pen to get her to look at him.

"What do you mean about changing the story because some people have issues?" he asked.

Whatever she told him, Laurie would be able to compare it with what really happened. If she told him something that was true that had been handed down to Bill by his great-great-great Grandad Pete, then Laurie would know that it was not all a dream. If she told him something that did not mesh with his memories, then he would know he was going crazy.

"You know how people are," said Maddy, her eyes gentle. "Nobody that I care to associate with, but back in the day our customers weren't as tolerant as they ought to be. After Bill and I discussed it years ago, we changed the story to suit. Nowadays, I'm too old to give more than a fart in a high wind what anybody thinks. We don't allow bigots anyhow, but the story is in place, so we just leave it like it is."

"You leave it?" Laurie asked. He shook his head. "What do you mean, leave it? What did you change?"

"The part about the little red fox that John found in the snow," said Maddy. "It wasn't a fox at all, it was a young man John brought to town. Bill's Grandad Pete always stated he didn't care, but there was talk that John and the young man—never got the name, but Grandad Pete always referred to him as Little Red—well, they were lovers. Back then, that didn't happen. So in order to avoid upsetting people, the story turned into how John had rescued a fox in the snowstorm, and there you have it, the ghost of Old Joe looking for his little fox friend in the snow."

Laurie's breath caught in his throat, for how she described it was exactly how it had happened. He'd *met* Grandad Pete, back in the day when he was a storekeeper with a dashing mustache and clean white apron.

"Adeline made the belt," said Laurie with numb lips. "She made beadwork by hand to make her living and she lived above Grandad Pete's store."

"How do you know that?" asked Maddy. Her eyebrows were high in her forehead. "Grandad Pete told Bill that her Arapahoe name was Summer Cloud Woman, but that the whites always called her Adeline. But how do you *know* that?"

"I'm sure Bill told me," said Laurie. "We were standing behind the chuck wagon and talking at the cookout."

Maddy shook her head, tapped the papers into a neat stack, and went back to her desk to file them away. Laurie trailed after her. The numbness had overtaken his entire body so hard he could barely feel himself sitting down.

"Did they really find John's frozen body in the spring like in the story?" asked Laurie.

He hated to think of it. Before, the story had just been an old yarn that he'd thought had been made up or conjured out of parts to entertain the newly arrived dude cowboys. He remembered being affected just the same because it was simply that sad, but it'd not been anything he was going to carry around with him and worry about.

"Well, no," said Maddy as she tidied up her desk, pausing with a pile of folders in her hands. She looked up at him as though embarrassed.

"I mean, yes, they did find him sitting in the chair wrapped in a quilt with his rifle over his arm, but it wasn't in the spring, it was in the fall of that year. And yes, he had died of hypothermia because all the windows were blown in from a storm. It was one of the worst fall blizzards the town had ever seen and lasted three days and nights, they say.

"Why he was just sitting there instead of cleaning up the glass nobody ever knew. As to how they found him, Grandad Pete and Summer Cloud Woman noticed he'd not been in town in a while, and he usually came once or twice a week, or so they say. They went out to check up on him after the blizzard and found him dead like that. Just like in the story Bill tells around the campfire."

Blinking back his tears, Laurie swallowed the hard lump that had formed in his throat. John must have come back from getting the rifle and the jackrabbit and found his Little Red was nowhere to be seen.

He might have hollered for Laurie, and he must have looked everywhere, but to no avail.

As to how long it had been before John had given up on Laurie ever coming back, Laurie imagined that it must have been a good long while. John would have kept on looking, except for the storm that had happened, a storm fierce enough to blow the windows in. And with the cabin being so cold to begin with, John might have just given up—

"Where's the journal?" asked Laurie suddenly. "And Bill said you had a picture of John, an old photo or something."

"We took those out of the case because they were starting to fade," said Maddy. "Would you like to see them? Here."

Maddy reached down into one of her desk drawers and drew out an old cardboard box. It was a little crumpled at one corner, but seemed sturdy as she opened the lid. The first item she pulled out was John's journal, the dull brown of the leather instantly familiar to Laurie's eyes. Maddy flipped open the journal, placed it on the desk, and turned it so that Laurie could see.

"Don't touch it or the paper'll crack," she said. "This is the page we like to show folks because here is where he talks about hunting buffalo wolves, which are now extinct. It adds a nice natural history touch, don't you think?"

Leaning forward, Laurie scanned the words written in John's looping, old-fashioned handwriting, the ink faded to brown where once it had been a crisp black. John described tramping through the snow as he followed the wolves' tracks upriver. He described the snow fort, and how long he waited in the cold before seeing the wolves. Then he wrote:

I confess that I did not dispatch the wolves as I had been ordered, for while they were great big hairy, gray beasts, they did not attack, and at the sound of the shots from my rifle trotted up into the hills where they will bother no one. I arrived back at the surveyors' cabin after dark, after having dallied along the river to watch the geese settle on the water in the purple twilight. For supper, there was fried antelope (the last of the meat), and biscuits and butter and honey. I washed and went to bed at the usual hour.

And that was it. There was nothing about Laurie and his antics, but then, there never had been. When Laurie had flipped through John's journal in the cabin, there'd been no mention of Laurie, even then.

Laurie remembered scanning this very page, thinking how words could not compare to the vivid memories of the sunset and the wild geese landing on the water for the night. Could not compare to the feeling of John standing so close their shoulders touched, or of the feel of John's hand over his mouth to get Laurie to be quiet for once.

"Where's the picture of John?" Laurie asked, his heart twisting at the thought of seeing an image of John.

"It's just one of those drawings from a newspaper clipping meant to look like a photograph," said Maddy. "But here. Again, don't touch."

She brought out from the cardboard box a plastic sleeve, no bigger than a three-by-five index card. Inside of it was a yellowed scrap of newspaper with a blobby black image that looked like it was supposed to be a man in a buffalo hide coat. Laurie squinted at it, desperate to see John's eyes. He tried to imagine he recognized those features, that stance, but it could have been anyone, anyone at all.

"Are you okay, Laurie?" asked Maddy as she put the items back in the box, and the box back in the drawer. "You're shaking again. Here, let me get you some more coffee."

Laurie didn't want coffee, but he trailed after her into the dining hall and into the large empty kitchen, where she poured coffee into two thick white mugs, the kind that John had in the cabin.

Laurie needed to get back there, back in time, back to where John was so he could be with John and they could continue their lives together. John made Laurie feel safe, and being with John brought a sense of calmness and peace he'd so easily lost in this modern world of cell phones and deadlines, with all the bright and shiny things that blinked and beeped. He didn't need any of that, he needed *John*.

"Bill said something about Iron Mountain," said Laurie. He took the mug of coffee from her and, before she could offer him cream and sugar, took a large sip of it. The coffee had cooled and the taste had turned slightly bitter and it was perfect, just like John made.

"What was that?" asked Maddy as she doctored her coffee.

Laurie watched her spoon go round and round in the white china mug. He had the feeling that she was really listening, not because he was a customer whose vacation had gone wrong, but because she really cared.

"He said that if there's a meteor shower and you see Old Joe's ghost and you make a wish while walking toward Iron Mountain, it'll come true."

"Oh my God, that Bill," said Maddy with a laugh. She shook her head and smiled at Laurie. "He gets worse every year, and that's not how it goes anyway."

"How does it go, Maddy?" asked Laurie, and if his question came out more sharply than he intended, he was immediately sorry for it. He needed her to tell him the truth about Iron Mountain. He needed to get home to John.

"Now keep in mind that this is just a legend, you see," said Maddy smiling. "But Iron Mountain doesn't grant wishes, it gives you your heart's desire."

"Bill said something like that at the time, but I didn't really know what he meant," said Laurie. "What's the difference between wishes and desires?"

"A wish is something you want," said Maddy, as though the discussion was completely ordinary and not about make-believe ideas at all. "A desire is something you really need, something that's in your heart. Like, you wish for a million dollars, but what you really want is to be safe and warm. It's a layer deeper than wanting tons of money. You see?"

"I guess so," said Laurie. He felt tired all over and was no closer to understanding how to get back to John. John was real, and his time with John had been real, but the way back to that life was fuzzy.

"The part about the meteor shower is true," said Maddy. "That's what they say anyway. They say the mountain is made of iron and the meteors are made of iron. So it's like the shooting stars are trying to get back home and, along the way, together with the mountain, they'll grant you your heart's desire."

A shiver went up Laurie's spine and the hair on the back of his neck stood straight up because that's exactly what John had said. Oblivious, Maddy swallowed the last of her coffee, and laughed a little to herself as she rinsed out their coffee mugs and put them on the draining rack to dry.

"It's all stuff and legends anyhow," she said. "Now, I can take you into town and get you a room at a hotel, would you like that?"

"I'd rather stay here, Maddy," said Laurie. "And get at least one night's sleep in a real bunkhouse." He made a face at her, pretending to feel chagrined at needing such a foolish thing after having, supposedly, nearly escaped kidnapping, abduction, and death.

"I guess that'd be all right," said Maddy. "Are you hungry? We've got frozen pizza I can make you, or I can order from town. I'm going to turn the heat on in the bunkhouse for you, and though they went through your stuff, its all still there. Tomorrow, the van'll pick you up and take you to the airport, and your refund check will arrive this week. You'll call me if it doesn't, right?"

"Sure, Maddy," said Laurie.

He wanted to rub his face and he wanted to curl up in a corner and he wanted to cry, all at the same time. He missed John so much, so hard, that his whole body hurt and his heart felt like it was drying up into a little kernel of flesh, worn out and sick-sore and not much use to anybody.

"You don't have to order. I can make the pizza myself."

"I have to go and feed my family," said Maddy. "Otherwise, I'd stay. And, hey, I should put you up in the hotel in town rather than have you stay here. You don't look so good."

"I'm fine," said Laurie, though nothing could be further from the truth. "I'm just tired. Being interrogated by a sheriff and his deputy and poked at by paramedics is enough to wear anybody out."

He smiled to get her to join in his little joke, hoping and praying that the humor would be enough to distract her. He needed to be alone, needed to think about what to do. He didn't want pizza, he just wanted to be alone.

"Okay, okay," she said, waving her hands in the air. "Here, come back into the office and I'll write down my personal cell number for you. If you need anything during the night, anything at all, you just call me, okay?"

"Sure thing, Maddy," said Laurie. "I'll be fine. Hot shower, good night's sleep, I'll be fine."

And he would be, if he could figure out a way to get back to John.

CHAPTER TWENTY-FOUR

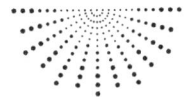

Laurie didn't know how to get back to John, or even if he should believe it had all been real. Grief and sadness lingered behind every thought, every breath, and would rip him apart from the insides if he let it.

Instead, he didn't let it, and focused on the solitude of the empty bunkhouse, the smell of dust, and the weight of the stillness without all the other dude cowboys around. One of the light bulbs flickered beneath its thin cowhide-looking yellow shade, and somewhere in the walls the wooden timbers creaked in the wind.

Compulsively, he went to his cell phone, which was still plugged in the outlet above the bathroom sink. Laurie flicked on the bathroom light, picked up the phone, and held it in his hands, then tapped it to life with his thumb.

There were dozens of texts from Maxton and Zach. He scrolled through them, and they were all the same: *Where are you? Come home! Be safe. We miss you.*

The voice message box was full, and he listened to a few. Most of them were from Zach, and the longest one told Laurie to not listen to the ones from the day before because Zach had been drunk and out of his mind with worry.

The last message Laurie listened to was from Maxton. The entire message was almost thirty seconds of pure silence before Maxton made a sound that could have been interpreted as a sob and hung up.

Laurie couldn't bear to hear any more. His friends had been frantic to find him, imploring him to return their calls, their texts. He didn't think he could bear any more of that *and* the thought of John sitting in the leather chair freezing to death in a cabin with broken windows, a howling wind whipping through, tearing everything apart with icy cold teeth. He just couldn't manage both of those, so he tapped the phone off and put it on the edge of the sink.

He wasn't hungry, but he needed to eat, otherwise his growling stomach wouldn't let him do anything else. He left the bunkhouse and went through the growing darkness to the dining hall, There, in the empty, echoing kitchen, he pre-heated the huge, commercial oven.

Before the oven was properly hot enough, he opened a frozen pizza box and put the pizza directly on the rack. Then he turned on the timer and stood by the stove, staring at nothing until the buzzer dinged. He turned off the oven, ate half the pizza, and threw the other half away. The taste of the pizza was too bland, though even if it had been New York style pizza from Grand Central station, it never could taste as good as John's fried cornmeal mush.

He wiped down the counter and swept up the crumbs from the floor. Tomorrow, he would be transported by plane and by shuttle bus to his apartment in Harlin. After a very warm welcome from his friends, he would go back to work and resume his ordinary life.

He would commute, drink overpriced coffee on a regular basis, work in a cubicle, and probably never look at a sunset again.

Never see the geese settling on the water.

Never carry an armful of wood, staggering for effect to get John to laugh at him.

Never roll over in a too-narrow metal framed bed into John's arms and be swallowed by warmth and tenderness and love. Never, never again.

A sob cut off his breath, and he staggered back to the bunkhouse, almost tripping over the threshold in the boots that John had bought for him. The clothes he wore were his only connection to John, and he stood there in the middle of the bunkhouse, slowly stroking the canvas of his trousers.

How long before the cloth faded? How long before the leather of the soles of his boots wore thin? How long had it taken the beaded belt in the case to grow stiff, the leather cracked with age along the edges? One hundred years or forever, it made no difference. Eventually all of this would be laid waste, and the world would forget the story of John and his Little Red.

He lifted his hands to his face, clasping his own cheeks as John would have done. Except Laurie's face was hot as flame, and his hands felt like ice, shocking him into stillness.

How could he get back to John? He needed to get back to John.

The mountain and the meteor shower played into all of this, he was sure, because when he'd fallen asleep there'd been a meteor shower overhead. When he'd woken up in the snowstorm and arrived at John's cabin, it was the same month and the same meteor shower was going on, even in 1891. As it was only a week later, in this time, the meteor shower was still happening overhead, night and day. But which meteor shower was it again?

Laurie went back to get his phone and opened a browser. He tapped in the words *meteor shower* and *October*. The results came up quickly, which only made sense, since the meteor shower was current and he wasn't the only person looking for information about it. It was the Orionid meteor shower and was created by dust and debris from Halley's Comet.

The meteor shower was happening right now, right outside the door of the bunkhouse. Just waiting for Laurie. Dust and starlight, all streaming through the night sky, headed for Iron Mountain as fast as gravity could take them.

It was then that he knew what he needed to do to get back to John.

He didn't let himself hesitate, but got undressed, and took the longest, hottest shower he'd ever taken in his whole life. He washed his hair three times, and put tons of conditioner in it before rinsing it out. He took so long in the shower, he was still beneath the stream of water when it began to run cold. And that was saying something, since the bunkhouse was set up to house up to 20 dude cowboys.

He used the toilet and washed his hands in the now-cool water, using plenty of easy-lathering soap. When the fog on the mirror had cleared, he shaved, using lavish amounts of shaving cream from the can. He flossed and brushed his teeth slowly and carefully, and then licked his teeth, watching himself in the mirror, laughing a little as he did this.

His hair was indeed a dark red, and in the light from the bare bulb over the mirror, he could see the streaks of gold that John had so loved. *The color of a summer fox's coat,* John had said. Now drying from his shower, and without the benefit of having used anything to style it, Laurie's hair curled across his forehead. He looked in the mirror and imagined John's fingers sweeping through his hair, lifting it away from his eyes so that John could look into them.

I'm coming home, John. I don't know how, but I'm coming home.

He got dressed in the sturdy clothes he'd arrived back at the dude ranch in. He thought about his buffalo hide coat, and his scarf and hat, but they were in Maddy's office. It would take too long to get them, and maybe they would make a nice addition to her antique collection.

Carefully stacking all of his worldly goods on one of the bottom bunks, he added his phone, now unplugged, to the pile. Anybody looking at the collection would know that Laurie had left everything where it was on purpose.

He didn't want his friends, or anyone, thinking someone had come and kidnapped him. He wanted them to know that he had left. That he was gone. They would not know that his intention was to get back to John, but they didn't need to know.

Zach and Maxton would mourn his loss, he knew that, and he would find a way, somehow, to get word to them that he was okay so they wouldn't be so sad. He hated the thought of it, but if he did not try to get back to John, then he would regret it all the days of his life. He could not bear the thought of John dying all alone like that, sitting in the leather chair facing the door while the wind howled through the broken windows, his cracked rifle on his arm, waiting for his Little Red to come home to him.

What he was about to do might not work, but he needed to try. For John.

LAURIE'S HANDS were empty as he stepped out of the bunkhouse and went around it. He walked in the darkness, then slid between the barbed wire that bordered one of the large pastures beyond the corral and walked toward Iron Mountain.

The air was chilly. With only a quarter moon low on the horizon, the sky overhead was bright with stars, making it light enough to see by. There was also enough darkness to be unseen in, for he didn't want Maddy to come upon him and stop him. But she was miles away in Farthing, and had no idea what he was doing.

He'd passed a herd of horses that was large enough he imagined Gwen would be among them. Some of the horses whickered at him in the dark, and he wished Gwen well and thanked her for being so sweet.

He was heading straight for Iron Mountain with nothing but the love in his heart and the desire, the true desire, to get back to John. It wasn't a want, he didn't just *want* this. He needed it to survive, he needed John like he needed air to breathe. If he couldn't get back there, to 1891 where John was, then there was no point, not to living, not to going on with his life, not to any of it.

Once he reached the other side of the pasture, he went through the barbed wire again, knowing Bill would scold him something fierce if he ever found out. But he'd never find out, for soon Laurie would be long gone. On the other side of the fence, he stood up straight, his legs braced.

Iron Mountain loomed like a giant with broad shoulders, shaded a darker dark than the night around it. Overhead, the shooting stars zoomed towards the mountain, streaking like soundless silver ribbons, bits of dust and starlight all headed home to the mountain.

I love you, John. I love you, I love you, I love you.

Laurie kept walking. He didn't say out loud what he felt inside. The mountain knew, it had known from the beginning. The shooting stars, silver streaks overhead, knew. The high prairie that had always been there waiting for him knew, and the dirt he was walking on with sturdy leather boots from 1891 knew. Everything knew.

The closer he got to the foot of the mountain where the rocks formed ragged edges, the harder the wind blew, as though racing fiercely to get at him. It was colder too, and without his Carhartt jacket he was shivering. With his arms wrapped around himself, his hands clutching his upper arms, he kept walking, his head bowed as it began to snow.

The snow was icy cold, the hard flakes batting at him, trying to make him turn back, almost testing him, it seemed. The whiteness of a storm swirled around him and took his breath away. Beneath his footsteps the ground grew uneven, and he felt himself teetering as though he were on a bridge that had suddenly given way.

When he stumbled, there was nothing to grab onto and nothing to stop him as he fell.

CHAPTER TWENTY-FIVE

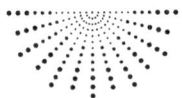

He landed on his knees, breaking through a hard crust of snow as a low wind howled across the icy surface. His arms felt every sting and, without his coat, even his sturdy canvas trousers felt paper thin. Snow got into his boots as he struggled to his feet. Barely able to keep his balance, he squinted across the white field, trying to get his bearings. There was only snow for miles, the blue ridge of mountains to the west a ghostly line.

But there, a block of brown against the white, was the cabin. He couldn't be sure that there was smoke coming from the chimney, or whether he was too late and the windows had blown out from the storm and John was already dead.

With panic filling him, a scream rose in his heart, and a roar of love escaped him.

Laurie stumbled across the snow. The white surface had been scudded by the wind into such hard, sharp dunes he broke through with every other step. He sank deep, up to his thighs, arms flailing. He was cold, freezing cold, both from his fall through time and the icy air all around. He wasn't going to make it back to John if he didn't keep going, so he had to, he had to keep going.

He managed to cross two more dunes of icy snow before he fell flat on his face, banging his mouth, tasting blood. As he pushed off the snow, he left dapples of blood behind. His hands had no feeling, only a raw numbness that went all the way up to his elbows. He needed to move, he needed to get back to John.

As he got to his feet, he staggered to a level spot between the icy dunes, hugging himself.

He was close enough now to see that the windows of the cabin were still intact, though there was no smoke coming from the chimney. In a breath of still air between gusts of wind, he saw that the curtains were drawn, at least on this side of the cabin, and that the shed door was closed.

All was well in that regard, but the cabin was so still without the bustle of industry that John usually brought to it. Everything was deadly still, as though nothing moved inside, nothing was alive.

"John." Laurie took a breath and shouted again, louder this time. "*John!*"

There was no answer, and still no movement from within the cabin. Laurie's heart hurt so badly that he placed his hands over his chest, clasped together, as if that could stop the pain of it, the anguish at the thought that he was too late.

But how could that be? The windows were intact. Maddy had been quite specific about the windows being blown out when they found John dead. Or maybe the windows had blown out after he died, and that's why he didn't clean up the glass?

"*John.*"

Laurie began to run, slipping on the ice. He reached the door just as it opened to reveal John standing there, dark-eyed and rough, a quilt falling away from his shoulders. Without a word, he stepped out of the cabin in his bare feet, grimacing, and grabbed Laurie and held him tight, almost too tight for Laurie to breathe.

Laurie didn't care, but held onto John just as hard, breathed in his scent, unwashed and sweaty, winced at John's unshaven face, and held on that much harder. His heart ached with the loss of Zach and Maxton, and the world that he'd known, his own world. But he was with John now. He had John.

Laurie grabbed John tightly around the neck and squeezed hard. Breathless, he wanted to pull himself inside of John's body where he would be safe forever.

John stepped back across the threshold of the open door. His hands were on Laurie's head, gentle and warm. Laurie heard the soft sounds in his ear as John whispered something over and over. His body next to Laurie's was hot, as though he had a fever, though the air in the cabin was almost as cold as the wind sweeping across the high prairie.

Turning to kiss John's cheek, Laurie let go long enough to smooth John's witchweed dark hair back from his forehead, and attempted to erase the worry in John's eyes.

"What are you saying, John?" asked Laurie.

"You came back," said John, his mouth trembling. "Why did you go away? Where did you go?"

"I'm sorry," said Laurie, and he meant it with everything that he had. He leaned back, his hips against John's hips, their chests still close together, and clasped his face. "I'm sorry I scared you, I'm sorry I made you worry."

John clenched his jaw, and it almost looked like he was struggling to decide whether or not he would revive his old opinion that Laurie was a tenderfoot who needed to be taken out to the shed for discipline. And surely in John's mind, running off without a word would qualify as supreme foolishness.

Laurie felt a pang in his heart at the thought that John might want to whip him, as though they might have to start from the beginning. The truth of it was, John seemed shaken to his core, and that made Laurie feel even worse.

"I didn't run off, John," said Laurie. He looked up into John's dark blue eyes, half-hooded, as though hiding all the thoughts that whirled in them. "I didn't run off. I got lost, and now I'm home again."

John drew back and held Laurie's head in his hands and together they stood in the open doorway. John looked at him, tracing the lines of Laurie's face with his eyes as though absorbing him, committing him to memory for Laurie's next long absence.

"I didn't go away on purpose," said Laurie, shaking his head as he clasped his hands over John's hands. "I promise you, John, I *promise* you."

John's eyes were still wide, as though with disbelief, and Laurie knew that now wasn't the time for a lengthy explanation. He wanted, *needed*, to get them back to their lives where they shared everything. Shared the chores, and the way the light changed in the cabin as day wore on to night. Get them back to the simple things, like the flicker of firelight while John wrote in his journal, or how Laurie would sit at his feet and oil two pairs of boots so that John could read out to them from the green-bound *Polar and Tropical Worlds*.

He wanted all of that, and he wanted John. More, he wanted John to be happy, which was so far removed from the sad-eyed man who looked at him now.

"I'm home for good, John," said Laurie as steadily as he could manage, given that his lungs couldn't seem to get enough air and all he wanted to do was to fall into John's arms and cry like a little kid.

"You're here," said John. "You're really here. Not lost."

"No, not lost anymore," said Laurie. He wanted some levity, otherwise his heart was going to break, for the thought of it, of John dying because of him being gone, was almost too much to bear.

Laurie took a breath and looked over John's shoulder. The cabin was dark with the curtains drawn, and the room was stone cold, as there was no fire. There were dishes on the wooden counter, and ash spilling out of the cast iron stove, the door left open and untended. There were clothes on the back of a chair at the table.

In the center of the room, facing the door, was the leather chair. The cracked rifle was on the floor beside it, as though John had just put it down when he heard Laurie shouting.

"What have you been doing in here, John?" asked Laurie, forcing lightness in his voice. "It looks like you've invited a pair of buffalo wolves in for a dance, only neglected to tidy up after."

With Laurie still in his arms, John cast a glance at the cabin, but only that, for his gaze came back to Laurie once more.

"You were gone a whole week," said John, his voice thick. "I came home from getting the jackrabbit and my rifle, and you were gone. I couldn't find any prints to indicate which way you'd headed, or if you'd fallen. There was no sign. I looked everywhere. When I couldn't find you, well, there seemed no point to anything but to wait for you."

The look on John's face, the unhappy tilt at the corners of his eyes, the slight shake to his jaw, all of this broke Laurie's heart. The story Maddy told him was true, then. John had waited for Laurie to return, and froze to death.

There was no way Laurie could make that funny, so he pressed himself against John, wanting to move into John's body and curl up inside of his ribs and never ever leave John on his own like that again.

"You're shaking, Little Red," said John. "You're cold. I'll start a fire and make you something to eat."

"I'm sorry, John," said Laurie, and he realized he was crying, and as hard as he tried to stop, he couldn't. It was all too much, and he feared that he was, in reality, still walking across the high prairie while the blizzard raged around him. "I'm so sorry—"

"It's all right, Little Red, it's all right," said John. He petted Laurie, held him close, and waited while the tears subsided. Drawing back, he used his thumbs to gently wipe the wetness from beneath Laurie's eyes. He brushed his fingers across Laurie's busted lip and shook his head. "What happened to your mouth?"

"I fell in the snow coming back to you," said Laurie, almost whispering.

"You need looking after, so come here," said John, stepping backwards. Inch by inch he moved them into the cabin until he could close the door behind them.

"You need looking after, too," said Laurie with a clogged voice as he let himself be drawn to the cast iron stove. He didn't want John taking care of him when it was so obvious that John had been neglecting himself while Laurie had been gone. "Don't just—we should take care of each other, you know? Let me take care of you, too."

With his hand on the open stove door, John's whole body stilled. He looked Laurie up and down, and Laurie knew he did not imagine that John's eyes lingered on Laurie's red hair, which Laurie had so carefully washed in the shower when he'd been in the future, just for John's benefit. Yes, he'd miss hot water showers, but he'd rather be with John than have all the modern amenities in the world. Showers could be replaced with a bath in a tin tub and, besides, John was one of a kind.

"You're right, Little Red," said John. "We'll do it together. But first, you need to sit down so I can tend to your mouth."

When John finally let go of him and went to put on his boots, Laurie sat down and took what felt like his first deep breath in a long while. The sight of John getting ready to go out was so familiar, that to be back in the cabin looking at it felt almost surreal. The smell of the cabin, traces of burnt coffee, and ash in the fireplace, and the faint odor of fried onions, all of it was familiar. He took in a breath, wanting to absorb it all into his skin, his very being.

John went out and quickly came back with a handful of snow wrapped in a cloth, which he directed Laurie to place against his lip. Then he drew some water from the pump and, gesturing that Laurie should pull the snow-cloth away, gently bathed his mouth and chin with a damp cloth.

All the while, he touched Laurie's face with his fingers, as though checking for more damage at the same time he was reassuring himself that Laurie was really there. Laurie couldn't blame him and leaned into the touch, his eyes almost closing as John tended to him.

"Put the snow-cloth back for a minute," came John's voice, echoing and soft, as though from a distance.

Laurie opened his eyes and did as John asked him.

"I'll go get some firewood and then I'll clean out the ash and lay some kindling," said John.

"Let me do that while you get the firewood," said Laurie. "I'll feel more normal if I'm busy, and it'll help warm me up, besides."

"You don't feel normal?" asked John, his eyebrows going up. He moved close and put his hand on Laurie's shoulder, and looked down at him with such tenderness that Laurie felt like crying all over again.

"I'm okay," said Laurie, scrubbing at his eyes with his hands.

He didn't want to discuss the effects that traveling through time had on his psyche, as he didn't understand it himself. Besides, such a discussion would delay the return to normal. So he took a long, shuddery breath and shook his head.

"I'm okay, but I'm hungry and I'm cold, and you need to make me some fried cornmeal mush. And after that, we need to cover the windows with tar paper or some wood from the shed so they don't get blown out in the storm."

"What storm?" asked John, showing his innate ability, once again, to parse Laurie's ramblings down to their essential parts.

"The storm that is coming," said Laurie. He knew this one future event, and after that he didn't know what would happen, except that he would be with John forever. "We need to clean up, and then we need to head into town to lay in some food before the storm comes, and cover the windows with something."

"You said that before," said John. "But what storm?"

"It's going to be a bad one, three days and nights," said Laurie. "But we'll be okay. The cabin is sturdy, and we'll be inside of it, but we need to make sure of the windows. Just trust me, okay?"

"I trust you," said John. He tilted his chin down and kissed Laurie gently. "I trust you."

He took the snow-cloth from Laurie's hand and tossed it in the basin on the counter. He dried Laurie's face afterwards with a corner of the quilt from the floor. This he folded carefully and put on the railing of the cast iron bed. Then, with a nod, his jaw square, he went out to get firewood.

Laurie went to the chest of drawers where he found his red union suit, nicely dry and folded. He took off his boots and clothes to pull on the woolen underwear, and was warmer even before he put his trousers and shirt back on. Then he shoved his feet into his boots and stomped on the wooden floor, and though he still felt a little shaky inside, he smiled.

He cleared the stove of ash. This felt right. More, it felt normal and good, the way it should be. It wouldn't take them long and they'd be back to their old life, him and John.

After he cleared the ash and laid the scraps of kindling he'd found in the wood box, Laurie went to the kitchen table, and put his hands on it, palms flat. The top of the table, and the edges as well, were smooth. A belt might slide right off of it.

He bent down and went on his hands and knees, getting grit on his palms, combing the floor with his fingers. He kept at it until he found a floorboard that rattled on its nails, as though it was loose.

Laurie pushed the chair out of the way and lifted the floorboard, which came up easily.

The stuff in the case is what we found in the dirt beneath the cabin when we tore it down.

There, lying in the dirt, was his Indian beaded belt. He'd found it, still safe, waiting for him, and his heartache eased.

The leather looked soft and new, and the beads sparkled in the low darkness. Laurie drew out the belt, shaking the dust from it as he stood up. He was about to slip it on when the door opened and John walked in with an armload of newly cut firewood.

"I found my belt," said Laurie to explain what he was doing with part of the floor pulled up. "One of the floorboards was loose."

"That's good," said John. "I tried looking for it, too, and couldn't find it. But now can you tell me where your coat and hat are? And your scarf? You're wearing everything you were wearing a week ago when you disappeared, except for those. What happened to them?"

"I don't know, John," said Laurie, grinning to himself at John's brusque tone. It seemed John was trying to get back to normal, too. Laurie slipped on the belt, buckled it, and admired it for a moment. Then he pushed the wooden plank back into place before he looked up at John. "I honestly don't know what to tell you about that."

And he didn't. How could he explain the vagaries of time travel, or how Maddy had hung his things up to dry in her office, and Laurie hadn't wanted to take the time to get them? Or how Iron Mountain had granted him his heart's desire? Which, come to think of it, had probably been why he'd been drawn forward in time, as he'd been wanting, quite hard, to share how happy he was with John with his friends back home.

"When we go to town, we'll get you another coat so you don't freeze," said John. He piled the wood in the wood box and eased Laurie out of the way as he hunkered on his heels to build a fire in the stove.

"That's exactly what we need to do," said Laurie. "You're out of groceries, and we need supplies for shutters. So, town it is."

Doing chores steadied Laurie in a way he'd not thought possible only a short while before. They worked together to clean up the cabin, to put the quilt back and to sweep and wipe the floor with vinegar.

John heated up some water, and washed and shaved. Laurie didn't even pretend not to stare, and John didn't pretend not to notice that Laurie was staring. And with each part of John's ritual, Laurie's heart slowed and he became more calm.

John drew Laurie close to the basin and lifted his chin, and examined his face, checking the swelling with gentle touches, followed by the gentlest of kisses, like butterfly wings.

"You're so clean, how did you get so clean?" asked John. He carded Laurie's hair with his fingers. "Your hair feels like silk."

"Only for you, John," said Laurie with a wink, striving for his normal sense of humor, though he was still rattled down to his bones. "Is it bedtime yet?"

"After we go to town for supplies," said John, his voice rough as a blush crept up his cheeks. "We'll definitely need to go to bed early, I should think."

Laurie smiled, and tipped his head to the side so that John could cup his cheek in his broad, warm hand. Everything was just as it should be.

CHAPTER TWENTY-SIX

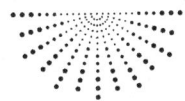

Except for the fact that Laurie almost froze to death as they walked into Farthing, on account of he only had a quilt from the bed to wrap around his shoulders and no coat, the trip to town was almost unexceptional. Nobody but John knew that Laurie had been gone, and John didn't say anything about it.

They went to Pete's store to put in their order for groceries, and to buy nails and other hardware John said he needed in order to cover the windows.

While John was talking to Pete, Laurie made sure to stop behind Adeline's table in the window, waiting till she noticed him. When she did, she smiled and stepped away from her beadwork. She was wearing the same leather dress he'd seen her in the first time they'd met, and her hair was done in the same two braids.

"I love my new belt," said Laurie. He looked down to show her, tracing his fingers across the beads "I almost never take it off."

"I'm glad to hear it," said Adeline. "The leather stays softer if you wear it. If you don't, the leather goes hard."

"Right," said Laurie, for he was fully aware of that, since he'd seen the sad state of the unworn version of the belt in Maddy's display case.

"But where is your coat?" asked Adeline. She looked at his half-naked state, the drape of quilt around his shoulders, and shook her head. "You'll half freeze to death in that cabin with no proper coat and hat."

"Yes," said Laurie. "That's why we're here. As to what happened, it's a long story and I don't really understand it myself. I lost some stuff in a snowstorm, I think."

"You think?" asked Adeline, her voice edged with confusion.

Laurie wanted to tell her, he really did, but he couldn't. It wasn't just the difficulty of parsing out the effects of a time paradox, which he didn't fully understand himself. It was that he didn't want them to think he was crazy. He wanted her to accept him. He wanted her and everyone in town to think of him as John's Little Red. He wanted to belong.

"I think I had a fever or something, and went out into the snow and lost my gear," said Laurie. It was the lamest of explanations, but Adeline's eyebrows rose, and she looked like she felt sorry for him. Back in 1891, a fever was probably nothing you wanted to fool around with. "Yes, it was a fever."

"Is John going to get you a new coat?" asked Adeline.

"Yes, that's why we're here," said Laurie. "And something to cover the windows because there's a storm coming."

"How do you know that?" asked Adeline. "My uncle, who's quite old, said just yesterday that there was a storm coming. It's going to be a bad one, he said, but then he's seen many winters, he knows the signs. I can't imagine how you would know, however."

"Just a feeling," said Laurie, doing his best to figure out a way to backpedal out of the conversation. "You know, nothing I can explain, really. Just a feeling."

"I see," said Adeline. "Well, you have time to prepare, and that cabin is as sturdy as they come. As long as you're ready, you can weather the storm."

Laurie looked over at where John was handing money to Pete and taking a bundle of clothes in exchange. The stack looked like it contained almost the same articles as John had bought for him the first time, although now there were a few more things that he couldn't identify. John was doing his best to make sure Laurie had what he needed and then some.

He wanted to tell Adeline that as long as he had John, he could weather anything. But, according to Bill's great-great-great Grandad Pete, who was standing only ten feet away, there was already talk in town about the two of them.

There was no way Laurie was going to make that worse by gushing how he felt about John. Except, when he looked back at Adeline, he saw an expression in her eyes, a softness. As she'd been looking at Laurie, who'd been looking at John, it was very likely that she already knew.

"You'll take good care of him, won't you, Little Red?" asked Adeline, keeping her voice low so that only Laurie could hear. "He's a good man with a soft heart, and he needs the tenderest of care."

"Yes, Adeline," said Laurie. He felt his eyes grow hot, and struggled to keep the tears back. "I know it, I do, and I'll take the best care of him. The best, you can count on it."

She placed her hand on his arm and tightened her fingers gently. Then, letting him go, she went back to her table in the window. Placing her braids behind her shoulders, she picked up her needle and string and continued with her beadwork.

Laurie sniffed and wiped his nose, then took a deep breath. He went over to John and poked him in the ribs as he began stuffing things into his rucksack.

"What did you buy, the entire store?" asked Laurie as loudly and as obnoxiously as he could.

John just smiled, his chin dipped down, that lovely blush playing behind his ears.

"You just go on in the back and put this union suit on."

"I already have a union suit," said Laurie. "I'm wearing it."

"Now you'll have two," said John. "Just do as you're told. Here's this new shirt and trousers, so you'll have two of everything. Here's your new coat and hat, you might as well put them on, as well," said John.

He handed Laurie a new, clean buffalo hide coat, a blue chambray shirt, a soft felted brown hat, and a brand new red woolen union suit.

"When you're dressed, we'll get some lunch at the hotel, and come back to get our groceries and then go home."

"Yes, sir," said Laurie, much in the way that John had said to him earlier. "I need a new scarf, too," he added, just for fun, in the voice of a spoiled child for whom nothing was ever enough. "I need a new scarf, and I'd like a pen knife of my own, and some bright red suspenders. You got all that?"

"In the back, *now*," said John, pointing, but he was smiling broadly, and Laurie could tell he knew Laurie was just playing up because he could and to make John laugh.

He went obediently into the storeroom in the back, and got dressed as quickly as he could. It was so satisfying to slip on the new warm woolen underwear and the thick trousers with the high waist and sturdy belt, and to put the Indian beaded belt over that so he could show it off to John. The blue chambray shirt was exactly like what John wore, so they'd be two of a kind as they made a home for themselves in the cabin in the middle of nowhere.

It was exactly the life he wanted. Exactly. He wanted for nothing more.

He slipped on his suspenders, leather for now, though he had no doubt that John was purchasing a pair of bright red ones for him to wear, this very minute. Then he stopped and closed his eyes.

He needed Iron Mountain to know that this, right here and now, was his heart's desire. That John was his heart's desire, only John, only being with John. That there was no need for the mountain to give him anything more, if indeed it was the mountain doing all of this in conjunction with the meteor shower overhead.

He might never know for sure, but maybe it would be a good idea to get away from such a powerful combination as soon as possible. But that could wait till spring, if ever, for if Laurie never forgot what his heart really wanted, then there was no way the mountain could take it away from him.

Stomping into his boots was its own kind of noisy pleasure, and he made sure to do it as loudly as possible so that everybody in the front of the store could hear. As he shrugged into his new buffalo hide coat, and tipped his hat onto his head, he felt warm all over, he felt right.

Pleased with himself, he strode out of the back of the store and paused with a broad sweep of his hands and a little *ta-da* gesture and jazz hands combination that he knew nobody would understand, not for years, at least.

"You look handsome," said Pete. "And decently dressed in that new coat."

"Thank you, Pete," said Laurie. "What do you think, John, am I decently dressed?"

"You look very well," said John.

Those dark blue eyes were half-lidded, and Laurie had a feeling that as much as John wanted to pull Laurie into his arms and kiss him very soundly, he was restraining himself. They were in town after all, and they'd made that mistake before.

They needed to be smart, and if they kept on being smart, even if there was talk in town, talk was all it would be. Those three guys that John didn't know from Adam could gossip all they liked about seeing him and John kiss. Laurie already knew that Grandad Pete didn't care, and Adeline didn't care, and if they didn't, probably most folks didn't.

"Here are your red suspenders," said John. He took the folded suspenders from the counter and stuffed them into his rucksack. "You can try them on for me at home."

That was a slip-up already, and a statement like that could get them into trouble if the wrong people were to read into it. But Grandad Pete was busy with something behind the counter, and nobody else was even listening.

"Better watch your mouth, John," said Laurie, stepping close, using his best John-in-a-scolding-mood voice, all gruff and bossy. "People'll get the wrong idea exactly what you mean there. Because are you suggesting I wear those suspenders *with nothing else on?*"

He could see that while John hadn't been thinking that, he was thinking it now, for the blush on his cheeks was a hard red. John looked away as he tied up his rucksack and hauled it on his shoulders, as though looking at Laurie might break him, but in the most delicious of ways. To reward this, Laurie butted his forehead against John's buffalo hide coat, laughing.

When he lifted his head, he felt flushed and warm, and happy all over, inside and out.

"Come on, John, let's go get lunch. I'm starving."

"I can hear your belly from here," said John. He looked as though he wanted to add something, but shook his head. "I should have known you'd come back. I'm sorry I doubted you."

"It's okay, John," said Laurie. "I'm glad I found my way back. Thank you for waiting for me."

They were very close to kissing now, right in Grandad Pete's store, which wouldn't do at all. So Laurie petted John's arm and stepped away, knowing they had time to be together, for he remembered that Maddy had said the storm had raged for three days and nights. Plenty of time to be alone and private in the glow of the fire.

When they returned to the cabin, they put away the supplies, stopping to kiss whenever they liked. Afterwards, they spent most of the afternoon in the shed building three sets of shutters.

John showed Laurie how to trim the planes of wood neatly with the smaller axe, and how to pound the nails in smoothly so they were level. Laurie handed John the square-headed iron nails and held his tools while their collective breaths clouded the air.

John had purchased boughten hinges, and so nailed those into place. Then together they went around the cabin and hung the shutters one by one. The shutters could be latched from the outside or the inside, and were sturdy and would protect the windows when the wind blew hard.

Inside the cabin, the shutters, now closed and latched, made the cabin even more cozy, though it was a little darker.

"That was a good idea, Little Red," said John as they took off their coats and hung up their outdoor things. "I should have thought of it, for blizzard or no blizzard, it'll take less wood to heat the cabin."

"Good," said Laurie. "I kept thinking if there was a hard wind, the glass might break. That would be expensive to fix, right?"

"Yes, it would be," said John, nodding. "That's quite sensible of you."

Laurie went to him and curled himself in John's arms and kissed his mouth and sighed.

"I'd like to become insensible if you'd let me," said Laurie, almost purring.

"Whatever are you talking about?" asked John. "We need to get supper going."

"Always with the chores, John," said Laurie with a huff.

But then he looked at John, and saw John's secret smile, and knew that John was teasing him in a way, drawing out the moment to build anticipation. He'd not forget his earlier agreement with Laurie that they should go to bed early.

John was a good man, but he was also a little shy, and being so openly in love with another man was still new to him. Laurie needed to be patient, to be kind, and yes, he needed to tease the hell out of John at every given opportunity.

Supper was a quick meal, rabbit stew with flour dumplings, and more potatoes than carrots this time, as John had not forgotten Laurie's preferences. They finished up with toast and jam, and then Laurie hustled to do the dishes and dry them while John built a fire in the rock river fireplace.

By the time Laurie was done wiping his hands on the towel and had swept the floor around the table, John had checked his pocket watch and put it on top of the chest of drawers.

Laurie watched as John dimmed the lamp. Then he pulled the mattress onto the rug and, in the glow of the fire, remade the bed.

"What are you doing?" asked Laurie, for he'd not expected this. It was all very romantic, John's version of romance. A warm bed. A golden fire. The light of the lamp turned down low. "Oh, John."

"Is this going to be all right?" asked John as he stood up. "While you were gone, I kept thinking and thinking what I would do, what I would say, if you came back to me. While I can't hardly think of all the things I want to say, I know I wanted to do this. So we could be together in front of the fire this way. So I could do nice things, things that you like, and you wouldn't leave me again."

"I didn't leave on purpose," said Laurie, his heart breaking all over again. "I swear to you, John, I swear it. I'll never leave you. Never."

He sidled past the newly made bed on the floor and circled his arms around John's neck and kissed him soundly and then kissed him again. Then, more gently, he slid John's suspenders from his arms, and started unbuttoning his shirt. The red woolen union suit's buttons followed quickly after until Laurie could tuck his hands inside of John's clothes and feel John's warm skin beneath his fingers.

"We should wash first," said John softly, looking down as Laurie looked up at him.

"You already washed today," said Laurie. "Besides, I want to taste you just the way you are right now, all sweaty and manly, with a bit of sawdust still in your hair from installing those shutters."

John made a low noise in his chest. With a hitched breath, he pulled Laurie into his arms, held him close and kissed his temple and his forehead, and circled his hands around the back of Laurie's head, as though cherishing him.

"I was so lonely without you," said John, whispering into Laurie's hair. "So lonely, Little Red."

"I missed you too, John," said Laurie, becoming breathless at the thought of it. "So so so much."

Laurie pulled back, his arms still around John's waist, and made himself smile.

"Now it is time for us to disrobe, all the way down to bare skin," said Laurie, as sternly as he could. "You will do as you are told, John, and strip to the skin. Right this minute."

"And you as well," said John, his eyes a little wide, as though this was quite a bold thing to do.

As John wasn't quite getting down to the task Laurie had assigned him, Laurie gave him a helping hand, and pulled off John's boots and then his own. He undid his Indian beaded belt and placed it carefully on top of the chest of drawers next to John's brass-lidded pocket watch. Then he raced through undressing them all the way.

When they were both left wearing only their union suits, which now hung from their waists, John reached for the chest of drawers. Laurie knew he wanted to put on his nightshirt, as they usually did, so he reached out and stopped him with a gentle touch to his wrist.

"Not tonight, John," said Laurie. "Tonight we're going to be disporting in the altogether between those sheets. And do you have something like bear grease or whatever?"

"Bear grease?" asked John, his brow wrinkling.

"Something to ease the way," said Laurie. He moved close to John and pressed his naked stomach to John's. "Because I'm going to be face down in the mattress, and you are going to push your person into me. You're going to *spend* inside of me, get it?"

With a grunt, John picked Laurie up with one arm. Laurie wrapped his legs around John's middle as John carried him into the kitchen and began rifling in the cupboard with his free hand. When he found what he wanted, he pulled out a small tin. Laurie didn't question what it was, only trusted that John knew that it would work.

John carried Laurie to the bed on the floor, and placed him back on his feet. He put the tin on the floor next to the braided rug with a small clink. Reaching for the kerosene lamp on the table, he dimmed it completely so the only light was coming from the fireplace, with an additional glow from the banked cast iron stove.

"Tell me what to do," said John, almost whispering in the flickering gold and blue firelight.

"You know what to do," said Laurie. "But I'll help you, so take off your woolen underwear and get into bed. I want your skin against mine with nothing in between. Here, like this."

Slowly, Laurie peeled off his woolen underwear, exposing his skin to the warmth of the cabin. John echoed his movements, never taking his eyes from Laurie's.

When John was fully naked, he stood there. Laurie admired all that he was, from his broad shoulders and his sturdy chest, all tanned from the sun, to his long thighs, and his belly, more pale from being covered in clothes all the time. And his cock, which stood up pink and red, curled against his dark pubic hair.

Laurie knew, in that moment, that he was the first person John had stood naked in front of. Laurie, naked to his skin, puffed out his chest so that John would know he wasn't alone in feeling a little nervous. Then he stepped forward and guided John down with him to the mattress, and snugged their bodies together as he covered them both with the sheet.

"There," said Laurie, with a little laugh. "Now nobody can see us be naked together."

He kissed John and realized that both of them were a little breathless.

"I want to spend inside of you," said John. "What do I do first?"

"Ever been with a woman and take her from behind?" asked Laurie in response, and he was not surprised when John shook his head. "I'll show you. You have to make the way ready, so that's what you need to do to me. Take your fingers and some bear grease and make me ready."

In the firelight, John's eyes were wide, his pupils dark, so Laurie knew he understood, and that he wanted them to be together like this. And as John reached for the tin and popped off the lid with one hand, Laurie knew they were going straight to it. But that was okay, because he didn't want to wait a second longer than he had to. He wanted John inside of him, fucking him, and he wanted it *now*.

Nothing was ever hurried when John did it, and this was no different. He circled Laurie's body with his arms and, taking a bit of the stuff from the tin, made slow traces of it on Laurie's bottom. Then, slowly, slowly, he moved the fingers of one hand closer to the cleft between his buttocks, and taking more salve from the tin, traced the pucker of Laurie's anus.

Always, he moved quite slowly and with tender care. And all the while Laurie was panting against John's neck, gritting his teeth, wanting John to go faster.

"Easy, Little Red," whispered John in his hair. "I'll turn you over soon."

John took more salve and pushed one of his fingers into Laurie, and eased it around, then pushed in two fingers, and kissed the top of Laurie's head. His arms held Laurie quite still, right where John wanted him so Laurie couldn't turn around and make John do what he wanted. Laurie growled, baring his teeth and huffed, pushing his hair from his damp forehead.

"Now," said John. "Now roll over."

"Don't forget to put that stuff on you," said Laurie, almost whimpering with his eagerness.

"I will, Little Red, I will," said John.

The bed was warm and the sheets were rumpled as Laurie rolled over. He was facing the fire now and reached out his hands to it, as though to gather the flames and hold them close.

John's hands cupped Laurie's hips and he shifted Laurie in the bed. He sank low behind him till John's hips were close, his thighs snug behind Laurie's thighs. John's cock was hard and hot against his skin, and he felt John take himself in hand to arrange himself and snub inside of Laurie's body.

Laurie let out a breath and urged John in his mind to just do it already and put Laurie out of his misery. But John went slowly and carefully, and pushed in to ease the way with his cock, and pulled out and shifted and pushed in, a little further this time. He took forever, it seemed, the sweat from his brow dripping onto Laurie's bare back.

"C'mon, John, push, push already," begged Laurie. "Please, please, oh, *please*."

"You will learn to be patient," said John and, with his voice so low and gruff, he reached around with his hand and squeezed Laurie's cock.

Laurie came then and there, spurting hard into John's hand. His belly turned concave as he curled his hips up to try and stop it, but it was too late.

"Now I can take my time," said John, his voice still low, but sweet, too, as he bent close to kiss Laurie's spine.

Laurie felt John trace his hole with his fingers, and then he pushed in, just a little, and then a little more and with a grunt, sheathed himself in Laurie's body. For a moment, they were still as Laurie breathed, relaxing into the feel of John inside of him.

John's heartbeat thudded hard against Laurie's back. Then John began to move, rocking slowly, curling his hips backwards and forwards. He would speed up and slow down until Laurie felt the rhythm and eased into it. He gasped out loud when John grabbed his hips hard and pushed all the way in, grunts from his chest in the darkness echoed by Laurie's own cry of pleasure as John came inside of him, three quick thrusts. And then all was still.

Laurie took deep breaths to calm himself, and felt John's breath slowing behind him. When John's softened cock slipped from his body, Laurie eased onto his back and looked up at John.

John was kneeling on the mattress, his chest still heaving, the firelight glinting off the sweat on his shoulders, the line of his neck. His expression when he looked down at Laurie was as though he'd done something so new, so unexpected, that he couldn't quite wrap his mind around it.

"Come here, John," said Laurie, gently. "This is the part where we hold each other, and don't worry about the sheets just now, they'll wash."

Obediently, John lowered himself into Laurie's open arms. They were both silent as they held each other while their breaths and hearts slowed, while their bodies cooled. Laurie tipped his head so that as John nuzzled his ear, he could have as much room as he needed.

"I've never spent myself inside of someone I loved before," said John.

Laurie opened his mouth, and his old habit of saying something jocular to ease the seriousness of the moment rose up before him. But he stopped it and changed it to what he really wanted to say.

"I've never felt so loved before," said Laurie. "Never felt loved the way you make me feel loved."

"I will make you feel loved all the days of my life," said John, his voice quite clear and sure as he said this.

Laurie wanted to weep at the simple beauty of it, this old-fashioned man who'd had such a hard life pronouncing how he felt in no uncertain terms, always so brave and so loving. Laurie wrapped his arms around John's waist and squeezed him so hard that John grunted.

"Easy there, Little Red," said John. "I'm a delicate flower, as you know."

"Are you, are you—" Laurie sputtered with laughter. "Are you making a post-coital joke, dear John?"

John moved their bodies so that Laurie's head was resting on John's bare shoulder, and the warmth of the fire could get to them both.

"I've no idea what that means, but yes, I'm attempting to be amusing," said John. "You always make me laugh, so I wanted to do the same in return. Isn't that what love is?"

Laurie knew he would quickly become addicted to the gooey, melty feelings that being with John made him feel, always saying sweet nothings in Laurie's ear, always taking care of Laurie, and most of all, opening his heart and making a place for Laurie at his side.

"I love you, John," said Laurie, his throat thick with the feelings that rose up inside of him. "And yes, that's what love is. Like thinking I wanted carrots and not being mad when I told you I'd rather have potatoes."

"And being with me in the firelight," said John, softly. "And in the sunlight. And in the gray of a snowstorm, so I'll never be alone again."

"No, you won't," said Laurie. He buried his face against John's chest, still damp from their lovemaking, and licked John's nipple with a rough tongue. He heard John gasp and thought he felt a twitch from John's cock where it was trapped against Laurie's cock between their naked bodies.

"Another round, I think," said Laurie with a growl, as though he was the one in charge. "You need more practice so we're going to keep doing this till we get it right or collapse, whichever comes first."

"Yes, sir," said John with a kiss to the top of Laurie's head. "Yes, sir."

CHAPTER TWENTY-SEVEN

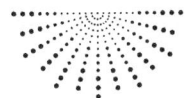

When the blizzard struck two days later, they were ready. John had walked his traps twice a day, and now half a dozen skinned and gutted jackrabbits hung frozen in the shed. Laurie had cut enough wood for a hundred cabins. In addition, John had gone back into town to bring home two fresh loaves of bread, more jam and butter, jars of pickles and rhubarb compote, dried beans and potatoes, as well as other supplies. There was no way that they'd starve or freeze to death.

The day the blizzard came, the storm clouds had gathered all day. Towards evening, the wind blew so fiercely from the east that it banged against the cabin with the sound like the slap from a large hand. John looked at Laurie as though he were a witch of some kind to have known the storm would be so bad. Laurie shrugged, for there was no way he could explain how he'd known about the storm.

He tried to smile to lighten his own mood, but he shivered instead. If he'd not come back, then he wouldn't have been able to warn John, and John would have died. The idea of it expanded in front of him, as if it was happening that very moment.

Seeing the shiver, John came to him and held him for a long while, and didn't ask any questions, for which Laurie was grateful.

When the temperature dropped at sunset, the wind increased and, when it did, the snow started to come down sideways in such a thick blanket that it blotted all the light. Pellets of ice rapped on the windows so hard they would have broken the glass had the shutters not been latched securely in place. The roof timbers creaked, and bits of snow hurled down the chimney, sputtering and sizzling to a fiery death.

"We're safe. We're snug," said John as he opened the door, his eyes wide at the storm. He closed and bolted the door, and turned to Laurie, rubbing his hands. "How about we start that checkers match now, best out of ten games."

"What does the winner get?" asked Laurie. He knelt in front of the fire and used the iron poker to move the logs around in the fireplace. He added another slender log so the firelight would be bright and cheery.

"I'll let you know when the match is over," said John, grinning. He came to the edge of the rug and stood over Laurie.

"Oh, so you think you're winning?" said Laurie, and he was about to protest further when he changed his mind. "I'll put my mouth on you as many times as you want if you win best out of ten, how about that?"

"And vice versa if you win," said John. "Tarnation, I don't know whether I want to win or to lose."

When he stood up, John was blushing. Laurie smiled and put his arms around John's waist. They stood toe-to-toe, the warmth between their bodies growing.

"Listen to that wind howl," said Laurie, as he cocked his ear to the low moan that was growing into a collection of shrieks. But the cabin stood solid against the gale, while the light from the fireplace and the stove and the kerosene lamp made it glow like a cave of hidden gold.

"Yes, it's pretty fierce," said John. "I'll have to be sure to write about it in my journal for the railroad company so they'll know, come spring, how bad the weather can get in winter."

"Speaking of spring," said Laurie.

He looked down at where their bellies were touching, and thought about peeling John's clothes off then and there to tend to his needs. But John liked it when the room was a little darker than it currently was, and besides, Laurie needed to talk about what would happen come spring.

"What is it?" asked John. He tilted his head at Laurie. His blue eyes were focused and attentive and it seemed he had all the time in the world to listen to whatever it was that Laurie wanted to say.

"Well, I think this is what we should do," said Laurie. "You hear that wind blow? It's going to be winter here all the way to April. That's a long time for winter to last, so when you get paid in spring, I think we should head out to where the winters aren't so rugged."

"Head out?" asked John. "You don't mean move back east, do you?"

"No, no," said Laurie. "I mean someplace south, in Colorado somewhere." His mind quickly traced his mental geography and his sparse knowledge of history. "Where nothing bad ever happens, like no floods or fires or wars or anything."

"What are you talking about?" asked John. "Sometimes, Little Red, I have no real notion what you are trying to say to me."

"Well this is what I'm trying to say to you, so listen up." Laurie kissed John, petted his belly, and tugged on his suspenders to make sure he had John's attention. "While I love living with you in this cabin, you run it like it's a hotel, everything at a certain time, everything very clean and tidy."

"I suppose that's true," said John.

"I think we should open up our own hotel," said Laurie, warming to the idea. "You like to make things cozy and pleasant, and people like that. They pay good money for it. We'd make a living doing something like that. You wouldn't have to risk falling into a ravine ever again, and I think we'd be happy."

"A hotel," John said, his brows coming together. "Taking care of strangers?"

"We'd make them feel welcome," said Laurie. "We'd find a town with a train that runs through it. They had lots of trains back in the day, didn't they?"

"Back in the day?" asked John. "Back in the day, they didn't have trains, they only had stagecoaches."

Now that he'd totally confused John, *and* planted the seed, Laurie felt comfortable enough to let the matter drop.

"Not a big hotel, mind you," said Laurie. "I wouldn't want us running around taking care of too many guests. We need to make it so we have plenty of time in the evenings to ourselves. If you know what I mean." Laurie waggled his eyebrows at John, and kissed him, and then took his hand to drag him over to the kitchen table.

"Checkers now," said Laurie as he got out the oilcloth board and laid the game on the table. The soapstone pieces were like silk in his hands as he placed them in their squares. "Winner gets all the blow jobs in the world."

Smiling, John pulled out his chair and sat down, placing his hands on either side of the board, as though marking his territory.

"You are losing this game, Little Red, you realize that, don't you?" asked John.

John was so handsome, sitting there in the light of the kerosene lamp that cast blue lights on his dark hair. He'd shaved in preparation for the evening because Laurie had asked him to so that John's cheeks would be soft to kiss, though Laurie didn't mind a little stubble burn once in a while.

John's blue eyes were bright as Laurie took the first move with his rust colored soapstone piece, which was usually how they started the game. Laurie would go first and then he would lose, because nobody in their right mind, and certainly not him, would ever hesitate to be the lucky guy to take off John's clothes and make love to him. Laurie was that guy, and he would be that guy forever. Time had given him a gift, and he was not one to squander that. No, not him.

Want to read another m/m time travel romance? Want to find out what happened to Laurie's friend Zach? Then check out Wild as the West Texas Wind! (http://readerlinks.com/l/1568462)

Love reading m/m cowboy romances? Try my Farthingdale Ranch series, starting with The Foreman and the Drifter. (https://readerlinks.com/l/1703675)

Would you like to read a sweet m/m Christmas romance? Try The Christmas Knife! (https://readerlinks.com/l/1568448)

JACKIE'S NEWSLETTER

Would you like to sign up for my newsletter?

Subscribers are alway the first to hear about my new books. You'll get behind the scenes information, sales and cover reveal updates, and giveaways.

As my gift for signing up, you will receive two short stories, one sweet, and one steamy!

It's completely free to sign up and you will never be spammed by me; you can opt out easily at any time.

To sign up, visit the following URL:

https://www.subscribepage.com/JackieNorthNewsletter

- facebook.com/jackienorthMM
- twitter.com/JackieNorthMM
- pinterest.com/jackienorthauthor
- bookbub.com/profile/jackie-north
- amazon.com/author/jackienorth
- goodreads.com/Jackie_North
- instagram.com/jackienorth_author

AUTHOR'S NOTES ABOUT THE STORY

The second book in my Love Across Time series is called *Honey From the Lion*.

Years ago, I came across the phrase "honey from the lion" from a poem I saw (or an article about the poem) called *Honey From the Lion* by Leah Bodine Drake, which was published in 1974 in a collection called *A Celebration of Cats*.

I wrote the phrase down at least 15 years ago on a 3 x 5 index card and stuck it on my fridge, looking at it often, and wondering what I was going to do with it.

The lovely, esoteric (to me) quote turned out to be something from the Christian bible (Judges 14:9), and is later referenced in Judges 14:18, with the idea being that there was something precious and valuable about taking something sweet from something strong and powerful.

AUTHOR'S NOTES ABOUT THE STORY

From there, the idea grew that I wanted to write a story about two men struggling through the winter. I was also very inspired by the *Little House on the Prairie* series.

I have a thing about chores, and the old-fashioned sound of the word makes me feel comfortable and safe. The Wiki article has this to say about chores: *The (series) also describes other farm work duties and events, such as the birth of a calf, and the availability of milk, butter and cheese, gardening, field work, and hunting and gathering. Everyday housework is described in detail. When Pa goes into the woods to hunt, he usually comes home with a deer and smokes the meat for the coming winter. One day he notices a bee tree and returns from hunting early to get the wash tub and milk pail to collect the honey. When Pa returns in the winter evenings, Laura and Mary beg him to play his fiddle, as he is too tired from farm work to play during the summertime.*

I also have a thing about Pa Ingalls. He's the father figure throughout the books, he's strong, and stern, but kind. He's consistent and fair and honest, and he doesn't suffer fools gladly. What's not to love? It's taken me a good long while to admit this obsession, but I figured it was time, and Honey From the Lion seemed a good story to do it in!

In the end, I decided I wanted it to be the title of a book that was a cross between *Brokeback Mountain*, *Little House on the Prairie*, and *Outlander*, so it's a bit of all three!

I wanted to linger over descriptions of sunsets and chores, I wanted cozy nights in front of a flickering fireplace, I wanted strong coffee in the mornings, and I wanted to write about a simpler time - I wanted to write what was in my soul, so I wrote *Honey From the Lion*.

I wrote about Laurie, and his sunshine personality.

I wrote about John, who was the grumpy one with the heart of butter.

AUTHOR'S NOTES ABOUT THE STORY

And I made them do chores together and fall in love. What could be better?

As for the location of the story, I entered the phrase "iron mountain" in Google, and it gave me, among other things, the location of a town called Farthing, Wyoming, which used to be called Iron Mountain, on account of the amount of iron ore nearby. Which then was the genesis for the idea of how time travel would work: that when meteor showers fall, they are trying to get home to Iron Mountain, and that's when you can make a wish!

When I write a book, I like to have a theme song attached to the writing process, so I can turn to it for inspiration. The song for this book is called *Sons and Daughters*. It is particularly slow and a little thoughtful, and describes how the two people want to be when they are with each other and, more related to *Honey From the Lion,* they talk about the chores they have and who will do them.

A LETTER FROM JACKIE

Hello, Reader!

Thank you for reading *Honey From the Lion* from my Love Across Time series.

If you enjoyed the book, I would love it if you would let your friends know so they can experience the romance between Laurie and John.

Best Regards and Happy Reading!

Jackie

- facebook.com/jackienorthMM
- twitter.com/JackieNorthMM
- instagram.com/jackienorth_author
- pinterest.com/jackienorthauthor
- bookbub.com/profile/jackie-north
- amazon.com/author/jackienorth
- goodreads.com/Jackie_North

ABOUT THE AUTHOR

Jackie North has written since grade school and spent years absorbing mainstream romances. Her dream was to write full time and put her English degree to good use.

As fate would have it, she discovered m/m romance and decided that men falling in love with other men was exactly what she wanted to write about.

Her characters are a bit flawed and broken. Some find themselves on the edge of society, and others are lost. All of them deserve a happily ever after, and she makes sure they get it!

She likes long walks on the beach, the smell of lavender and rainstorms, and enjoys sleeping in on snowy mornings.

In her heart, there is peace to be found everywhere, but since in the real world this isn't always true, Jackie writes for love.

Connect with Jackie:

https://www.jackienorth.com/
jackie@jackienorth.com

- facebook.com/jackienorthMM
- twitter.com/JackieNorthMM
- pinterest.com/jackienorthauthor
- bookbub.com/profile/jackie-north
- amazon.com/author/jackienorth
- goodreads.com/Jackie_North
- instagram.com/jackienorth_author

Made in the USA
Middletown, DE
17 January 2024